TABLE OF CONTENTS

PROLOGUE
The Child

The small girl stepped out of the swirling-colored lights into the morning sun. Guardians greeted her with deep roars and large teeth, and the child shivered in fright. She had never seen such creatures. Tears streamed down her cheeks, and she desperately wanted to return to the safety of home. She turned her head back to the lights, but they had vanished.

The leader of the guardians ambled toward her. Sniffling, the girl managed a smile, hoping to gain its favor. The four-legged creature stopped inches from her face and gazed into her teary eyes. He raised his nose to gain her scent. Judging her agreeable, he stretched out his head and nuzzled her. She smiled and touched him, feeling the softness of his mane. The beast purred in delight, and she hugged him. Now the other guardians came to her side, and she hugged them all. After a few minutes, the leader nudged her forward. She gave her new friends a wave and departed.

Mid-morning found the girl walking into a small town, her white dress tattered and dusty from her walk-through scrub brush and along a dry dirt path There was a crowd gathered listening to a man talk, and curiosity got the best of her. She walked up to the crowd and wriggled her way through to the front. There she saw a middle-aged breaded man talking. She judged his face as being kind and listened to him.

"Truly I tell you, some who are standing here will not taste death before they see the Son of Man coming in his kingdom," he said, then looked down at the child and smiled. She immediately experienced a warm tingling traverse her body. With it, her mind opened to an unknown world. She felt both elation and fear and then heard in her mind, "Do not be afraid, I am with you always." The words calmed her, and she turned and made her way back through the crowd. Near the back, she saw a teenage boy staring at her. Their eyes met. He held a blank face. She nodded to him, gave him a smile, and moved on. When she cleared the people, she paused and looked back at the preacher. The listeners blocked her view of him, so she took a deep breath and continued on her way.

Cassius Marcus, recently promoted to Centurion, led his three men toward Capernaum. It was there he would meet up with his new command of a hundred soldiers. The distance to Capernaum was still forty miles away. The warmth of the day was fading to a chill, as the sun set lower in the sky.

"We need to make camp soon," Marcus said, looking up at an early evening sky.

"Centurion, there is a clearing at the base of those rocks—to the left," one of his men said, pointing the direction.

"Yes," Marcus agreed. "And there are trees. We will have ample wood for a fire." The four horsemen made camp. They rested and nourished by the fire.

"Decanus Varius," Marcus addressed the man of a sergeant's rank. "You have been in this land for a few years; what are the Jews like?"

The decanus stirred a bit and cleared his throat. "The Jews are a religious sort yet hard working. They resent our presence. With the appearance of the zealot, many people have turned into sheep following him and his every word. We are always keeping an eye on him."

"And violence?" Marcus added.

"The sheep, no," Varius answered, warming his hands. "They are pacifists. Their religious leaders resent the zealot and stir up trouble against him. I think they are more of a threat."

"And what of this zealot? Is he a threat to the empire?" Marcus continued, reclining against a rock.

"I haven't seen him. I only know he goes here and there preaching about his God."

"This is just great," Marcus said sarcastically. "My first command, and I have to defend the empire against a religious fanatic." He shook his head and took a long draw of wine. His comments brought a chuckle from the men. They, too, drank wine.

As the evening cooled and the wine took effect, the conversation lessened. The men alone with their thoughts stared into the fire. Then a rustle came from the trees. The men's attention sharpened, and they sat upright with their hands on the hilt of their swords. They relaxed as a straggly-haired four-foot-tall girl emerged into the light of the fire. She wore leather sandals and a dirty and frayed white dress. Her eyes focused only on the fire. She paid the men no heed and walked to the edge of the campfire and sat. After a moment, she reclined into a ball, using her hands as her pillow.

Centurion Marcus scooted up to her and said, "Child, where are your parents?" The girl stirred, lifted her head, and stared into his eyes. Marcus felt her gaze deep inside his mind. It caused him to pause as significant moments of his life flashed before him. He shook his head to reset his thoughts and find words. He refocused on the girl, but she was fast asleep. Not wanting to wake her, Marcus ordered his men to check the area for others.

His men had noticed the change on his face, and they exchanged quizzical looks. He sternly reissued the order. They took torches and searched the immediate area, finding no one. Satisfied, Marcus took his cape and draped it over the sleeping child. He would have answers from her in the morning.

"Oh, Cassius, come, let's go down to the river," called out a girl's voice.

The teenager peeked over the balcony of his parent's grand house. "Claudia, I still have lessons."

"Cassius, you can do those later. It's me! And we will be alone!"

The dark-haired beauty was too much to resist for a fourteen-year-old with rushing hormones. He relented and they went down to the river. There, her soft skin, playful dark eyes, and a sweet kiss overcame him. They discovered the innocence of youth.

Cassius Marcus sighed and unconsciously pulled his cape to his chin. Then his eyes snapped open. He had placed his cape on the child. He looked to where the child slept. His cape was there, but not the child. He scrambled up and surveyed the area in the faint light of early dawn. His men were sleeping, and they seemed to have placid faces. He checked the horses. They stood unflustered. Marcus then walked around the area searching for her footprints; she left none. He took a deep breath, relieved himself, and returned sitting by the dying fire. Gazing at the glowing embers, he could only think of the child and how she had affected him. And the dream! He had not seen Claudia since he joined the army, and that was some twelve years ago. During his absence from her, he had entertained many women, and she was but a faint memory. Did the child cause his dream? He shook his head in response to his question. But now it was time to hit the road.

"Sun's up," he said in a loud voice. His men didn't stir. Marcus took his sword and tapped each one on the foot. That brought groans from the soldiers. "Up, men!" he commanded. They awakened, rubbed the sleep from their eyes, and willed themselves to stand. They were out of character. "What is it with you men?"

Decanus Varius cleared his throat and said, "Sir, I have never had such sound sleep, and my dreams."

"What about them?" Marcus questioned.

"Sir, ah, my dreams were so wonderful. I'm not sure how else to put it."

"And what about you two?" Marcus asked the others.

"The same," they said in unison.

"Sir, where is the child?" Varius asked.

"I do not know. She wasn't here when I got up," he replied dryly. He didn't tell them his dreams were like theirs. If he did, it would place the moral tone of authority in jeopardy. "Now get yourselves ready. We need to be on the road."

After two hours they neared Capernaum, a town along thebanks of the Jordan River. As they approached the town, an Optio, named Balbus, and three of his subordinates greeted them. Optio rank was equal to a lieutenant.

"Centurion Marcus, I'm your first officer, Optio Balbus." He and his men saluted Marcus.

Marcus returned the salute. "Optio Balbus, where is my garrison?"

"Sir, in Capernaum two miles from here."

"Very good." They marched on.

Approaching the town, Marcus noticed a group of people lined up at Jordan's riverbank. In the river, a sackcloth man stood. Individuals at the bank went to him and he performed some sort of ritual on them. Marcus and his men stopped and looked on with curiosity.

"Optio, is that the zealot who is stirring up all the trouble?" Marcus asked.

"Not 'the zealot,'" Balbus answered. "This one is a zealot, but a minor one. He is not a concern."

"Really?" Marcus returned. "He has a following."

Balbus laughed. "Sir, they are mere sheep."

"And what is he doing to those so-called sheep?"

"He baptizes them in the name of his God. The people call him John the Baptist."

Marcus nodded and then his focus narrowed on the line waiting for baptism. There was the little girl! *How did she get ahead of us?* "Optio, do you see that little girl in line?" He pointed to her.

"Yes, sir."

"Do you know her?"

"No, sir. I have never seen her before."

"I need to talk to this child," Marcus said.

"Sir, I suggest we meet the garrison and get quartered. There is a nasty storm coming in fast." Balbus pointed west. The sky had turned ominously dark with lightning bolts dancing. Pearls of thunder boomed over the area. Even now the wind had picked up. "Sir, after the storm passes, I will find the child and bring her to you."

"No, I want to see the child now," Marcus demanded as the girl stepped into the river and waded up to the Baptist.

John the Baptist smiled at her. "Child, you are alone." The small girl looked up at him and fixed her eyes on his. John hesitated and nodded. "You are a blessed child." He reached down into the river and scooped water up in his hands. "I baptized you with the water of repentance in the name of the One God." He then poured water on her head. As he did, he added, "And He will come and baptize you. Yet you are already baptized in the spirit." When he finished, there was a strike of lighting and an earthshaking clap of thunder. Neither John nor the child shuddered. John patted the girl on the head. "Behold the power of God. Now go, child. I sense danger for you."

Centurion Marcus led the way to the child as she was being baptized. On approach, lightning struck, and the ground shook. His horse reared up, as did several other horses. He fought the reins to gain control. As he did, the wind gusted. He and the others had to shield their eyes from the dust; then the rain came in a torrent. Each horseman strained against the wind, rain, and frightened horses. After a few minutes, the wind and rain subsided, and Marcus looked to the river for the child. Only the Baptist stood with his hands raised to the sky. Marcus glanced in all directions for her. She had vanished, but not from his mind.

He met with his garrison and gave them a briefing of what he expected of them. When he finished, he took with him several of its best horsemen to search for the girl. His mind required—no, pleaded—for answers from her.

CHAPTER ONE
In The Beginning

*I*n the beginning God created the heavens and the earth. Dhiel Tl'Rak continued reading the first chapter of the Bible in the solitude of his cabin. He concentrated deeply on the story of creation.

And God created man in His own image; in the image of God, He created him; male and female... And the Lord God planted a garden toward the east, in Eden; and there He placed the man whom He had formed.

And out of the ground the Lord God caused to grow every tree that is pleasing to the sight and good for food; the tree of life also in the midst of the garden, and the tree of knowledge of good and evil.

...But from the tree, which is in the middle of the garden, God has said, "You shall not eat from it or touch it, lest you die."

And the serpent said to the woman, "You surely shall not die! For God knows that in the day you eat from it your eyes will be opened and you will be like God, knowing good and evil."

...She took from its fruit and ate; and she gave also to her husband with her, and he ate... .

Then the Lord God said, "Behold, the man has become like one of us, knowing good and evil; and now, least he... Take also from the tree of life, and eat, and live forever."

Dhiel Tl'Rak, completely engrossed with the prospects of living forever, and knowing man couldn't, eagerly read God's response. God banished Adam and Eve from the Garden of Eden and placed a cherub, an angel, with a flaming sword, which turned every direction to guard the way to the tree of life.

Dhiel Tl'Rak paused, took a sip of wine, and read about the descendants of the first couple, and their eventual life of corruption and evilness. So vile were the people that God destroyed every life thing by a flood; all except Noah and his family, righteous people.

By God's command Noah built an ark, which he filled with two of every living creature, himself, and his family to ride out the flood. From Noah and his family and the animals from the ark, Earth replenished itself.

Tl'Rak read of Moses, who further demonstrated God's power through the plagues cast upon the Egyptian Pharaoh and his people. Pharaoh held Moses' people in bondage. Then there were the other great men of the Old Testament who demonstrated God's power. Many were gifted with prophecy, and all with wisdom and a firm trust in God. There were also great miracles in the Old Testament.

Tl'Rak paid close attention to Elijah, another man of God. Elijah went up to heaven in a chariot of fire. He never died on Earth. Tl'Rak found that only Elijah and Enoch from the book of Genesis never died. He wondered if by a gift from God they were able to eat from the tree of life.

It was the New Testament that grabbed Tl'Rak's attention the most. The God that created all, sent his son, Jesus Christ, to Earth. Jesus Christ, the most significant man of all time, showed the glory of God through miracles and profound wisdom, kindness, and love. He was a man for all times, only to be crucified by His own people.

Three days after His death, He rose from the dead, and forty days later ascended into heaven. His death and resurrection proved in the deity of Jesus Christ as God and that everyone who believed in Him would have his sins forgiven and gain eternal life.

After His ascension into heaven, Jesus' disciples carried on for Him, spreading the gospel of Jesus Christ. Most of them performed miracles, and many were executed for their faith.

The final book of the Bible, Revelations, detailed the end times of Earth, the conquering of evil and the return of Jesus Christ. The end came with a great battle between evil, headed by Satan, and good, led by Jesus Christ. This time good won with Satan and his followers, the unbelievers being cast into the eternal lake of fire, and the believers being delivered into heaven.

Tl'Rak found it interesting in the book of Revelations that two men appeared and gave witness of Jesus Christ with works of wonders. They were eventually killed only to rise three days later and rise to heaven in the presence of their enemies. Tl'Rak wondered if the two men were Enoch and Elijah from the Old Testament.

Finally, the Bible ended with both a warning: I testify to everyone who hears the words of the prophecy of this book: if anyone adds to them, God shall add to him the plagues which are written in this book.

And if anyone takes away from the words of the book of this prophecy, God shall take away his part from the tree of life and from the holy city, which are written in this book.

He who testifies to these things says, "Yes, I am coming quickly." Amen.

Dhiel Tl'Rak closed his reader and rocked back in his chair. His eyes were tired from the non-stop reading, but his mind was working overtime processing all that he had just read. He concluded the Bible was a descent piece of literature, a combination of fiction and nonfiction to inspire people to believe in God and His son, Jesus Christ. But was Jesus Christ truly a supernatural being, taking human form on Earth, or just a man of flesh and blood being made into a god?

Since Tl'Rak didn't believe in gods, he saw Jesus Christ as a man like any other on Earth. True, Jesus Christ had a charisma about him that swayed people's feelings and beliefs, so much so that he shaped mankind and ultimately the universe. And that, Tl'Rak, vowed he would change.

The miraculous powers of Jesus Christ and others in the Bible, Tl'Rak attributed to magic or outside forces working with a magician to perform the feats. He felt everything written in the Bible had a plausible explanation.

Finally, his mind succumbed to fatigue. He wearily rose from his chair and dumped himself into bed. Tomorrow he would begin his move to change all that Jesus Christ had established.

CHAPTER TWO
The Plan

*I*t took a beeping alarm to jolt Dhiel Tl'Rak from his sleep. He couldn't remember the last time he slept so soundly. Then again, he had not read a book the length of the Bible, or any book in his adult life cover to cover in one sitting. It was too much for his eyes and mind. Yet he was up and ready to start the day that would change everyone's life.

After changing into his exercise attire, he was off to the gym for his morning workout. He wouldn't skip his exercise; it kept him fit and mentally alert. Others who frequented the facility in the early morning greeted him with nods. He exercised vigorously for an hour, stretching, lifting weights, and doing aerobics. Thoughts of the upcoming day blocked out the pain of his strenuous workout.

He returned to his cabin, showered, donned his uniform, and had a leisurely breakfast. Then it was time for duty. With his blood hot with determination, he strode onto the bridge of the warship he commanded. His ship would be a warship again!

The five crew members hardly took notice of his arrival. Such was the apathy aboard the ship. Tl'Rak noticed the disease months ago, but tolerated it. He had the contagion too—until last night!

"We have new orders!" he barked, sitting proudly in his command seat. That caught the crew's attention, who seemed to perk up in their seats. "This ship will shortly embark on a mission that will restore glory to our empire and change the galaxy as we know it. We will rule and subjugate every race to us." A pause as he shifted in his seat.

"Navigator, plot a course to Ul'tarus. Normal cruise speed."

The young navigator looked startled at his commander. His eyes shifted to the first officer for confirmation.

"Commander," the first officer said, rescuing the navigator, "Ul'tarus is off-limits to all ships, except patrol ships. Are we to be one?"

"No," Tl'Rak replied with a wry smile. "Our order is to proceed there."

"We haven't received an order relieving us of our current mission, Commander," the first officer returned.

Tl'Rak waved a dismissing hand. "Of course not, M'Catis. Our new mission is too sensitive for reception over normal comm channels. I received the orders at our last port-of-call."

"Commander, what is the mission that requires us to proceed to Ul'tarus?" M'Catis asked.

"M'Catis, Nh'Got to the briefing room," Tl'Rak said, rising from his seat.

The veteran first officer and young tactical officer followed their commander into the briefing room and settled into their respective seats. Both officers sat pensively awaiting Tl'Rak's update. He got right to the point. "We are doing time travel." His statement raised the heart rates of his officers. They knew full well that time travel was a treasonable offense. The punishment being death.

M'Catis' parted his lips to speak, but Tl'Rak raised a hand, stopping him before a word escaped. "I know what you are going to say." He paused and gave the man a thin smile. "This mission is top secret. The secrecy level is such that there is no official record of the order." He paused again and held his stare at his subordinates to let the words sink in. Satisfied, he continued, "We are going back in time and travel to Earth. We will use the slingshot maneuver around Ul'tarus and arrive in the Earth year 33 A.D. Nh'Got, you will make the calculations for the transit to take us to this date. I trust you can do it."

She swallowed with difficulty, her mouth turning to cotton. "Commander, it will take some time," she managed. "There are many variables to account for. May I ask why the central command didn't provide you with the calculations for this maneuver?"

Tl'Rak chuckled, confounding, both M'Catis and Nh'Got. "My orders were verbal; such is the secrecy of this mission. They couldn't trust me to remember all the formulas and calculations, lest I miss one number. You understand?"

Nh'Got nodded. "Of course, Commander."

"And once we are there, Commander?" M'Catis asked.

"We will assassinate the man responsible for the course of Earth's history and the galaxy." Another pause.

M'Catis's eyebrows furrowed, thinking hard about who this person might be. Nh'Got's eyes widened; she knew the person.

"Commander, that would be Jesus Christ," she said.

"Correct, Nh'Got," Tl'Rak said with a broad smile. "And how did you know that?"

"Commander, I studied Earth history as a minor at the academy. Jesus Christ claimed to be a god. Most on Earth consider him to be the Creator."

"Yes, and as a result has molded history, including ours. Well, I don't believe in gods. Jesus Christ is only a man and is mortal. His people executed him."

Nh'Got responded, "But Commander, he rose from the dead and ascended into His kingdom."

"They called it heaven," Tl'Rak said. "No matter, I'm sure there was an outside force keeping him alive after his crucifixion. As the story goes, he rose from the dead three days later. I'm sure whoever was aiding him made this happen. And forty days after this, they made it look like he ascended into heaven. Likely, they took him to their spaceship. All this was to keep his persona as a god alive. And it worked!"

"Commander, we may not have to kill this Jesus Christ," M'Catis commented. "We just need to find and destroy the spaceship that kept him alive."

Tl'Rak waved a dismissing hand. "There may be no spaceship. If there is one, we'll destroy it too, killing Jesus Christ in the process. It would save us time searching for him planet side and killing him."

"Commander, if there is a spaceship, we need to determine the who, when, and where, of it," M'Catis suggested.

"Absolutely. And that will happen," Tl'Rak agreed. "Likely, whoever is in that spaceship is still determining the course of the galaxy. And that means our empire too. Nh'Got, you have work to do. The trip to Ul'tarus will take six days. Neither of you are to speak a word about this meeting or this mission to anyone. Understood?" Two heads nodded. Both hoped their faces didn't give away the displeasure they felt. "Good. Dismissed."

The orders troubled Z'mia Nh'Got. She couldn't believe Tl'Rak had received them. The emperor had publicly forbidden time travel under the penalty of death. Tl'Rak must have gone mad, severely affected by apathy and depression. So much so that he would attempt to alter the natural flow of time, change history, and the future. She needed to stop him. The question was, how?

Nh'Got had a restive night as her mind conjured a way to thwart Tl'Rak. The simplest solution would be to kill him outright. The crew might tolerate it if they knew the reason for it. Central command and the emperor would condone her actions and make her a hero. But what if they sanctioned the mission? Tl'Rak's death would only lead to another attempt, and her slow torture and ultimate death.

Then there was Subcommander M'Catis. What were his thoughts about Tl'Rak's order? He, too, seemed taken aback by Tl'Rak's revelation. Yet he didn't vigorously challenge him. For the time being, she had to count M'Catis on Tl'Rak's side.

She thought about the situation. *The emperor was enjoying her highest popularity amongst her subjects.* She sighed, not relishing the thought of dying at a young age. There had to be another way. Until she discovered it, she would carry out her orders.

It was mid-afternoon the next day that she came to a means to thwart Tl'Rak. In calculating the time travel jump, the weight of the ship was a variable in the formula. Currently, it was one metric ton too heavy to make the time jump to the old Earth date 33 A.D. That meant jettisoning some non-essential material. Hidden inside the debris would be the means to stop Tl'Rak, at least she hoped.

Within the debris, she would place a science probe transformed into a transmitter. She would make the probe look like it had outlived its usefulness. After twenty-four hours, it would start transmitting a message. It would be for the Supreme Fleet Commander, Sen Tr'Tala, eyes only, alerting him of Tl'Rak's proposed action. She hoped and betted her life that he and the emperor didn't sanction Tl'Rak's order.

Supreme Fleet Commander Tr'Tala was the key figure for the time travel prohibition. Two years ago, on orders and against his protest, he took his ship, the *Tigerii,* back in time to old Earth. The purpose was to kidnap a twelve-year-old human boy. The boy's name was Ross, who in the future would be a starship commander for the United Planets Alliance, the UPA. Until recently, central command considered him to be a major thorn in the empire's side.

The sanctioned story was that an alien woman had also returned in time to old Earth at the same time. She convinced Tr'Tala that his future and the galaxy would change and not for the better if he kept the Ross boy. Tr'Tala released the boy and returned home to his own time.

The emperor lacked knowledge of the kidnapping scheme. Someone, possibly the alien woman, alerted her about the plot. Appalled that someone went behind her back, she had the ones who devised the scheme executed. Supreme Fleet Commander U'Litia was the last to die, after watching the others go before him. She elevated Tr'Tala to Supreme Fleet Commander in honor of his moral character and wise decision-making.

These two people certainly wouldn't compromise th eir values and approve time travel. The emperor was enjoying her highest popularity amongst her subjects. The Valeriian Empire was at peace with its long-time enemy, the UPA. People had jobs, plenty of food, and excellent health care. More importantly, sons and daughters were not being killed in war.

But politics was politics, and it led those thirsty for power to do strange things. Was there again a hidden agenda by a person or people? One to depose the Supreme Fleet Commander and possibly overthrow the emperor.She would have answers only if she could get her probe into space, the transmitter worked, and someone heard the message and forwarded it to Tr'Tala. Many ifs and they were unsettling.

Subcommander M'Catis believed Tl'Rak was acting on his own. He needed to stop him, but how? He, too, valued his life and didn't want to do anything to jeopardize it. And what were Nh'Got's feelings on the matter? He noticed her startled face at the meeting. Yet over the last two days, she carried out her orders without hesitation. It would be another sleepless night for him.

At the morning meeting, day three, Nh'Got gave her report to Tl'Rak. He listened to her, vaguely glancing at the data on the holo screen. When she finished, he nodded and looked expectantly at M'Catis. "Subcommander, begin gathering and removing weight to meet Lt. Nh'Got's calculation. I want it done by midday. "

"Yes, Commander," he replied with a fractional nod.

"Commander," Nh'Got piped. "I would like to go with Subcommander M'Catis. I need to verify the weight and what is being discarded." She gave M'Catis an apologetic look. "No disrespect, Subcommander. But what you and the department heads think is unnecessary material, I may view as useful in this mission. The ship may sustain damage during the transit. Some items may be necessary and some stripped for parts."

"Very well." Tl'Rak agreed, approving of her rationale before M'Catis could respond to her. "Take T'Som with you too. After all, he and his team will be the ones making any repairs."

"Commander," Nh'Got said, "I suggest you leave the engineer out. He is currently out of the loop on this mission. There is an old human idiom: loose lips sink ships. Meaning beware of unguarded talk. Why jeopardize the mission?" She glanced at M'Catis for support.

He saw a change in her eyes. Did she have a plan to subvert this mission? He took the cue. "Commander, I agree with Lt. Nh'Got. No need to include anyone else. I'm sure Lt. Nh'Got and myself can determine what is useful to the ship."

Tl'Rak nodded. "Leave the engineer out. Anything else?" They shook their head. "Okay. Begin your job. Dismissed."

As the two left the room, Subcommander M'Catis needed to know what the young officer's feelings were about Tl'Rak's plan. Time was running short, and he didn't want to act alone, though he would if he had to.

"Lieutenant," he said to her as they made their way from the briefing room. "How should we proceed?" His voice was soft. He wanted her to know his question wasn't dealing with the acquisition and disposal of material.

She looked him in the eyes that beckoned for reassurance. Her own eyes were searching for a purpose. He too held the gaze, and after a pause, nodded. He saw what he hoped and needed. She nodded back at him. They agreed feeling relief.

Finally, she answered, "Have all department heads bring all non-essential materials to the hanger deck. We will sort, weigh, and begin disposal. Don't give them a reason for your order."

"My thoughts exactly," M'Catis said. "Does your department have any non-essential material? He assumed she had a plan, and it involved the debris.

"Of course. I'll see you in the hanger deck in thirty minutes with my nonessentials. Then help you with the disposition of the gathered items."

"That sounds good to me," M'Catis said. "Thirty minutes." She nodded at him and strode confidently down the hall. She had two stops to make.

CHAPTER THREE
Storm of Uncertainty

On schedule, Nh'Got entered the hanger deck pushing an anti-gravity sled oaded with unnecessary materials, save one, a half-meter long, six-centimeter diameter cylinder, hidden beneath the pile. It was a science probe turned into a transmitter, albeit without transwarp capability. It held her message to Supreme Fleet Commander Sen Tr'Tala that would continuously repeat itself. She hoped it had the strength to reach a transmitter relay buoy.

"Lieutenant," M'Catis acknowledged her arrival. At his side were two crewmen weighing other departments' discarded materials. "I see you brought a selection of items."

"Yes, Subcommander. I've wanted to get rid of this junk for some time. I'm glad Commander Tl'Rak finally made an order to clean house." She made sure the two crewmen heard her explanation. She didn't want them to have a hint of what the ship was about to do.

"And this is all non-essential, Lieutenant?" M'Catis asked.

"Every piece, Subcommander."

"Start unloading the sled," M'Catis ordered his assistants. As they did, he cursorily inspected each item and then weighed it. He noted the battered scientific probe, yet said nothing. *Is it a bomb?* He shuddered inside. He didn't want to die in stopping Tl'Rak.

After weighing the last item, he ordered his assistants to place all items on the growing pile at the hanger deck's massive space door. While the underlings were at the space door, M'Catis whispered to Nh'Got, "Your plan?"

"In the debris," she murmured.

His heart skipped a beat. The scientific probe was the only item in her discarded materials that could stop Tl'Rak, meaning it had to be an explosive. "Bomb?" he mouthed.

She shook her head as the assistants returned. "Let's see," he told his helpers, "only the engineering department has yet to bring its debris." As if on cue, two men from engineering entered the hangar deck, pushing two sleds of items.

"If you will excuse me, Subcommander," Nh'Got said. "I must get back to my post. Give me the final weight of the discarded materials, so I may recalculate the correct weight of the ship."

"Of course, Lieutenant." As she left, M'Catis stood perplexed, wondering about her plan and what was inside the probe that could make a difference.

As Nh'Got rode the lift to the bridge, the ship slightly shuddered. She knew the space door had opened, and the debris jettisoned by the violent decompression of the hanger deck. She mentally checked off part one of her plan. In twenty-four hours, she hoped to check off part two when the probe began transmitting her message.

Twenty-four hours later, amid the flotsam, the small tubular transmitter came to life. It first oriented itself to the empire's homeworld, turning 210 degrees on its axis. Seconds later, Nh'Got's coded message went out. It would repeat until the probe's batteries drained or destroyed by an outside force. The batteries had a duration of ninety days.

While her insides churned acid, Nh'Got tried to appear calm at her tactical post on the bridge. She had just given Tl'Rak the final calculations to make the time jump back to ancient Earth. He approved her work with a grunt and a nod of his head.

She acknowledged him with a "'thank you." From her station, she let out a controlled sigh, hoping the probe was transmitting. If it was, the message would take five and a half hours to reach Valerii. She figured Supreme Fleet Commander Tr'Tala would answer quickly via light speed transmission. As she saw it, he had two options of orders for Tl'Rak. One, turn over command of the

Lionare to M'Catis. The other, find the traitor who was trying to subvert this covert mission. If the latter option, she would be a suspect, tortured, and executed. She decided not to rat out M'Catis. He would be the last chance to stop the mission.

Finally, her curiosity got the best of her. She directed a long-range scan back to her transmitter to determine if the probe was sending. To her relief, it was. She checked her chronometer. In about five hours, she would know her, the ship, and the future's fate. As she leaned back in her chair to draw a relaxing breath, the comm-technician called for Tl'Rak's attention.

"Commander, I am picking up a distress call. It's garbled. Something about an ion storm—ship without power."

Tl'Rak swiveled his seat to face the man. "ID on the ship?"

"It is the *Ry'Tec.*"

"Commander, it's a bulk freighter," M'Catis advised.

"What is its position?" Tl'Rak demanded, unconcerned about the ship. He wanted to know the location of the ion storm and if it was on its way to Ul'Tarus.

Anxiety registered on Nh'Got's face. The storm could bisect her probe and the homeworld, preventing or disrupting its transmission. "Sector 6-C. Approximate coordinates: 101 by 23 by plus 10," the technician answered.

Tl'Rak sighed, relieved. The storm wasn't on its way to Ul'Tarus. Nh'Got paled, though she hoped it didn't show. The storm was directly between her probe and Valerii.

She still had hope. The storm may not be large enough to affect the probe's transmission. It could also dissipate or move on quickly. Both would allow the transmission to proceed unaffected. She would scan the ion storm to get her answers.

Off to Tl'Rak's side, M'Catis noticed Nh'Got's sudden facial change. She was in distress. Whatever her plan was, the storm had interfered with it. He drew Tl'Rak's attention to himself to prevent him seeing Nh'Got's distress. "Shall I implement a course change to rendezvous with the *Ry'Tec,* Commander?" He didn't expect him to do so.

"Negative," Tl'Rak barked, glaring at his first officer. "We are on a priority mission. Another ship will rescue the freighter. Maintain our present course.

"Will do, Commander," M'Catis conceded.

Nh'Got's scan of the storm showed it to be large; covering most of the sector, and it was moving slowly. Her calculations showed the storm would clear the sector in forty-eight hours. The Supreme Commander would then have twelve hours to act. Would that be enough time? She drummed her fingers, pondering whether to stay the course or conceive of an alternative plan. The latter would be to destroy the ship.

CHAPTER FOUR
The Message

The empire's primary space station sat in high orbit over he homeworld. It homeworld. It contained their main communications center. From it, central command could contact any planet or ship in seconds. The exception was the extreme outlying areas that could take a several minutes.

It was near the end of the day shift for a blurry-eyed second lieutenant. He was about to finish a double shift, remaining on duty due to his replacement calling in sick. Adding to his fatigue was a very busy day. Only a few minutes to go before his substitute took over. To his relief, he saw him enter the room. "One last check of the scanning antennas and then I am out of here," he whispered. To his surprise, a faint low-frequency message came through, and it kept repeating. The message was security coded.

"I'll take over Trac," the replacement said.

Second Lieutenant Trac La'Hal lifted a stopping hand. "I've picked up something very low power." He was raising the gain as he talked. "It's coded for the Supreme Commander."

"Let's hear what it says," Second Lieutenant Mh'Nah said, scooting into an adjacent chair.

"We can't do that," La'Hal protested. "This is for the Supreme Commander only. Anyway, we don't have a decoder for this message."

Mh'Nah smiled. "Yes, we do. I've rigged one." He reached over and started touching in a sequence on the screen. Before he could complete it, La'Hal slapped his hand away.

"Idiot. What are you doing?" Mh'Nah protested.

"Preventing you from decoding the message. It would be treasonous to do so."

"Problem here?" boomed a female's voice from behind. The two men turned in their seats to face the shift commander. Before either could answer, she continued, "Lieutenant La'Hal, you have finished your shift. Log off."

"Yes, Subcommander," he answered, and logged off. As he started to stand, the shift commander placed a restraining hand on his shoulder.

"Lieutenant Mh'Nah, log on."

"Yes, Subcommander."

"Now, Lieutenant, reenter the code that you had on the screen," Subcommander Sl'Zahah directed. "It's the one La'Hal interrupted you from inputting."

"It was nothing important, Subcommander," Mh'Nah said nervously. "It was a joke, and I know they aren't permitted while on duty."

Sl'Zahah smiled. "I understand, Lieutenant." Mh'Nah deflated with relief. "It's been a long day for me too," she continued. "I could use some levity. Let me see the joke."

Mh'Nah shrugged. "It's personal."

"Now!" she barked. "The exact sequence."

Mh'Nah swallowed with difficulty. "Yes, Subcommander."

As he entered the sequence, La'Hal sat sweating with anxiety. Ma'Nah's career, possibly his life was over. Was his, too?

Both junior officers' foreheads showed beads of sweat as the decoder popped up on the screen.

Decode incoming message, yes, or no? the screen read.

Lieutenant Mh'Nah held a finger over the input board awaiting the Subcommander's order.

"La'Hal, is there a coded message coming in?" Subcommander Sl'Zahah asked.

"Yes, Subcommander, for Supreme Commander Tr'Tala." He hoped by naming the Supreme Commander as the recipient, he could defuse the situation—at least his. Mh'Nah was on his own. Sl'Zahah now had to decide how to handle the message.

There was a pause as she pondered her decision. She wanted to hear the message. It could contain useful information for her rapid advancement in the military. In her twenty-two years of service, she had seen leaked information used as a blackmail tool for such a purpose. It was common practice in the empire's history.

But, could she trust the two junior officers to keep their tongues quiet even under oath?   Either of the two men could use it against her. Worse, the Supreme Commander would find out and her career would end.

She pondered her decision. Mh'Nah still held his now-shaking finger over the input board. She took a breath and reached over him and touched, no. "Forward the message to the Supreme Commander, now."

Mh'Nah complied. Both he and La'Hal released a sigh of relief, but they weren't out of the woods. Mh'Nah would have to pay for his intended act of treason. La'Hal was unsure of his fate.

"Lieutenant La'Hal, remain at your post until I find a replacement. Security," she said, waving a hand to the officer on duty. A very large man came to her side. She pointed to Mh'Nah and said, "Place this man under arrest."

Supreme Fleet Commander Sen. Tr'Tala leaned back in his chair and smiled. Tonight, promised to be wonderful. His wife's starship, formerly his, had returned to port. She had been in week-long meetings with United Planets Alliance representatives. It was to tidy up loose ends of the recent peace treaty between the two foes. The meeting took place on a planet, equal distance between the two powers.

The peace agreement came about after the time travel incident involving the empire. They had sent a ship, commanded by himself to old Earth to abduct UP Captain Mark Ross when he was child. His first officer, now his wife went down to Earth and kidnapped the boy.

Later on, while still in orbit around Earth, she persuaded her future husband to return the boy to a traveler from their future. He would have the boy treated for a near-fatal head injury incurred in a game called baseball. The boy would become Captain Mark Ross, a man of their time. The traveler turned out to be Captain Ross's son. It was a very complicated matter, one Sen Tr'Tala and the emperor vowed never to happen again. If not for his wife's actions, Tr'Tala wouldn't be the Supreme Fleet Commander.

Now Commander Te'ana Zh'Cata was both a starship commander and diplomat. She had first-hand knowledge of Earth, its customs, and its people. Her meetings with UPA diplomats, included a reacquaintance with Captain Ross. During the meetings, cultural exchange was high on the list. She learned the customs of the other inhabitants that made up the UPA. In return, she shared information about her people and the other races that made up the empire.

Tonight, she and her husband would dine with the emperor at the palace. She had secured a bountiful supply of the UPA's finest wines, especially those from Earth. On recommendation from Captain Ross, she selected a French Merlot for tonight's dinner. She delivered it to the palace chef.

Sen Tr'Tala was also looking forward to time alone with his wife. After several years of pretending not to be in love with each other, they were still catching up on lost intimacy. Even now, in his office, he could feel her soft body against his and the brush of her tender lips to his.

Suddenly his annunciator beeped, jolting him from his daydream. He took a breath to clear the scent of his wife from his mind and stabbed the "answer" bottom.

"Yes, C'Realk," he barked.

His aide cleared his voice, fearing the wrath of his superior. C'Realk knew how important this evening was for his boss. He cringed at having to interrupt him at this hour.

"Supreme Commander, sorry to bother you. There is a coded priority message on channel one. It is for your eyes only."

A pause. "I will take it," Tr'Tala harrumphed. "But no more messages. Understood."

"Yes, Supreme Commander."

Tr'Tala cursed under his breath and touched the view screen to call up the message. "This had better be very, very important," he told the screen. The screen replied and a nervous lieutenant appeared. He didn't recognize her, nor the location she was addressing him from. He found out as he listened to her message.

He couldn't believe what he had heard. To be sure, he let the message repeat before he saved it on a data chip. He touched his annunciator. "C'Realk! Get me Commander Tl'Rak, of the starship *Lionare,* ASAP." He sucked in some air, his mind returning to Lt. Nh'Got.

She appeared nervous, and her face looked troubled. The thought of being part of a conspiracy to change the past, present, and future was frightening. But he also sensed the turmoil she was going through. She didn't know if Tl'Rak was acting on his own or following orders from the Supreme Fleet Commander. The young lieutenant decided Tl'Rak was a madman and acting on his own; a correct one at that.

Tr'Tala doubted the emperor went behind his back and ordered Tl'Rak on this mission to old Earth. If Lt. Nh'Got survived, a medal of valor awaited her. If she died in the battle to stop Tl'Rak, she would be memorialized as a hero.

Until now, Tl'Rak was a very competent commander, yet one with an aggressive command style. He showed his loyalty to the empire many times. But the winds of change were blowing across the empire. Now it was obvious. Tl'Rak took exception to the way the landscape was changing. The man wanted to return it to the warlike old guard. To do so, he would put his life and the integrity of the future on the line by going back in time and killing Jesus Christ. Allowing him to do so was out of the question.

His annunciator beeped again. "Yes," he snapped.

"Supreme Commander, the *Lionare* isn't responding," C'Realk responded.

Tr'Tala slapped a hand on the desk in disgust. "Damn! Get me Commander Fr'Tet, unit commander for Ul'Tarus defense. And have him hold."

"Yes, Supreme Commander."

Tr'Tala touched his viewer, calling up his channel to the emperor. Her secretary answered.

"This is Supreme Fleet Commander Tr'Tala. I need to speak to the emperor, code U-1-A-2B."

A pregnant pause. "One second, Supreme Commander."

While he drummed his fingers on his desk irritated by the delay, C'Realh beeped him again, announcing Commander Fr'Tet was waiting for him.

Finally, the emperor appeared. She was as attractive as ever; her black hair was up and her dark eyes bright and penetrating. Her thin lips parted with a smile. It disappeared as she saw the tension in Tr'Tala's face. She was expecting the call to be social regarding the upcoming evening.

"Sen," she addressed him informally. "Is there a problem with this evening?"

"Possibly, my Lady." He gave her the details. When he finished, he could see her face pale. She hadn't ordered Tl'Rak's mission.

Her first words came out in anger. "Stop this madman!"

"We will, my Lady. The three ships on picket duty around Ul'Tarus, though each smaller than the *Lionare,* collectively can stop him. That is if their commanders aren't in on the plot."

The emperor was thinking the same. The empire had a history of subversion and subterfuge as a means to gain power at all ranks. She had vowed to put an end to it, especially after the Captain Ross time travel incident. She had eliminated those responsible for it. Now treason and treachery were raising their heads again. "Who's the lead commander of the picket ships?"

"Commander Fr'Tet," he replied dryly.

"Sen, you don't sound confident about him."

"My Lady, I'll get a plan to Commander Fr'Tet to stop the *Lionare.* Tl'Rak's scheme will fail."

"I want to listen to your conversation with Commander Fr'Tet; secretly of course."

"Certainly, my Lady. Right now, I need to get my wife and her first officer into my office. They were with me when I made the previous time jump. Their input will be most helpful. When we have a plan, I will contact you and Commander Fr'Tet."

"I will wait." The link closed.

With a blank screen staring him in the face, Tr'Tala felt helpless. He wanted, no— needed, —to be at Ul'Tarus. Halting Tl'Rak required a competent commander, and he laced faith in Fr'Tet and the other ships' commanders.

The madman Tl'Rak was a loyalist to the old ways and the most capable tactician. He would know that the picket ships would be ready and waiting with orders to stop him at all costs. To his advantage was the fact that those on picket duty were there due to incompetence. He would use it against them and devise a plan to evade them and make the run around Ul'Tarus.

"The run around Ul'Tarus," Tr'Tala said to himself. "I made it. What approach did I take?"

He shook his head unable to remember. The mechanics of the operation were left to the tactical officer and the first officer—his wife. Both would know the route Tl'Rak would use having the same class of ship.

He touched his annunciator. "C'Real, find Subcommander R'Zoha, assigned to my wife's ship. Have him come to my office now."

"Yes, Supreme Commander."

Tr'Tala then touched his viewer and activated the code for his wife.

Seconds passed. "Damn! Te'ana answer." He reached to touch the code again, but she appeared suddenly. Her smiling face took his breath away. *How could I have dismissed this woman all those years we were together on the Tigerii? A great mistake.*

"Sen," she said. "I was in the—"

"Yes, yes," he dismissed her excuse with a waving hand. Her smile disappeared.

"Is there a problem?"

"How fast can you be in my office?"

She shrugged. "Twenty minutes."

"Ten," he countered.

"Fifteen." She gave him a persuasive smile.

"Fifteen, then." He gave her a look that spoke volumes of concern. She read it and nodded.

"So that's the situation," Tr'Tala said to his wife and former tactical officer, now the commander of the *Tigerii*. "Given that the *Lionare* and *Tigerii* are of the same class, Tl'Rak will use the exact approach we did. I need to know what it is, so Fr'Tet can get his ships in position to stop him."

"Supreme Commander," R'Zoha said. "The *Lionare* will have to use an equatorial approach to the sun's right to get the full effect of the sun's counter-clockwise gravitational pull. Remember, Tl'Rak is going farther back in time than we did. He will need a greater acceleration curve to make the jump."

"I concur, Sen—Supreme Commander," Zh'Cata said, making a slip of protocol with her first officer present. The man held a stoic face unphased by the slip. "He must know that we will block this path and will use a secondary course." She looked to her first officer for help.

He shook his head. "I don't see a successful alternate approach, Supreme Commander. He needs the full pull of the sun's equatorial force to be successful." A pause as he and the others looked at the slowly rotating three-dimensional yellow sun center desk. Three small dots representing the picket ships floated in a triangle about the sun.

Then R'Zoha spoke again. "Tl'Rak could swoop into the equatorial plane from above or below and then make the run around the sun. But the stress on the ship would be tremendous, possibly ripping it apart. That would be his only other option."

"But is it a genuine option?" Tr'Tala asked.

"I would need to do the calculations, Supreme Commander." Tr'Tala gave him that *then do it look.* "I will have them shortly, Supreme Commander."

With his superiors' eyes glued on him, R'Zoha worked at the computer. He sweated as he tried every angular approach, starting at equatorial zero and moving up a degree until the ship destroyed itself repeatedly. The calculations completed below the equator mirrored the results of those from above the equator.

"There it is, Supreme Commander," he said. "Tl'Rak can swoop into an equatorial course from above or below from zero to thirty-two point eight degrees. Past thirty-two point eight, the *Lionare* will rip apart." He shaded the approach area before the rotating sun in red.

Tr'Tala ran a hand through his dark hair. "That's sixty-five degrees of area that three frigates need to cover. Three ships can defend the equatorial plane approach, but not the whole red zone. He could sneak through."

"We can reduce that possibility, Supreme Commander," Zh'Cata said matter-of-factly. "We mine the equatorial plane using proximity mines except for the approach area we want him to use. Let's say we use his current course. The position of the picket ships needs to be here." She moved the three ships on the holograph. "Position one ship at equatorial zero. The other two ships at positions five degrees in from the edges of the approach area. All the ships need to be just outside the effect of the sun's gravity field. Using this configuration, Tl'Rak will have to use a more central approach. He wouldn't dare come in at the extreme angle, because even the smallest hit on his shields from the frigates' weapons will be too much for his ship's shields to deflect. Given the stress already on them, the destruction of his ship is certain." She again looked to R'Zoha for confirmation.

"I agree, Commander," he said.

"And we can further reduce the approach area by using the proximity mines in the gap area between the three ships just ahead of them," Tr'Tala added. He was suddenly feeling good about stopping Tl'Rak.

"That would certainly do it, Supreme Commander," his wife agreed.

"Supreme Commander, Commander," R'Zoha piped. "My calculations were done, given Tl'Rak's shields being at one hundred percent. Any decline in their strength significantly reduces the approach area and the possibility of his success getting around the sun. The minimum shield strength needed to make it around the sun is 98.87 percent. It would only take two plasma cannon shots to bring them to that level. And one mine could take them out entirely or destroy the ship."

Zh'Cata smiled. "We have him, Supreme Commander."

"So, it appears." But his smile disappeared. "Let there be caution. We cannot claim victory until his ship is out of commission. Now, I must contact Commander Fr'Tet and give him new orders." Before he did, he reopened the channel to the emperor.

"My Lady, everything is ready. I will contact Commander Fr'Tet to give him the plan. One second."

She nodded.

Again, he touched his screen, and it split into four blocks. The emperor was in one and Fr'Tet in another. The others remained blank.

"Commander Fr'Tet," Tr'Tala addressed him.

"Supreme Commander." He bowed his head in respect. It wasn't every day the Supreme Fleet Commander talked directly to a field commander, unless it was something important.

"Commander, get your unit commanders on this channel now."

"Yes, Supreme Commander."

Quickly, the other two commanders appeared on both Tr'Tala's and the emperor's screen. Tr'Tala spelled out the situation to the three commanders and gave them the defensive plan. He ended his briefing by saying, "Now if any commander in this unit balks at any of my orders, then the others will destroy his ship. If all three of you are in on the plot, then you had better make the time jump with Tl'Rak, as I will hunt you down."

There was a pause as Tr'Tala let his words sink in. "Of course, I trust that all of you are loyal to the empire and won' let me or the emperor down." The three commanders nodded.

"We are loyal to the empire," Fr'Tet answered boldly for his group. "We will stop Commander Tl'Rak, giving our lives." He and the other commanders knew that if they stopped the *Lionare,* praise and glory would be theirs and a reassignment to the battle fleet. They had their fill of the mind-numbing picket duty.

Tr'Tala gave a curt nod. "Start implementing the plan. When you encounter Tl'Rak's ship, open this channel to my office. I will watch the battle."

"Yes, Supreme Commander," Fr'Tet replied.

"Good hunting," Tr'Tala said and severed the comm-link with them and returned his attention to the emperor.

"Very good, Sen," she praised. "I will watch it too. The galaxy's future is at stake."

"Yes, my Lady. I will contact you once I'm contacted."

"How much time until Tl'Rak's ship reaches Ul'Tarus?"

"About three hours, my Lady."

She blew out a heavy breath. "Not much time, but for us, it will seem to creep by."

"That it will, my Lady."

She bobbed her head, feeling unsettled.

Along the UPA-Empire border, the UPA frigate *Sparrow* cruised slowly. The ship, outfitted with enhanced sensor arrays, monitored communications within the Valeriian Empire, especially between command and starships. Since the peace treaty between the two powers almost all communiques intercepted were ordinary. The duty was becoming ho-hum.

Toward the end of the evening shift, Chief Larson's eyes grew tired as he viewed his monitors that displayed the sensors' data. The incoming data was all nominal, mostly background static. He took a deep breath to clear the boredom from his body and massage his weary eyes. As he relaxed back into his seat, one monitor flashed an alert for new data. Larson shook his head. "Probably just a routine ship movement order," he whispered to himself. He touched the record and decode icon and waited for the translation to display on the monitor. It started: *For Fleet Commander's eyes only. Alert, alert....*

"Holy Toledo," he voiced out loud. There was no one else in the room. He stabbed the comm button. "SIC (sensor information center) to Bridge."

"Bridge, Lt Diaz." Diaz was the evening shift duty officer.

"Sir, Chief Martin. I have what appears to be a top-secret intercept. Can you come to the SIC?"

"On my way. Bridge out. Ensign Mayo, you have the bridge," Diaz said. He exited to the SIC that was one deck below.

Diaz read the message and tapped his annunciator. "Captain Kelley, Lt. Diaz."

"What is it?" Kelley asked gruffly.

"We have a Valeriian intercept of the highest priority. You need to read, sir."

"I'll be right there." Kelley with the rank of Commander entered the SIC and read the message. He uttered a few expletives. "Route this message to my cabin. I will contact CIC (commander-in-chief) Fleet Ops."

Luckily, it was morning at Fleet Ops and Admiral John "Jack" Reid was in his office. He was having coffee before he tended to the never-ending reports and dispatches. Suddenly his viewer beeped, and he glanced at it. The message read, "For your eyes only. Incoming transmission from Commander Kelley, *Sparrow*." He keyed in his passcode and Kelley's face appeared. It looked grave.

"Admiral," Kelley began, not even wishing his superior *good morning*. He read the intercept to Reid. After finishing, both men took deep breaths.

"Thank you, Commander," Reid said. "Keep listening and keep me informed. God speed." He cut the link before Kelley could say, aye, aye. He then opened a link to the president's office.

CHAPTER FIVE
Truth and Consequences

The *Lionare* was now speeding at maximum velocity for a rendezvous with destiny. Commander Tl'Rak sat confidently in his command seat, watching the stars pass swiftly. Behind him, Lt. Nh'Got sat pensively, hoping her message had made it through and Central Command had come up with a plan to stop the crazed commander. To Tl'Rak's right, First Officer M'Catis sat stoically. His mind was continually turning over alternatives, just in case Nh'Got's message had not gotten through. He surmised the probe was transmitting a distress call to central command.

"Commander," the comm-officer piped up, jolting Tl'Rak from his godlike aura. He turned to Sl'Hut, annoyance scowled on his face. The young man didn't flinch at the look and simply gave his report. "There is an incoming message from Central Command. It's the Supreme Fleet Commander's office." He held his breath.

Suddenly, Nh'Got's heart skipped a beat. M'Catis managed a dry swallow. The timing was right for the ship to receive a message from Central Command. Now it is time for truth and consequences.

"Cut the transmission," Tl'Rak ordered in an even tone. "We are beyond the recall point."

"Yes, Commander," Sl'Hut breathed, shocked that his commander spurned the Supreme Fleet Commander.

M'Catis and Nh'Got exchanged stunned glances. Both knew now Tl'Rak was a lone wolf. With the call from central command, they suspected Tl'Rak had to be suspicious why the Supreme Fleet Commander was calling him. He had to know that central command was on to his plan and that someone on the ship ratted him out. Both shivered inside wondering if he would accuse them of being the snitch.

Other than the comm-officer, all eyes fixed on Tl'Rak. He felt their weight, and his left hand dropped to his side, finding his weapon. "Is there a problem with my decision?" he asked, looking back at his junior officers.

Heads shook and turned back to their stations. Tl'Rak grinned with satisfaction. "Tactical. Cloak the ship."

"Yes, Commander, cloaking now," Nh'Got replied crisply. She didn't want to die today.

"Lieutenant Nh'Got," Tl'Rak said stiffly.

"Yes, Commander," she said, holding her breath, waiting for him to accuse her of conspiring against him.

"Set forward sensors to long-range scan. Find those three picket ships around Ul'Tarus. I suspect that they will have orders to stop us."

"Yes, Commander," she clipped, deflating inside. M'Catis hid his sigh of relief. Nh'Got repositioned the forward sensor array. "Commander, the scanner is detecting three ships at the sun."

"Of course," Tl'Rak said, straightening in his seat. "Helm, stop the ship."

"Ship to stop," was the repeat. As the ship slowed, Tl'Rak said to Nh'Got, "Put those three ships on the main." Instantly the sun and the three picket ships appeared in a 3-D display.

"As I suspected," Tl'Rak harrumphed. "The Supreme Commander has positioned them in a triangle to block our approach. Yet he must know I can dive the ship onto the approach course from above or below. Tactical, scan for mines."

"Scanning for mines, Commander," Nh'Got said, knowing full well they were there. The Supreme Commander had the reputation of being a brilliant tactician. He wouldn't overlook all routes to and from the sun. Sure enough, hundreds of them showed up on her screen. "Commander, mines are present. They appear to be proximity mines. I will add them to the display."

"Damn!" Tl'Rak cursed and stabbed his comm button. "Engineer, to my briefing room now! Nh'Got, you're with me. Helm, hold this position. M'Catis, you have the bridge." The first officer felt uneasy being left out. Or should he? For all he knew, Tl'Rak would accuse Nh'Got of conspiracy against the ship with the ship's engineer as a witness and then shoot her.

Tl'Rak stood, his left hand still on his plasma gun. Satisfied his crew was placid, he left the bridge with Nh'Got in tow. As she followed him, her heart pounded, anxious about what would happen next. Was Tl'Rak going to confront her about how the Supreme Fleet Commander had gotten wind of his plan? Or did he simply want to go over a strategy about how to get by the picket ships?

With him off the bridge, M'Catis studied the tactical display and concluded Tl'Rak's only option was to retreat. They would become the prey for Tl'Rak's treasonous action.

In the briefing room, Nh'Got opened the tactical hologram center table. Tl'Rak came right to the point of the meeting. "How can the *Lionare* get past the picket ships and mines and make the run around the sun to ancient Earth?" He shifted his eyes back and forth between the officers.

Nh'Got felt appeased that the situation was impossible. The time continuum was secure. Yet she was sure her life would end. The madman would attempt the run regardless of any recommendations.

"Commander, it is strictly forbidden to go back in time," the ship's engineer, T'Som reminded. "Is there a reason we need to?"

Tl'Rak returned a disapproving glare to his engineer, a man he trusted for many years. He owed his life to him many times during the heat of battle. He softened his stare. "At present, it is a need to know, and...." The engineer nodded his understanding. He had heard those words before from Tl'Rak. It was when missions were clandestine and in the best interest of the empire. Why would he doubt him now?

T'Som took a deep breath and studied the holo-image. "Commander, to make a run around the sun, the ship's shields need to be at one hundred percent to protect us from its heat. The safety margin is 1.5 percent if we are lucky. The shields will hold against the blast of one proximity mine and two direct cannon shots. They will be weak, well below the minimum of 98.5 percent without hope of surviving the sun's effect."

There was silence as Tl'Rak stared at the hologram. "We will make the run cloaked."

Nh'Got's brows knitted and said, "Commander, their scanners must have detected us by now. They will look for us even if cloaked."

"And Commander," T'Som added, we cannot make the run around the sun cloaked at greater than light speed with the shields up. The power expenditure is too great and will cause an imbalance in the main reactor. They will go offline or worse, explode. Only an uncloaked ship can make the run around the sun."

That's not what Tl'Rak wanted to hear. He continued to stare at the hologram. The tension in the room was high. "Then we will have to take out the pickets?"

"Commander, surely you don't mean to attack our ships?" T'Som protested.

"That's exactly what I intend to do. Our mission is so secret they don't even know what it is." It was a lie. "And my order is to complete the mission, no matter the cost. Even if it means taking out our ships." Another lie. Only Nh'Got knew it, but she held her tongue. Another pause as Tl'Rak shifted his eyes to his officers to see their reaction. Nh'Got was ready and kept a straight face. The engineer's eyes were wide with surprise. "T'Som," he said to him. "Once we are back in time, I will reveal the 'why' to you and the crew. What I need now is your loyalty and expertise to keep the ship intact and functioning to complete our mission. I expect you to do that." It was not a question but an order.

T'Som managed a swallow and said, "Commander you have my loyalty."

Tl'Rak looked at Nh'Got. "I know you are loyal." She nodded; a lie on her part.

"T'Som, return to engineering. I want the shields up to hundred and five percent. Push the reactor past the red line. Funnel every bit of energy into them, even if it means diverting power from life support. Those shields will not fall below hundred percent, regardless of the hits they take. Do you understand?" Again, it was not a question.

T'Som's mouth gaped to protest, but thought the better of it. "As you order, Commander." He bowed and left the room. The order to T'Som confirmed to Nh'Got that her commander had lost sanity. The man was going to make the run, and if the ship disintegrated, so be it. He summoned the first officer to the briefing room. He arrived and took a seat next to Nh'Got and listened.

"Subcommander, the chief engineer has assured me that he can have the shields at hundred and five percent. That will give us a 6.8 percent safety margin against any attack and the sun's heat when we make the run." It was yet another lie. T'Som hadn't given any such assurance. Nh'Got withheld her dissent of the lie. Tl'Rak continued, "Nonetheless, we have to plan our run to minimize any hits to the ship. I need your thoughts." His eyes shifted between the two officers. They stared at the holo-display.

M'Catis sighed. "I don't see any option that would negate less than six cannon shots to the ship. Six hits would take down our shields. The ship wouldn't survive the run around the sun."

"I agree with Subcommander M'Catis," Nh'Got said. Both hoped their analysis would dissuade their commander from committing suicide.

"That's if we make a dead-center run," Tl'Rak concurred. "If the ship drops into the run from a wing positioned ship, we would only have to worry about that ship's cannons." As his subordinates started to protest, he held up a hand. "If you're concerned about mines, don't be. We will blast our way through the mines while attacking the wing picket and make our run." He tapped the table with his hands, grinning from ear to ear.

"It may work, providing the other ships don't reposition quickly and attack," M'Catis said.

"The first mine explosion coming out of cloak will give us away," Nh'Got advised. "The other ships will certainly close on us as we blast through the other mines." A pause. "And we cannot do that at light speed," she added, anticipating Tl'Rak's next move. There was silence as the mad commander eyed the tactical display.

"Yes, of course," he harrumphed. Both M'Catis and Nh'Got were relieved. But it was short-lived as Tl'Rak said, "Then the best option is going up the middle enroute to the sun. We'll take on the lead ship, destroying it, and make the jump to light speed before the wing ships close." He gave them a devilish smirk of satisfaction. Both subordinate officers nodded, conceding Tl'Rak's plan had a hint of success. Likely it would fail, and the timeline would remain intact.

"Commander," Nh'Got spoke hurriedly, feeling distraught her life would end with this plan. "Let me add in the time travel course and see the position of the pickets before we make the run."

"Do so," Tl'Rak motioned to the holo-display. Nh'Got moved her fingers over the controls and a red line appeared. She moved it toward the sun and around its equator and back on a parallel course. The course bisected the lead picket ship.

"Do we have the name of the ship and it's unfortunate commander?" Tl'Rak asked.

"It's the *Selfor.* The commanding officer is Commander Fr'Tet," M'Catis replied. "He was one class ahead of me at command school. He is a capable officer. It would be unfortunate to lose this man." M'Catis tried to appeal to his commander's benevolent side if it was still present.

"Not that capable. Picket patrol at the sun is scut duty," Tl'Rak said, waving a dismissing hand. M'Catis wanted to rebut him but held his tongue. Anyone in command of a ship was a competent officer no matter his assigned duty. "He won't be a loss to the empire." A pause. Tl'Rak's dismissive attitude about fellow Valeriians left M'Catis and Nh'Got wide-eyed and mouths parted.

Tl'Rak ignored their looks and said, "I see it this way. We sneak up on the frigate while cloaked. Then decloak and hit the frigate with a sustained siege cannon blast. With its shields weakened, two torpedoes separated by one second will finish it off. With the way clear, we jump to hyper-light and make the run for the past and to a new glorious future for the empire." His grin broadened even more. "To the bridge!"

In his office, Tr'Tala; his wife, Commander Zh'Cata; and her first officer, R'Zoha stared at the main viewer. It showed a wide, real-time view of the sun and the three picket ships. Tl'Rak's ship, the *Lionare,* was not visible, but assumed to be ahead of the blockade. At the palace, the emperor viewed the same on her main screen.

"How long has it been since the *Lionare* cloaked?" Tr'Tala asked.

"Sir, coming up on four hours," R'Zoha answered.

"Tl'Rak must be going mad trying to figure out a way past the frigates," Zh'Cata said.

"He already is mad with this treasonous plot," her husband added.

"Maybe he has reconsidered and fled the area," R'Zoha suggested.

"I don't think so," came the emperor's voice. "He'll act without concern for his life, crew, and ship."

"I agree, my Lady," Tr'Tala said.

"There!" R'Zoha said, pointing at the screen. "A ripple in space."

"I saw it too," Zh'Cata said. "It has to be the *Lionare.*"

"The cloak shouldn't cause a ripple-like that, especially at a dead stop," Tr'Tala stated.

"It could if there was a power fluctuation," R'Zoha advised. "Tl'Rak must be shunting power from all available systems to the shields once he decloaks. That would explain the ripple, a momentary decrease in power to the cloak."

"Then that means he's going to attack and Fr'Tet's ship is on the point and will be hit first," Tr'Tala said, stabbing a Comm button. "Commander Fr'Tet."

"Fr'Tet here, sir."

"Did you see that ripple in space a moment ago?"

"Yes, sir. I think it was the *Lionare's* cloak that experienced a power variance. Commander Tl'Rak is routing all available power to his shields."

Tr'Tala nodded, surprise that Fr'Tet had rendered the same conclusion. Possibly he had misjudged the man, and mistakenly assigned him to monotonous picket duty. But right now, he was happy that he had placed Fr'Tet in command at Ul'Tarus.

"I believe the attack on the *Selfor* is imminent," Fr'Tet said. "We are ready. All ships have shields up, ready to move on the quick with weapon locked and loaded."

"Very good, Commander," Tr'Tala praised, more impressed with Fr'Tet. "Now we wait."

"What was that?" Tl'Rak shouted from his command seat on the bridge. No one answered. He turned to Nh'Got his face angry red. "The distortion on the main. Did you see it?"

"No Commander. I was checking weapons status."

"M'Catis?" He eyed his first officer.

"I noticed nothing," he admitted.

"Did anyone see it?" He looked around at the remaining bridge crew.

"Sir, I think I saw a quick blur," the helmsman said. "But I dismissed it as a film on my eye."

"It was no film on your eye!" Tl'Rak shouted, then tapped his annunciator. "Engineering. What was that, ah, film, distortion?"

"Commander, the cloak may have had millisecond power fluctuation," the engineer advised. "It likely happened as I routed the power from nonessential systems to the shields per your order."

"You idiot!" Tl'Rak shouted, his face flushed with fury. "You may have given away our position and intention!" He closed the link to engineering never hearing T'Som's apology. Again, the bridge went quiet, as Tl'Rak fumed, rethinking. "We must assume they saw us and know we are planning a dead-on attack. I am open to suggestions."

"Commander Tl'Rak," came the helmsman.

"Go ahead," Tl'Rak waved an approving hand to the young officer.

"Sir, ah, why don't we circle the sun and attack from behind. We can sneak up, decloak, and hit them point-blank. They'll never expect it. Then we, I mean you, sir, can make a leisurely time travel run around the sun." The helmsman closed with a hopeful smile.

Tl'Rak nodded his approval to the helm and turned to Nh'Got. Inside, she was pale, as was M'Catis. The helmsman's suggestion was ingenious and had a high probability of success. "Nh'Got, your replacement sits before you," he said to her, motioning to the man. "To keep your job, you better prove yourself in the upcoming attack and this mission. If not, you will be the new helmsman. Do I make myself clear?"

"You do, Commander," she clipped crisply. *At least he doesn't suspect me of contacting the supreme commander.* When Tl'Rak turned from her, she glanced over to M'Catis. He lowered his head, acknowledging her thoughts.

"Helm, slowly back the ship a hundred kilometers."

"Yes, sir," replied the now confident helmsman.

"Navigator, plot a slow wide course around the sun. Bring us in the middle of the three picket ships."

"Plotting the course now, Commander," the navigator replied.

Tl'Rak relaxed back into his seat, satisfied.

CHAPTER SIX
Ready, Set, Jump!

The atmosphere in Tr'Tala's office was tense. The officers sat watching the tactical screen of the sun and the picket ships. The emperor herself felt anxious as she viewed the same scene at her palace. The past, present, and future were at stake not only for her empire but for the entire galaxy. Allowing Tl'Rak to travel back in time wasn't an option. All means to stop him were on the table. She hoped the rogue commander had abandoned his doomed plan and fled the area. Better yet, there had been a mutiny on the *Lionare*. Time seemed to tick by slowly at the empire's home planet.

"You would think Tl'Rak would have made his move by now," Commander Zh'Cata commented. She stood and stretched to relieve the pent up tension.

"Three hours have passed. What is he waiting for?" Subcommander R'Zoha added, shaking his head.

"Damn!" Tr'Tala shouted, slamming a fist down. "He's attacking from the rear. He's made a counterclockwise transit around the sun. Fr'Tet!"

The *Lionare* came up from behind the picket ships undetected. Tl'Rak had taken them by surprise. He gave a wry smile, inched to the edge of his seat, and said, "Tactical. Weapons status?"

"All weapons locked and loaded on targets. Ready at your command," Lt. Nh'Got replied with a steady voice. Her stomach churned with disgust and remorse for what was about to happen.

The *Lionare* crept closer to the pickets, almost at point-blank range. Everyone on the bridge edged up in their seats. They knew full well the damage and destruction the *Lionare* was about to inflict.

"Tactical decloak and fire," Tl'Rak ordered. Nh'Got hesitated a breath, uncloaked the ship, and fired. Quickly, she turned to the main screen to see the result of her actions. Six torpedoes, fluorescent green in color, streaked from the *Lionare*, two per frigate with orange balls of plasma following from the *Lionare's* cannons. They hit their marks, lighting up the area with multicolored flames and explosions. The wing frigates held their place in space for only a few seconds before turning to flotsam. Fr'Tet's ship was still intact after the initial barrage. It was scorched and vented gases from a hull breach. He had heard Tr'Tala's call and was able to strengthen his rear shields, but the damage to his ship was severe. He blindly fired with all available weapons at the shielded *Lionare.* All missed. The *Selfor* slowly moved away.

Tl'Rak beamed broadly. He leaned back in his seat, satisfied." Lt. Nh'Got good shooting. You have secured your position as tactical officer."

The helmsman's ego deflated, but asked, "Will we pursue and finish off the *Selfor?*"

M'Catis jumped in before Tl'Rak answered. "I suggest we let the *Selfor* flee. Our luck has been good. Let's not chance it. The *Selfor* might hit us with a lucky shot. Its commander and crew will have to answer with their lives to the emperor for their failure here."

"I agree with the first officer," Nh'Got chimed. "Save the shields for the run around the sun." With an already sour stomach, she didn't want to sicken it further by destroying the *Selfor.*

Tl'Rak sucked in a breath as he watched the *Selfor* oozing life and limping away. "Helm, return the ship to our original position before our attack and hold station there." The helmsman talked back the order.

In Central Command, mouths were agape; a cloud of disappointment hovered over everyone. Tr'Tala felt wounded as he was the one who planned for the defense of the sun to make sure no ship ever made a trip back in time. He began second-guessing himself. *Should I have had more ships there? Stronger ships? A more competent group commander?* The answer to these questions would come later. He had to react now to save the past, present, future, and his fate.

"Commander Zh'Cata," he said, looking at his wife. His wife's grimaced with sorrow for her husband and the lost ships. "Recall your ship's crew. Prepare *Tigerii* for immediate departure. I will join you there shortly. We must hunt down Tl'Rak before he gets to ancient Earth.

Tl'Rak sat in his seat, staring at the sun. He had his armrests in a secure position to hold him in place when the ship started its run around the sun. "M'Catis, what is the ship's status?" His voice was calm.

"All stations are manned and ready. Engineering is reporting shields at one hundred and five percent. There is no life support in non-personnel areas. The ship is a go."

"Very good. Bridge crew, secure your positions. Helm, ready, set, jump!" he said with enthusiasm. In a blur, the *Lionare* was at light speed and accelerating toward the sun and an appointment with history.

CHAPTER SEVEN
Time Revisited

Admiral Reid couldn't believe the Valeriians were attempting time travel again. Two years had passed since the last incident. This incident was worse; a rogue starship commander was doing it. He immediately requested an emergency meeting with the president.

Within the hour, he was in the situation room ten floors below the West Wing of the White House. Joining him were the president's chief of staff, the Director of Intelligence (DI), and members of the Joint Chiefs of Staff. All stood when the president entered. She motioned for them to sit as took her seat.

"You have the coded message received from the *Sparrow,*" the president said. "The situation is critical. At any moment, one or more of us may not exist. Even the world, the galaxy as we know it may change. I contacted the Valeriian Emperor, and she assured me she didn't sanction Commander Tl'Rak's actions. They attempted to stop him, but he successfully made the time jump. She said they are taking measures to hunt him down."

"Madam President, that would mean they are sending another ship to the past," Reid said. "The move itself could alter the present and the future. Also, there is no guarantee the ship could go back to the exact time that Tl'Rak did. And there's no telling the precise date Tl'Rak ended up in. Any time travel to the past by anyone could accidentally alter the timeline."

"I and the Valeriian Emperor understand all this, Admiral," the president said. "Supreme Fleet Commander Sen Tr'Tala is tasked to hunt down Tl'Rak. As you recall, he was the one who went back in time to kidnap Captain Ross." Reid nodded. He had taken the *Trafalgar* back in time to stop him.

"Tr'Tala has taken the mission to stop Tl'Rak personally and will use all means at his disposal to do so. To show you what a madman Tl'Rak is, he destroyed three empire ships guarding their sun to make the time jump. Another reason for Tr'Tala to go on the hunt himself. I offered our help, and the emperor declined. She cited an increased risk to the time continuum if further ships engaged in time travel. She thanked me and closed the link. Her demeanor seemed stressed."

"Madam President, of course you're going to send a ship back to stop this Tl'Rak?" asked the chief of the army.

"We have to," the president affirmed. "Admiral Reid, since the empire is sending back Sen Tr'Tala, we should send Captain Ross with his ship. They both know each other and jointly can work together to stop Tl'Rak."

"Madam President, I agree. However, Captain Ross and his ship are days away from the Earth's solar system. There is no time to recall him for this mission. The only heavy cruiser available is the *Orion.* Her captain is capable, but not in time travel. Ross is the only captain in the fleet with time travel experience. It would be a crapshoot sending the *Orion.*

"You're experienced, Admiral," she came back. "You can take command of the *Orion* and go after Tl'Rak."

"Madam President, I had a group of seasoned officers with me that made the trip to and back successful. That wouldn't be the case with the *Orion,*" Reid countered.

"Madam President," the Director of Intelligence (DI) Bob Katz interrupted, rescuing "There is another. The asset, Kay're. She is Captain Ross's wife and is currently here on the planet, and her vessel is in orbit. She is familiar with Sen Tr'Tala and time travel."

"And Madam President, her small ship would be undetectable to Tl'Rak and Tr'Tala if she made the trip," Reid added.

"And she could neutralize Tl'Rak quickly," Katz affirmed. "And return home without the Valeriians knowing she was there."

The president paused, then nodded her approval. "Activate her. She has the authority to use any means necessary to stop Tl'Rak and put an end to this nightmare. The *Sparrow's* intercept and this mission are beyond top secret.

Understood?" Heads nodded. "We will reconvene when the asset begins her time travel run. That's it, gentlemen, and pray we are still here to meet again."

Kay're was apprehensive as she piloted her craft toward the sun and trip back in time. She didn't care about the mechanics of time travel. The intel boys made all the calculations and loaded the program into her craft's computer. The techies had double-checked her ship's systems. They were a go. All she had to do was engage the program and sit back and enjoy the ride. Her worry was the same as everyone involved in the mission; the timeline could alter at any minute. She thought of her husband. The sensitivity of the mission prevented her from contacting him. *If my ship malfunctions, I may never see you again. The prospect of being lost in time for eternity isn't appealing.*

"Kay're, are you ready?" DI Katz asked, his determined face appearing on her main screen.

"Ready," she replied, refocusing her attention.

"Good luck!"

"Thanks, Bob," she said, smiling.

"Three, two, one!" Kay're touched an icon on the control panel, and her ship raced ahead to a meeting with Jesus Christ.

In the past, coming out of time travel had left her dizzy and disoriented. This time was no different. She closed her eyes and gave her head a quick shake. After several slow breaths, she opened her eyes to see a beach-ball-sized blue planet in the distance. It had to be Earth. She moved her ship closer and scanned for Tl' Rak's ship; it wasn't in orbit. Possibly he had cloaked it. Further scans showed no man-made orbiting objects; a good sign. Hopefully she arrived at the right time.

She wondered if Tl'Rak would cloak his ship. He had to know Earth at this point lacked the technology to scan the atmosphere for orbiting objects. Cloaking his ship wasted energy, unless he believed the empire would send lieved the empire would send a ship to hunt him down. She set her sensors to scan for an ion trail. Even a cloaked ship left a residual one, but there was none. The tech boys were good. They got her to Earth before Tl'Rak's arrival. Or was it weeks, months, years after his arrival? Had the timeline changed? Too many questions without answers. She shook the uncertainty from her head. Exercising caution, she cloaked her ship and proceeded to Earth. She needed to verify the period.

On approach, she scanned the planet for broadcast signals. There was none. She then scanned for a sizable population. She could have shot so far back to a time when the Earth lacked a significant population or any people! The scans showed people present. Most living within defined boundaries on all continents except Antarctica. To sustain her relief, there was a lack of industrialization. The populace was alive before the invention of the steam engine. The only way to confirm her arrival time was to beam down to the planet and ask for the date. Of course, if she found Jesus, that would be confirmation. She remembered her childhood encounter with him. She shivered in joy, thinking she may meet him again. Then she felt a bit of panic. What if she met her childhood self?

Was it even possible to have two of herself present? If so, what would she say or do if they met? Then there was... She gasped at the thought and blew out a breather to relax. Her past would be her present again; time revisited. She settled her craft into a geosynchronous orbit over Israel and cloaked it. As she began to select a custom appropriate for the time, she disappeared in a sparkle.

The *Lionare* violently decelerated from its trip around the Valleriian sun. The bridge crew reoriented themselves from the physical stress of the sudden slowing. All stared at the main viewer. The sun and stars all looked the same, and space showed no evidence of their attack on the picket ships. They had made the jump to the past. The crucial questions were: how far back did they travel? Did they indeed arrive at the time Jesus Christ lived on Earth?

"Tactical, do we have a time date?" Tl'Rak asked anxiously.

"Commander, we're too far from the home planet for scanners to verify a date," Nh'Got answered her eyes focused on her monitor. "We will need to establish an orbit around the planet."

"That will not happen," Tl'Rak gruffed out. "Supreme Commander Tr'Tala will be hot on our trail. I'm sure he will take the *Tigerii* back in time to hunt us down." The statement gave M'Catis and Nh'Got a mixed message. They exchanged dubious glances. There was hope for maintaining the time continuum. Likely they would die in a space battle.

"Commander," M'Catis piped in. "The Supreme Commander wouldn't know the exact date we have traveled to. And we do not know it either."

"Even if he had the date, the chances of returning to that exact time are astronomical," Nh'Got added, covering herself. "One minute difference from our entry acceleration or deceleration will place the *Tigerii* in another time. Even a small change in any of the variables will do the same. I believe the Supreme Commander knows this and will not chance time travel to hunt us down."

There was a pause as Tl'Rak suspiciously eyed the two officers. His gaze sent a shiver down their spines. "Tr'Tala will take the chance, albeit on orders from the emperor herself," he finally said. "There's too much at stake for them. I have a feeling he knows the exact date too. How he got it, I don't know, but there will be time to figure that out. Right now, the *Lionare* is heading to Earth at best speed. Regardless of the date we are now in, we will change the course of Earth's history that will benefit the empire." What he didn't add was that it would benefit himself. "Helm, to Earth, full light speed," he commanded, waving his hand.

The *Tigerii* left orbit for the sun. Tr'Tala and his senior officers gathered in the command center to discuss the hunt for the *Lionare.* "With all respect Supreme Commander," First Officer R'Zoha said, "I don't see how we can go back in time to find the *Lionare.* We don't know the date Tl'Rak was shooting for. In reading earth history, Jesus Christ's life span was some thirty-three earth years. Which year did he pick?"

"He is right," Commander Zh'Cata said to her husband. "Returning to Jesus Christ's birthday is the only sure way for us to intercept him. Then wait for the *Lionare* to show up. Theoretically our wait could be thirty years."

Tr'Tala rubbed a hand through his hair, feeling the weight of the moment. "You're both right. I did my research by reading the Earth book, the Bible. It references Jesus Christ's birth and nothing until his later adult years, about the age of thirty. Around his birth, his parents took him to a country called Egypt. There was no mention of returning to his home country. So, I doubt Tl'Rak would travel to this time. There's too much uncertainty. That leaves the years around 30 to 33 A.D. old earth date. We can rule out the first two years of Jesus Christ's later life. He was unknown then, and Tl'Rak would have a hard time finding him. He will make the jump to the last year of Jesus Christ's life. It was then that he was in the public eye and stirring up the biggest controversy. That likely will be the time of his torture and execution."

"Having studied Earth's history, I completely agree," Zh'Cata said.

"But why would Tl'Rak go back to kill him, when the man will die at the hands of his people?" R'Zoha questioned.

"Because, the Bible says Jesus Christ rose from the dead three days later. Then after forty days he ascended into heaven," Zh'Cata answered. "Tl'Rak will try to kill Jesus Christ after his resurrection from the dead or before his execution. There are theories that Jesus Christ survived his execution. His followers took from the burial tomb and aided his recovery. For forty days Jesus Christ roamed the area before rising into the clouds. Obviously, he had help, likely from an alien ship in Earth's orbit. Jesus Christ may not be a human but an alien in disguise. His mission to shape the course of earth's history. Regardless, Tl'Rak won't leave Earth unless he is sure Jesus Christ is dead. And if there is an alien species involved, he may deal with them too, and the consequences may alter the future." She paused to let her last comment sink in. There was deep concern on her husband's face.

"Supreme Commander," R'Zoha said. "Maybe Jesus Christ's ascension to the sky was Tl'Rak's doing. He transported him to the *Lionare* and made off with him. If so, we would be the ones who could change the future by stopping Tl'Rak."

R'Zoha's point was sound. The concern in Tr'Tala's face turned to distress. He looked to his wife, whose forehead wrinkled with uneasiness.

"We will never know by sitting here, sir," she said. "We need to make the jump to the time of Jesus Christ's execution. We can reevaluate the situation then and decide on a course of action." She gave him a hopeful look.

"Do it, Commander," he said, nodding to her.

The *Tigerii* hung motionless in the blackness, the sun roiling in the distance. The bridge crew waited pensively for the ship to begin racing to the past with all its uncertainty. And there was no assurance they could return to the current date. Commander Zh'Cata, looked over to her husband. He smiled at her as if it was his last and nodded. She returned the same and look at the main screen. "Helmsman engaged the time travel program."

"Engaging, Commander."

The *Tigerii* accelerated, and time seemed to blur. Minutes passed, and the ship started decelerating and the blur of time refocused. Finally, the ship slowed to a crawl, and the crew blinked away their disorientation.

"Engineering, ship's status," Zh'Cata called over the comm-link.

"The reactor is nominal, Commander," the chief replied. "There are some blown circuits scattered throughout the ship. No serious damage. I have crews making repairs."

"Keep the first officer appraised," Zh'Cata said and swiveled to her tactical officer. "What is the date?"

"Unknown," was the reply.

She then turned to her comm-officer. "Can you reach central command?"

"No, Commander," replied the junior officer. "And I'm not picking up any transmissions across the frequency spectrum." It was a sign they had traveled past the pre-radio wave era. But how far?

"Supreme Commander, will we return to the planet to find out the date?" Zh'Cata asked her husband.

"Commander," the tactical officer interrupted before Tr'Tala could answer. "The scanner is detecting a faint ion trail that is consistent with the emissions of a star drive. It has to be *Lionare's*."

"Well done!" Tr'Tala exclaimed, pumping a fist, and standing. "There is no time to check the date. Follow that ion trail before it dissipates."

"Lieutenant Se'Say, can you tell how old the trail is?" Zh'Cata asked the tactical officer.

"It's very faint. And the only reason I picked it up was the lack of frequency traffic. Comparing the standard decay rate of star drive emissions to these, I say these are at least a week old. It appears our jump put us behind the *Lionare* by that amount of time. I have extrapolated the heading and it is toward the UPA territory."

The excitement in Tr'Tala's face faded on the news. "One week," he said to no one in particular. "During that week he could change the future and the here and now, and...." He lacked words to finish the sentence. At any moment their lives could change or even be nonexistent, and everyone on the ship knew this. Their lives and the future were in limbo. He looked down at his lovely wife in despair. She returned a hopeful smile of encouragement. He managed a smile and nodded at her.

"Se'Say, feed the extrapolated ion trail up to the UPA border to helm control," Zh'Cata ordered. "Helm, once you get the coordinates, full light speed. Once we reach the UPA border, we will scan for the ion trail again." Zh'Cata hoped Tl'Rak never changed course, as the scanner couldn't track the ion trail at light speed. Then again Earth was the only destination to find Jesus Christ.

CHAPTER EIGHT
The Well

Kay're stretched the sleepy fog from her body and opened her eyes to a cloudless azure sky. The air was warm and arid with a hint of a breeze in the quiet of the moment. She looked side to side to see only parched ground and gray rocks. Sitting up, she pondered the how and where. Her short-term memory was absent.

She stood and gazed eastward to see the sun winking over the distance hills. It was morning and that was a foreboding sign in the already warm air; and she was thirsty. When the sun peaked, she knew it would bring a scorching heat. Doing a 360 survey, she saw a landscape that was rocky, dry with little vegetation. Water was her priority and soon. To the south she noticed several birds circling. With a nod of her head, she headed that way.

During her walk, she failed to break the amnesia of the events leading to her current situation. She wondered if someone had drugged her and she was still under its influence. Maybe in a few hours her muddle would clear and the when, where, and why would be answered. She sucked in a breath and made for the next hill knowing that she had been in worse situations.

An hour later and parched she crested a hill to find a woman below drawing water from a stone well. The woman had long graying hair and wore a dark brown sack-like dress. She had sandals on her feet. Kay're's uniform for her slim tall defined figure was a tight blue jumpsuit with ankle high black boots. She was out of costume for the time and area. Her short slightly curled dark brown hair was likely foreign to the area too. Yet she needed water and answers.

Approaching the woman, she cleared her throat to announce her arrival. The local turned, showing her sun aged face. She startled and backed away a few steps eying her unexpected visitor from head to toe.

Kay're smiled and lifted a hand to her mouth indicating she needed to drink. The woman nodded and returned to the well and drew another bucket of water. She handed the bucket to the stranger. Kay're drank to the full. The water was surprisingly clear and cool. She smiled and returned the bucket to the lady.

"Kay're," she said, pointing to herself.

"Miriam," the lady replied, bowing, and placing a hand to her chest.

Kay're raised a hand and moved it around as means of asking where she was. She wanted to hear the stranger talk to determine the language and the land.

The woman spoke, but Kay're didn't recognize the language, though she thought she had heard it before. The where and when she couldn't remember. She held up a hand and touched her left ear to activate her translator. Again, she motioned for the woman to repeat.

"Samaria. This is Jacob's well," the woman said.

Kay're had heard the word Samaria before, but couldn't place it.

"You are obviously Roman," the woman continued. "I'm surprised you're alone out here. You're beautiful, not dressed appropriately, and without a canteen. Have you been cast out by your husband?"

Kay're chuckled. "No. I am simply lost." The words were in the woman's own language. "Thank you for the water, Miriam. You have returned life to my soul. May you be forever blessed." Kay're reached out and touched Miriam on the shoulder.

"For a Roman, you are very kind," Miriam said.

"I'm not Roman," Kay're said softly with a smile.

"You're not a Samarian or even Jewish?"

"I'm a stranger from a very distant land."

"Do you seek the prophet?"

"The prophet?" Kay're returned, surprised.

"The great one that asked me for water as you did several weeks ago. He said that whoever drinks from the water he gives will never thirst. Yet he gave me no water like this." She pointed the bucket. "Yet inside I felt satisfied and filled with new life. I cannot explain the feeling."

On hearing Miriam's words, a cold shiver ran Kay're's body. She knew the where and when. "Yes, I seek the prophet. Where may I find him?"

"In your heart," Miriam replied, touching her chest.

"Yes, I know. But I want to see him. Where?"

"I heard he was heading to Galilee; to the northeast." She pointed in that direction.

Kay're nodded. "Miriam, you are more blessed than I could ever be. Thank you." Miriam nodded and watched Kay're walk away.

CHAPTER NINE
The Four Horsemen

Heading toward Galilee was no less fatiguing. Walking up and down dry craggy hills taxed her energy. They seemed to be never-ending without any hint of life. There was no scrub brush or plants from which she could suck moisture to wet her lips and tongue. Swallowing was a challenge as her throat felt raw. Every so often, she would stop and look back to see if anyone was following her. Hopefully, someone with water, but there was no one. She was alone in the hills of Israel with the sun baking her. Not even an occasional cloud passed by to give her a few minutes of shade. *Oh, I how she wish for a wide-brimmed hat to keep the sun off my face.*

Two hours passed and her thirst was overwhelming. She wanted to be back at the well with Miriam and feel the pleasure of cool water going down her throat. Never again would she dismiss the simplicity of downing a glass of water. Despair was setting in, but she continued to push herself.

Finally, after another hill, there was a hint of life, a dirt path, and a few blades of grass. She dropped to a knee and pulled up the grass and chewed it. The grass gave little moisture, but enough to wet her tongue

Standing, she gazed at the path that was heading to the northeast. She decided to follow it, hoping it would lead to a village and water. If she was lucky a stranger bearing water would be walking her way.

After another hour her optimism began fading. Completely dehydrated, she sat and looked up at the sky, hoping rain clouds would appear. The sky remained cloudless, and she wondered if she could trek further. The prospects of finding a water source seemed to be nil.

Then there was noise! She heard coordinated pounding coming from the rear. She turned and saw a dust cloud. From it appeared horsemen. Four of them, three clothed in similar knee-length grey tunics over a red wool shirt. They donned metal helmets with red plumage down the center and rode either side of the fourth man. He wore a white tunic with gold trim, a metal chest plate, and a scarlet robe over the shoulders. All had swords and canteens. She judged them to be Roman soldiers, likely on patrol, and they might be trouble. Yet they had water. Could she risk waving them down and asking for water without them being menacing toward her?

As thirsty as she was, she decided against it. She surmised that if they were around, local people would be too, and a town. She dropped her head and moved off the path, hoping they would dismiss her and pass. In her current attire, likely not. She was right. They galloped to her side as she kept walking with her head down.

"What do we have here?" asked the leader, moving his horse to block her.

"Centurion Marcus, I surmise a whore, given her costume. Look at it," said one of his men.

Damn! They're going to be a problem. Ready yourself, girl.

"Or lack thereof," added another.

"I agree," the centurion said. He dismounted and lifted Kay're's chin with a finger.

She stared into his face and recognized him as someone from her past. She kept a stoic face, though her heart was racing. The sunburn on her face hid her blush.

Her eyes caught the man by surprise. His head balked back as if someone had stabbed him. He regained his composure. "A feisty one," he added. "And looking very thirsty too. I can quench your thirst and you mine." He gave her a wry smile.

"Please, I am not a whore. Just a lost traveler from a distant land. As a man of authority and education, you can see I am a stranger. As a gentleman, please offer me your welcome and water to quench my thirst." She focused her eyes on his and entered his mine with the simple word, "Please." He turned uncomfortably to his men to break the link. Somehow, she was affecting his mind as the child had.

"Do you believe her?" he asked his men.

"No, Centurion," they chorused. "She is a whore!"

"I have seen whores dressed like this," one lied.

Centurion Marcus turned back to the woman. "You're right. I am an educated man and a gentleman to refined ladies. And you are not that." He felt uncomfortable lying as he recognized her as a decent and unique woman that was telling the truth.

"We don't tolerate women of your kind," he continued his lie. "So, being a gentleman, I will look the other way and spare your miserable life." He paused and smiled at her again. "But only after you comfort me and then my men with your...." He eyed her from head to toe. When he looked into her face, his lustful smile suddenly turned to panic. She had knifed her fingers into his throat, something she felt terrible doing. He reeled back, gasping, holding his crushed windpipe. His soldiers quickly dismounted, but Kay're was ready. The first soldier she side-kicked in the face, her boot collapsing his nose. He turned away in pain, spewing blood. Returning to her feet, she ducked down and leg-whipped another from his feet. With her other leg, she kicked the other man in the groin, dropping him to his knees. Catlike, she kicked a sword from his hand as he raised it to strike.

The first soldier, somewhat recovered, wiped the blood from his face. He grasped his sword and swiped at Kay're. She adroitly dodged the blade and reverse spin kicked him in the face again. She felt and heard the crunch of his facial bones. He reeled back with a yelp of pain. The other man was up and tackled her, taking her to the ground. She lost her breath from his weight falling on her chest. He loomed over her, his face twisted in anger and ready to kill. Bracing one hand on her chest, he raised a fist to silence her, but never landed the punch as she thumbed one of his eyes. He arched back howling, and she punched him in the throat. With the man gasping for air, she pushed him off her body and scrambled to her feet. The man she had kicked in the groin came at her with his sword raised.

"Stop!" she shouted, hoping the man would do so. He kept coming set on revenge. She stepped toward the soldier and side kicked him in the face, his helmet flying off. He paused from the blow, a mistake, as she again kicked him in his bloodied face, caving it in. Stunned and blind with blood, he swung his sword wildly. Kay're evaded the swings and kicked the man's left knee, crumpling it, bringing him to the ground. An ax kick to the head finished him.

The soldier with the crushed face and distorted vision came at her with his sword. She back flipped to avoid the sword and sprang to a fighting stance as he stumbled toward her. He was easy prey. As he raised his sword, she did a flying jump kick and planted a heel on his mangled face, forcing bone into his brain. He staggered and fell face first. He was dead.

Now there were two men left, both gasping for air. The centurion had propped himself up against a rock and watched in horror. The woman without a weapon took apart three of Roman's finest without so much as a scratch to herself. The other soldier took one last gasp and joined his two fellow soldiers.

Kay're glanced at the centurion. He was in no condition to offer resistance. Feeling spent, she placed hands on her knees and sucked in several deep breaths. Yet she kept an eye on the centurion, a man who would figure prominently in her life. After regaining her wind, she approached, hunched down, and looked at him. Still struggling for air, he eyed her and placed a hand on the hilt of his sword. She shook her head and his hand dropped to the ground.

"What happened to that gallant soldier who placed his robe on a cold little girl that slept by the fire?"

His eyes widened in surprise. "How could you know that?" he wheezed. She smiled and inched closer to him and stared into his eyes. "You!" he gasped. "How?"

She stood and looked around and went to one horse. Its blanket still had some straw entangled in it. She checked each twig until she found a hollow one and returned to the centurion. "I'm going to save your life. Trust me." She squatted down and stared into his eyes and reached into his mind. Centurion Marcus felt peace and saw Claudia smiling at him. He nodded.

She reached into her hip pocket and produced a penknife. Slowly she brought the knife to Marcus's throat. His eyes widened in fear.

"No," he tried to say, shaking his head.

"I'm going to slice an opening in your neck; not to kill, but to give you a chance to live. And you will thank me in the future." Using her other hand, she felt for his Adam's apple while still holding the straw and made a one-inch vertical cut. The centurion felt the pain but remained still. She separated the tissue, cut through the windpipe cartilage, and inserted the straw. Immediately Marcus gave a raspy sigh as he gained more air. He nodded his thanks. She smiled and then took his canteen and rinsed his face. The act brought her happiness. She gave it to him and told him to take sips. Finally, she took his robe that was on the ground and draped him. Once again, she gazed into his eyes and returned his memories of happier times.

She then retrieved canteens and food bags from the fallen soldiers. Quickly she drank one canteen empty. Never in her life did water taste so good. While watching the centurion, she nourished herself with dried meat and grain wafers.

"Centurion Marcus, you are a gallant and proud man. I know you didn't mean what you said about me to your men. I took no offense. Then you let your teenage lust get the best of you. I had to act. I hope you understand?"

"I do," he mouthed. "How do you know my name?"

She scooted up to him and clasped his face with her hand and gently kissed him. "I just know. Remember, my dear. Rest now. Your salvation is near."

CHAPTER TEN
Trapped

It took seven days for the *Lionare* to reach the Earth's solar system. It was a tense time for Lt. Nh'Got and Subcommander M'Catis. They worried Tl'Rak would question them about how the Supreme Fleet Commander got wind of his scheme. He never did. The crazed commander was intent on reviewing every detail about Jesus Christ and this time. Yet he and his officers lacked knowledge of how far back they had traveled in time. His research could be for naught.

"Commander," Nh'Got said, "the ship is about to enter the Earth's solar system."

"Helm, reduce speed to sub-light slow," Tl'Rak ordered.

"Reducing speed," the helmsman replied. Eyes stared at the main viewer that showed a few of the nine planets of various sizes orbiting a star. The blue third planet grew with each passing second. It took three hours to reach Earth. When it did Tl'Rak ordered Nh'Got to scan for satellites and ships around the Earth.

"The scan is negative, sir," she reported.

"Helm, establish a stationary orbit over the country of Israel at two hundred kilometers."

"Entering orbit now, Commander," the helmsman said. Several seconds passed and the helmsman announced the ship was in a stable orbit.

"Commander, I'm scanning for transmissions," Nh'Got said, anticipating the order from Tl'Rak. She was eager to determine they had arrived at the time of Jesus Christ. There was a brief pause. "No transmissions are coming to or from the planet. We arrived before the Earth's industrial period. One second as I scan for life." Another pause. "There are life forms, with the Mediterranean area having the highest concentration of humans. We have arrived around the time when Jesus Christ could be on the Earth. Only a survey team to the planet's surface can tell the exact earth date." She hoped Tl'Rak would send her and M'Catis to the planet alone. They would warn Jesus Christ if he was present of their commanders' plot.

M'Catis was thinking the same. "Per standard protocol, I will lead the survey team," he said. "I'll take only Lt. Nh'Got. The less the better and we will dress to look like humans of this time."

"Nothing is standard anymore," Tl'Rak snapped. "You will stay with the ship." M'Catis stiffened at the rebuke. "I and Nh'Got will transport to the surface."

"Commander, will we carry weapons?" Nh'Got asked, hoping for an affirmative answer. With an opportunity, she would shoot him and end this fiasco.

"Me only," Tl'Rak said stiffly, tapping his sidearm. Nh'Got nodded, composed though deflated.

At mid-day Israeli time, they beamed down to an area devoid of human life outside of Jerusalem. Their costumes consisted of tattered-looking dark brown tunics and leather sandals. Accompanying cloth headpieces covered most of their head and mouth. Tl'Rak had a rope tied around his waist that defined his robust chest. Nh'Got's tunic hung loosely. They looked ordinary for the time. Neither spoke any Earth languages. Their annunciators also worked as translators. They started their trek to Jerusalem with the sun high and the air hot.

"Commander, we needed to bring canteens. It's much warmer than I expected," Nh'Got commented, wiping sweat from her forehead.

"We'll not be here long," Tl'Rak said. "The town is ahead and once we find this Jesus person, I will blast him. Then we beam up and you can drink all you want in the glory of the new empire. We'll get drunk together!" He was grinning ear to ear. Nh'Got's stomach soured.

"Look, some humans are coming toward us," Tl'Rak said. "Your affable voice is the best suited for these humans. Ask them where we can find Jesus

Christ."

"Yes, Commander."

"Nh'Got, use no titles while we are on Earth. Doing so is too obvious." She nodded, understanding.

Two middle-aged men approached and Nh'Got raised a hand to stop them. "Excuse me. Do you know the location of Jesus Christ?"

They gave her quizzical looks. One spoke: "We don't know that name."

"What about Jesus of Nazareth?" Tl'Rak asked in his deep voice.

"That name we heard," the other local said, nodding. "We heard he is in Capernaum and we're going there to meet him. Will you join us?"

"How far is it to Capernaum?" Nh'Got asked.

The two men exchanged dubious glances. "You must not be from this area," one man said. "It's five days' travel on foot."

"Five days!" Tl'Rak boomed.

"Are you still going to join us?"

"No," Tl'Rak answered. "We will get there on our own."

"Then we bid you Good day," they said in unison and walked on.

When the men were a distance away, Tl'Rak said, "We will return to the ship, refresh, and beam down to this town, Capernaum."

Nh'Got sighed relieved. Not only did she want to bathe, Jesus was still safe, and there was the possibility of stopping Tl'Rak on the ship.

He called the ship. "M'Catis, transport us back to the ship."

Aboard the *Lionare,* M'Catis felt sick when he heard Tl'Rak's beam-up order. Could he have found Jesus Christ in such a short time and killed him? He would know once the mad man was back aboard. "Yes, Commander," he returned. He decloaked the ship, called transporter control, and gave the order to beam Tl'Rak and Nh'Got aboard.

He waited, knowing Tl'Rak would walk onto the bridge and boast of his killing. The wait seemed to be longer than usual. *Did Tl'Rak bring Jesus alive on the ship and is interrogating him?* Then he got a call from the transporter chief. "Subcommander, I can lock onto the away team, but the transporter isn't functioning."

"Use another one," M'Catis ordered.

"I have tried them all. None of them are working."

"Get the chief engineer and find out what's going on?" He didn't care if Tl'Rak returned, but he wanted Lt Nh'Got back.

As he waited, Tl'Rak called again. There was fury in his voice. "M'Catis, what's the delay?"

"Commander, the transporters are offline. Engineering is working on the problem. It shouldn't take long."

"Make it quick!" Tl'Rak snorted.

Some thirty minutes later, the chief engineer stepped onto the bridge, his face demurred. "Subcommander, all transporter systems are out. I'm at a loss on why they aren't working. I even tried transporting a box to the surface, and it was a no go. I lack an explanation." He raised his hands in frustration.

"The timeline has changed with the killing of Jesus Christ," M'Catis said, shaking his head. His words had a sobering effect on those on the bridge. He could see it in their faces. "I will let Commander Tl'Rak know." He called down to Tl'Rak and gave him the situation and his conclusion.

Immediately Tl'Rak screamed out, "I haven't killed Jesus Christ or anyone!" The mouths of the entire bridge crew dropped, astonished. "Send a shuttlecraft down to get us and I don't care if anyone sees it!"

"Yes, Commander," M'Catis said, somewhat relieved that Jesus was still alive, at least for now. The next question: who would pilot the shuttle? He decided he would do it.

Within minutes he was ready to guide the shuttlecraft into space and down to Earth. As the hangar bay decompressed and the bay doors opened, he engaged the startup sequence, but it didn't work. He tried again, then again. The shuttle was dead, but there were three others available.

After the hangar bay reestablished standard atmosphere, M'Catis went to the next shuttle. It, too, was dead. He repeated the same with the others, and they, too, were inoperative. Tl'Rak was furious when heard the report and the thought of mutiny entered his mind. Was M'Catis lying and using it as an excuse to leave him and Nh'Got on the planet and take control of his ship? He demanded to speak to the chief engineer to confirm M'Catis's reports.

The chief engineer relieved his fears, confirming the transporters and shuttles were down. He suggested moving the ship to see if the *Lionare's* propulsion drives were functioning. Tl'Rak agreed. M'Catis gave the order to move the *Lionare* to a higher orbit. The helmsman worked the controls, but the ship failed to move. M'Catis ordered more power and still, the ship held its position. The ship was trapped in space! He relayed the information to Tl'Rak, and the news made him even more furious. He stomped the ground, swore, and glared at Nh'Got as if it was her fault.

She brushed it off and said calmly, "We need to find water and then figure out an action plan. Tl'Rak still re-faced, nodded. They entered Jerusalem and secured water and food, the latter with sleight of hand. They left town and settled for the night under some trees. Nh'Got gathered wood, and Tl'Rak used his weapon to ignite a campfire.

Nh'Got remained quiet, waiting for Tl'Rak to speak. "There must be some unknown power working here," he finally said.

Nh'Got nodded. "I agree. I wonder if Jesus Christ is the source. I read that he returned people from the dead and performed many other miracles. He must be an alien with powers beyond humans and ours. That would also explain him rising from the death and ascending into the clouds."

"I have been thinking the same thing from the beginning," Tl'Rak said. It was a lie.

He's such a liar and it makes sick!

"Likely he is a powerful alien that has shaped the course of the galaxy," Tl'Rak continued. "We cannot allow this alien to subjugate our empire. He must be eliminated so we and the rest of the galaxy can determine our destiny. That's why I planned this mission."

The man had a point, Nh'Got told herself. "Sir, the past has already happened, and the future is still ours to make."

"And we will!" Tl'Rak exclaimed, waving a hand. "Trapped on this planet, our future starts now. I won't allow some alien to determine it. I will rule this planet. I will be king, and you will be my queen!" He pounded his chest proudly. "Together we will establish a superior race and change the Earth's history and that of the galaxy."

There is no way I am going to let this man with delusions of grandeur impregnate me, she told herself. "Sir, we need to find this Jesus Christ and seek his help with getting off this planet. I for one don't want to live with humans in this primitive time. What about your ship and the crew? Will you let them die in space?"

Tl'Rak's forehead wrinkled in thought. "They are unfortunate causalities."

Nh'Got was about to protest when a rustling sound came from the trees. Tl'Rak reached for his sidearm. Out of the darkness walked a small child. She moved up to the fire and stood and stared into Tl'Rak's eyes. In his mind, he heard the words, *peace be with you,* and he felt his body relax. The child reclined and curled up in a ball by the fire. Tl'Rak shook his head to clear it.

Nh'Got noticed the change in her commander. "Are you okay?"

He waved a hand. "I'm fine. Child," he addressed her. The girl didn't respond. She was sound asleep.

"Humans are strange," Nh'Got said. "They let this small child wander alone in the night. Even animals take care of their young."

"That is why we have to rule over them," Tl'Rak said. He didn't tell his lieutenant that this human had entered his mind. Or was this child, an alien like Jesus Christ? He would have answers in the morning.

CHAPTER ELEVEN
Perfect Time to Kill

*I*t was two hours past sunrise when Nh'Got willed opened an eye. She didn't want to rise from such a beautiful sleep, having dreamed of love with the man of her fantasy. In her wakeful life, she hadn't met him yet or found love. Now she savored the last few minutes of the man's face before he disappeared from her mind. Blinking her eyes open, she saw Tl'Rak sleeping with a thin peaceful smile on his face, a look she had never seen before. What about the child? She glanced at the smoldering campfire for her, but she wasn't there. Sitting up, she looked around, but didn't see her. Again, she eyed Tl'Rak. He was still asleep. *I could end his life now with one of these rocks or a kick to his throat. I could save the timeline and be a hero. But a hero where? On this planet with humans?*

Reality was sinking in that this was likely her fate, stuck on Earth forever. *And how long can I keep my disguise? Once found out I will be hunted. Tl'Rak's weapon has a limited charge, rendering me defenseless against a horde of hunters. Maybe I can find this Jesus and reason with him to release the ship and return me to it. What if he refuses and keeps me, a prisoner, here?*

There were too many ifs and unknowns. She looked at the rock and then Tl'Rak. It was a perfect time to kill. She decided and stood. She took a step to Tl'Rak, paused, and walked past him into the trees to relieve herself. When she finished, she peeked out to see Tl'Rak sitting up and stretching the sleep from his body.

"Nh'Got, where are you? he yelled, looking around the campsite.

"Here, sir," she replied, moving out from the trees.

"Why didn't you wake me?" he asked, standing. *And why didn't you kill me? I know you are against my plan and likely tipped off the Supreme Commander.* He kept his thoughts to himself, not wanting to give her a bonified excuse to kill him.

"You looked so happy in your sleep. I didn't want to wake you."

And I was. Dreams of romance. Dreams I wish never ended. And the child, I saw her too in my dreams, but she was an adult? Dreams are strange. He held the thoughts to himself as well. "I must have been more tired than I thought. Where is the child?"

"I didn't see her when I awoke. I looked for her, but didn't find her." She held out empty hands.

"I wanted to talk to her. Did you call the ship?"

"No," she said, shaking her head.

"I will." He walked to the trees to refresh himself. After a few minutes, he returned to the campsite. "There is no change with the ship. We will walk to Capernaum and find this Jesus. When we find him, I will force answers from him and have him release my ship."

"And if he returns control of the ship to you, then what will you do?"

He gave her one of those I do not believe you looks.

Nh'Got nodded soberly. *I should have killed you. I might get the chance again. It's five days until Capernaum.* Without food or water, they started the trek north.

CHAPTER TWELVE
Command Decision

Commander Tl'Rak and Lt. Nh'Got followed a path along the Jord River north to Capernaum. They nourished themselves on the plentiful wild dates and almonds. Only a few locals were on the road. From them, they learned that Jesus of Nazareth was moving about the area near the Sea of Galilee. Late afternoon of day three, they were within sight of the sea.

"I can see a town by the shoreline," Nh'Got said. "Maybe we can barter figs for fish. It's only a few more kilometers."

Tl'Rak agreed and pointed ahead. As they walked, Tl'Rak contacted his ship for an update. The ship's status remained unchanged. They trekked toward the town and encountered two approaching men. The strangers nodded in passing, then turned and jumped Tl'Rak and Nh'Got from the rear. One man put Nh'Got in a headlock. The other man wrapped an arm around Tl'Rak's neck and stabbed him on the right side under the ribs. Tl'Rak yelped out and grasped the blaster beneath his tunic. He pointed it under his arm and fired. The attacker gasped and stumbled backward to the ground. He had a smoking hole in his chest where his heart used to be. The other man's eyes widened in fear. He released his hold on Nh'Got and started running. He only made it a few steps before Tl'Rak blasted a hole in the attacker's back. He then reached to his wounded side.

"Are you okay, sir?" Nh'Got asked.

He held up a blood-soaked hand and collapsed to his knees. Nh'Got rushed to his side and pushed away his tunic to view the wound. It was hemorrhaging. She tore a piece of her tunic to make a bandage and placed it over the hole in his side. "Hold this," she said to him. "I need to make a wrap to hold it in place." Tl'Rak nodded and Nh'Got tore his tunic into lengths and used them to secure the bandage.

"I need to get you into the shade. Do you think you can stand?"

"I think so," he gurgled. With Nh'Got's help, he stood. She guided him to some trees off the path and slowly lowered him against one. He nodded his thanks. "He got me in the kidney. I'm not going to make it."

"I need to find a surgeon in that town ahead," Nh'Got said.

"I don't think they have any in this primitive time," Tl'Rak coughed.

"They must have a healer that can help. But first I need to make a fire to keep you warm. The night is coming, and it will be cold." Nh'Got gathered dried twigs and brush and piled them before Tl'Rak.

"Sir, I need your blaster to start a fire." He was now shivering and looking very pale. He didn't respond to her request. She reached under his tunic for the weapon. As she did, his hand caught hers. She paused and looked into his eyes. They held each other's gaze, and then Tl'Rak's hand loosened and fell to his side. Nh'Got took his weapon and stood. Once again, she could maintain the present and preserve the future. It was like fate was demanding her to forsake Tl'Rak and do her duty for the empire—for the galaxy! She felt the weight on her shoulders.

Through slit eyes, Tl'Rak saw her turmoil. "To be a commander, you need to make command decisions," he coughed. "Are you capable of making them?" He looked at the blaster in her hand and back to her face. He managed a faint smile and dropped his head back to the ground.

Nh'Got took a deep inspiration, nodded to her commander, and pointed the weapon. Tl'Rak coughed a laugh, and she pressed the trigger. Tl'Rak managed a breath and went limp. She dropped the blaster to her side, kneeled, and put an ear to his chest. "I decided." She rose and looked west to see the sun dipping behind the hills. In the twilight, she walked toward the seaside town.

CHAPTER THIRTEEN
The Man of Wisdom

The confrontation with the Roman soldiers left Kay're feeling drained both mentally and physically. Although she consumed the provisions scavenged from the fallen soldiers, her hunger persisted. The journey to Galilee was depleting her energy reserves. Having already felt the need for water, she also required additional food to elevate her low glucose levels. Her stomach growled in protest, but she silenced it by taking a sip of water from the Roman canteen.

She continued moving ahead through an unchanging landscape. It was now mid-afternoon, and the sky was still cloudless. Ahead at the base of the hills, she spotted a long-haired, bearded man dressed in a brown robe. He was sitting on a rock near the footpath eating berries from a bush. She didn't sense he posed a danger. The sight of the berries made her mouth water.

She approached the man, who, without turning, beckoned her with a hand. "Sit, woman," he said in an even tone. She took a seat on a rock a meter from the man. "Eat." He motioned to the bush without looking at her. While picking the red berries, she sneaked a sidelong glance at the man. His face appeared calm, but she couldn't see his eyes to read him. She eagerly downed the sweet berries and helped herself to more.

"Please excuse my etiquette," she said, with a chuckle. He gave her a nod. She noticed his eyes were bright and full of life, and sensed kindness, but couldn't access his mind. She had an inkling they had met before. "I'm not a Roman." She waved a hand over her attire.

"Yet you are shouldering a Roman canteen," he said.

"Oh, yes. I got it from a Roman." She failed to tell him how she happened by it, not wanting him to know she killed to get it.

She turned her head to listen. "I hear nothing."

"Only Roman soldiers have horses that ride with the wind. Perhaps they want their canteen back," he said, his smile turning thin. "You must go now. There, past those rocks." He pointed the way. "Once over them you will see a large boulder. Behind it is a narrow path. It will lead to Capernaum, and from there you can find directions to the Master and a change of clothes. Now go, quickly."

She rose and started in the pointed direction. After several meters, she turned and asked, "Will you be safe from the Romans?"

"And you would protect me?"

"You can come with me." She waved to him to follow.

"I will be safe. They don't seek me. Now go."

She nodded and hustled to the rocks. There she spotted a large boulder and the path. Then she heard hooves. The man had keen hearing. She hustled down the path a few meters and then paused. She listened, and the horses passed without stopping. Surely, they would have stopped and asked the man if he had seen her, even with the threat of death. Did they slay him on the run without stopping? She wanted to go back to see if the man who had great wisdom needed help. Yet inside she had an overwhelming desire to move ahead to Capernaum. She kept moving with the man's words in her head, *"Currently, it is rare for a woman...."*

CHAPTER FOURTEEN
Healing

*T*he sun was setting, and Centurion Cassius Marcus sat rasping against a rock. Only a straw in his windpipe kept him alive. Several times he tried to rise and get to his horse, but he lacked the air for such a simple task. In the sky, he saw buzzards circling. ***Will I join the dead soldiers and be dinner for the birds?*** Even now, one landed next to one of the dead men. It eyed its meal and then Marcus.

Marcus unsheathed his sword and waved it feebly at the bird. The buzzard stared him down, knowing he was near death. Then another joined his feathered friend, and then more. They eyed him, waiting for him to take his last breath before they began their feast.

"To die alone in this forsaken land," Marcus murmured to his audience. "At the hand of a woman." He shook his head in disgust. "I will have my flesh picked to the bones rather than be given the honor of a centurion's funeral." Suddenly, the birds spooked and took to the air. "Great," Marcus coughed. "Just what I need—a lion." He tightened the grip on his sword and looked at the horses. They were in place and calm, and from between them, a man came into view. He was middle-aged, bearded, and dressed like a local.

The man walked up to him and hunched down. Their eyes met, and Marcus felt kindness coming from him. "May I have a drink of your water?" the stranger asked.

Marcus nodded. "I won't need it much longer," he whispered and handed the man his canteen. The man took a long drink and returned the canteen to Marcus. He then assessed the straw in Marcus's neck and removed it. Marcus panicked as he struggled for air. The man touched Marcus's throat and raised his head to the sky and mouthed a few words in an unknown tongue. Instantly Marcus felt a warm flush come over him and his breathing returned.

The stranger stood and said, "Behold the power of the living God, who is, who was, and will come again. Believe and have eternal life." He smiled down at Marcus and walked away. Marcus sat in awe as he watched the man disappear amongst the rocks. Then he touched his neck. It was tender where the woman had cut him, but the wound had closed. *And this man! Is he the zealot that raised the dead and healed the sick?* Marcus wanted to rush after him to find out. With the help of his sword, he tried to stand, but vertigo overcame him. He sat to recover. To satisfy his thirst, he drank a canteen of water. With his thirst quenched, he made it to his feet, fighting off the dizziness, and sucked in several deep breaths. *The man healed me!* He smiled and looked skyward at the buzzards. "You won't dine on me or any Roman today."

In his weakened state, it took him over an hour to gather wood, build a funeral pyre, and cremate his fallen soldiers. After one last word of remembrance, he gathered the horses and mounted his horse. He rode to Capernaum hoping the mystery woman would be ahead. As much as he wanted to settle the score with her, he needed answers to the many questions she left in his head.

CHAPTER FIFTEEN
Confirmations

It was sunset when Kay're arrived on the outskirts of a small village. Only a few people were milling around. "The man said I would find a change of clothes here," she whispered to herself. Looking around, she saw some hanging from a rope tied between two trees. Were they for her? The thought of stealing clothes didn't thrill her. Especially in a primitive culture, where clothing may be a person's only possession. Then again, she couldn't go around dressed like she was without drawing attention to herself. She made the decision to steal them if they were still there when night fell.

They were, and as she crept toward them, she froze, hearing footsteps from behind. Glancing back, a woman came into view.

"Excuse me, you must be the stranger the Teacher said would come," the woman said.

"Am I?" Kay're questioned, carefully eyeing her. *The man knew the scriptures, so maybe he is a teacher. And I wonder if he is still alive.*

"You're a beautiful woman! My name is Mary. I have clothes and sandals for you."

"My name is Kay're. Thank you for your kindness, Mary."

"You are welcome. I like your name. It is most unusual."

Kay're smiled and said, "I'm from a distant place and custom. I came to see the Master."

"Some refer to the Teacher as the Master," Mary said. "Hurry and change now to avoid attention from the locals. You can stay with me. I have food and you can clean yourself."

Kay're changed into her new costume and followed Mary to her small abode. On the way, she wondered if the man she had met was the Messiah, Jesus Christ. If so, the Roman soldiers couldn't kill him now. She hoped to meet him to see if the Teacher and Master were the same person. Once inside, she refreshed herself and the two sat down to dine on dried fish and bread.

"Kay're, I have noticed other strangers in the area that must be from distant lands. They came to see and listen to the Teacher, yet no one dressed like you. The material of your clothes is so different." Mary rolled it in her fingers. "Do all the women in your land dress like you?"

Kay're chuckled. "No. Men and women wear many styles made from various materials, some even wool like yours. That's my work uniform."

"What kind of work do you do?"

Kay're took a bite of the fish as she thought of an answer. "I'm a goodwill ambassador for the government. I travel to foreign lands to interact with the people and learn new customs that I take back to my country."

"I can see you doing this. You're a refined woman and very kind."

"And you are a very kind person, Mary, and very observant. You would be a good ambassador for your people."

"Thank you."

"Mary, you appear to be unwed. How do you support yourself?"

Mary chewed into a loaf of bread to avoid answering the question. When she looked up, Kay're could read her. "I understand," Kay're said, and tapped Mary on the knee to say it was okay.

"You are much like the Teacher—nonjudgmental and forgiving."

Kay're chuckled again. "I'm far from being like the Teacher. I have many faults and I'm not pleased with some things I have done."

"The Teacher forgives," Mary said. "He will forgive you if you ask."

"I know. Will we see him tomorrow?"

"I don't know. He wasn't here today. Tomorrow, we'll go down to Capernaum by the sea. He frequents there."

The morning was sunny with a few white clouds. With their heads covered, they made their way through the village. Mary carried a basket with a couple of bread loaves that she would barter for fish. Kay're toted a water jug. One man asked Mary who her new friend was and if she was available. Mary dismissed him with a wave. "I'm sorry you had to hear that," Mary said to Kay're as they walked on.

"Don't apologize, Mary. I have heard it many times. Most recently by some Roman soldiers while on my way here."

"That is typical of Roman soldiers. Did you...?"

"No, no," she said, laughing.

"So how did you fend them off? They don't take no for an answer, especially if they saw you wearing what you had on yesterday."

"I used my diplomatic skills, and they lost interest."

"Really! I'm impressed," Mary said, nodding. "Look, down there by the sea, Roman soldiers. They come and go, but use Capernaum as a base camp."

"I see them," Kay're said, feeling uncomfortable. She wondered if they had found the dead bodies and the centurion. If so, they would be on the lookout for her. She would need to be careful to keep her face covered as much as possible, even in this costume. They entered the fishing village. The locals were busy carrying on with normal daily life and didn't take notice of them. Nor did the Roman soldiers as they passed them on their way to the shoreline.

"Where is the Teacher, Peter?" Mary asked the fisherman.

"I don't know. He left us yesterday and said he would return in time. I worry for him with the Pharisees trying to stir up trouble against him. And these Roman soldiers may side with them, and seize him or worse. And who are you?" He glanced at Kay're.

"I'm Kay're, a new follower of the Teacher." She bowed her head, feeling excited she may have met Peter the apostle.

"You need not bow to me, woman. Only the Teacher is worthy."

"Sir, does anyone refer to the Teacher as Jesus of Nazareth?"

"He is the same person. And you don't need to call me sir, either. Call me Peter."

"That I will, Peter," Kay're said with a smile.

"Peter, I have bread," Mary said.

"Andrew," Peter called to his brother at the boat. "Mary has bread for us. Fill her basket with fish." Andrew waved Mary to the boat, and they exchanged food. "I haven't seen you before," Peter said to Kay're.

"I'm new to the area and Mary has offered her friendship that I have accepted."

"And did she tell you what kind of woman she was?"

"Peter, it is what she is now that is more important."

Peter nodded. "You're a kind and wise woman."

"And Peter, you are and will continue to be a great man." She looked into Peter's eyes to hush the rebuke he was about to give. Peter smiled and nodded.

Mary struggled up from the shore with the filled basket. Kay're noticed and came to her side, taking a handle. "Peter, if the Teacher returns today, send young John to let us know," Mary said.

"Will do, Mary. Nice to meet you Kay're."

"And you, Peter." The women walked away. After a few meters, several Roman horsemen and one horse-pulled wagon passed them. Kay're kept her head down to hide her face.

"Fisherman," called out a Roman. "How was your catch last night?"

Kay're blinked in surprise upon hearing the voice. It was from a man she knew, and her heart raced. It was the centurion! "Mary," she whispered. "I need to see that Roman's face. I think he was one of the Romans I met yesterday, but I don't want him to see me."

"Let's duck behind this cart and you can get a look." Mary pointed ahead. They took a position behind the cart and listened. Kay're peeked out to watch the Romans.

"Your catch was good," the centurion said from his horse, looking down into Peter's boat. "I need all your fish for my army. And I will pay you a better than fair price."

"I can agree with that," Peter answered, surprised. "Do you agree, Andrew, James, and John?"

"We do," they chorused, amazed at the offer.

Kay're eyed the centurion, and when he turned his horse in her direction, she confirmed it was him. She felt her heart skip a beat with joy. The cut she had made to his throat appeared red, but closed, and he was acting as if never injured. She concluded he had encountered Jesus, who healed him. *The experience humbled him. That would explain his generous offer for Peter's fish.*

"Is that him?" Mary asked.

"It is. And he must have met the Teacher yesterday. I would like to ask him about it."

"You think that is wise?"

"No. Let's go back to the house."

CHAPTER SIXTEEN
Light of the Fire

Twilight had given way to the night when Lt. Nh'Got entered the seaside village. The near full moon that provided light was now peeking in and out of the clouds. Her priority was finding water. She also needed a canteen to carry the water. To her relief, she spotted a water well. No one was around it. She ran to it and drank to the fullest. Now she needed food to quell her hunger.

Looking around, she saw only faint glows coming from a few structures, but down by the seashore she saw a fire. Staying in the shadows, she made her way toward it and saw several men sitting around the fire and eating. The aroma of what they were roasting enhanced her hunger.

"Woman, come out of the darkness and partake with us," said a man with his back to her. Nh'Got wondered how he knew of her presence as she had stayed quietly in the darkness. She cleared her throat and stepped into the light of the fire. "Sit and eat," said the same voice. He scooted over a bit, making room for her. Nh'Got sat. The other men eyed her, but said nothing. "Here," he said, and gave her a fish on a stick. "It will satisfy some of your hunger."

"You're most kind," Nh'Got said, thanking him, wondering what he meant by "some of your hunger." Like the other humans, they heard her words in their language through the annunciator she wore that modulated her words into the local language. Such was the wonder of twenty-fifth-century technology.

She took a bite and savored the taste. Quickly, she consumed the fish. With the last bite, she gave the men a sidelong glance. They seem amused watching her. She felt ashamed of her impolite eating behavior. The man across from her offered her another fish. She hesitated.

"Woman, it is okay. When you're hungry, you must eat," said the man who invited her to sit. She looked at him and their eyes met. Nh'Got gave a start. The man seemed to reach into her soul to quench another need—one of peace. He smiled and nodded for her to take the fish. She took it and started biting into it, but more slowly. The men approved with smiles.

"You're from a very distant place," the man said.

Nh'Got felt exposed, yet not threatened, as his voice was gentle and not accusing. "I am," she replied.

"Not to worry," said another. "You're among friends." The other men nodded.

"What do you seek here?" asked the man who had reached into her soul.

"Tonight, food and water," she answered. "And I have found both, and generous people too." She smiled at the men.

"And tomorrow?"

"I will seek the one called Jesus of Nazareth." The men shared glances, and she noticed. "It appears you know this man. Where may I find him?"

"You will find him in your heart," said the one who invited her. Suddenly, the wind picked up. In the distance, thunder clapped.

"I seek not his spirit, but his physical presence," Nh'Got countered.

"And when you find him?"

"It's hard to explain." Nh'Got stumbled for words. "I need help and he is the only one who can help me."

"Maybe we can help you," offered one of the other men. "What is your need?"

She glanced at him, then at the others. "Oh, I wish any of you could. My problem is unique. Only Jesus of Nazareth, who has what they claim, heavenly power, can help."

"And what do you say is 'heavenly power'?" the man asked, poking the fire with a stick.

"The power that gives life to the dead and heals the sick."

The man continued stirring the fire as the others remained silent. The thunder sounded again, and it was closer. Lightning flashed to the west, and the wind gusted. "Do you believe he has the power to calm the storm that is approaching?"

"I'm not sure."

"Woman, there is no need to worry about tomorrow," he said. "Tonight has problems of its own. You should seek shelter now and return in the morning when the sun rises. Then you may find a solution to your problem." He smiled at her. She returned a thin smile hoping his words were prophetic. More thunder sounded, and the wind was now strong and constant.

"You're both kind and wise," Nh'Got said, standing up. "Thank you for the food. Gentlemen." She bowed and turned to leave.

"Woman," the man called out. Nh'Got pivoted back to him. "You will need this." He handed her a sheepskin canteen. "And take this extra fish."

"Thank you so much," Nh'Got said. She bowed and hurried away as lightning danced with increased frequency.

Once she cleared the village, she started trotting. She hoped to reach the spot where she had left Tl'Rak before the rain drowned her campfire. After a few minutes, she could see the light of the fire. Large raindrops were now falling, and she knew soon a wall of blowing rain would hit.

She reached the campfire as the rain came in a torrent. Lightning was unceasing, and she feared being struck by it while under the tree. Several meters away, a lightning bolt hit a tree, exploding it with an earthshaking boom. Reflexively, she flattened herself on the ground next to the still body of Tl'Rak. The words of the man, "Tonight has problems of its own," were visionary.

CHAPTER SEVENTEEN
Pensive Time

The atmosphere aboard the *Tigerii* was tense and contemplative as it madeits way to the UPA border. Everyone knew that at any moment their life could end or change. Supreme Fleet Commander Tr'Tala hoped he could stop the madman Tl'Rak before he killed Jesus Christ. Doing so would secure the current timeline.

"Commander, we are approaching the UPA border," announced tactical officer Se'Say.

"Helm, slow to sub light," ordered Commander Zh'Cata. "Lt. Se'Say scan for the *Lionare's* ion trail and any other ship traffic." She wanted to be sure the UPA of this time lacked space travel.

"Scanning," repeated the lieutenant. A pause. "I have an ion trail. It must be from the *Lionare.* Extrapolation shows it heading toward Earth's solar system. The scan is negative for other spaceships."

"Excellent work, Lieutenant," Zh'Cata praised. She smiled at her husband. "Helm plot us a course to Earth and go to full light speed."

The great ship accelerated. The trip took another tension-filled five days. Finally, the *Tigerii* slowed to sub-light as the ship approached the Terran's solar system.

"Tactical, any sign of the *Lionare?*" Commander Zh'Cata asked.

"Nothing in the immediate vicinity, Commander," Lt. Se'Say reported. "We're too far from Earth to scan for orbiting satellites or ships. Commander Tl'Rak may have cloaked his ship. I will know more once we get closer to the planet."

"Helm continue the approach to the Terran solar system and cloak the ship," Zh'Cata ordered. It took several hours before Earth was a blue orb on the *Tigerii's* primary screen.

"Commander, scanners are detecting a single spaceship in orbit above Earth. There are no artificial satellites," Se'Say piped.

"Commander, scanners are detecting a single spaceship in orbit above Earth. There are no artificial satellites," Se'Say piped.

"I don't believe it," Tr'Tala commented. "Tl'Rak didn't cloak his ship. He had to know we would come after him."

"He was so certain that we couldn't figure out the exact time of his return," Zh'Cata said. "The odds were in his favor. Now they are on our side. It is a costly error on his part." Her husband nodded his agreement.

"Helm, bring the *Tigerii* into the same orbit as the *Lionare*. Maintain a kilometer distance between ships. Continue the cloak," Zh'Cata ordered. She turned to speak to her husband, but the helmsman interrupted her.

"Did you see that?" he blurted, pointing to the primary screen. "They're gone!"

"What did you see?" Commander Zh'Cata asked, as all heads turned to the primary screen.

"I'm not sure, Commander. I thought I saw very large ghost-like figures with wings around the *Lionare*. They were there for a second and gone the next. Maybe I'm seeing things."

"Lt. Se'Say, did the scanners show any energy fluctuations around the *Lionare?*" Zh'Cata questioned.

"No, Commander. Space is nominal."

"Did anyone see anything?" Zh'Cata asked loudly. Heads shook around the bridge. There was a pause. "Helm, finish your approach to the *Lionare.*" She had an uneasy feeling. Was this pensive time fatiguing the crew, including herself? The two ships hung in space, though only one was visible to the other.

"Lt. Se'Say, is there life aboard the *Lionare?*" Supreme Commander Tr'Tala asked.

"Yes, sir. And the *Lionare's* systems are normal with its defensive shields down."

"Lieutenant, scan the planet for life and any audio-visual transmissions," Zh'Cata ordered. "We need to know if we travel back to the point when Jesus Christ was alive." She looked at her husband feeling confident in her order. Again, he nodded.

A pause. "There are humans in various densities scattered about the planet. There are no transmissions detected nor evidence of industrialization," Se'Say conveyed.

"Very good," Commander Zh'Cata said with a smile of satisfaction. "I defer further orders to Supreme Commander Tr'Tala." She looked up to her husband with eyes saying, *It's all yours, dear.*

"I'm transporting to the bridge of the *Lionare* with a security detail," he said. "We'll take them by surprise. I'm heading to the transporter room. Commander Zh'Cata, on my command, decloak the ship, and I and the security team will transport over. I'll contact you once I have control of the *Lionare.*" He quickstepped it off the bridge.

Five minutes later, Tr'Tala and six security men, with sidearms at the ready, stood ready for transport. "Set weapons to stun," Tr'Tala ordered. "I want everyone on the *Lionare* alive." Heads nodded, and everyone set their weapons. "Commander Zh'Cata, decloak."

"I have decloaked the ship," Zh'Cata voiced over the intercom. Supreme Commander Tr'Tala nodded to the transport tech. The man activated the transporter, and the men disappeared in a shimmer of light.

CHAPTER EIGHTEEN
Stalemate

Subcommander M'Catis sat in the command seat staring out at Earth. The chief engineer had just told him he couldn't fix something that wasn't broken. The man lacked answers for the sudden problems the ship was experiencing, so M'Catis sucked in a breath and pondered whether to update Commander Tl'Rak on the ship's status. As nothing had changed, he dismissed the thought.

"Subcommander," piped the comm-officer to get his attention. "Many crew members report seeing large white ethereal figures outside their windows. The figures were present only for a few seconds before disappearing."

"Did anyone on the bridge see anything?" M'Catis asked, looking around at the crew. All shook their heads.

"Very strange," M'Catis said. "I'm not ruling out anything. They could be entities tied to Jesus Christ. If they are gone, maybe the ship is functioning normally now. Helm, expand the orbit by one kilometer."

"Yes, sir," replied the helmsman with renewed vigor. He worked the controls and deflated. "The ship is unresponsive. There is no change."

M'Catis blew out a sigh. "Very well, maintain the status."

"Subcommander," said the fill-in tactical officer. "I've picked up another ship in orbit."

"Put it on the primary screen," M'Catis ordered. All eyes turned to the screen. But what they saw was seven individuals materializing on the bridge. M'Catis stabbed a button on the seat. "Security to the bridge!"

"That won't be necessary," said the central figure of the group that appeared on the bridge. "Security is here."

"Supreme Commander Tr'Tala!" exclaimed M'Catis, rising from his seat.

"Everyone, maintain your positions!" Tr'Tala's voice boomed. "Security, keep your weapons on them." As he finished the command, the *Lionare's* security team, with weapons drawn, stepped onto the bridge. "Stand down!" Tr'Tala ordered them. When they saw who gave the command, they froze and holstered their sidearms.

"Subcommander, where is Commander Tl'Rak?" Tr'Tala asked.

"Supreme Commander, he and Lt. Nh'Got are on the planet."

"Tactical officer," Tr'Tala addressed the man. The young officer straightened in his seat. "Lock on Commander Tl'Rak's annunciator."

"I have a lock, Supreme Commander," he clipped, beaming with confidence. It was a rare occurrence the Supreme Fleet Commander would give the sub-lieutenant a direct order or even be on a front-line ship.

"Send the coordinates to the transporter control. Security chief, take three men with you to the transporter room and arrest Commander Tl'Rak once he is aboard." They left the bridge with their weapons at the ready.

"Supreme Commander, our transporters aren't functioning," M'Catis said. He filled him in about the ship's status since Commander Tl'Rak and Lt Nh'Got transported to the surface. Included in his brief for Tr'Tala was the crew's sighting of the large, ethereal figures outside the ship. He concluded by telling him the *Lionare* was stuck in space.

"Understood Subcommander," Tr'Tala said. He touched his annunciator. "Commander Zh'Cata, this is Supreme Commander Tr'Tala."

"Go ahead, sir," she replied.

"Commander Tl'Rak and a lieutenant are on the planet's surface. The *Lionare's* transporters and ship propulsion drives aren't functioning. We have a transporter lock on Tl'Rak and the lieutenant. I'm having their coordinates sent over to your transporter chief. Have a security team ready in transporter control. When they're in place, beam up Tl'Rak and the lieutenant. Put Tl'Rak under arrest. The lieutenant was the one who sent the original warning message. See to her immediate needs. Then, transport me back to the *Tigerii.*"

"Understood Supreme Commander," Zh'Cata replied. A pause. "Transporter control has the coordinates. Security is on the way. I will contact you once we have them aboard."

"Very good. Tr'Tala out."

A simple task that should have taken a few minutes dragged on beyond ten minutes. Tr'Tala was becoming impatient and paced back and forth on the bridge. Finally, a call from Commander Zh'Cata. "Supreme Commander, our transports aren't functioning. Engineering is working on the problem."

Tr'Tala dragged a hand through his hair, worried that *Tigerii's* fate was like the *Lionare's*. "Commander, move the ship out of orbit now. No questions. Just do it and leave the channel open."

"Helm, take the ship out of orbit, now!" Zh'Cata commanded.

"Taking the ship out of orbit," said the helmsman, working his controls. A pause. "The ship isn't responding."

"I can see that," Zh'Cata said. "What is the problem?"

"I don't know, Commander. Everything looks normal, but the ship isn't responding."

"And it will not!" Tr'Tala's voice roared over the *Tigerii's* bridge. He told his wife about the situation on the *Lionare.*

"Supreme Commander, do you believe that Jesus Christ is the source of the problems?" Zh'Cata asked.

"I lack any explanation. He must be an alien entity with certain abilities foreign to us. And those white things reported in the immediate space may be the same alien entities."

"Supreme Commander, what do we do now?" his wife asked.

"I'm going to contact Tl'Rak. His presence on the planet seems to be the focal point."

"I agree, sir. But he is deranged. He won't listen to you. I hope the lieutenant can get the jump on him and kill him. I hate to say it like that."

"I know. She may be our only hope. But I want you and engineering from both ships to work on a solution to this problem. The aliens have to have a weakness somewhere."

"And we will find it," Commander Zh'Cata affirmed.

"Excuse me, Supreme Commander," interrupted the young replacement at the tactical station. All eyes turned to him. "Maybe the aliens are invisible in space around our ships. What if we fire weapons from both ships in a broad dispersal pattern and see what happens? We may hit them and disable their control of our ships."

Tr'Tala's face wrinkled in thought.

"Sen, I think it's worth a try," his wife said, breaking protocol.

"Let's do it," Tr'Tala said. "Tactical officers set plasma cannons to wide dispersal, range, four hundred meters. That will give two hundred meters of a safe distance between ships."

"Weapons ready," chorused both tactical officers.

"Fire!" Tr'Tala ordered.

Both ships shuddered as brilliant green explosions erupted along their perimeters.

"Helmsmen, move the ships out of orbit," Tr'Tala ordered.

Both Helmsmen worked the controls, but the ships' positions remained unchanged.

"It was a good suggestion, Sublieutenant," Tr'Tala said, nodding to the young tactical officer. Nothing will deter us. Everyone, put on your thinking caps. Offer suggestions no matter how absurd. We need to break this stalemate. I'm contacting Tl'Rak."

CHAPTER NINETEEN
A Helping Hand

Finally, the storm passed, leaving the night air cool. Soaked and shivering, Lt Nh'Got needed to relight the fire. With the moon shining, she could see the tree that had exploded was still smoldering. She hustled over to it and gathered enough kindling for a new fire. Using the blaster, she restarted the fire and nuzzled close to it to warm up and dry off. As she lay there trembling, she glanced at Commander Tl'Rak. Unbelievably, the man she had given up for dead showed shallow chest movement. She crawled over to him and shook him. He managed a weak moan. Mustering up her last bit of strength, she dragged him closer to the fire to provide him warmth in his last hours.

Curled up by the fire, the day's events replayed in her mind. Surely, by morning, she would be on her own. Suddenly fearful roars and growls interrupted her melancholy. She grasped the blaster and sat up. In the dim light, she could see several large four-legged beasts. They were tearing into the bodies of the two men that Tl'Rak had killed. One beast with a large mane looked up, stared at her, and let out another roar. It was like a warning to stay clear. Nh'Got lowered herself to the ground, and the beast returned to his feast. The beasts devoured their meal in less than an hour, dragging off the remains into the hills. Finally, Nh'Got felt safe and closed her eyes. With her adrenal rush over, sleep came to her.

The morning broke with bright sunlight. Nh'Got blinked her eyes awake, wondering what the day would bring. Then she heard voices. She looked at the path and saw several groups of people headed in the direction of the seaside village. "Nh'Got." The voice was weak. She looked at Tl'Rak surprised he had the strength to talk. The man's eyes were open, and he was mouthing her name.

"I'm here," she said, scooting to his side. Incredulous the man was still alive, she propped his head up and gave him water from the canteen the strange man had given her. "Drink slowly." He took several swallows and nodded. She laid his head back on the ground.

"I need to find you a healer."

Tl'Rak coughed and managed a nod. Nh'Got got to her feet, walked to the path, and greeted a group of four men. She kept one hand under her tunic on the blaster. "Excuse me. I need help. Some men attacked me and my partner yesterday and he suffered a stab wound. I fear he will die. Is there a healer in the village?"

"We're not from that village," said one, shrugging.

"Maybe the Teacher can heal your friend," offered another. "People say that he doesn't shun Samaritans like you. And we shouldn't even be talking to you." They turned and resumed their walk toward the town.

"Who is the Teacher?" Nh'Got yelled. "I'm not a Samaritan. Is the Teacher Jesus of Nazareth?" The men ignored her, leaving Nh'Got cursing in frustration.

She returned to Tl'Rak. "We need to get to town. Do you think you can walk?"

"I am very weak," he whispered and closed his eyes.

Nh'Got nodded. It was a matter of minutes, maybe an hour, before Tl'Rak died. As she pondered her next move, Tl'Rak's annunciator beeped.

"Get it," he mouthed.

"Lt. Nh'Got, here."

"I want Commander Tl'Rak," boomed the voice.

Nh'Got's eyes widened. It wasn't Subcommander M'Catis. "Who is requesting? And where is Subcommander M'Catis?"

"This is Supreme Commander Sen Tr'Tala!"

"Supreme Commander," she gasped. "You got my distress message. Are you in orbit about Earth?"

"I received your message. We are in orbit. I want to speak to Tl'Rak."

"Supreme Commander, Commander Tl'Rak is near death and too weak to speak."

"What happened?"

"Yesterday locals attacked us and Tl'Rak was stabbed. He has lost a lot of blood. We need urgent transport up."

"I would if I could. Both the *Lionare* and *Tigerii* are disabled. I'm currently on the *Lionare* and cannot return to my ship."

Nh'Got felt despair for herself, but a bit of relief that Tl'Rak would die and the problem of him killing Jesus put to rest. "Sir, I believe the solution to our problem lies with Jesus of Nazareth, who Commander Tl'Rak wants to kill."

"I agree. Is there any possibility of you meeting this individual?"

"Sir, I have learned that Jesus of Nazareth is in the town a few kilometers ahead of our current position. I will attempt to take Commander Tl'Rak with me to this town and see if Jesus will miraculously heal him. It's said that he heals the infirm and raises the dead."

"Lieutenant, you want this Jesus to heal Tl'Rak so he can kill him? Lieutenant, have you now sided with Tl'Rak?"

"No Supreme Commander. I don't want Commander Tl'Rak to kill Jesus, but I can't leave one of our own here to die."

"Do you have his blaster?"

There was something in his tone that sent a shiver down Nh'Got spine. "I do, sir." She knew what was coming next, but his order stunned her.

"You hold on to it at all costs. At no time is Tl'Rak to have his hands on it, healed or not. If he attempts to regain the weapon, shoot him dead. Understood?"

"Yes, Supreme Commander." She managed a dry swallow.

"Your new order is to find this Jesus, who I believe to be an alien and have him release our ships. If necessary, use force. Once our ships are free, we will transport you and Tl'Rak up. Commander Tl'Rak will face justice for his crime. Now go to that town and find this Jesus."

"Yes, sir," Nh'Got answered crisply. The connection ended, and she glanced over to Tl'Rak. He heard the conversation and managed a wry smile.

"Help me sit up," he mouthed. She nodded and took his arms, pulling him to a sitting position. After letting him sit for a few seconds, she ducked under one of his arms and brought him to his feet. His legs were wobbly, and he was heavy; it would be burdensome for her to walk and support him. They made it only a few meters before she needed to pause and regain her breath. She didn't dare let Tl'Rak sit, knowing she lacked the strength to bring him to his feet again. They traveled another few meters and rested, then again and again. From behind, Nh'Got heard a sound. She craned her head sideways to see what was coming. Stepping up to their side was an older man riding a donkey. His dress was more regal than other locals.

"It appears you need help," the man said. He dismounted and supported Tl'Rak on the other side.

"My friend is near death. We were attacked yesterday and he was stabbed," Nh'Got gasped, out of breath. "I am trying to get him to a nearby village, so one called Jesus of Nazareth can heal him. Do you know him?"

"Not personally. But I know of his heavenly powers. I'm heading that way to hear him speak. Let's get your friend on my donkey and we will make the town to see and hear Jesus."

"You are very kind," Nh'Got said with a smile. "I assure you we're not Samaritans."

The man laughed. "I know by looking at you. But it would make no difference to me if you were. We are all God's children and are called to look out for the well-being of one another. Unfortunately, many people are prejudiced. Some are evildoers, like the ones who attacked you." They hoisted Tl'Rak onto the donkey. "Hold on to the animal's neck," he instructed. Tl'Rak nodded.

The trio started ahead. "Do you have a name, sir?" Nh'Got asked.

"Please excuse me for not introducing myself. I am Joseph from Arimathea."

"I am Nh'Got and he is Tl'Rak."

"Where do you call home?"

"We're from a very distant land unknown to you," Nh'Got answered somewhat evasively. "We have traveled to see Jesus of Nazareth."

"Just as I have, but not from too far away," he said, smiling. "It's said that three noble foreigners, much like yourself, traveled from afar to pay homage to

Jesus when he was an infant."

"We're far from noble," Nh'Got said, giving Joseph a thin smile.

"But you are!" corrected Joseph. "You have traveled a great distance to see Jesus of Nazareth. It surprises me people beyond Judea know him. The three noblemen indeed have spread the word of Jesus throughout the lands far from Israel. Is Jesus of Nazareth known in your land?"

"He is."

"In these modern times, news spreads quickly," Joseph said, shaking his head.

If he only knew what modern times are like.

CHAPTER TWENTY
Romans, Robbers, and Roars

The following morning was overcast and cool, perfect for sleeping in. Kay're had blinked an eye open at sunrise, but close closed it and curled into a ball to resume her sleep to mid-morning. Mary was up with the sun and prepared a small meal for her and Kay're of bread, figs, and pomegranates. After refreshing herself, she went to the well for water and returned to find Kay're up and stretching.

"Good morning, Mary," Kay're greeted her.

"And good morning to you, Kay're. You must have been very tired."

"I was." She yawned. "All the travel finally caught up to me. Is there anything interesting going on? Any signs of the Teacher?"

"The Teacher, no. But the Roman soldiers have all the women and children out in Capernaum. The centurion is inspecting them. I wonder why?"

"Let me see," Kay're said, stepping outside. She nodded and said, "I know why. He's looking for me. I'm taller and paler then most of the women around here."

"Then why the children?" Mary asked.

"The centurion is asking them if they had seen me. Children are truthful." It was close to a white lie. Mary would never understand the real reason. "Mary, the centurion will come here. Enough people in this village have seen me, and they'll likely point me out to the centurion. I need to leave now and take my clothes with me. When the centurion comes, tell him I left at sunrise for Nazareth to find the Teacher, Jesus of Nazareth."

"Is that where you are heading?"

"No," Kay're said with a smile and gathered her belongings.

"Kay're, you have to be very careful traveling alone around here. There are robbers who will kill you for whatever you are carrying. And there are lions that will attack."

"You say lions?" Kay're asked thoughtfully.

Mary nodded. "They're not afraid of people."

"Yes, I remember," Kay're said, thinking back to her youth. "Mary, don't worry about me. I'll be careful and we'll meet again. You are a wonderful woman." She wanted to tell her that in the future many will write stories and make movies about her and her life with Jesus. "I'll go now." She hugged Mary and turned to the door.

"Oh, Kay're, don't forget your canteen. I don't want the centurion to find a Roman canteen in my home. And here, take this food." Mary gathered up the breakfast and placed it in a small cloth bag.

"Thank you, Mary. And God bless you."

Mary gave her another hug. "And may the God of our fathers bless you too." She watched Kay're disappear into the hills behind the house.

An hour later, the Romans came to Mary's village, Magdala. Led by Centurion Marcus, they came directly to Mary's home. Mary stepped out and greeted them. "May I help you?"

"You have a woman staying with you that I want to talk to," Marcus said.

"I did. She left at sunrise."

Marcus turned to his soldiers: "You four, draw swords and search this house."

"Do you need to draw swords against a woman?" Mary asked, sarcastically.

Marcus didn't want to say that the woman he searched for was dangerous. "Step aside, woman, and let my men enter."

"Very well, but she isn't here." She stepped away, and the soldiers entered with swords at the ready. After a few seconds, they emerged shaking their heads.

"The woman isn't inside," said one.

"So, woman, tell me. Who was your guest?" Marcus asked.

"My name is Mary, and her name is Kay're."

"Okay, Mary, where is this Kay're from?"

"She didn't say. Only that she was from a distant land of different customs—a traveling ambassador for her land. In the short time she was with me, I found her to be a genuinely kind, caring, and wise woman. One I'm proud to call a friend."

"And where did this woman say she was heading?" Marcus continued dismissing Mary's assessment of Kay're.

"She told me Nazareth to find the Teacher, the one called Jesus."

"This Jesus of Nazareth is the zealot."

"He isn't a zealot or stirring up any trouble," Mary protested. "He is a great healer, teacher of scripture, and the Son of the living God. If you met him, you would discover this to be true."

Marcus didn't tell her or anyone that he had met this man called Jesus and that he had healed him. "So, is this Jesus in Nazareth now?"

"That I don't know. He travels this area. We were hoping he would be here today. Since he wasn't, Kay're left."

"Woman, did Kay're say why she wanted to see him?"

"She didn't say. But I assume to greet him as the ambassador of her country."

"Will she be returning?"

"She assured me we would meet again. However, she didn't say when."

"Very well. You have been most helpful. Mount up, men."

"May God bless you, Centurion," Mary said to him when he was atop in horse. Marcus just turned his horse and led his men away. They galloped off southeast toward Nazareth.

"Centurion, do you believe that prostitute?" asked Marcus's new decanus.

"She has found religion from this Jesus person. I find her responses credible."

"Centurion, forgive my ignorance," continued the decanus. "Why are we pursuing this woman? Has she committed crimes? And what about this child we are on the lookout for?"

She only killed three Roman soldiers and nearly killed me; Marcus didn't tell the young officer. To do so would show his weakness. "Decanus, as you heard the woman say, this Kay're is an ambassador from another country. I believe she is the mother of the child and they got separated somehow. As a courtesy, we are going to find and reunite them." It was a partial truth. Marcus wanted to find out how they could enter his mind and where they were from. More so, he wanted to know if they could be the same person. Incredibly, as it seemed, he didn't rule it out.

"Centurion, I am somewhat confused," rambled the decanus. "Why would the woman go to Nazareth to seek this Jesus person and not her child?"

"Decanus," Marcus's voice rose, "this is the last question I will answer." He gave him a stare of displeasure. The young decanus nodded. "Likely she believes Jesus will use his so-called godlike powers to tell her where her child is. Maybe even produce her on the spot. They say he can raise the dead."

"Of course, Centurion Marcus. I hope to have your wisdom as my career develops."

Marcus shook his head in disbelief. *Rome is sending all the rejects to Israel. I hope they don't see me as one.* "Decanus, a word of advice. Career advancement is achieved by demonstrating unwavering loyalty to the empire. And by obeying your orders, carrying them out effectively, and keeping your mouth shut." He gave him that certain stare of authority. The young soldier's face demurred, and he fell back a few paces from his commander's side.

Kay're headed south through the hills that bordered the Sea of Galilee. After a few hours, she was on the outskirts of another seaside town. From the bluff overlooking the town, she saw many Roman soldiers roaming the streets. At the seashore, there were fishermen tending their nets and preparing and selling fish. Farther to the south she saw another town, smaller, with fewer people in the streets and no soldiers. There, she would go for rest and food.

After another swig of water, she restarted her trek. After a few steps, some falling stones stopped her. She looked up to see a man jumping from the rocks toward her. She sidestepped him, but he clipped her, knocking her to the ground. The man rolled as he hit the ground. Then another man jumped, landing on his feet.

Robbers, she thought. Quickly, she crouched, spun, and leg-whipped the standing robber, toppling him. Now in a fighting stance, she faced the first man who was now on his feet with a knife drawn. He came at her. She took one step toward him and did a snap kick to his face; her heel breaking his nose. He yelped as blood spewed from his face. The second man sprang up and tackled her by the legs. She went down hard on her back, taking some of her breath. The tackler got to his knees and loosened one hand to reach for a knife at his waist. With an opening, Kay're got a leg up and into his chest. With a grunt, she pushed him away. As he went back, she used her other leg to plant a weak kick to his face. It was enough to disorient him.

She sprung to her feet as the man with the bloodied face, who was yelling expletives, came at her. He slashed at her with his knife, but she adroitly avoided it. He lunged his knife at her and she sidestepped it, grasping his wrist. With his arm outstretched, Kay're slammed her elbow down on his upper arm. He howled in pain as his arm snapped. With his arm limp, she released it and side-kicked his lateral right knee, collapsing it. The man fell to the ground in agony; his right side was completely useless.

The other man tackled her again and sat on her chest. " W o m a n , you die now!" he swore, reaching for a rock. As he did, it allowed Kay're a bit of movement in her right arm. She reached up, grasped his genitals, and squeezed as hard as she could. It was the loudest cry of pain she had ever heard. The man dropped the rock and his hands went to his groin, giving her room to wiggle one arm free. She kept a vise grip on his genitals. With her free arm, she knifed him in the throat with her fingers and pushed him off as he fought both pain and the lack of air.

She looked at the crippled man. He had grasped his knife and shifted it into a throwing motion. He flung it at her, and luckily the hilt hit her in the chest. She scrambled to her feet and stepped toward the man as he reached for a rock. His hand never reached it as she stomped on his hand. He rolled onto his back with more pain. Putting a foot on his throat, Kay're glanced back at the other man. He withered in agony and was gasping for air.

Returning her attention to the man below her, she said to him, "You're a foolish man." She increased the pressure on his throat with her foot to crush it. Before doing so, she looked into his eyes and paused. His face stirred her memory. "Your time to die isn't now. You and your friend's date with destiny is yet to come." She took a breath, lifted her foot off his throat, and kicked him in the temple. He blacked out.

Now her attention returned to the other man. He was lying on his side gasping, still holding his groin. When he saw her approach, his wide eyes widened in terror.

"No, no," he wheezed. '

Kay're stooped down and placed the back of her hand close to his face. She felt for the strength of his breath; it was still noticeable. He would survive. Reaching under his tunic, she found his coin purse. Looking inside, she saw coins and gold jewelry. She discarded the jewelry and went to the other man and took his purse. It contained the same. She emptied its contents, minus the jewelry, into the first one and rested on a rock to collect herself. After several minutes, she rinsed her face, scratches, and took long draws of water. Satisfied she had neutralized the danger, she continued on her journey.

It was mid-afternoon when she approached the town. Once again, she was hungry and thirsty, having consumed all her food and water. She spotted a spring just north of town where the locals were drawing and drinking water from it. With her head down, she went to the spring to drink and refill her canteen. She needed to keep the Roman canteen hidden from view lest it draw suspicion. She took a drink and found the water warm, almost hot. "I would I love to take a bath in this," she whispered to herself. Looking around, she produced the canteen from under her robe and filled it. As she did, a man came to her side. Her breath caught, and she tensed, ready to defend herself again.

The man took the gourd and drank. "The water is warm, but refreshing when thirsty," he said without looking at her. She gave him a sidelong glance. He was older and dressed like a local. She held words. "How does a woman have a

Roman soldier's canteen?" His voice was not accusing—more like amused.

"I came about it on my journey."

"It appears your journey was hard," the man commented, looking at the dusty and scratched woman. "And Roman soldiers don't lose their gear. I suggest you keep it hidden, lest they arrest you and...."

"I understand," Kay're said and gave him a smile. She could tell immediately that he was a kind man. "Sir, I'm a stranger to this land. Is there a place where I can find shelter and some food? I have money to pay for my keep."

"I can help you," he said with a smile. "And I don't need your money. Follow me." She nodded and kept up with the man's swift pace. "My name is Cleophas."

It was another name she had heard before, but couldn't place it. *If only my memory would return.* "I'm Kay're."

"Kay're, a most unusual name, uncommon in this part of the world."

"I'm from a land a great distance from Israel."

"I can tell by your pale skin tone. What brings a woman, alone, to Israel?"

"It's a long story. But in short, I came here to see the one called the Teacher, Master, and Jesus of Nazareth."

"Many seek him—some to listen, some to rebuff, some out of curiosity. Why do you seek this man?"

"To affirm my belief that he is the Son of God. And for answers to my long story. And to witness history in the making." She smiled at him.

"You're a believer!"

"Are you?"

"I am. Here, we are at my home." They entered. "This is my wife, Mary. Mary, this is Kay're." They bowed to each other.

Kay're chuckled. "Are all the women around here named Mary?"

Mary laughed. "It's a common name."

"Kay're is a believer in Jesus of Nazareth."

"You are! That is so wonderful. Bless you." Mary hugged her. "Please sit and tell us your story."

They all sat on wooden stools around a small table. "Before I tell you my story, is there a hot spring where I can bathe? I need a bath."

Mary smiled. "Yes, there is. It's a warm pool where only the women go to bathe. I will take you there at sunset. Now let us break bread and talk."

Kay're related her story, excluding the part of her taking the lives of three Roman soldiers. The act still pained her. She did tell them about her encounter with two robbers and being able to fend them off. That impressed Cleophas and his wife.

"To think, a woman almost killed two men with her bare hands!" Mary exclaimed.

Kay're continued, saying that she had amnesia of how she ended up in the area. She hoped that Jesus would return her memory, providing answers to all her questions. Her hosts told her she was in a town called Hamat. They then gave her their accounts of meeting Jesus and becoming believers.

"You know, Kay're," Cleophas continued, "I have three sons your age: James, Simon, and Thaddeus. Jesus of Nazareth called my sons to follow him. James did. The others balked at first but then went out to join the followers. They're with him now, but we don't know where."

"I hope Jesus and your sons return soon. I want to meet them."

At sunset, Mary led Kay're to the hot spring for women only. Other women were present and Kay're smiled at them. They nodded their greeting to the newcomer. She undressed and immersed herself in the hot water. A sigh of delight spread across her face; a bath never felt so wonderful.

"Centurion Marcus," the young decanus dared to address his commander again. "It has been hours. We should have overtaken the woman by now. The prostitute has lied to us."

The man had a point. He didn't want to admit his mistake in trusting the woman. "She may not have followed a direct path and has stayed in the hills and woods to avoid detection. Men, keep your eyes on the periphery. We'll continue to Nazareth. I would like to meet this Jesus of Nazareth to judge his authenticity."

Minutes later, a man called out. "Centurion, to the left. There is a young girl." The horsemen stopped. Marcus saw it was the child that had visited his campfire and placed dreams in his head. She was at the base of the hills amongst the trees. Marcus trotted his horse in her direction with his men following. As they approached, a pride of lions emerged from the trees. They roared at the Romans and started running toward them. The soldiers' horses reared and turned, galloping from the beasts.

The cats chased the horses for several meters before stopping. Marcus and his men reined in their horses and looked back to see their pursuers. The lions gave one last roar, turned, and trotted toward the child.

"Centurion, they'll attack and eat the child," said the decanus, his voice panicky. "Will we try to scare them off?"

"They scared us off," Marcus said, shaking his head, disappointed. He would never have the chance to talk to the child. To his and the soldiers' amazement, the lions slowed down and walked up to the child. They nuzzled up to her as if she was one of them. The child looked up and stared at Marcus. Even at this distance, Marcus could sense her thoughts in his mind.

Peace be with you, he heard. The child turned and walked into the tree with the lions at her side.

"She is a demon," voiced one of Marcus's men. "Only a demon can command lions." Others mumbled in disbelief.

"Centurion, do you think the lions killed and ate the woman we are searching for?" the decanus asked.

"No," he replied. "The child would never permit it." He didn't say that the child and the woman could be the same person. And if he did, his men would judge him crazy and he would lose their respect. "We continue to Nazareth."

CHAPTER TWENTY-ONE
Miracles

Joseph and the two Valeriians arrived on the outskirts of the village. They saw a few people heading south. Joseph questioned one couple about Jesus. He learned that the Prophet had been preaching on the hills south of the Sea of Galilee for the last three days.

"How far is that?" Nh'Got asked.

"About a two-hour walk," Joseph answered as he turned his donkey in that direction.

Nh'Got checked Tl'Rak. He was pale and with labored breathing. "He won't make it," she demurred.

"He is in God's hands. Let us continue," Joseph said.

After a few kilometers, they came upon a small girl wearing a dirty and tattered white dress, now browner than white, and sandals. "My child, are you lost?" Joseph asked her. She glanced up at him and smiled, shaking her head. Joseph felt a warm joy inside him. *Did this child cause this feeling?* he wondered.

"Where are your parents?" he asked her. She pointed a finger at the sky. *How sad*, Joseph thought. *Her parents had died and gone to heaven*. Yet he sensed the child was content and happy.

Even Nh'Got understood the girl's situation. "Who takes care of you?" the lieutenant asked her. The child touched her chest. Nh'Got and Joseph exchanged glances of amazement with a touch of pity.

"Your friend appears very sick," the child said, walking up to him. His head hung low from being draped on the donkey.

"He is," Nh'Got confirmed.

The child put her hand on the man's face. He didn't stir, and his eyes remained closed. "Are you taking him to the Son of God for healing?"

Joseph's mouth went agape and Nh'Got blinked in astonishment. That was the first time either had heard Jesus of Nazareth referred to as the Son of God.

"We are," Nh'Got replied. "But I'm not sure he will survive to meet this person you call the Son of God."

"Child, who is the Son of God?" Joseph asked with excitement.

"Jesus," she said, again touching Tl'Rak's face. This time he opened an eye, and she held his gaze. After a pause, she withdrew her hand and Tl'Rak closed his eye.

"He belongs up there," the child said, again pointing to the sky.

"We all do, in time," Joseph said, smiling.

"No, he belongs up there," countered the child, again pointing upward. She looked up to Nh'Got. Instantly, the lieutenant felt her mind probed and knew what the child meant by "up there." Without a word to the child, her thoughts affirmed such and regretted being here in this time. The child nodded and said, "Let us hurry to see, Jesus."

The group stepped up their pace to the hills where people had gathered to see and hear Jesus of Nazareth. Joseph quizzed the child on how she knew Jesus. She told him she had seen him before and knew inside that he was the Son of God. Her responses and wisdom at such a young age astounded Joseph.

Nh'Got wondered about the child's ability to reach inside her mind. And how did she know Tl'Rak and herself were alien to Earth? The child accepted the fact like it was an everyday occurrence. The little girl was most unusual.

Finally, they reached the crowd. "I don't see many Jews here, mostly Gentiles," Joseph said. "I'm out of place while you and your friend are in good company." He gave Nh'Got a smile and a wink to the child.

Most of the crowd sat on the ground with their eyes staring up the hill There, a man was sitting on a rock speaking. The newcomers were too far away to hear what he was saying. Sitting below the man were several other men Nh'Got gasped as she recognized the speaker. He was the man who had invited her to the fire last night and gave her fish and a canteen of water. The other men were the same ones that sat around the fire. "Is that Jesus of Nazareth?

"That is him; the Son of God," the child declared, pointing to him.

"He needs to heal my friend now," Nh'Got said.

"In time," Joseph replied, patting her on the arm.

Nh'Got checked Tl'Rak. His breathing was shallow and labored—he was near death."I must get him to Jesus now." She took the donkey's reigns and started through the crowd toward the hill.

As she progressed, Jesus stood and called out, "Bring me the lame, blind, and infirm for healing." Many stood and started toward Jesus as he came down to greet them. He laid his hands on them and prayed. Then the lame walked, the blind saw, and the infirm breathed without pain and distress.

He came to Nh'Got and smiled. "The water I gave you last night will give life to your friend. Give him the water again." He moved past her to the next person.

"But we need your help to get back...." She called out as a rush of people brushed her aside as they surrounded the Healer. Sucking in a breath, she guided the donkey holding Tl'Rak down to the base of the hill to Joseph and the child.

Joseph shook his head, dismayed, seeing the dying man not healed. "He refused to heal your friend?"

"He told me to give him a drink of my water and he would have life," Nh'Got answered. "Help me get him down." Together, they lowered Tl'Rak to the ground. Joseph held the dying man's head up as Nh'Got coaxed him to drink. He was too weak to part his lips. The child scooted up to him, lifted one of his eyelids, and stared into his eye. After a few moments that seemed like forever to Joseph and Nh'Got, his lips parted. Nh'Got spilled water onto them, and Tl'Rak mouthed them onto his tongue. Slowly, his mouth widened as he took in a gulp full.

After a minute he whispered: "More." He even raised his arms for the canteen. Nh'Got' jaw gaped in amazement. She gave him the canteen and Tl'Rak managed several swallows and took a deep breath. "The air is filling my lungs with energy. I feel...."

"Normal," the child said. Her face showed a wide grin.

Tl'Rak blinked his eyes and fell into a deep sleep, snoring. His color had returned to normal. "It's a miracle," Joseph proclaimed. "Truly, Jesus is the Son of God." The three returned their attention to the crowd. All the people were standing quietly.

"What are they waiting for?" Nh'Got asked, coming to her feet.

"Maybe they are waiting to hear him speak the word of God," Joseph suggested.

"For another miracle," chimed the child.

"And what miracle could that be?" Joseph asked, smiling at the girl.

"See!" She pointed at Jesus.

Jesus told the crowd to sit. All sat. He took seven loaves of bread and a few fish and looked up to the sky and gave thanks and broke them. He then gave them to the men near him with instructions to distribute them to the crowd. It numbered four thousand men, not counting the women and children. Everyone ate to the fullest and when finished there were seven basketfuls of leftovers. After which, Jesus instructed the crowd to return to their homes.

"Jesus has healed your friend," Joseph said, wiping the crumbs from his face. "I will take my leave of you now."

"Joseph, you have been most kind," Nh'Got said and gave him a hug.

"It has been my privilege to help. Will you be returning to your home now?

Nh'Got paused, unsure of a reply. The child looked up to her and then at the sky. *How does she know? I wonder if she knows we can't go home.* "Hopefully soon," she finally replied and glanced back at Jesus to see him and his men heading toward the sea. She needed to talk to him about returning to her ship. The miracles he performed confirmed he was responsible for the situation in space.

"And child, where will you be going?" Joseph asked her.

She looked around and then up to the sky. Her look was hopeful, and Joseph felt sad for the child. He knew she would only go to heaven to see her parents when she died. "You may come and stay with me," he offered, stooping down. She stared into his eyes and he gave a start and stood shaken by the experience. "May the peace of God be with you," he muttered and took the donkey's reigns and walked off.

Nh'Got noticed his shaken response to the girl. *What did she put into his mind? Can I let her stare into my eyes?*

Before Nh'Got spoke to the child, the girl said, "I'm thirsty." She said it in Valeriian and looked at Nh'Got's canteen.

Nh'Got's jaw went slack hearing the child speak Valeriian. "Of course, child," she stammered, and handed her the canteen. She wondered what effect the water would have on her. *And what effect would it have on me after I drink from it again? And how does this child know Valeriian, unless she is an alien like Jesus.*

The girl drank and handed it back. "Thank you. Will you leave for the sky now?"

"I wish we could. How do you know my language and that we are from the sky?"

"I just know. Why can't you go to the sky?"

"I don't know. I think Jesus of Nazareth knows and can help me and my friend.

Then it struck Nh'Got. *Maybe the child can help me. After all, she always points to the sky. Yes, she must be an alien.* "Are you from the sky too?"

"I think so."

Nh'Got nodded, happy her assertion was correct. "Are your parents in the sky?"

"No, they live on the ground, but far away beyond the sky."

"Can you get there now?" She hoped they could rescue her, Tl'Rak and the girl too.

The child shook her head.

"So how did you get here?"

"Through the lights."

"The lights?" Nh'Got quizzed. "What are the lights? Where are they?"

"That way," she pointed to the west. "But they disappeared."

"Will they come back?" Nh'Got persisted hoping that they may be the key to getting back to the ship. "

awakens, we can search for Jesus and ask for his help."

"Only if Jesus wants them to."

"Then we must find Jesus, so we can all go home. When my friend awakens, we can search for Jesus and ask for his help."

"Jesus will help you as you are a kind lady. But your friend has evil in his mind. He needs to seek forgiveness. Jesus will forgive him, but he must ask. I will go now." She smiled and walked toward the south, leaving the lieutenant slack-jawed again.

CHAPTER TWENTY-TWO
Missed Opportunity

Centurion Marcus led his men into Nazareth. To him, it was another typical Israeli village. The few people in the open took notice of the Romans and went about their business. Marcus came up to a small outdoor shop where a man was carving timber.

"Carpenter," he called to the man. The worker paused and gazed up. "Is there one called Jesus the Nazarene here?"

"If you are referring to my son, he is not."

Marcus dismounted his horse and walked up to the bearded man and looked him over. "So, you're the father of the one that calls himself the Son of God. You don't look like a god. I see one of your fingers has a cut and that it bleeds. Gods don't bleed. Can they die by the sword?" He put a hand to the hilt of his sword.

"I'm not God," the carpenter replied

"Yet you have a son that claims he is the Son of God."

"He is not my son by blood. He is of God."

"And who is his mother?"

"I am," came a female voice, stepping up to the carpenter's side.

Marcus apprised her. She was beautiful for a local. "Did you give birth to the one called Jesus of Nazareth?"

"I did."

"And this man next to you is your husband?"

"He is Joseph, my husband."

"But he's not the biological father of your son, Jesus?"

The woman dropped her head and didn't reply.

"So, you have disgraced your husband."

"She hasn't disgraced me," Joseph said with a raised voice and put an arm around his wife.

"The pious ones," Marcus chuckled. "Not so holy after all. Tell me, woman, who is your son's real father? Or are you too ashamed to say?" who is your son's real father? Or are you too ashamed to say?"

"His father is God," she replied firmly.

"You don't know who the father is," Marcus said, laughing.

"His father is God of all creation," Joseph said, coming to his wife's defense.

"I will give you this, carpenter; you are a nobleman to defend this woman who bore an illegitimate child."

"My son is who he claims," the woman declared. "He is the savior of mankind."

Marcus continued laughing, and his men joined in. They were enjoying the exchange between their commander and the Jewish couple.

"Mary, they don't know the scriptures and will never understand until the Day of Judgment," Joseph said. Mary nodded.

Marcus chuckled and his men did too. "Your day of judgment will come now if you don't tell what I want to know. Once again, is your son here?"

"He is not," Mary snapped. "We haven't seen him for several weeks."

"Your pretty face has a bit to it," Marcus said, smiling. *Much like the woman that entered my mind.* "Is this your house?" Marcus asked gesturing at the small home.

"It is," Joseph said.

"Decanus, search the house," Marcus ordered. The young dismounted his horse and entered the small home.

After a quick search, he came out shaking his head. "There is no one inside."

"One more question," Marcus said. "Have either of you seen a tall young woman that would be out of place or a stranger in this town?"

"We have seen no strangers other than you and your men," Joseph replied impatiently.

"What about a small female child, about the age of five? She travels alone." Both Mary and Joseph shook their heads.

"Very well," said Marcus and remounted his horse. "Decanus, there is still four hours of daylight. We will head south toward the Sea of Galilee. The woman must have turned and gone there."

Or eaten by the lions, the decanus thought.

Three hours later, with the sun drifting toward the horizon, the Romans were near the Sea of Galilee. Up ahead were rocky hills and beyond them the seacoast.

"Centurion, look! Buzzards." the decanus said, pointing to the sky.

"I see them," Marcus said. "It is likely a dead animal."

"Or a dead person!" the decanus said excitedly.

Marcus shook his head. The decanus was wearing on his nerves and wondered if he as a junior officer was a pain to his centurion. He waved his men forward toward the hills and buzzards.

After some minutes they came across the reason for the circling buzzards. Lying on the ground were two men moaning in pain. Marcus had seen this scene before. He wondered why these two weren't dead like his men. He dismounted and came up to the injured men.

"What happened?" he asked.

"Attacked, by robbers," one huffed. Marcus glanced at the other, who was wheezing and holding his neck with one hand and his groin with the other. He bobbed his head up and down.

"Really," Marcus said, bending down and picking up a handful of gold jewelry and jewels. "Would robbers leave this treasure?"

"They only wanted our coins," assured one man.

"Coins over gold and gems," Marcus said, shaking his head. "You were the robbers and the one you tried to rob got the best of you. He grasped the man by the collar. "Did a woman do this to you?" The man shivered. Marcus tightened his grip, demanding an answer. He nodded. "How long ago?"

"Maybe a few hours," the man coughed in pain.

Marcus pushed him to the ground. "Decanus, bind these two. We'll take them to the next village. From there, other troops will take them to Jerusalem for trial. They have committed the crimes of robbery and likely murder. Gather the gold and gems. They will be evidence at the trial and seal their fate."

"As you command, Centurion."

Marcus mounted his horse and scanned the surrounding area for the woman. She wasn't in sight. Another missed opportunity.

CHAPTER TWENTY-THREE
The Path

Kay're stayed the night with Cleophas and his wife. At dawn, she and Mary went to the well to draw the day's water. There, a man was boasting of the miracles Jesus of Nazareth. Performed in the hills south of the Sea of Galilee. He claimed the man healed many and fed thousands with a few loaves of bread and fish.

"I need to go there," Kay're said to Mary. "I have to find Jesus."

"Of course, my dear. But first, you must eat for strength."

After the meal, Kay're said her goodbyes, and headed toward the Sea of Galilee.

Again, the sun blazed in a cloudless sky; the air was arid and hot. After two hours, she saw a few trees in the distance and made her way for them to rest in the shade. On approach, she spotted an elderly man with his donkey sitting under the trees. She sensed him to be harmless.

"May I please join you?" she asked.

"Your company will be welcome." The man smiled, standing to greet her. "My donkey is a poor conversationalist. I'm Joseph from Arimathea."

Kay're chuckled, finding the man amusing. "I'm Kay're." She bowed to him.

"No need to bow to me. I'm not a king." Joseph proffered to her to sit.

As they sat under the trees, Kay're again had that feeling of recognition. *I know him. But from where and when? Why can't I remember?* She wanted to stare into his face to see if it would uncloak her memory, but it would be rude. Maybe some conversation with him would stir her memory.

"Let's share some water," she started off, producing her canteen. "Oh!" she exclaimed as her Roman canteen came into view.

It surprised Joseph. "You're Roman. Are you the wife of a soldier as this is an army canteen?"

"No, to both," she said with a smile, looking at his eyes. "I'm a foreigner in this land and was very thirsty in my journey and by a miracle of God, I happened upon it." It was a partial truth.

"God works in mysterious ways," Joseph said. He studied the woman's facial reaction to his comment and then gave a start.

Kay're noticed the change in his face. "Is there something wrong?"

Joseph shook his head. "No. It's just—that I feel we have met before and shared bread and drink. Yet that can't be, as I have never met you before. Then again, you seem so familiar—your eyes, smile, and manner. I can't explain it."

"I have that feeling many times too."

Joseph shook his head and took a drink from his leather water bottle. "You said 'by a miracle of God.' What God do you believe in? I hope I'm not being rude?"

"You're not, Joseph," she said in a soothing voice. She read his thoughts. "I believe in your God—the God of all creation, and his Son, Jesus Christ."

Joseph's mouth gaped in amazement. "Praise God, another believer, yet I have never heard the Son of God called the 'Christ.'

"Where I come from, He is the 'Christ' and called the 'Son of Man.'

"The 'Son of Man,' 'Jesus Christ,' Joseph murmured. "Where do you come from?"

"I come from a very far distance, and we know about Jesus and His divinity. We believe He and the Father are one as it says in the scriptures, 'And he will be called wonderful, Counselor, Almighty God, The Everlasting Father, the Prince of Peace.'

"I know that verse," Joseph said, "yet I never put it together as you have. You're a wise woman."

"Your words are kind. But I have done many foolish things in my life."

"We all have, child." Joseph patted her on the knee. Then he realized, the child! She was like the girl with the two strangers. He stared into her face. *Could it be? No. Yet....*

"What is it, Joseph?" she asked, her mind spinning about a child. She broke eye contact to refocus. *What is it about this man? Why is he so important? And a child?*

Joseph let out a breath. "Now I remember. You remind me of a small girl I met on this very path on the way to see Jesus perform his miracles."

"What about her? What happened to her?" she asked anxiously.

"I don't know. I left her with two strangers who were from a distant land. One was a woman about your age and the other a man who was near death from a stab wound that Jesus healed. I met them on this very path too. There's something about this path."

"Did the child have a name?"

"I never asked," Joseph lamented. "I just called her 'child.' She is probably an orphan. When I asked about her parents, she pointed to the sky. I take it she meant they died and went to heaven. I offered her my home, but she declined. She is such a sweet little girl, all alone in a dangerous world. I hope that the couple takes care of her." A pause. "Where are you heading to?"

"I'm heading to find Jesus Christ. I too need a miracle from Him."

"Kay're, you look very healthy, hardly in need of a miracle."

"To tell you the truth, since I entered this land, I'm experiencing amnesia. I'm not sure why, but I don't remember how I got here or how to get home, or where home is. I was hoping Jesus would clear my mind, so I could go home."

"That is a unique problem," Joseph said, stroking his beard. "I'm sure Jesus will heal your mind. After he performed his miracles, he and his disciples headed toward the Sea of Galilee. I then left. It's possible he is still nearby."

"Then I must take my leave from you and hurry," she said, standing.

Joseph stood to bid farewell and paused. "I hear something."

"I do too," Kay're concurred, looking toward the hills to their right.

"Lions!" Joseph exclaimed, pointing to them. There was a large make with four females at his side. "We have no defense," Joseph sighed. "Have courage, my child of God. We will be with our creator, God Himself, shortly."

The five cats made their way down from the rocks toward them. Kay're patted Joseph on the shoulder and smiled. "We won't see the face of God the Father today." She walked out from under the tree toward the approaching lions and held up a hand. "It is me, Kay're," she said in a soothing voice She then held out both hands to the large cats. They slowed their approach. The male let out a great roar.

"It is me, Kay're," she repeated and walked toward the pride. Joseph stood, mouth agape.

As the lions approached, the females growled. The male came up and sniffed her. She touched his head and looked into his eyes. The large male gave a roar and stood on his hind legs and draped his forelegs over her shoulders.

"How are you, big boy?" she said, steadying herself under his weight. She gave him a big hug. Finally, he dropped to all fours, and the females came up to Kay're's side. She bent down and let them nuzzle against her. They purred and gently pawed her. She gave each a hug.

Joseph stood shocked. *How could this be?*

Kay're smiled at Joseph and said to her animal friends, "That is Joseph. He is my friend. Don't harm him." The male lion roared as if agreeing.

"Joseph, do you have any fish?"

"Yes, I have two."

"Good. Will you share them with my friends here?"

"I—I guess. Sure."

"Come," she said to the pride and led them to Joseph. Joseph shaking reached into his cloth bag for the fish.

The lions roared as they came up to Joseph who was wide-eyed and trembling. He reached out a piece of fish to the male, who grasped it from his shaky hand. He repeated his offer to the other cats. Kay're chuckled as she watched Joseph nervously feed the beasts.

"Joseph, you now have new friends forever."

"Control over these lions! You are a blessed woman of God. It's a miracle!"

"I guess God has blessed me with this gift to befriend animals." The

"Truly amazing," Joseph said, letting out a breath.

"Well, Joseph, I need to take my leave of you to find Christ."

beasts nuzzled Joseph and reclined at his feet.

"Truly amazing," Joseph said, letting out a breath.

"Well, Joseph, I need to take my leave of you to find Christ."

"And the lions?"

"They will watch over and protect you until you send them away."

"How do you know that?"

She winked at him and stooped down to the cats. "Now watch over Joseph and listen to what he says. Okay?" The male roared his acceptance. "You will be fine, Joseph." She stood, hugged him, and left.

Joseph watched her walk away and said, "Now it is you five and my donkey. We go now." Joseph took the reins of his beast and restarted his journey home. He gazed back, and the pride followed.

CHAPTER TWENTY-FOUR
We Are Aliens!

At the base of the hill, Lt. Nh'Got sat alone with her thoughts. Jesus and his followers had left. The crowd had returned to their homes, and the girl and Joseph had departed. Tl'Rak with his color back to normal snored in peace. He even seemed to have a thin smile on his face. *Did the girl plant pleasant thoughts into his mind, possibly the need to abandon his drive to kill Jesus?* She hoped he would be thankful Jesus had healed him and give up any thoughts of killing him. She would know when he awoke from his slumber.

The sun was setting and Nh'Got gathered wood and started a fire. She held the blaster at the ready in case the four-legged beasts returned and bandits too! As she was settling into a reclining position, her annunciator beeped. "Lt. Nh'Got," she answered.

"This is Supreme Commander Tr'Tala. Status report."

"Sir, Tl'Rak will survive," she said and filled in the Supreme Commander on the day's events. Concluding, she said to him, "Sir, I couldn't follow Jesus and leave Commander Tl'Rak asleep. The area is dangerous with bandits and ferocious animals roaming about."

There was a pause. "Of course," Tr'Tala concurred.

"And sir, the child I mentioned, she knows we are aliens!"

"How can that be?" Tr'Tala asked.

"Sir, somehow, she can read our thoughts. She told me Commander Tl'Rak had evil intentions and needed to repent before he asked Jesus Christ for help. I also think she has some healing powers. She seemed to give Commander Tl'Rak extra strength when he was near death by looking into one of his eyes and touching his head. I can't explain it."

"Humans don't have that ability," interjected Commander Zh'Cata, who was listening. "I have studied them, and their mental powers aren't extraordinary. And this child spoke to me in Valeriian. She must be an alien."

"Most interesting," Tr'Tala said, surprised. "And what of the 'lights' the child mentioned?"

"Sir, she said they disappeared and maybe Jesus could bring them back," Nh'Got answered.

"Sir, the 'lights' could be a post transporter effect or a portal," Zh'Cata added.

"If the former, then that could mean there is a ship in orbit," Tr'Tala said. "Tactical officers, both ships, focus scanners for a cloaked ship."

Both tactical officers failed to detect another ship in orbit above Earth. "Supreme Commander, there still could be a cloaked ship," his wife said. I'm sure there is one. Due to superior technology, it has evaded our scanners. Or they detected our sweeps and moved out of orbit." She paused, allowing time for her comment to sink in, then continued, "Jesus isn't a god, and the child likely snuck away from his ship."

"That's likely," her husband agreed.

"And sir," his wife continued, "after the humans kill him as detailed in the Bible, he will beam back to his ship for resuscitation. When he is better, beam back to Earth for a fake resurrection. Forty days later, he will ascend into heaven, which is transporting back to his ship. Then the ship will leave for its homeworld."

"Then what you are saying is we need to let the events play out to preserve the timeline," Tr'Tala said.

"Yes, sir. But we have to make sure Tl'Rak doesn't kill Jesus."

"Lieutenant Nh'Got, did you hear the exchange?" Tr'Tala asked.

"I did, sir. Yet I have witnessed miracles that no mortal being can do."

"Lieutenant, are you saying you believe that Jesus is a god?" Tr'Tala quizzed.

"Sir, what I saw points to that conclusion. I don't discount the child came to Earth through a portal. That may be why you can't detect a cloaked ship, because there isn't one."Nh'Got bit her lip, hoping her answer was not insubordinate.

"Lieutenant, no matter what you believe, your job is to prevent Tl'Rak from killing Jesus. At least until we can figure out a way to get the transporters working. Hopefully, Tl'Rak will come to his senses as you said and give up on his idea of killing Jesus. He may even work with you in finding Jesus and persuading him to release our ships. I want to go home with the timeline maintained."

"Sir, Commander Tl'Rak may abandon his plot to kill Jesus," Lt. Nh'Got said. "However, I don't think he will help us. He knows his life will end once you gain control of the ships. He would rather die here than at your hand. I shouldn't have tried to save his life."

"Lieutenant, you did what was necessary," Tr'Tala said. "You still have a job to do, and you will use lethal force on Commander Tl'Rak if he is uncooperative. Preservation of the time continuum is a must. We'll work out a solution, so we can transport you and Tl'Rak up and then return to Valerii."

Nh'Got took a breath. "I understand your orders, and will comply."

"Lieutenant, until we know Tl'Rak's disposition when he wakes, you must bind him and get some sleep. Tomorrow will be busy for you."

"Will do, Supreme Commander. I will contact you in the morning."

"Have a good night's sleep. Tr'Tala out."

CHAPTER TWENTY-FIVE
Close Call

After leaving Joseph with the lions, Kay're headed toward the eastern shore of the Sea of Galilee. There, Joseph witnessed Jesus perform the miracle of feeding four thousand people. She hoped Jesus was still nearby. On her trek, she met a few people returning from the miracle. They gushed over what they witnessed, but they couldn't confirm if Jesus was still there. Daylight was fading, and she had only made it to the tip of the southern shore. Up ahead, a seaside town loomed. *Could there be quest lodging and a restaurant at this point in history?* She didn't have faith in meeting anybody like Cleophus and his wife again.

Approaching the town, she saw many Roman soldiers and felt crestfallen. *They could be trouble especially if the centurion was among them. I need to be careful.*

Keeping her head down, she walked to the town's well. There, she took a long drink and then quickly submerged the Roman canteen into the bucket to fill it. When she finished the fill, it went under her dress, and just in time, as another woman stepped up to the well.

Kay're smiled at her and the woman nodded back. "Excuse me," she said to the local woman with graying hair. "I'm a traveler and new to this area. Is there a place I can rest for the night? I can pay for my stay and food."

The elderly woman eyed her suspiciously. "Do you have a husband?" she finally spoke.

"No, I'm alone, and not a prostitute." She could read the woman's thoughts.

The woman blinked in surprise. "Then you must be one of those following this Jesus person around."

"I'm trying to find him. Others I met told me he was in the area. Is Jesus of Nazareth in town now?"

"He hasn't been here," the woman replied dryly, suspicious of the strange. "Most of the travelers are coming from Gergesa. They tell stories that Jesus performed many miracles there. I heard he drove demon-possessed swine off a cliff."

"Wow," Kay're said as three Roman soldiers came to the well. She dipped her head to hide her face. The older woman did the same and tugged on Kay're's dress and began walking away. Kay're got the message and followed her. The soldiers ignored them and drew water.

When the women were some distance away, the local said, "You can't trust Romans. You're young and alone, they would have...."

"I know," Kay're said, cutting her off. "I had my experience with them and bandits. And none of them violated me; I fought them off."

"Oh my," the woman said, putting a hand to her mouth. "It is true then."

"What is true?"

"Not here. Come with me."

The woman took Kay're by the elbow and scurried home. Inside was another older woman. She asked, "Who is this woman?"

"She is the one of the rumors." The other woman's eyes widened and stood, but didn't approach Kay're who's face showed a quizzical look.

"Is it true you beat two bandits nearly to death with your bare hands?" the first woman asked. Kay're's mouth gaped, unsure what to say.

"They were two of the most notorious thieves and murderers, and you beat them up!" exclaimed the second woman

"How do you know this?"

"Roman soldiers found them near death in the hills," answered the second woman.

"The soldiers in town are talking about it. They say the bandits conf -essed that a woman attacked them."

"Of course, they attacked her first," added the woman from the well. "Are you that woman?"

"Yes," Kay're said, nodding, leaving the woman slack-jaw.

"Whoa!" exclaimed the second woman, eyes wide with surprise. "Then you need to spend the night here. I heard the centurion is looking for you. And he doesn't want to thank you for disabling the bandits."

"It appears he has some sort of grudge against you," the first woman added. "I heard him curse today when some of his men brought you up in conversation. Did you do something to him?"

"I took a canteen from one of his soldiers. I was very thirsty." Kay're produced the water skin from under her dress. The women's mouths gaped in surprise. "And the centurion wasn't happy about it. Let's just say the encounter didn't end well for him. Please, don't give me away."

"No, my dear," the second woman said. "We hate the Romans and what they represent. They have mistreated our people and abused many women. Any hurt done to them is welcome. Do you have a name?"

"I am Kay're."

"I am Sarah," said the second woman.

"And I am, Hannah. Sarah is my sister. We are widows."

"Such beautiful names," Kay're said with a smile. "Thank you for inviting me into your home. God will bless you."

"God can bless us by making the Romans disappear," Hannah said sarcastically. "Let us eat and then you rest." They ate and Kay're told them she was from a distant land and had some memory loss since coming to Israel. She hoped Jesus could restore her memory and help her find a way home.

"My dear, if Jesus is who he claims to be, he will help you," Hannah said.

"But I have to find him," Kay're said soberly.

"It's late, and darkness is falling," Sarah said. "As you have found, Israel isn't a kind land, especially for a foreigner. In the morning when our minds are fresh, we can talk about a plan to help you."

The morning broke with sunlight and Kay're and the women refreshed themselves and then sat for a meal. "So, what is your plan?" Sarah asked.

"I will head to Gergesa with hopes of finding Jesus of Nazareth. If I am lucky, I will run into him between here and there."

"So far luck has been on your side. May it continue," Hannah said. "Would you please go to the well with me to draw water for today's needs?"

"Of course, Sarah. And if there is a market, I can buy food for all of us."

Hannah stayed behind and Kay're and Sarah took cloth bags and water jars to the main square. Kay're gave Hannah coins to buy food while she went to fill the jars. As Kay're filled her jars, she noticed Roman soldiers led by Centurion Marcus coming into town. He was on a horse. Amongst the soldiers were the thieves she had encountered in the hills. They looked pained. Kay're smirked, knowing they got what they deserved for attacking her with the worst yet to come. She dropped her head as the Roman garrison approached.

At the well, the centurion stopped. "Decanus, do we have enough water to make it to Jerusalem?"

"We have sufficient supply, Centurion. Unless unexpected actions sidetracked us. There are no wells on the main path to Jerusalem. I suggest we top off our barrels and canteens."

"Make it so," Marcus ordered. He dismounted his horse. "Woman," he said to Kay're, as she walked away, head down. She stopped, but adrenaline surged inside her. "Have you seen a small orphan girl in this village?"

"No," Kay're said, shaking her head, not looking at the centurion.

"Woman, when you talk to a Roman you look at them," he said, stepping up to her. He was about to reach out and spin her around when the decanus drew his attention.

"Centurion, there in the boat; the child!" The decanus pointed and eyes turned toward the sea. In a boat stood a small girl. She looked back at the centurion as the boat's owner raised the sails.

Marcus quickly mounted his horse and raced to the seashore. Kay're turned as the centurion rode off and gasped as she recognized the girl as her childhood self

How can this be? she wondered, eyes watering with emotion. She continued watching as the centurion yelled for the sailor to turn the boat back to shore. The man either didn't hear him or ignored the command as the boat moved away as a gust of wind filled the sails. Marcus cursed as he again missed a chance to take hold of the child. Kay're scurried off, bursting with emotion and confusion.

"How far is it across?" Marcus asked the decanus as he came up to his side.

"It's about eight miles, Centurion. But it looks like the boat is turning to the north and that will make the distance further."

Marcus stared at the boat as it became smaller with each passing second. Frustrated again, he looked back to the spring. His garrison was replenishing their water. *That woman! Could she be her? Or visa-versa? Where is she?* He scanned the area. He couldn't find her in the gathering crowd. *She could be anywhere now. Do I dare waste time searching for her and be late for my new assignment in Jerusalem?* He shook his head.

CHAPTER TWENTY-SIX
Curses and Confessions

*C*ommander Tl'Rak woke in the middle of the night to find both his hands and feet bound. He glanced over to Lt. Nh'Got. She was sleeping

He called out to her, "Nh'Got, Nh'Got." She didn't stir. Tl'Rak smiled and noticed a rock close by. He rolled over to it and vigorously rubbed the binding on his wrists against it until his hands were free. He untied the bindings on his ankles and crawled over to Nh'Got. Stealthily, he took the blaster and her canteen. After a drink, he stood a nd sucked in a large breath of cool air, then another. He felt strong.

"Lieutenant, you're a fool," he snickered and pointed the blaster at her, pretending to pull the trigger. "You should be dead for betraying me. I knew all along it was you. For saving me, I will spare you. Now you're on your own. I'm off to find Jesus of Nazareth and glory." He thumped his chest and walked off into the night.

At sunrise, Lt. Nh'Got's eyes blinked open. Her sleep was restful, and she stretched out the kinks from sleeping on hard ground. In doing so, she noticed the bindings she used to secure Tl'Rak were in a pile. In panic, she sat up and reached to her side for the blaster, but it wasn't there. She scrambled to her feet and looked around for Tl'Rak. The man was nowhere in sight. She mouthed a curse and felt for the canteen; it too was missing! Another curse. She was weaponless and thirsty in a dangerous land with a madman on the loose. It was obvious he was still hell-bent on murdering Jesus of Nazareth even after the man saved his life. She took a breath and called the ship, knowing she would get a good scolding from the Supreme Commander.

"What? How could you let that happen?" was the boisterous reply from Supreme Commander Tr'Tala after she told him Tl'Rak had fled with the blaster.

"Supreme Commander, I take full responsibility for letting Commander Tl'Rak escape. His recovery was more than I expected—a miracle. I will find him, and he won't get away again." She took another deep breath.

"And how will you find him?" Tr'Tala asked with frustration in his voice. "He could be anywhere, and at any moment he could kill Jesus Christ. Then we could all wink out of existence."

"Sir, since the timeline is still intact, I will concentrate my search for Jesus of Nazareth. Once I find him, then Tl'Rak will show and I will be ready for him." Nh'Got felt proud of her answer.

"With what, Lieutenant, your bare hands? He has the blaster," he said sarcastically.

Nh'Got cringed. *He's right.* "I'll think of a way."

"I hope so. But this time you will kill him. I don't care where or how he dies. He dies! No hesitancy or questioning on your part. Do you understand?" Tr'Tala's voice gave no option for an alternative.

"I understand, Supreme Commander."

"Lieutenant, get moving. Time is of the essence."

"Yes, sir. Lt. Nh'Got out." She closed the link and managed a dry swallow. She had a cotton mouth. Her conversation with the Supreme Commander only added to it. Now she needed water. She looked on the ground to see if there were footprints. There were many from the crowd, but only one that resembled a boot, and it headed southeast. She started her walk in that direction.

Kay're had slipped behind a market stall and hid until the Centurion and his garrison moved out of town. Feeling safe, she walked back into the square and found Hannah. "That was close," she said to her. "I will be okay now. I heard the centurion say that he and his troops were heading to Jerusalem."

"Did you see the two thieves?" Hannah asked.

Kay're nodded. "They were the ones I encountered in the hills."

"I'm still amazed at what you did to them. What will you do now?"

"I will head to Gergesa."

"I have food for you." Hannah handed Kay're a sack of fruit and dried fish.

"Thank you. Did you get some for yourself and your sister?"

"I did."

"Here are the water jars. Do you need help with them?"

"No, I can manage," Hannah said, taking them. "You need to leave now just in case the centurion unexpectedly returns."

"I will. Let me hug you and wish me luck." The two embraced, and Kay're began her journey to the northeast along the shoreline.

The day was the hottest since she had arrived on the surface. As the sun rose higher in the sky, so did the temperature. Nh'Got's physiology was human-like, but different enough to not be able to withstand the heat as well. She hadn't acclimated to the arid and hot climate that was sapping her strength. Without food and water, it made her situation worse. She was feeling desperate. Looking around, she saw no one. There was only dirt, dust, and scrub brush. She longed for a shade tree and rest. *Maybe over the next hill, there will be water and trees, hopefully, some with figs.*

She dragged herself to the crest of the hill and dropped to her knees. There was no water, only a few trees. She staggered toward them and collapsed against one. Shade never felt so good. She looked up to see if they bore fruit—none. With despair, she sank with her back against the trunk. Quickly, she felt drowsy and her mind started wandering in and out of a dream state.

She dreamt of seeing Tl'Rak killing Jesus and suddenly winking out of existence. In another dream, she dazzled onto a street in her small hometown on Valerii. The town lacked the vibrancy she remembered from her teenage years. The buildings were dirty and in disrepair; trash littered the streets. The townsfolk looked downtrodden. "No, no," she moaned and shook her head, awakening to the heat and the thirst of reality.

"I have to stop Tl'Rak," she said to the air. "If he only knew that killing Jesus would be detrimental to Valerii. Yet I lack the strength to move on. Maybe the ships are back to normal and I came transport up." She touched her annunciator and called the ship. The ships' status remained unchanged. She told Tr'Tala that her situation was dire. He encouraged her to sum up internal strength and kick in her survival training. "I will do my best," she said, closing the link.

She sucked in a breath and gazed out at the cloudless sky. Overhead, she saw several large black birds circling. She wondered if they were a sign that water was nearby, maybe over the next rise. She managed another dry swallow of hope and placed her hands on the ground to push herself up. As she did so, a bird landed several feet away. Nh'Got shivered at its sight. It was hideous looking with long talons and eyeing her ominously.

"The bird of death," she whispered and kicked dirt at it. The bird just moved back a few feet. Soon more of its kind landed on the ground. "I must be close to death," she whispered. Then she thought of Jesus Christ. *If he is God, then he can hear my prayer.*

"Jesus Christ, when I was in need before, you gave me food and drink. I have seen you work miracles feeding the hungry and healing your enemy in Tl'Rak. I confess you are God, the God of all creation. Please, help me again and provide me with water." She let out a "Jesus Christ, when I was in need before, you gave me food and drink. I have seen you work miracles feeding the hungry and healing your enemy in Tl'Rak. I confess you are sigh, waited, and hoped.

The birds held their vigil, waiting to feast. Suddenly, they flapped their wings and hopped back. Coming from Nh'Got's left was a person. With her eyes dry and blurry, she couldn't make out if the newcomer was a man or woman. She hoped the person wasn't a bandit. She lacked the strength to defend herself. Nh'Got sighed with relief as the stranger was a smiling woman. The woman bent down and gazed into her face. Nh'Got shuddered. *I have seen those eyes before.*

The woman handed Nh'Got her canteen. "Drink as much as you need," the calm voice said. Nh'Got nodded and took several long draws and handed the skin back to the answer to her prayer.

"You speak my language!" Nh'Got exclaimed, wondering how this stranger could speak Valeriian.

Kay're smiled and said, "You're a Valeriian." She sat across from the woman, and knew immediately that she had met this woman before; a very long time ago. "I thought it would be appropriate to speak in your native tongue."

"But, how do you know I'm a Valeriian?"

"I don't know. I just know you are."

"Where did you learn to speak Valeriian?

"Again, I don't know."

"Somehow, I have this feeling that we met before," Nh'Got said, "But I know we haven't. I have another question and it may seem silly to you, but I need to ask."

Kay're nodded to her.

"Did God direct you to bring me water?"

Kay're wanted to chuckle, but knew it would be rude. "Perhaps. And this may seem strange to you, but I was looking for the Son of God and my search took me to you. Possibly, it is His will."

Nh'Got's mouth dropped in amazement. "You're looking for Jesus Christ?"

"I am. How do you know about Jesus Christ?"

"I have met him twice and seen the miracles he performed, and they made me a believer that he is the Son of God. I was dying of thirst right here, and I prayed to Jesus Christ for a miracle to save me. Then you came along and spoke Valeriian! He answered my prayer and gave you the knowledge to know that I'm a Valeriian and speak my language."

"I guess it is a miracle," Kay're said, smiling. "I was following the shoreline, and I saw the buzzards circling, so I came to see what they were flying over and found you."

"They're buzzards?" Nh'Got pointed to one that was still on the ground.

"Yes. Some people call them vultures and they prey on the dead flesh."

"If you didn't come along, I would have been their dinner."

Kay're chuckled. "Do you have a name?"

"I am Z'mia Nh'Got." She left off her title lieutenant.

"That is a pretty name. I like it. I'm Kay're."

"Just Kay're?"

Kay're's forehead furrowed. "I think I have a surname, but don't recall it.

I have amnesia, and that is why I'm seeking Jesus Christ. I hope he could return my memory and then I could go home."

"Kay're, so you don't know where your home is?"

"No," she replied, shaking her head. "I know it is in a distant land."

"What about your family? Like your mother or father? Or husband?"

"I don't remember if I have a husband," Kay're demurred. "My parents—I feel like they're in the sky, as strange as that sounds."

Nh'Got's mouth gaped again. *The sky is where the little girl pointed when asked about her parents. And this woman's eyes and voice seem just like the child. But they can't be the same.*

"You seemed more surprised than amused."

"I met a small wayward girl yesterday that reminds me so much of you. Same eyes and when I asked her about her parents, she just pointed to the sky. Have you lost a daughter here?" Nh'Got wondered if this woman was alien to Earth and the mother of the child. Together they had traveled through the lights and got separated.

Kay're shook her head. "No, I'm alone here." Yet she knew Nh'Got had met her small self.

"Are you from Earth?" Nh'Got boldly asked.

"To be honest, I'm not sure."

"Do you remember coming through any bright lights?"

"All I remember is waking up on a hill some days ago. As to how I got there, I don't know. I need to find Jesus. He will have the answers to all my questions. May I ask, what is a Valeriian doing on Earth? And how did you get here?"

Nh'Got's gaze turned toward the lone buzzard as if it had answers to Kay're's questions. The bird flapped its wings and flew off to join its brethren who were soaring away. They knew there wouldn't be a meal here. Nh'Got's eyes returned to Kay're. *How do I tell this woman from ancient times that I am from the future? And that I'm here to stop my commander from killing Jesus Christ?*

Kay're could read her conundrum. "The truth is always the best," she said with a smile. "And I'm not judgmental.

"Kay're you are wise, as was the child. I wish I could have got her name. You seem to see through me, as did the child. I'll tell you the truth." She took a breath. "I'm an officer in the Valeriian military, and from your future; some twenty She hesitated to see Kay're's reaction that remained stoic. "I came to Earth in a spaceship, but not by choice. My commander ordered our spaceship to travel back in time so he could kill Jesus Christ. He believes that by doing so, the course of time will change and return the lost glory to our empire. He is on Earth now, around here somewhere. He has an advanced weapon that can kill." Nh'Got took another breath and filled in Kay're on her and Commander Tl'Rak's time on Earth.

Kay're bobbed her head. "Z'mia Nh'Got I'm glad you told me. It must have been very hard for you to do so." Kay're reached out a hand and touched Nh'Got's arm to console her. "And I believe you. Since we both need to find Jesus Christ, can we do it together?"

Z'mia Nh'Got grinned and nodded. "Kay're, you are a kind woman. One I will call, friend."

"And you are my friend too," Kay're added. "This is a nice place to rest for the night. I have food. Tomorrow, we will set out to find Jesus of Nazareth."

CHAPTER TWENTY-SEVEN
Meetings and Greetings

By morning, Tl'Rak reached the south shoreline of the Sea of Galilee. There he found several fishermen tending to their night catch. He inquired if anyone had heard of Jesus Christ and had seen him recently. They admitted knowing of him. One man said he saw him in a boat heading toward the western shoreline yesterday. They returned to removing fish from their nets that perturbed Tl'Rak.

"Fisherman, take me to that area now!" he boomed.

"We aren't going anywhere," the man replied. "And you are a Gentile. We don't associate with your kind."

"Fisherman, you will sail me to the other shore," Tl'Rak demanded, his tone menacing. He pulled out his blaster and pointed it at the man.

"What is that?" the man asked nervously.

"The instrument of your death if you don't take me to the shoreline where Jesus Christ is." Tl'Rak pointed the weapon at a floundering fish on the ground and fired. The fish exploded into many pieces. "That will happen to you if you don't do as I say."

The man gulped a dry swallow and motioned for the others who were slack-jawed to push his boat out into the water. Tl'Rak boarded and pointed to one of the younger men. "You will help your friend sail to the other side." The man nodded and joined the other in the boat, and it was off with the wind.

Morning broke, and Z'mia Nh'Got woke feeling renewed. The food that her new friend provided, along with a good sleep, allowed her to regain her strength. She was ready to move on to find Jesus of Nazareth.

Kay're's eyes fluttered open to see the Valeriian staring up at the clear blue sky. "Are you ready for a day of hiking?" she asked.

"I am," Z'mia replied, sitting up.

"Good. I suggest we head to the shoreline. We may encounter some fishermen who might have seen Jesus or Tl'Rak." Nh'Got agreed. The women refreshed themselves and set off. After a two-hour trek, they reached the Sea of Galilee. There they saw two beached fishing boats and several men sitting around a fire.

"I smell the aroma of fish roasting," Nh'Got said, remembering the time Jesus had invited her to sit and eat. "I want something more than fruit."

"Me too," Kay're agreed, licking her lips. "Perhaps these men will be kind enough to offer us some."

"I hope. Maybe Jesus of Nazareth is one of them."

"Let's go find out."

They approached the men. Nh'Got's heart saddened as she didn't recognize any of the men. Kay're took the lead. "Good day, gentlemen." She bowed to them. The men eyed the two women suspiciously. They remained seated. Kay're didn't sense the men were a threat, but that they were both curious and wary.

"What do you want?" one man asked.

"We seek information," Kay're said, not immediately pursuing the desire for some cooked fish.

"You two are Gentiles," another man said. "We don't socialize with people of your kind."

"We are not Gentiles," Nh'Got said in a soothing manner that surprised Kay're. "We are travelers from distant lands in search of the one called Jesus of Nazareth."

"And what is that to us?" asked another man.

"He is Jewish like you and is known far and wide for performing miracles," Kay're interjected. "We want to meet this great Jew."

"Great Jew, bah. He is just stirring up controversy."

"Still, have you seen him?" Nh'Got prodded.

"Woman, we saw him in a boat yesterday heading west. Now leave us." The man waved a dismissing hand.

Kay're sensed the man was tense and worried. "Sir, you seem upset about something." The man gave her a long look but said nothing. Kay're could read that the man wanted to talk, but not to a woman. Kay're sat down a few meters from the man and his friends so as not to enter their personal space. She motioned for Nh'Got to do the same. "I have fruit," she continued, "and I will share it with you." She hoped to gain their confidence. She took the cloth that held the fruit and spread it open on the sand. "Please help yourself." The men eyed the fruit. It was a change from smoked fish.

After a long pause, one man took a fig, then another did the same, then all were munching on various figs and berries. Kay're and Nh'Got sat, hoping the men would offer them some fish. Finally, the leader noticed Nh'Got eyeing the fish.

"Here," he said and reached to the fire and took two sticks holding fish and gave them to the women.

"Thank you, sir. You are most kind," Kay're said, giving him a smile. "We haven't eaten any flesh for some time."

"You cook fish very well. This is delicious," Nh'Got praised. "You should open up a shop and sell your cooked fish. You would make a nice profit."

"I would be a customer," Kay're added. "Better than fixing it yourself. Stop at your shop, get your fish, and eat on the run. If you add a drink, all the better. You would have a fast-food establishment. Call it 'fish on a stick.' You men would make a fortune."

The lead man stroked his beard in thought. He looked at the others and nodded. "That is a good idea," he admitted. "But right now, we are short two men and don't know if they will come back." His mood darkened with worry.

"Where are they?" Kay're asked

"On the water heading toward the east bank," the leader said.

"They are with a stranger that has a weapon that shoots lightning," said another man.

"He demanded they take him across the lake to find Jesus or he would kill them," added yet another man. Nh'Got's heart raced with the news. She described Tl'Rak to them, and they affirmed her description.

"So, you know him?" asked the leader.

"I do," Nh'Got nodded. "He is a terrible man and sadly needs to die soon or everything in life and this land will change for the worse."

"To stop him, we need to leave now," Kay're said, standing.

"How can one man change life for everyone?" asked the lead man.

"Because he plans to kill Jesus of Nazareth," Nh'Got answered.

"So, he kills Jesus. No loss."

"We can't explain it in a way you would understand," Kay're told the men.

"But with his weapon, he can take control of all the world," Nh'Got added. "And when he does, you'll wish the Romans were back in control. That is how bad he is."

The men exchange sidelong glances. "So, you two women will stop this man," said the leader mockingly. "With what? Your bare hands?"

"I know him, and he knows me," Nh'Got said. "He will let me get close to him because I'm a woman and he likes women. If you know what I mean." The men's heads bobbed. "And he will let both of us hang on his arms like prostitutes, and when he does, we will get the jump on him and kill him."

Two of the men laughed. "You are a scrawny woman, and he is a big man. You can't take him."

"Did you hear the rumor of the woman that beat up two bandits?" Kay're asked.

"We did," they chorused.

"I'm the woman they attacked and beat them to the point of death. They're alive only because of my kindness."

"Would one or two of you men be kind enough to take us across the lake to where Jesus is?" Kay're asked. "I will pay you in coins for your trouble."

The men looked at each other and nodded. "My son and I will take you two to the west bank." They stood and motioned for the women to head to the boat. After an hour of sailing, they spotted a sail heading their way. "That's Thaddeus's boat," the son said. "He's the one that took the man you seek across the lake. And Phillip is with him. They met in the middle of the lake.

"Are you both okay?" the leader asked.

"Yes," they chirped. "We dropped him off and left. Who are these women? And what are you doing with them?" Thaddeus asked curiously.

"They know that man and mean to kill him. We are taking them across the lake, so they can find him and do what they must."

Phillip laughed. "These women against a madman who has a weapon that shoots fire."

"Sir," Nh'Got interrupted. "Don't delay us with talk. This is urgent. We must stop him. Your friend here will tell you the story after he drops us off."

"Let us go," the leader said. "We will talk when we return." The boats separated and two hours later, Kay're paid the men for their taxi service. The women walked into Migdal, a town Kay're knew full well. With Nh'Got in tow, Kay're headed toward Mary's home.

"Kay're!" Mary greeted her friend at the door with a hug. "I worried about you. But you look fine. And you have a friend."

"Yes, Mary. This is Z'mia. We met recently. She, too, is in search of Jesus from Nazareth."

"It is nice to meet you, Z'mia." Mary hugged her too. "Please come in and refresh." Kay're and Nh'Got sat while Mary brought food and water.

"Mary, I never found Jesus," Kay're said. "So, my memory is still lacking. But Z'mia has met Jesus twice and seen him perform miracles."

"Please tell me," Mary prodded, sitting. Nh'Got related her encounters with Jesus and included the healing of Tl'Rak.

"Now I regret taking my friend to Jesus for healing because he is a very evil man."

"Why is that?" Mary asked.

"Because he wants to kill Jesus, believing it will bring him great glory He is very delusional."

"We followed him by boat to Migdal," Kay're added. "We need to stop him Mary, did you notice a stranger in town a few hours ago?"

"I saw two fishermen land their boat and a large stranger get out. The fishermen set sail immediately. The large man started talking to a few of the locals in the market and then left town on the road to Nazareth.”

“That has to be him,” Nh’Got said. “How long ago was that?

“About two or three hours ago.”

“Mary, have you seen Jesus recently?” Kay’re asked.

“The Master was here yesterday. I heard he was heading to his hometown, Nazareth.”

“Oh my,” Z’mia said. “We need to leave now.”

“You can’t leave now,” Mary protested. “It will be dark in two hours and it is a five-hour walk to Nazareth. Even the man you are after will not reach Nazareth by foot before darkness. It is too dangerous to be out in the darkness.”

Nh’Got bobbed her head, remembering the storm and the large beasts. “We’ll leave at morning’s light.” She looked to Kay’re for confirmation. Kay’re nodded in agreement.

“If this man is so bad, why do you call him a friend?” Mary asked Nh’Got.

“He really isn’t my friend, but my superior. We both work for our government and he is my boss. Like Kay’re, we are from a distant land. He forced me to go with him to Israel for his purpose, to kill Jesus of Nazareth. Our government didn’t sanction him to kill Jesus. When he was near death from a stabbing by bandits, I had him in control. But when Jesus healed him, I didn’t bind him securely enough, and he slipped away during the night. I should have killed him.”

“It is difficult to kill someone who was spared from death by a miracle,” Mary said. “I couldn’t have done it. Don’t feel too bad. You will find him.”

Z’mia managed a thin smile.

“Kay’re,” Mary continued, “speaking of bandits, did you hear about the woman who fought two of them, almost killed them? I thought about you when I heard the news.”

“I was that woman,” Kay’re admitted, touching her chest.

“Whoa!” Mary whistled. “You continue to impress me. First with your kindness and wisdom and now with your strength.”

“It’s not so much strength, but position, balance, counterbalance, and timing. I learned it, but I don't recall where or when or who taught me."

"When you meet Jesus, it will all come back to you," Mary consoled. "Now let us refresh ourselves and eat and rest. Tomorrow will be a big day for you." Kay're and Z'mia nodded.

As the sun slid below the horizon, the night air quickly cooled. Though recovered from his stab wound, Tl'Rak hadn't regained all his stamina and was leaking energy. With the cool of the evening, he felt fatigued to the bone. Ahead were some trees. He would spend the night under them in case of rain. He reached the trees and gathered some twigs and lit them with his blaster.

The warmth of the fire felt good, but he was hungry. He cursed himself for not checking Nh'Got for food. The pangs of hunger would prevent a restful sleep and make tomorrow's hike to Nazareth trying. He settled against a tree and closed his eyes, but an ominous roar nearby snapped them open.

"I heard that sound before, but where?" he whispered to himself. After some time passed, he fell asleep.

CHAPTER TWENTY-EIGHT
More Roars and Romans

Another typical Israeli morning broke; dry and sunny. The three ladies rose with the sun, refreshed themselves, and ate a meal of bread, fried

eating an insect. Kay're laughed, took a locust, and popped it in her mouth. Her bite made a crunching sound.

Nh'Got made an ugly face as she bit into one. "Hmm," she murmured. "It's rather good. It tastes like a foul we eat in my land."

"Like chicken," Kay're giggled.

"What's a chicken?" Nh'Got asked.

"You don't know what a chicken is?" Mary said, surprised. Nh'Got raised her palms, shaking her head.

"It is a large ground bird common on Earth raised for eggs and meat," Kay're said.

"Sure," Nh'Got said, trying not to show any more ignorance. "Where I'm from, we call it something else."

After eating breakfast, Kay're said, "Mary, as much as we would like to stay, we must be off."

"Of course. Please be careful," Mary cautioned. "There still may be bandits around and Roman patrols. They may stop you and...."

"I understand," Kay're said with a thin smile. "We'll be very careful."

"Mary, thank you for your kindness," Z'mia Nh'Got said, hugging her. Kay're did the same, and the two departed with some food and one roman canteen of water.

Tl'Rak slept well past sunrise. It was the sound of pounding hooves that stirred him from his slumber. The sunlight poured into his eyes, and he shielded them with his hand. Squinting, he saw several men wearing military uniforms riding large mounts. They were heading east on the road, and didn't notice him in the shade of the trees. "Good fortune," he told himself, looking at the trees and bushes to see if they bore fruit. He was hungry, and the growl of his stomach affirmed the fact. They were bare. His good fortune had disappeared. He still had water, but there was little of that left. After taking a long swig, he returned to the road and followed it west.

During their walk, Nh'Got told Kay're about her life growing up on Valerii and her military career. Kay're had a nagging feeling she already knew about Valerii and their military. It seemed there was a fog shrouding that knowledge. Nh'Got continued to say that her world and Earth were at peace after many years of war. The peace pact evolved after another Valeriian time travel incident to Earth's past. It involved an important human that went from bad to good. Upon hearing this, Kay're grasped the sides of her head.

"Is something wrong?" Z'mia asked, concerned.

"Somehow I feel like I know this." She shook her head, trying to bring back the memories. "But I can't remember. Maybe I want to recall everything no matter the time, whether I was there or not."

"Amnesia is very frustrating, though I have never experienced it," Z'mia said.

"Do you know the name of the human and why the person was so important to your government? The name may jog my memory."

As Nh'Got was about to reply, she grabbed her abdomen. "Those insects don't agree with my intestinal tract. I need to go over to the bushes."

"Certain foods don't agree with me either," Kay're said, laughing. "I will go over to the other bushes."

Several minutes later, Kay're was back on the path waiting for Nh'Got and then she heard her scream. Kay're rushed over and saw several lions creeping toward Z'mia. She yelled out to the cats. They paused and looked at the newcomer. The large male roared and ambled toward her.

"Run, Kay're!" Z'mia shouted. Kay're smiled and waved at her. The large lion came up to her and raised himself on his back legs and draped his front legs over her shoulders.

"Good boy," Kay're soothed the enormous cat, hugging him. Then the other lions came to her side, and she talked to each one. She told them not to hurther friend. The ca.ts glanced at the terrified Valeriian and roared. "They're my friends," Kay're called out to Z'mia. "Come over and say hi to them."

"I will stay here," Z'mia affirmed, shaking in fear.

"Nah," Kay're said with a chuckle, and led the cats to Z'mia who stood frozen.

"I saw beasts like this eat the two people Tl'Rak killed after they attacked us. Yet they are like pets to you."

"These are lions. Feel how soft the male's mane is." Z'mia lifted a hand and hesitated. "Go on and touch him. He won't harm you."

"How do you know that?" Z'mia asked, and reluctantly stroked the lion's mane. The big cat purred. Then the others came to Z'mia's side and brushed up against her.

"I told them not to hurt you because you are my friend. And theirs, too."

"I don't understand," Z'mia said, petting the females on the head. "How do you come to command these animals?"

Kay're shrugged. "I guess it is a gift. By the way, do you feel better?"

"Yes, thank you. And seeing these beasts kind of cleaned me out. If you know what I mean."

Kay're laughed and hugged the male lion. The cat agreed with a roar. Even Z'mia laughed.

"We better get going," Z'mia said. "Will the lions follow us?"

"I'm going to send them away."

"Just like that?"

"Yes. Now big boy and girls, head into the hills." Kay're pointed in that direction. The male gave a gentle growl and nuzzled Kay're and led his companions away. The two women watched the lions disappear amongst the rocks.

Z'mia shook her head dumbfounded at what she experienced. "Kay're, you continue to amaze me. You have many talents."

"Sometimes I amaze myself. I just wish I could remember my past and how I got here."

"You know, what's affecting our spaceships could be causing your amnesia."

"Right now, anything is possible. Have you called your spaceship to see if there has been any change?"

"I did when I was in the bushes. No change. They're able to track Tl'Rak's annunciator and he is twenty kilometers ahead of us."

"That would likely put him in Nazareth," Kay're surmised.

"I was thinking. If Jesus of Nazareth is the Son of God, then he is immortal. Meaning, Tl'Rak is wasting his time."

"But he died at the hands of his people," Kay're countered. "On Earth he is human, so he is mortal. The question is: would he allow someone other than his people to kill him?"

"Then it's possible for Tl'Rak to kill him," Z'mia said, worry creasing her face. "He could sneak up on Jesus and shoot him with his blaster."

"You have a point there. Somehow, I have a feeling Jesus would know if someone was trying to get the jump on him."

"True, but Tl'Rak's weapon has a kill range of fifty meters. He doesn't have to be that close to him."

"This is all too confusing," Kay're confessed, shaking her head. "You were about to say something about the human in the other time travel incident."

"Yes, at the time we were at war with Earth and its partner planets, and things weren't going well for us. A certain human spaceship commander always bested our spaceships when they engaged in battle. Central command decided they needed to put a stop to that. The way to do it was to go back in time and kidnap this human when he was a child. He would grow up on Valerii and be a spaceship commander for us. Our current fleet commander was the one who went back in time to do the kidnapping. He is now in orbit on one of our ships."

Kay're's forehead wrinkled, deep in thought. "Again, I feel like I know all about this. But I can't remember. Do you know this man's name?"

"His name is...."

Kay're raised a hand, stopping her mid-sentence. "I hear the pounding of horses, and that means a Roman patrol."

Nh'Got craned her head, trying to hear the sound. She shook her head. "Oh! I hear them now. What do we do?"

"Hopefully nothing. Keep your head down. If they stop, stay silent. I will talk. We may have to fight. Do you know any martial arts?"

"What are martial arts?"

"Hand to hand combat skills."

"I have had such training at the academy."

"Good. Let's hope it doesn't come to that."

Ahead, they could see a cloud of dust moving toward them. The women stepped off the road to let the soldiers pass. Unfortunately, the soldiers slowed down and stopped before them.

"So, what do we have here?" the decanus asked. Seven other riders came to his side.

"Simple women on our way to Nazareth," Kay're replied, keeping her head down.

"Not so simple. That is a Roman soldier's canteen," the decanus said, pointing to it. "How would a Jewish woman have one?"

"I found it on the ground," Kay're replied. "We aren't Jewish nor Gentiles, only women from a distant land. I didn't know it was a Roman canteen. I will give it back to you." Kay're looked up into the soldier's face. The man balked as he felt his mind probed.

"You are a sorcerer! You're in my head!" he claimed, pointing his lance at Kay're.

One of the other horsemen did the same to Nh'Got. "I think this one is a prostitute. She has the face of one."

"Maybe this sorcerer woman is one too," the decanus said, smirking. "For your services to me and my men, I'll let both of you continue on your way. If not, well, you will still serve us anyway. Then we will bind you and take you to Jerusalem to face charges of sorcery and prostitution. Your fate is stoning or crucifixion. Make it easy for yourself."

"We aren't prostitutes, and we won't make it easy for you!" Kay're exclaimed. "Now Z'mia!"

Without hesitation, Z'mia grasped the lance fixed on her chest and pulled it out of the man's hand. She jabbed its blunt end into his face. The man yelped in pain and his horse reared, toppling him to the ground. The light in his eyes turned dark. Quickly, she snapped the blade end up and stabbed the next horseman in the thigh. Blood gushed as he screamed out.

Kay're quickly pushed the decanus's lance off her chest and grasped the horse's bridle, twisting it as hard as she could. The horse went down to its side, pinning the soldier underneath. He cried out in pain as one leg fractured. She then stepped up to the closest horseman who was trying to rein in his panicky horse. She jumped high and reverse chopped the man in the neck. He let go of the horse's reins, gasped, and fell to the ground. Kay're crouched, eyeing two other soldiers.

Nh'Got had two men down. She positioned the lance into a throwing position and let it fly, hitting another Roman in the side. His breath went out, and he fell off his horse, hitting the ground with a thud. The next closest Roman charged his horse with a lance aimed for the kill. She dove in front of the horse before the point found its target. One of the horse's hooves grazed her head, causing her to see scintillations. She lay on the ground, disoriented, and the horseman turned and raced to finish her off.

Kay're glanced over to Nh'Got and saw the man's intent, sprinted toward the horseman, and leaped, grasping him by the leg. She fell off, hitting the ground hard, taking her wind. The move was enough to cause his lance to miss Nh'Got by inches. Another horseman raced toward Kay're. She rolled away from his lance. Then the other came, and out of position, she sucked in a breath, knowing the end was coming. But the soldier fell off the horse, hitting the ground with a thud. Kay're glanced over to Nh'Got who was up with hands on her knees. She had flung a rock, hitting the man in the head.

Six Romans were down and two still on horseback faced the women. They charged. Kay're ducked behind a riderless horse for cover. The stab from the rider missed her. She saw a lance on the ground, picked it up, and stepped out into the open, waiting for the next assault.

Nh'Got dropped and rolled to the rider's opposite side as he came at her. He missed his jab. As Nh'Got stood, she felt something pulling her leg.She looked down to see the man she had stabbed in the thigh locking onto her leg. His free hand held a sword, ready to slash her. He never got a chance as she smashed her free foot into his face. He went limp. She took hold of his sword and spun to face the horse soldier again.

This time he dismounted and came at her with his lance. He thrusted, and Nh'Got parried it off with the sword. Again and again, she fended him off. But he was too big and strong and Nh'Got was tiring. In desperation, she flung the sword at him. The hilt hit him in the chest, with the blade catching him in the face. His cheek and nose spewed blood, and Nh'Got raced at him and did a jump kick, hitting him square in the head. He faceplanted into the ground.

Kay're, poised with her lance, blocked the first prod from the charging rider. The next pass, she again blocked the lance and ran after him. He couldn't turn his horse quick enough and she pierced him in the shoulder. He wailed out in pain, dropping his lance. Kay're used the blunt end of the lance and poked him in the jaw. He fell off his horse and lay motionless with eyes closed. Kay're turned to see how Nh'Got was doing. She was out of breath but gave Kay're a thumbs up.

"Whoa!" Kay're gasped. "Now that was exciting!"

Z'mia just laughed, shaking her head. "I hear groans coming from some of these men. Should we finish them? After all, they tried to kill us."

"I don't want to kill them," Kay're said, waving a hand.

"But they will come after us."

"By the time they recover, if they can, we will be far away. We'll hogtie them and take their horses."

"What is hog tying?"

"I will show you." She went to one fallen soldier, rolled him onto his belly, and took off his sandals. Using the bindings from them, she tied his hands and feet together behind his back. "That is hog tying. It will be some time before he gets out of that."

"That is how I should have tied Tl'Rak," Z'mia said as she went to the next Roman and did the same to him, and then the next. Finally, she stepped up to the man she had hit in the side with the lance. To her surprise, he was still alive. His face was deathly pale and his breathing labored. "I don't think this one will live long."

Kay're came to the man and bent down and assessed him. "This is bad. He has a collapsed lung. Help me get him sitting." They got him up and Kay're took the man's knife from his belt and cut his tunic open, exposing his wound. She then cut a long length of his tunic and wrapped it several times around his chest, covering the wound. "This will suffice until he gets medical help or...."

"Dies," Z'mia said, finishing the sentence. "Do we bandage the man I stabbed in the leg?"

"Yes, we need to," Kay're said. They dressed his wound and hogtied him along with the rest of the men, except the man with the chest wound. Kay're just tied his wrists. She didn't think he would live.

As they stood assessing the tied men, the decanus cried out, "We will hunt you down and kill you!"

Kay're walked up to him, stooped down, and looked into the man's eyes. Through his hate, she saw the agony of pain torturing him. She placed soothing thoughts in his mind and smiled at him. His twisted face softened, and he struggled to curse her.

Kay're stood. "Z'mia, you need a canteen."

Z'mia nodded and reached down and snatched one from a soldier. "And food too." The women helped themselves from the Roman food bags and took a few for their trip to Nazareth.

"We can get to Nazareth faster if we ride," Kay're said. "Do you think you can ride one of these horses?"

"We have similar on Valerii and I can ride," Z'mia said. She eyed the horses and chose one that was ambling toward her. "This one likes me."

Kay're chuckled. "Appears so. I will take this one." She took the reins of a chestnut.

"What about the others?" Z'mia asked.

"They will follow us."

"Why would they do that?"

"Because I will tell them to," Kay're said, smiling.

"Like you spoke to the lions?"

"Yep, just like that." Kay're grinned.

The women mounted their horses. Kay're looked at the six other horses and placed a thought into their heads. "Okay, my friends, let us go," she said to them. The two women started on their way to Nazareth with the horses following them.

CHAPTER TWENTY-NINE
The Vanishing

T l'Rak finally made it to Nazareth. He was both hungry and thirsty, having exhausted his water supply. His first stop was the town's well. He drank to the full and filled his canteen. Food was next on his agenda. As he looked around for a source of food, a small girl came to the well. He looked down at her. The girl stared into his eyes and smiled. Tl'Rak did a quick headshake, suddenly uncomfortable.

"Do I know you, child? It feels like I have met you before."

"I have seen you before. You were near death."

"Hmm," murmured Tl'Rak. "At the time, I was in no condition to remember anything."

"Jesus healed you," the girl said matter-of-factly.

"I wouldn't know that," he harrumphed.

"Why do you seek to harm him?"

The question took Tl'Rak by surprise. "I suppose my friend who was with me when I was near death said that to you. Well, believe nothing she told you. She is a liar."

"She didn't tell me anything about you. I could tell that you wanted to hurt Jesus."

"I was out of my mind with fever and probably said things I didn't mean," Tl'Rak said, waving a hand.

"I don't think so."

"You're a child. What would you know?"

"I know you are very hungry." She smiled at him and reached into a cloth bag tied to her waist and produced a chunk of bread. "Here, eat this."

Tl'Rak took the bread but didn't eat it. "Child, you will need this for yourself."

"No," she replied and reached in her bag again and retrieved a cooked fish. "Take this too. They will fill you."

He accepted it, and the girl looked into his eyes and affirmed his desire for the food. She walked away, leaving Tl'Rak's mouth agape. He sat and ate.

Kay're and Nh'Got rode at a gallop to Nazareth. At the swift pace, words were at a minimum. As they neared Nazareth, Kay're slowed. Z'mia came to her side.

"We can't enter Nazareth on Roman horses," Kay're said. "It would draw attention and there could be Roman soldiers there too. We need to dismount now and send the horse away."

Z'mia nodded and pulled her horse to a stop, then dismounted. Kay're did the same and grasped her horse's nose. She reached into its mind and told it to run off. She looked at the other horse. "Now follow the leader. Go!" She released it, and the other horses trotted off to the trees.

"Now we have to find Tl'Rak and Jesus," said Z'mia. "I hope we aren't too late."

"If we had been late, we probably wouldn't be talking to each other now," Kay're said, starting the walk to Nazareth.

Tl'Rak finished his meal and stood. Approaching the well was a woman with water jars. He nodded his respect to her as she reached the well. She ignored him and started drawing water. "Woman," he said to her, dismissing her lack of respect to him, "is there a man here called Jesus of Nazareth?"

She paused and pointed down the street. "He is in the synagogue." She returned to filling her jars.

Without a "thank you," Tl'Rak started in that direction. He reached the place of worship and approached the open door. He looked into the dimly lit room to see a middle-aged man standing in the center. He was reading a scroll to a crowd of men of varying ages. Tl'Rak didn't enter but listened to see if this was the man referred to in the Bible as the Messiah, Jesus of Nazareth.

After finishing the reading, the man handed the scroll to an attendant and said, "Today this Scripture is fulfilled in your hearing."

"Is this not Joseph's son?" some men questioned.

He replied back, "Surely you will quote this proverb to Me: 'Physician, heal yourself!' Do here in your hometown what we have heard that you did in Capernaum. I tell you the truth. No prophet is accepted in his hometown. I assure you that there were many widows in Israel in Elijah's time when the sky was shut for three and a half years. And there was a severe famine throughout the land. Yet Elijah was not sent to any of them, but to a widow in Zarephath in the region of Sidon. And there were many in Israel with leprosy in the time of Elisha the prophet, yet not one of them was cleansed—only the Naaman of Syrian."

Tl'Rak appreciated the man's wisdom and judged him to be Jesus of Nazareth. He reached a hand under his robe for the blaster. Yet to his amazement, the crowd inside turned furious with the son of Joseph. They surrounded him and started pushing him out of the building. Tl'Rak moved aside as they passed him and into the street. Tl'Rak followed and the furious men continued moving Jesus outside of town to a cliff.

"Let us shove him off and be done with him!" they shouted.

Tl'Rak smiled and said to himself, "No need for me to kill him. His people will now!" He stepped into the crowd and yelled, "Yes, throw him off!"

As they were about to do that, Jesus walked right through the crowd and went on his way.

"Where did he go?" was the cry. Tl'Rak was without words. He glanced around for Jesus and didn't see him.

The small child kept her eye on the man who had evil on his mind. She saw him enter the temple and then leave with an angry crowd that was pushing a man toward a cliff. To her surprise, it was the same man that had opened her mind in the town by the sea. Her eyes teared as she watched him about to be shoved to his death. Then her eyes brightened as she saw him walk through the furious men and disappear. *Where did you go? Did you go to the sky?*

Kay're and Nh'Got reached the edge of Nazareth in time to see a crowd of men pushing a man out of town. Nh'Got gasped. "That's Jesus! The one who gave me food and healed Tl'Rak!"

"He is the one I met on the road after I—" She hesitated, not wanting to say she killed some Roman soldiers. "After I found the Roman canteen. How could I be so dumb as not to recognize him?"

"Why are they so rough with him?" Z'mia asked.

"I don't know. They don't look happy. Let's follow and see what is going on." The two women kept their distance as the crowd approached a cliff. Then they heard the chorus, "Shove him off!" Kay're and Z'mia exchanged sidelong glances of disbelief. Then they heard a booming voice, "Yes, throw him off!"

"That's Tl'Rak's voice," Z'mia said. "But I don't see him. They're going to kill Jesus now!" Kay're's heart raced. The crowd was about to kill her only hope for memory recovery. The women looked on with sad faces. Then, to their surprise, Jesus turned, walked right through the angry crowd, and disappeared

"Did you see that? He vanished!" Z'mia gasped.

"I did," Kay're whispered.

"How did he do that?"

Kay're shook her head. "I don't know."

"Now what?"

"You wanted to get Tl'Rak. Now is your chance. And I will help."

"I don't see him," Z'mia said, watching the crowd filter back toward town.

"Are you sure?"

"I'm sure. I don't see him."

"Let's check these men out," Kay're said. The women walked toward the men that were waving their hands in the air and arguing with each other. Kay're stepped up to a man and asked, "What is going on?" The man glared at her and made a guttural sound and stormed away. Z'mia was looking amongst the men for Tl'Rak but didn't see him.

After the men separated and went their respective ways, Kay're and Z'mia stood alone in the street. "Tl'Rak must have left town," Z'mia said. "But which way?" They looked in all directions but didn't see him.

"Now I wish we still had the horses," Kay're said. "We would find him easily. He couldn't have traveled far on foot."

"But with us walking, it would be pure luck for us to find him," Z'mia said. "And only if we start trotting now."

"Well, are you up to it?" Kay're asked, hoping for a negative response. The fight with the Romans had taken much of her energy.

"No," Z'mia said wearily.

"Let's spend the night here and plan for tomorrow," Kay're said.

Tl'Rak slipped away from the mob after Jesus disappeared. He headed south into the hills. When he was cleared of the town, he touched his annunciator. "This is Commander Tl'Rak to Supreme Commander Tr'Tala."

"This is the comm-officer. State your business."

"I want to talk to the Tr'Tala, not a minion. Now get him for me!"

The comm-officer's face reddened in anger, but touch an icon to get the supreme commander, who was off the bridge.

Supreme Commander Tr'Tala sat in the captain's quarters on the *Lionare,* staring blankly out the window at Earth. The planet was causing great stress to everyone. He was on one ship and his wife on another, and both ships were unable to move or transport anyone. Only bio-life systems, communications, and weapons worked. Then there was the madman on the surface bent on murder and changing the timeline. Everyone on both ships knew the situation was filled with perils. They could wink out of existence at any moment or be living a different life, and likely not in a good way. Everything depended on a junior officer on the planet's surface.

Suddenly, a call from the comm-officer jolted Tr'Tala from his melancholic thoughts. "Supreme Commander, I am receiving a call from Commander Tl'Rak; he wants to speak to you, sir."

"I'm on my way to the bridge." Within seconds, Tr'Tala was standing next to the command seat. Sub-Commander M'Catis was sitting in it and rose to give it up to his superior. Tr'Tala motioned for him to remain seated.

"This is Tr'Tala," he said to the main viewer, knowing the image of

Tl'Rak image wouldn't appear.

"This is Tl'Rak, and I just saw this Jesus person who claims to be God disappear before my eyes. Before he vanished, I judged him to be an ordinary person, likely an alien. He must have transported to a ship in orbit. Scan space for a ship."

"We already did that and didn't find another ship in orbit," Tr'Tala said.

"Do it again, you pompous scrod!" Tl'Rak cursed. "It's cloaked. Refine your scan."

"You will pay for your insolence," Tr'Tala declared.

"I don't care. Rescan!"

Tr'Tala turned to the tactical officer. "Go ahead and focus the scanner to the finest detail."

"Yes, Supreme Commander." There was silence as the man did his job. "Sir, scanners are picking up something."

"I knew it," blurted Tl'Rak as the comm link to the ship was still open.

Tr'Tala came to the tactical officer's side and studied the scanned image. "Can you refine it?"

"Doing it now, sir. There is something out there about twenty kilometers off our port side. It's not big, about the size of a shuttlecraft."

"Put it up on the main," Tr'Tala ordered. All eyes on the bridge turned toward the main viewer. All they saw was space. Tr'Tala harrumphed, shaking his head.

"Supreme Commander, I think it is a cloaked ship," assured the tactical officer.

"Okay, Tl'Rak, we found a cloaked ship." Tr'Tala said. "And you think Jesus is on it?"

"He has to be. Try contacting it."

"Comm, open me a general hailing channel," Tr'Tala ordered.

"It is open, sir," came the reply.

"To the cloaked ship, this is Supreme Commander Sen Tr'Tala of the Valeriian Empire. Identify yourself and your intentions." There was silence. Tr'Tala repeated the hail and still nothing.

"Are your weapons still functional?" Tl'Rak asked.

"They are," Tr'Tala replied.

"Then blast that vessel to pieces and kill that imposter and whoever else is with him!"

There was a pause on the bridge as Tr'Tala pondered Tl'Rak's suggestion. Then he said, "If we destroy that ship, we may never get control of our ships, and we will remain in orbit until the ships run out of power and you know the rest."

"But if you destroy it, you could free yourself of its hold," Tl'Rak countered.

Another pause as Tr'Tala thought. "Get me Lt. Nh'Got on the surface."

"You have her, sir," came the reply.

"Lt. Nh'Got, this is Supreme Commander Tr'Tala."

"I read you, sir."

"Commander Tl'Rak has contacted me and the channel to him is open now. He claims to have seen Jesus of Nazareth transported away a few minutes ago. Do you know anything about this?"

"Yes, sir. We saw that too. Jesus simply vanished."

"Lieutenant, we have found a small, cloaked ship in orbit and it is unresponsive to hails."

"Yes!" Nh'Got exclaimed, pumping a fist. "I knew it all along. Jesus may act like a god, but he is an alien." She completely dismissed her previous confession that Jesus was the Son of God.

"Tl'Rak wants me to destroy it, hoping to free our ships."

"Supreme Commander, I don't think that would be wise," Nh'Got said. "Even though he may be an alien, he is benevolent and kind and has shaped Earth's history and the galaxy's. Killing him will alter the timeline. He still has to die at the hands of these humans and rise from the dead as written in their Bible. We can't interfere."

Tr'Tala sighed. "You're correct, Lieutenant."

"You are all cowards!" Tl'Rak shouted. "When he returns to Earth, I will kill him, and you will see I was right and Valerii will return to its greatest glory.

Then you will heap praise on me."

"Tl'Rak!" Tr'Tala screamed.

"Sir, he closed the channel," said the comm-officer.

"Lieutenant Nh'Got, are you in visual contact with Tl'Rak?"

"No, sir. He slipped out of town with the cover of a crazed mob that seemed angry with Jesus of Nazareth. They wanted to kill him."

"Lieutenant, my order still stands. You're to hunt down Tl'Rak and kill him."

"Sir, you can lock onto his annunciator and fire a cannon burst at his location. Then he will be dead."

"That's a good idea," Tr'Tala mused. "But there may be others around him. Killing friendlies could alter the timeline too."

"I heard that," came Tl'Rak's voice.

Tr'Tala turned his head to the comm-officer, who grimaced an apology.

"I'm tossing my annunciator now," Tl'Rak said. On the bridge, they heard a few clanks as the annunciator hit rocks. Then it went silent.

"That ends your idea, Lieutenant," Tr'Tala said. "It is up to you now."

"Yes, sir," she clipped, and the link closed.

CHAPTER THIRTY
Oh My!

Tl'Rak's departure from town didn't go unnoticed. Wondering if he knew where Jesus had vanished to, the child at the well followed him discretely. When he was some distance from the town, she saw him stop, talk to the air, and then throw something into the rocks. When he continued his walk into the hills, she searched amongst the rocks for the object that he had discarded. She noticed it reflecting sunlight, picked it up, and curiously turned it over in her hand. It was oval and glossy metallic—something she had never seen before. To her it was pretty; she would keep it. Suddenly it made a sound!

Aboard the *Lionare,* the comm-officer's board blinked. "Supreme Commander," she called to Tr'Tala who was now sitting in the command seat. "Commander Tl'Rak's annunciator just opened."

"So, he didn't toss it after all." Tr'Tala smirked. "I wonder what he wants now. Give me the link."

"You have it, sir," said the comm-officer.

"Tl'Rak, so you still have your annunciator," Tr'Tala said.

There was a pause and finally, a small child's voice sounded, "Who is this? Where are you?"

Everyone on the *Lionare's* bridge looked surprised to hear the voice of a child. "What language is that?" Tr'Tala asked everyone.

Everyone on the bridge shook their heads. "I'm running it through the translator," the comm-officer said. "It's having trouble recognizing it." After a minute, she said, "it is Aramaic, an ancient Earth language."

"I can speak your language," came the small voice in Valeriian. Everyone's jaws went slack. "Where are you? I hear you but can't see you."

"Child," Tr'Tala said in a soothing voice. "You can only hear us through the object you hold. We are far away and can't see you either. How is it that you can understand and speak our language?” *She must be the same girl Nh'Got encountered earlier.*

"I don't know. I just can."

"How old are you?"

"I'm five."

"Are your parents with you?"

"No, I am alone. They're in the sky." Her voice had a touch of sadness to it, and those on the bridge noticed. To them, it meant that the child's parents had died, and according to human beliefs, went to heaven in the sky.

"Then who takes care of you?" Tr'Tala asked, continuing in a gentle tone. "Are they nearby?"

"I take care of myself."

"All by yourself?" Tr'Tala echoed, amazed. "Where did you get the talking object?"

"I found it after the bad man threw it away. It is very pretty. I didn't know it talks. Do you have one too?"

"I do, but I am talking to you by other means. Do you have a name?"

"I am called Kay're."

"Kay're. That is such a beautiful name." It was a name he had heard before. The mysterious woman who was involved in the Mark Ross's time travel incident had the same name. *A coincidence? Or is she the same person? And how does she know Tl'Rak is a bad man? How would a small human from ancient Earth know Valeriian unless she's a time traveler too? That would explain why she said her parents were in the sky. The cloaked spaceship is theirs and somehow, she got separated from them. Is Jesus her father?* "Oh my," he blurted out, drawing curious looks from the crew.

"What was that?" the child asked.

"I was just thinking," Tr'Tala replied. "Kay're, do you know someone named Jesus?"

"I know him."

"Is Jesus your father?"

She giggled. "He is God.

That wasn't the answer Tr'Tala expected. "How do you know him?"

"He spoke to me."

"I see. Do you know where Jesus is now?"

"I don't know. He disappeared when some men were trying to hurt him."

That matches both Tl'Rak and Lt Nh'Got's account, Tr'Tala thought to himself. "So, Kay're, have you always lived in Israel?"

"No," was the soft reply.

"Where else have you lived?"

"I don't know the names of the places."

"How did you get to Israel?"

"I came through the lights"

"The lights," Tr'Tala muttered. *Is this the same child Lt. Nh'Got said had healing powers and came through lights?* "Kay're, please tell me about the lights?

"They are just lights." The voice was now timid. "I need Jesus to bring them back so I can go home." She sniffled back tears. Her response confirmed she was the same child Nh'Got encounter earlier.

"Sir, they're possibly transporter effects," Subcommander M'Catis added.

Tr'Tala nodded in agreement. "Likely from that cloaked ship."

"What is that?" the child asked, hearing the conversation on the bridge.

"It's the lights," he said to her.

"Can you bring them back? I want to go home." Her voice cracked with sadness.

"Yes, I know, child," Tr'Tala soothed. He wondered if he would ever have children. "I would like to bring the lights back, but right now they aren't working. Once they are, I promise I will get you home."

"I hope so," she cried and squeezed the annunciator and inadvertently closed the link. She waited for the man's response but none came. "Are you there? Are you there?" she cried out and shook the annunciator, but man's voice didn't return. Sniffling in her tears, she stuffed it into her food bag and wandered off.

"Kay're! Kay're!" Tr'Tala called out.

"Sir, she closed the link. I'm beeping it, but she isn't responding. It's likely she mistakenly closed it and doesn't know how to activate it."

"Yes, of course," Tr'Tala demurred. "Hail it every so often. Maybe she will accidentally activate it again."

"I will, sir."

Kay're and Nh'Got found lodging for the night at a local's home that had an extra room. There, they bathed themselves using a bucket of water provided by the keeper.

"If only this town had hot springs to bathe in," Kay're commented.

"I haven't had a bath since I have been on the planet's surface," Z'mia said, toweling off her face. Are there any of these hot springs in the area?"

"Yes, in a small town south of Capernaum. It felt so wonderful to soak in one. Now I smell like a horse."

Z'mia laughed. "I hate to say what I smell like. Do you think tomorrow we can head to that town with the hot springs?"

"I don't think we will find Tl'Rak or Jesus there," Kay're said, shrugging.

"He can wait," Z'mia sighed. "My body is sore and stinky, especially after riding that horse and fighting soldiers. I need a hot spring to soak in." She rubbed her lower back.

Kay're chuckled. "Your boss wouldn't want to hear that."

"He isn't a woman. He probably doesn't mind being smelly. I'm sure he hasn't been riding lately to feel the after-effects. I'm going to be stiff in the morning."

"As will I," Kay're agreed, massaging her neck. "Yes, the hot springs should be first on our list. Then we should head to Jerusalem. There, with the blessing of the Romans, the Jews will execute Jesus. I'm sure Tl'Rak will head there to kill him before they crucify him. He'll lay in wait there or outside of town to make his move on Jesus."

"Jerusalem will be dangerous for us as the city will be crawling with Roman soldiers," Z'mia said. "They will have found the soldiers we fought and be on the lookout for us."

"You're right. We may have to separate as they will look for two women together." She didn't mention there was a Roman centurion already searching for her.

Z'mia nodded in agreement. "I hope it doesn't come to that. I enjoy your company. You're my friend."

Kay're smiled. "You're my friend, too. Let us eat and sleep. Tomorrow will be a challenging day for us."

Tl'Rak indeed headed to Jerusalem. He took the direct route through the mountains. He was sure Jesus would be there to fulfill his destiny as written in the Bible. Tl'Rak wished he had a transporter available to make the hundred-kilometer distance. Without such, his trek would take him several days to make it to the city. He had eaten all the food the small girl had given him, leaving him only a canteen of water. He hoped to stumble upon a village or some other source of food and water. Taking a deep breath, he trudged upward only to see the hills turn into mountains on the horizon.

Several hours passed and he hadn't found a water source nor seen a living thing. He was thinking he had made the wrong decision going directly to Jerusalem. The sun was setting, and he knew the night would be cold. There wasn't even a tree or any scrub brush he could use for a fire. With his large size, the walk up and down rocky slopes was tiring and burned many calories. He was hungry and feeling desperate.

After topping another hill, he spotted some brush. At least he would have a fire tonight, albeit one without food roasting over it. He made the fire and called it a night.

Morning broke in Nazareth and Kay're and Nh'Got rose with moans from their aching bodies. "I'm glad we don't have horses to ride," Z'mia groaned. "My inner thighs hurt so bad I couldn't sit on a horse. Even walking will be painful."

Kay're laughed. "Mine too. Once we get moving, our legs will be better."

"Are you sure?"

"I hope so," Kay're chuckled, reaching into her food bag. She picked out locust and popped it into her mouth. "You want one?"

"Nooo," Z'mia said, shaking her head.

"I heard these things help muscle strain." Kay're tried to hold back her laughter.

Z'mia gave her friend a dubious look. Finally, Kay're burst out laughing. Z'mia joined in rolling on her side. They had a good laugh.

"They say laughter is the best medicine," Kay're said. "I feel better already."

"You know, I do too," Z'mia agreed. She willed herself to stand and did a toe touch stretch. Kay're stood and copied her. After eating and tending to their personal needs, it was time to leave. They thanked the housekeeper and started their walk back to Mary's house.

CHAPTER THIRTY-ONE
Me, Myself and I

Tl'Rak's rumbling and gnawing stomach woke him. Sitting up, he stared at the embers of the dying fire. He took a single swig of water, hoping to find more soon along with food. He stood and eyed the sun rising in the east. Using it as a bearing, he started his walk to the southeast toward Jerusalem.

About mid-day, Tl'Rak rested on a rock, exhausted. With his water down to a gulp, he admitted to himself he had made the wrong decision heading this way to Jerusalem. Up until now, he had made all the right moves to get to ancient Earth to fulfill his quest. Now glory for himself and Valerii had faded away. He shook his head in disgust. In his haste to kill Jesus of Nazareth, he had sealed his fate to die in the barren mountains of Israel. He licked his dry lips and suppressed the desire to drink the rest of his water. He stood, put one foot in front of the other and would do so until he succumbed.

Kay're and Nh'Got began their walk back to the Sea of Galilee. After a few hours, they settled under a canopy of trees to rest. Sitting felt so wonderful.

"You know, when we start again, our bodies are going to scream in pain," Z'mia said.

"That's for sure," Kay're returned, wiping the sweat from her forehead. "Yesterday when you contacted your superior, you claimed Jesus was an alien. Before that, you believed he was God. What changed?"

Z'mia blew out a breath. The question made her feel uncomfortable, and Kay're could read it. "Before I came to Earth, I didn't believe in God or a supreme being. But when I was dying of thirst, I prayed to Jesus to save me. After all, he healed Tl'Rak and if he could do that, then he could give me a miracle and save me. You arrived as an answer to my prayer. It was then that I decided Jesus was God. Then, with the news of another spaceship in orbit and seeing Jesus vanish, my thoughts changed. He disappeared as if he were transported from one location to another. Likely, he went to the other spaceship. It caused my scientific mind to kick in and overcame my emotions. The evidence says Jesus must be an alien; albeit one of exceptional power and benevolence."

"I see," Kay're said. "Yet I can tell you're unsure about your reasoning."

"Is it that obvious? Z'mia asked with a thin smile. Kay're nodded.

"But you still believe he is God?" Z'mia asked.

"I do. I sense he is God. When I first met you, I could sense you were an alien. I don't sense he is an alien; only the Son of God."

"You remind me so much of a little girl I met. She could tell Tl'Rak and I were aliens, and that Tl'Rak was evil."

Kay're smiled. She wanted to tell Z'mia that the girl and she were the same person. Yet her friend would never understand, nor could she. She still wrestled with her amnesia of how and why she was here in Israel. Adding to her confusion was how she could exist as an adult and as a child at the same time. All she wanted to do was talk to Jesus. He would decode her mystery.

After having a small meal, they stood. Standing was painful. They started their walk and did so until sunset and called it a day. Hopefully, the night will be peaceful.

At sunset, Tl'Rak could barely put one foot in front of the other. Like his stomach, his canteen was empty. He looked ahead and saw another hill, and shook his head, knowing he lacked the energy to climb any further. He settled down against a boulder, knowing this would be his final resting place. He closed his eyes and blew out a breath. "In a hundred years, someone will come across my bones and discover my blaster," he murmured. "For that person, it will be the discovery of a lifetime. Would it hold a charge that long?" He pulled out the blaster and held it across his chest and waited for death. But a sound interrupted his solitude.

His eyes blinked open, and he heard it again—bah, bah. "It is an animal, but where?" He stood and gazed in all directions yet saw nothing. Then the bah sounded again. It was to his left, behind some rocks. He stumbled toward the sound and peaked around a boulder to see a mid-size animal that had a coat like wool. All the better, it was drinking from a small pool of water that had trickled from some rocks. There was even some scrub brush beside the water. He didn't know the name of the animal, but it was food to him. He adjusted the blaster setting and fired. The animal dropped.

An hour later, Tl'Rak had a fire and a leg of the animal roasting over it. He had quenched his thirst and filled his canteen. Soon, he would fill his belly. Tl'Rak wondered what this animal's meat would taste like. The roasting leg smelled good, and his mouth watered in anticipation of the first bite. When he judged the meat cooked, he sampled it. It was delicious! After stuffing himself, he roasted two more legs. They would sustain him for the rest of his journey to Jerusalem.

Sunset found the women in a familiar spot, the place where they fought the Romans. Discarded bindings, broken water skins, and dried blood littered the area. The soldiers were nowhere in sight.

"Looks like they got out of their ties," Z'mia said, dismayed.

"Or rescued," Kay're added, checking some bindings. "These were cut."

"Maybe one untied himself and cut the others free," offered Z'mia. "Look, there are parallel gouges in the dirt trailing off to the east."

"Stretchers," Kay're said. "Pulled by horses. Look at the hoof prints in front of the stretcher marks."

"I wonder if their horses returned."

"It's likely," Kay're agreed. "If another group of soldiers rescued them, they would have sent out a party after us."

"And we would have seen them by now."

"Agreed. We can expect a patrol in the area tomorrow. Let us camp here tonight under those trees and rise early and keep to the rocks."

"I bet Capernaum and Mary's town will be swarming with Romans looking for us," Z'mia conjectured.

Kay're nodded and motioned to the trees. There, they prepared for the night. As they settled down to sleep, noises in the brush made them bolt upright. In the moon's light, they could see shadows creeping toward them. They stood and braced themselves for an attack. Finally, the shadows came into view—lions. But were they friendly? Kay're called out to them. There was a roar, and the lions ambled up to them. "Friends!" Kay're affirmed.

The cats purred and nuzzled them. Both women gave the cats hugs. After the greeting, the women laid down to sleep with the lions joining them. The women would sleep safe and sound tonight.

The sun peeked over the horizon and Kay're and Z'mia stretched out their kinks and sat. The lions had departed, likely to find breakfast. After eating, the women refreshed themselves and secured the area. They returned the area to a natural state as if no one had been there. The women followed the edge of the rocks to the east, noting hiding places if needed. Frequently, they paused and listened for pounding hooves. They finally came.

Kay're and Z'mia scrambled up into the rocks and hid behind a boulder just as Roman horsemen appeared. They slowed down and stopped. Kay're peeked out to see the soldiers surveying the area. They looked at the rocks and Kay're ducked out of view. Was it quick enough? They heard the horses coming their way.

"Did they see you?" Z'mia whispered.

"I hope not. There are at least a dozen. They're not taking chances with a lesser number of men."

"Should we scramble up the rocks? They would have to dismount. We can outrun them."

Kay're shook her head. "Some are archers. They would get us." They waited. Then there was a noise from above and behind. They turned to see lions and not a few, but lots of them. The cats adroitly moved past them and lumbered into the view of the Romans and roared. The Romans didn't want any part of the beasts and quickly galloped off.

"Thank you, Jesus!" Kay're gasped.

"I recognize some of the lions, but the others? I hope they are friendly," Z'mia said, wiping sweat from her forehead.

"Big Boy," Kay're called out to the large, dominant male lion. He turned and looked at the rocks. Both Kay're and Z'mia jumped out of their hiding place to greet their feline friends. They hoped the new cats would accommodate them. Kay're closed her eyes and mentally called them. They came with tails wagging in a friendly manner. The usual lions came to the women's side and then the new ones nuzzled them too.

"We have more friends!" Z'mia exclaimed. "I can't believe I'm hugging and petting man-eating beasts as if they were house pets."

Kay're chuckled. "Thank you, boys and girls," she said to the cats. After the meet and greet, Kay're and Z'mia continued on their way with the lions keeping pace. Later on, the cats took off, leaving the women feeling vulnerable.

The sun was setting and Kay're and Nh'Got were still far from the seaside towns. Staying close to the rocks slowed their journey. They would have to spend another chilly night in the open without a campfire. It would draw attention to themselves and likely bring Roman soldiers. Thankfully, the night was uneventful.

In the morning, Nh'Got contacted her ship to find the situation in space unchanged. It irritated Supreme Commander Tr'Tala that Tl'Rak was still tramping around Israel. He told Nh'Got that Tl'Rak had thrown away his annunciator and a young girl found it. She accidentally contacted the ship. Tr'Tala believed her to be an alien from the cloaked spaceship and explained his reasons.

Nh'Got immediately thought of the strange child she met and told Tr'Tala about it. They agreed the small girl was the same person. Tr'Tala ended by saying the child's name was Kay're. Nh'Got gasped and glanced at Kay're who was listening. Kay're held a straight face. The comm-link ended without Nh'Got giving away her new friend's name.

"Kay're, do you know that child?" Kay're kept a calm face without saying a word. "Are you the mother of the child?" Kay're shook her head. Then Z'mia's jaw went slack and this time Kay're nodded her head as she read Z'mia's thoughts.

"How is it possible?" Z'mia asked.

"I don't know. Like I don't know how I got here or how my child-self did too." Her voice cracked, and tears trickled down her cheeks. Z'mia came to her side and hugged her.

"Thank you," Kay're sniffled. "Normally I don't get emotional, but this is tearing me up."

"I know," Z'mia comforted. "I don't know how you can hold it together, knowing the two of you exist at the same time. How long have you known?"

"For a few days. I saw her, or myself, in a boat leaving Capernaum. The centurion was after her."

"A Roman centurion?" Z'mia quizzed. "Why would a centurion be after a small girl?"

"Because I entered his mind when I was a child. Like I did a few weeks back. It disturbed him greatly, and he also feels we are the same person."

"How and why?" Z'mia asked, captivated by the story.

"One night when I was a child, I was cold and tired. I came upon the campsite of the centurion and three of his men. I laid next to the fire, and the centurion asked me who I was, and I entered his mind and fell asleep. In the morning, I woke up and found the centurion and his men still sleeping. Being a playful girl, I put happy thoughts into their minds and left."

"No way!"

"Yep, I did," Kay're snickered. "Then last week, he and his men came upon me as I am now. They were like the Romans that greeted us. I defended myself and killed three of his men and nearly him. I felt bad about it. I did a minor surgical procedure to save him and left him in God's hands. Jesus must have come upon him and cured him. Since both encounters, the centurion has been hot on my trail, as an adult and as a child. When he finds out or maybe already knows we beat up more of his men, he will step up the search for me and now you too."

Z'mia exhaled in amazement. "Whoa! I'm not sure what to say. It is obvious the centurion never found you as a child or you wouldn't be here as an adult now."

"Not necessarily. Maybe he did, and this is the result."

Z'mia shook her head. "This is so confusing. Anyhow, is that ship in orbit yours?"

"I don't know. It could be."

"Are you from another planet?"

Kay're shrugged. "If we can find me as a child and question her, maybe she can provide us some answers."

"Does the child even know you or that she is here as an adult?"

"I think so. Our eyes met when she was sailing off."

"One thing is certain: one of yourselves did time travel."

Kay're laughed. "Yeah, me, myself, and I. And now we're in search of three people, Jesus, Tl'Rak, and me."

CHAPTER THIRTY-TWO
Be On the Lookout

Centurion Marcus made it to Jerusalem and sat in his tent pouring over reports. He was now in charge of cavalry patrols and and prisoners. All he seemed to do was clerical work. He routed patrols here and there, managed prisoners, and oversaw executions. The latter obligation was distasteful. Marcus deemed himself too educated and refined for such a task. Most of the time he relegated the job to an optio. It was only the more politically charged executions that he supervised. Thankfully, they were few.

As he sat writing the day's orders, he paused and thought of the child and the woman. It was likely he wouldn't see them again holding his current position. He shook his head and called for his decanus.

"Yes, Centurion," Decanus Varius replied, and saluted his commander.

"Decanus Viviani's patrol was due in yesterday. Have they returned?"

"No, Centurion. I take it they have experienced a delay."

Marcus rolled his eyes. "Do you think, Varius!"

"Well, yes, sir."

Outside the tent, a commotion drew their attention. Marcus rose from his seat and glanced out. It was Viviani's patrol. All the men appeared beaten and wounded. Marcus waggled his head in disbelief. "Where is Viviani?" He didn't see the man leading the patrol.

"Here, sir," was the cry. Marcus walked over to the voice while glancing at the battered patrol. The decanus was lying on a makeshift stretcher behind a horse. He had a splint made from tree branches on his left leg.

"What happened?" Marcus asked.

There was a pause. Viviani cleared his throat and said, "We had a skirmish."

"With who?"

"Sir, I would rather tell you in private."

A bad feeling settled in Marcus's stomach. "Okay, get the rest of the wounded to medical, and no one is to talk about the incident until I say so." He then waved for two soldiers to bring Viviani to his tent. Marcus returned to his tent and Decanus Varius followed the stretcher inside. "Help this man into a seat and then you and Decanus Varius leave us." The men carried out the order and departed. Disappointment showed on Varius's face as he left the tent. He wanted to hear the story.

"Okay, Viviani, let me have it," Marcus said, taking his seat behind a desk.

Viviani coughed and swallowed. "Centurion Marcus, we were ambushed." Another pause.

"By who?"

"Ah, by two women," he stuttered.

It was as Marcus feared, though he suspected one woman, not two. "You say two women? The decanus nodded. "Why would two women attack a Roman patrol of eight men carrying lances?"

"I don't know, sir. They just did." The decanus's voice was not assuring.

"And these two women, disabled you and all your men?"

"Yes, sir."

Marcus shook his head in disbelief. From experience, he knew it was possible. "The women, did you kill them?" He hoped not. He wanted them alive.

"No, Centurion. They got away."

"Got away!" Marcus said. "How could two women best eight of Rome's finest lancers and get away?"

"They were quick and skilled fighters. They fought like no soldiers I have ever encountered."

"I see," Marcus said, knowing one must have been the woman who dismantled him and his three men. "Didn't you go after them?"

"We couldn't, Centurion. They tied our hands and feet behind our backs and then took our horses. And my men were in no condition to pursue once we freed ourselves. Geraldi took a lance in the chest. He is barely breathing. Corsi had his thigh pierced and is in great pain and unable to stand. I have a broken leg. The others sustained head injuries, causing them severe headaches."

"So, back to why the women attacked you. I want the truth." He bore his eyes into the man. The decanus sat silent. "I see the truth is painful to you." Marcus had a thin smile on his face. "Let me guess. You came across the women and found them attractive and accused them of being prostitutes. You promised them you wouldn't arrest them if they pleased you and your troops. Of course, they didn't like your proposition. Am I right?

"You're right, Centurion," Viviani admitted somberly.

"What did they look like?"

"Well, they were both tall and slender with beautiful faces. Both had short dark hair, which is odd, as the women in Israel all have long hair. They must have been foreigners."

Marcus had to give Viviani points for being observant and knowing the locals. He, himself, never deduced that but wondered if they could be identical twins or even the same person. Right now, he would believe anything. He still had the lingering thought that the child and the woman were the same person. "Did the women look alike?"

"No, Centurion. Both had short dark brown hair, but of different shades and their facial features weren't the same. And one other thing. The woman that caused my broken leg—well, I think she was a sorcerer. I sensed her getting into my head." For Marcus, that detail sealed the fact that one woman was the one he was after.

"And the other woman. Could she do that too?"

"I don't know, sir. Lancer Nitti may know, as he had his lance on her chest when we confronted the women."

"Okay. I heard enough." Marcus rose and stuck his head outside the tent. "Attendants, remove the decanus to medical and bring me, Lancer Nitti."

Seconds later, Nitti entered on his own. His left eye was black and blue and swollen shut. He saluted his superior. "At ease," said Marcus. "Decanus Viviani told me his story, but I want to hear yours. What happened to your face?"

"I caught the blunt end of a lance in my face."

"By a woman?"

"Yes, Centurion."

"Was it your lance?"

"Yes, Centurion."

"And how did a woman get hold of your lance and butt you in the face?"

"She took it from my hands, sir."

"I don't believe it," Marcus commented, shaking his head. "You let a woman take the lance right out of your hands." Nitti held his tongue but managed a dry swallow. Marcus noted the man's discomfort. "I would be silent too, if I let a woman beat me." Marcus was silent too, about the real reason his patrol died when questioned.

"Viviani mentioned that the woman who broke his leg was a sorcerer—that she got inside his head. Was the woman that took your lance able to get inside your head?"

"No, Centurion," Nitti replied, surprised by the question. "I didn't get the sense that she was a sorcerer."

"Is it true that your patrol came upon the women and accused them of being prostitutes?"

Nitti paused for another dry swallow. "Yes, Centurion."

"And you made them a certain offer for their freedom?"

"Decanus Viviani did, sir," Nitti admitted. He hoped his answer would gain him a bit of favor considering his incompetence."

"But of course, you would go along with the deal?"

Nitti cleared his throat. "I'm not sure, Centurion."

"Somehow I find your answer hard to believe," Marcus harrumphed. "I heard enough from you. Go."

"Yes, Centurion." He gave a breast salute and left.

Marcus blew out a breath. "Two women now," he whispered. "Both foreign, and lethal, when pushed." He knew they could have killed the men if they wanted to. *What is it about them? Is the other releated to the child too?* He took a drink of wine. Knowing Decanus Varius was outside the tent, he called for him.

Varius eagerly stepped inside. Marcus noticed the quickstep and the slight smile on his face. He must have heard the exchange. "Centurion, shall I order a patrol to hunt down the persons that attacked Viviani's patrol?"

"Yes, do so. Get a description of the attackers from Viviani and Nitti. No, you already know. Keep it to yourself. I want you to lead the patrol. Take twelve of your best men including a few archers. Tell your men to be on the lookout for two women traveling alone who could become victims of the robbers. I suspect the women know we'll be looking for them and be on the defensive making them more deadly. They won't be traveling the main road so they will be hard to find. If you find them, encircle them and don't appear too threatening. Give them the chance to surrender peacefully."

"And if they don't?" Varius asked, fidgeting.

"Have the archers point their arrows at them and throw them some leather straps. Have one woman bind the other. Then you and a few of your men bind the other woman then get them on a horse and bring them to me. Be careful, one woman and maybe the other can get inside your mind and twist it disorienting you. They could do that to your men too. So, hold any conversations with them to a minimum. Above all, I want these women alive!"

"Yes, Centurion."

"If you kill them, you and your men will forfeit your lives for disobeying my order. Understood?"

"Perfectly, Centurion. Is that all?"

"One more thing," Marcus said, standing. "Be on the lookout for that small child we saw before; the one with the lions. If you see her, take her into custody too. If you can fulfill your orders, then I see a promotion for you."

"Yes, Centurion," Varius said, grinning.

"You can smile when you have the women and or child standing before me. Now you have a job to do. Get to it."

"Yes, Centurion." Varius gave the breast salute and dismissed himself.

CHAPTER THIRTY-THREE
Wanted Women

It was late afternoon when Kay're and Z'mia Nh'Got approached Magdala, the small town Mary lived in. They took a position in the hills above and observed the area's activity before slipping into town.

In the town of Capernaum, they noticed a group of Roman soldiers had set up camp on the shoreline. The men were eating and ignored the local fishermen who were getting ready for night fishing. It all appeared quiet in Magdala. Only a few people were in the street going about their daily chores; the town lacked any Romans.

Satisfied, Kay're and Z'mia moved from the rocks into town and walked up to Mary's home. As Kay're was about to knock on the door, a nearby woman called out, "If you are looking for Mary, she isn't home."

Kay're turned to the voice. "Do you know when she will be back?"

The woman eyed the two strangers. "I have seen you before." She pointed an accus finger at Kay're.

Kay're smiled. "Yes, I have been here before, as has my friend." Z'mia nodded to the woman. "We are friends of Mary."

"By the looks of you, I can see why," the woman said sarcastically. Kay're could read her thoughts.

"We aren't what you think," Kay're corrected the woman. The woman's eyes widened in surprise that her thoughts were transparent. "We are friends of the changed Mary, and we came to see her."

"Oh, you two must be followers of the prophet."

"Yes, we are believers," Kay're said with a smile.

"Well, the prophet was here yesterday. When he left town, Mary and the other women went with him."

"Do you know where they were heading?" asked Z'mia.

"To Jerusalem."

"May I ask; has there been any unusual Roman activity in the area lately?" Kay're queried.

"Yesterday, no, but the day before a Roman patrol came into town and they had all the women come out. They made us take off our head coverings. I asked why, and the leader didn't answer my question. He demanded I remove my headscarf. I did, and then he told me to undo my hair that I had up. I let my hair down and then he dismissed me and checked the other woman. Whatever he was looking for, he didn't find. He and his men left town, heading toward Nazareth. I found it all very strange."

"That is odd," Z'mia agreed, giving Kay're a sidelong glance. Kay're nodded in return.

"Well, I need to go. I have work to do." The woman turned and left them.

"They're looking for us, two women with short hair," Z'mia said, touching her hair wishing it were long.

"When we were in the fight with the Romans, our head coverings came off," Kay're said. "One man was very observant."

Z'mia nodded her agreement. "That's for sure. We should have killed them."

Kay're blew out a breath. "Let's use Mary's house for the night. I don't think the Romans will return."

"I hope you're right," Z'mia said, and she and Kay're ducked into Mary's home.

After they settled in for the night, there was a knock on the door. Kay're and Z'mia jumped up. "Cover your head," Kay're whispered to Z'mia and went to the door.

"Hello," came a man's voice. Kay're cracked the door to see a middle-' aged, bearded man smiling at her. He smelled like fish and had teeth missing.

Kay're read the man's intentions, yet asked him, "Can I help you?"

"You and the other woman sure can," the man said, grinning. "We know Mary isn't home and my friend and I saw you and another woman enter her house. We figured you are friends of Mary's and judging by your beautiful looks are in the same line of work. Well, we have money to pay." He held up a bag of coins and jingled it.

Z'mia didn't need to be a mind reader to know what he and the other man wanted and nudged Kay're. She nodded and said to the men, "We are not interested." She started closing the door, but the man put his foot inside, blocking the door. Kay're pushed harder, but the man was strong, and he pushed past her into the room with his friend following.

"Leave!" Z'mia demanded.

"We're not leaving until we get what we want," the other man said. He stepped up to Z'mia and eyed her. He then reached out to put his hands on her shoulders; it was a big mistake. Z'mia brought her arms up under his, grasped his head and pulled it down onto her knee. There was a dull cracking sound, and he fell face-first onto the floor.

His partner reached under his garment for a knife. He never touched it. Kay're snap kicked him in the face. He yelped as blood gushed from his nose. She then did a spin kick, hitting him flush on the side of his head. He crumpled to the floor, out cold.

"What is it with human males?" Z'mia said. "They only have one thing on their mind."

"Is it different on Valerii?" Kay're asked.

"No," Z'mia replied, rubbing her knee. "Men are the same all over the galaxy." She burst out laughing. Kay're laughed too.

"That guy had a hard head," Z'mia said through her laughter. "My knee is sore." Kay're laughed harder.

"What do we do with these two?" Z'mia pointed at them.

"They are going to be a problem. We cannot leave them here tied up. We won't get any sleep. And if we throw them out, they will wake up and come after us, and likely with friends."

"That means we need to leave and spend another night without shelter," Z'mia groaned.

"That's the only thing we can do. We'll need to leave the area too. In the morning they'll tell the Romans about us and they'll come calling."

Z'mia shook her head. "First the Romans are after us, now the locals. We are wanted women and on the run."

Kay're chuckled. "It's exciting."

"You have a wonderful sense of humor about it. I suppose we need to gag and tie these creeps up and hit the hills."

They did just that. Kay're took their money bags and said, "For services rendered." She and Z'mia wearily left town and into the hills with the moon being their guiding light. After two hours hiking, they found an outcropping of rocks with a smooth base to sleep on. The fatigue of the day swiftly overcame them.

CHAPTER THIRTY-FOUR
Pathways

Roused by a deep rumbling noise, Kay're opened an eye. Looking up, she saw blue sky. She glanced over to Z'mia. Her friend was asleep and decided not to wake her. She continued to lay flat on her back, listening for that rumbling sound, worrying it could be a Roman patrol. The sound came at irregular intervals and seemed distant, so she dismissed it. With her friend still asleep, she decided to try mediation as a means to release her amnesia.

She went deep inside her mind following synaptic pathways, searching for memories. The ones she encountered showed clouded images and muffled voices. Undaunted, she turned another corner to find the same. Backing up, she turned down another pathway only to see swirls of flashing lights. As beautiful as they were, they offered no answers to her amnesia.

Doing an about-face at the neural junction, she tried another route. Moving slowly, she listened and looked for clues to her past. She did see recent events starting with her first encounter with the Romans and so on until last night. Then she saw a corridor to her left, made the turn, and crept on.

At first, there was darkness, then she saw a white light in the distance. The light seemed to beckon her. She took baby steps forward, and the light became brighter and brighter. Continuing ahead, the light gave off an intense feeling of love. The lure was powerful, and she started running toward it. Closer and closer she came, giving herself up completely to the greatness of the source. Finally, she stood before the radiance, bowed her head, and dropped to her knees. She was in the presence of God! Trembling, she asked, "Please release me?"

"It isn't time yet," came a gentle voice. She dared look up to see a large, winged, ethereal figure standing before her. The angel was beautiful.

"Where is God?" Kay're asked.

"God is everywhere," the angel answered.

"I want to see God in person," she begged.

"You will when His Son comes in glory. Now you must return to your body."

"I don't want to go," she pleaded. "I want to stay in this place of great love."

The angel smiled and took her hand and started guiding her away from the glorious light. Even in the presence of love, she was shedding tears, wanting to stay.

"No, no, please," she sobbed and wiped the tears from her face. Yet tears continued to flow, and she couldn't keep pace clearing them from her face. In the end, she shook her head and opened her eyes to a dark sky that was crying rain. She looked to Z'mia to see her standing under the rock overhang.

"Finally, you're up!" Z'mia exclaimed. "You were so sound asleep; I couldn't wake you. Come out of the rain."

Kay're sat up and looked up to the heavens. The rain felt good on her face and soothed her sadness. She took a deep breath to regain her composure and stood. Slowly, she began removing her clothes.

"What are you doing?" Z'mia asked, disbelieving what she was seeing.

"Cleansing myself; both body and mind. Frankly, I stink and need a shower, and God provided me the water." Z'mia nodded and raised an arm and sniffed herself. Quickly, she was standing in the rain nude next to her friend. They giggled and danced with joy.

"This is fun," Z'mia said laughing. "I hope no one sees us."

"Only God."

"What is it with you and God this morning?"

"I was standing in His presence a while ago and asked God to release my memory. But an angel told me it wasn't my time yet and guided me back to my body."

"But you were just lying there sleeping!" Z'mia exclaimed, astonished by Kay're's story.

"I woke up earlier when you were asleep and started meditating to see if I could unblock my memory. While doing so, I saw a neural pathway and followed it, and it led me to heaven and God. I didn't see Him but felt His presence that radiated pure love. I didn't want to leave, and begged and cried to stay, but an angel took me away. Then the rain woke me up."

Z'mia shrugged. "I think while you were meditating you fell asleep and dreamed. Dreams can seem so real. Now that I think about it, I had one recently here on Earth that took me to my hometown on Valerii. It showed something different from what I remember. Everything was bleak and rundown. All because Tl'Rak caused the timeline to change."

"I don't think it was a dream," Kay're said. "More like a vision from God. He uses various ways to communicate with the chosen people, and visions are one of them. In the Bible, there are many instances of people having visions from God. Many of those experiencing a vision had their lives transformed. The vision you had is an affirmation that you must stop Tl'Rak. And when we find him, you can tell him you saw the future and what it is like if he kills Jesus."

"He won't believe me. The man is mad and without reason. And what about your vision if it was one?"

"I don't think it was a vision. I saw my brain's nerve pathways."

Z'mia's mouth gaped in skepticism. "Come on. Are you telling me that you can see nerve pathways in your brain?"

"Only this morning. I believe God allowed it; one of his means of communication."

"It seems odd that God would allow you to see your past and not unlock your memory in the alert state, like now." She gave her friend a quizzical look.

"God works in mysterious ways." She smiled and began shaking out her hair.

Z'mia rolled her eyes. "While you were standing before God, you should have asked Him to release the spaceships. Or at least miraculously make our hair long."

"I didn't think of it. The emotions I experienced clouded my thinking." A pause. "Well, I feel clean now." As she reached down for her clothes, the rain stopped, and the clouds parted, revealing the sun. She looked up to the sky and smiled. "See, after God cleansed us, he stopped the rain and brought out the sun."

Z'mia shook her head. She didn't have a response to her friend's statement. Both women wrung out their clothes and dressed. The sun would dry them in a short time. After eating a small meal, the women continued their journey.

CHAPTER THIRTY-FIVE
Feast and Frustration

Little Kay're wandering over the last few days brought her to the rock wall that had conveyed her to this foreign land. The child thought this unknown land was very crude compared to the modern world she was accustomed to. Most of all, she missed her parents. Many nights she dreamed of them and their love. Most nights she cried herself to sleep with no one to comfort her.

She stumbled about the rocks and pushed the rock wall, hoping it would activate the lights. If the lights appeared, she would run through them and return home. Nothing she did made the lights appear. With tears flowing, she threw stones at the wall, hoping they would turn on the lights. She even talked to it, commanding it to turn the lights on. Her final effort was to use her mental abilities to will the lights to appear. That, too, was for naught.

Tired, thirsty, and hungry, she sat and sniffled to clear her nose. She looked up to see the sky turning dark. Unfazed by the threatening weather, she continued to sit and stare at the rock wall. She knew only a miracle would return the lights. Minutes went by and the rain came. It started with sporadic small droplets giving way to a torrential downpour. Kay're smiled and stood with her face to the sky. She opened her mouth wide and took in the raindrops. The rain quenched her thirst, and she danced in a swirl, enjoying the moment.

After the rain passed, the drenched, hungry girl walked to the town where the nice man opened her mind. She hoped he would be there and that he could make the lights appear. Her walk turned into a run as she sensed evil from behind.

"Stop, child," came a man's voice from the rear. Kay're didn't stop. Her little legs moved swiftly, but she could hear two sets of footsteps closing. Finally, gasping for air, she slowed and stopped and turned to her pursuers.

"You're a rascal," said one of the bearded men. Both men were sucking air from the chase.

"Where are your parents?" asked the other man, even though it made no difference to him or his partner. They intended to kidnap the girl. She pointed to the sky.

"All the better," said one with a thin smile. "You will bring good money when sold." He reached into his waist for a binding to tie her hands. "Now give me your hands." Kay're shook her head. The man raised a hand to threaten her. She looked into his eyes and went deep into his mind, planting a painful thought. The man winced and shook his head.

"What's wrong?" the other asked and stared down at the child. Kay're did the same to him. He reeled back and she started running again, this time toward the rocks. As she gained the rocks, a hand grasped her leg and pulled her to the ground. "You're a witch. What did you do to me?"

The other man yanked her up by the tunic. "She is possessed and trouble. We should slit her throat. She will be more trouble than the money will get for her."

"Nah. Once she's tied up, she'll be no trouble," the other said, still feeling the effects of her intrusion into his mind. He took hold of her hands and secured them together. He avoided looking at her face. "There, now start moving." He pushed her forward.

"I'm hungry and need to rest," she protested.

"Well, that's too bad." The man pushed her again and she fell to the ground.

"Get up," ordered the other man, kicking her in the leg. She did and smiled at the men. "Don't look at us! Get moving." She shook her head and yelled, "No!"

"You do not say 'no' to me," the man said, lifting his hand to strike her. As he was about to strike her, there were roars from behind. The men knew the sound and their eyes widened in terror. They started running. They didn't make it far as the lions pounced on them.

Kay're stood and watched unnerved the lions tearing into the screaming men. Minutes later, the large male cat came to her side. She held out her hands and asked the big cat to break her binding. With one careful bite, she was free and hugging her friend. The lion purred in delight. She thanked him and together they walked over to the leftovers of the men. She felt no pity for them. Taking a food bag one man dropped, she sat with her friends. She dined on bread and fish, while the cats ate human flesh. After everyone had their fill, they moved to the shade of the trees. Kay're fell asleep. The lions yawned and reclined.

At sunrise, Kay're rose. The lions had departed, leaving her alone with vultures dining on the men's remains. Kay're walked close to the birds' meal and shook her head in disgust. She noticed another small bag on the ground near the birds and picked it up. The vultures ignored her as they partook. Inside the bag were coins of various sizes. She had seen people paying for food with such items; she tucked the bag under her dress. Waving to the birds, she continued her journey to find the man that opened her mind.

Centurion Marcus sat at his desk having his mid-day meal. He ate alone, having too much on his mind to be interrupted by company. His thoughts centered on the child, the two women, a longing for Rome, and love. Would he ever find love in Israel? The thought of Claudia and her soft skin and tender kiss brought a thin smile to his face. It was so long ago, yet the woman had returned the memory of his youthful love. Would Claudia be available or was she now in the arms of another man? Maybe with children of her own? He sighed.

"Centurion Marcus," was the call from the entrance of his tent.

Marcus recognized Decanus Varius's voice. *Did he find the women and child?* "Come in."

Varius entered and saluted his superior. "I have two women, sir."

Marcus smiled and quickstepped from his tent. The two women had their heads down and uncovered, and Marcus could see they had short hair. He lifted the chin of one woman and stared into her face. Their eyes met and Marcus shook his head. There was no visual or mental connection with her. This woman wasn't the one that entered his mind. It was the same with the other women.

"I have never seen either of these women before," Marcus said, shaking his head, unhappy.

"But one of them may have been in the skirmish with Decanus Viviani.

Marcus lifted a hand as if to strike them. In unison, they cowered in fear. "They're not fighters. Look at their thin, scrawny bodies. They couldn't hurt a fly. Let them go." Marcus waved a dismissing hand.

"But sir," Varius said.

"But what?" Marcus returned. "You brought me two women that are—I don't know what they are, definitely not the women I'm after. I'm looking for women that will be defiant to authority and will fight, not duck for cover. Varius, do these women have those characteristics?"

"No, Centurion," Varius admitted sheepishly.

"You still have a job to do. Get to it!" He returned to his tent, flopped into his seat, and took a long swallow of wine. "I need to return to Rome," he said to himself and finished the wine in a single gulp.

CHAPTER THIRTY-SIX
Near Miss

Kay're and Z'mia Nh'Got reached the outskirts of the town, Tiberias. From their mountain perch, they could see the town held a small garrison of Roman soldiers. It was late afternoon and many of the soldiers were bathing in the hot springs. They also had a view of the tiny village of Hamat that lay south of Tiberias. It was there that Kay're met Cleophas and his wife Mary. With Mary, Kay're enjoyed a bath in the hot spring. She and Z'mia longed for the opportunity to soak their tired and sore bodies in the spring set aside for women. There were no soldiers in Hamat, and Kay're and Z'mia made their way to the village.

Staying in the long shadows, they reached Cleophas's house. Kay're knocked on the door.

"Who's there?" was the answer.

Kay're recognized Cleophas's voice and smiled. "It's Kay're and a friend."

The door opened and a smiling Cleophas greeted Kay're with a hug. "Who's your friend?"

"I'm Z'mia Nh'Got," she answered with a bow.

"Please come in quickly. Mary, look who is here."

"Oh, my," Mary gushed, racing to Kay're and embracing her. "I see you have a friend."

"Yes, this is Z'mia," Kay're introduced her.

"Any friend of Kay're must be a blessed person," Mary said, and hugged Z'mia too. "Please sit and sup with us and tell us about your journey since you were last here."

Kay're told them about her travels and how she met Z'mia who was also searching for Jesus. Z'mia related how she and her injured superior met Jesus.

Out of kindness, Jesus healed him. She continued to say she needed to find Jesus so he could help her find a way home much like Kay're. She said her superior was mentally disturbed and was out to kill Jesus. That brought frowns of concern to Cleophas and Mary's faces. Kay're reassured them that she and Z'mia would find him before he attempted to kill Jesus. Kay're recounted their skirmish with the Roman soldiers and that they were now women on the run.

"That would explain why the Roman soldiers were checking all the women in town a few days ago," Cleophas said. "What I don't understand is why they wanted everyone's headcover removed."

"That's because we have short hair," Kay're answered. "Israeli women all have long hair."

"Of course," Cleophas said, nodding.

"Kay're, you continue to amaze us," Mary said. "Fighting off Roman soldiers. And Z'mia you are great, too."

"I believe God gave you the strength to fend off the Romans and travel safely," Cleophas said. Z'mia dipped her head as she was still struggling with the existence of God.

"Did I offend you?" Cleophas asked.

"No. It's just that—I'm not sure if there is a God."

"Even after witnessing the miracle cure of your superior?" Cleophas asked. "And Kay're finding you after your prayer for help?"

Z'mia shrugged. "I'm a practical woman and somehow don't believe in a higher power. I think Jesus is simply a man with exceptional ability and kindness." She didn't want to say she believed him to be an extraterrestrial, and that she was one too. They wouldn't comprehend that intelligent life existed beyond Earth. "Please, I respect you and Kay're's belief in God and that Jesus is His son. I will keep an open mind on the subject."

"That is good, my child," Cleophas said, patting her on the knee. "I'm sure God will further reveal Himself to you and change your mind."

Z'mia politely nodded. "What Kay're and I want now is to soak in the hot spring."

Mary laughed. "I can understand. When the sun dips behind the hills, we will go to bathe."

At twilight, the three joined the other women there. "This is pure delight!" Z'mia exclaimed, submerging herself to her chin.

"Mmm," Kay're murmured as she soaked in the soothing water. With her eyes closed, and relaxed, she hoped to see heaven. She willed herself along various pathways in her brain. Her first stop was at the prefrontal cortex. To her chagrin, the barricade to the episodic memory cells was still present.

These cells encoded her personal experiences both temporally and spatially into long-term memory. She backtracked to a neural junction and found the path that led to the bright light. The light was far away. She raced down the path and the brightness grew and grew until it was blinding. Again, unconditional love overcame her. She fell, prostrate before the light. As she lay there, a hand touched her on the shoulder. She raised her head to see the same angel.

"My dear, it's still not your time," the angelic voice said. "Arise, and let me guide you home once more."

Without protest, Kay're stood and took the angel's hand. Together they returned to the neural nexus. The angel smiled at her and wiped away her tears. "Your time is coming soon. Be faithful and strong." The angel left her.

"Kay're, are you okay?" Z'mia asked, noticing tears rolling down Kay're's cheeks.

Kay're nodded. "I saw the brilliant light of God again and felt His unconditional love. Yet, as before, an angel said it wasn't my time and guided me back to the here and now. Z'mia if you had my experience, you would believe in God."

Mary went slack-jaw hearing Kay're. "You saw God?"

"You can't gaze upon God," Kay're replied. "You only see this light that is brighter than the sun and feel His eternal love."

"But you saw an angel! What was he like?" Mary asked.

"The angel was very large with ethereal wings. He had a melodious voice that was gentle and pure. He was beautiful and so kind."

"The angel was male?" Z'mia quizzed.

"Yes, he was. I'm not sure how I know, but the angel was male."

"Z'mia, are you married?" Mary asked.

"No."

"A boyfriend?" Kay're queried.

Z'mia sighed. "No boyfriend."

"Why?" Mary asked. "You're a pretty woman. You should have plenty of men falling over themselves for you."

"I wish. Cooped up on a spa—ship," she caught herself again, "you don't have anyone asking you for a date. Everyone on the ship is too busy doing their jobs. When you are off duty, you don't want to strike up an intimate relationship with someone you see every day. Frankly, the men on the ship are—well, not anyone I would want a relationship with." She didn't say that she had a crush on First Officer M'Catis and suspected he had a similar feeling toward her.

"So, you are on a sailing ship?" Mary asked.

"Yes, it is a sailing ship." *That flies amongst the stars.*

"So why are you here in Israel?"

"My superior had heard of Jesus and his greatness and wanted to meet him. So, we sailed to Israel and came ashore. He asked me to join him to search for Jesus. Somehow, my superior lost his mind and wants to kill him. Then one morning I awoke to find him gone and myself alone and lost. Then Kay're found me."

"That is some story," Mary said. "When you get home, you should request duty on land and find a nice man to marry. It's not good for a woman of your age to be alone in life." Z'mia smiled and nodded.

"And Kay're, I'm sure you have a wonderful husband," Mary said to her. "Once your amnesia clears, you will see his face." Mary smiled and tapped her on the knee.

"Enough talk. Let us relax in this nice water," Z'mia said. All nodded.

On the bridge of the *Lionare,* Supreme Commander Tr'Tala sat in the command seat staring at the blue planet. It frustrated him being helpless. Everyone's existence and future depended on Lt. Nh'Got. She had to stop Commander Tl'Rak from killing Jesus, as well as finding him and convincing him to release the ships. And then there was the child called Kay're. Though the child didn't admit she was the daughter of Jesus, Tl'Rak still believed it was a possibility. Were they both from the small ship in orbit?

And the name Kay're kept repeating in his head. He thought back to the mysterious woman with the same name. She was the one that prevented him from kidnapping the boy, Mark Ross. In the future she would be Mark Ross's wife. It sounded so crazy, but in time travel everything was possible. Kay're eventually met with the emperor on Valerii and developed a friendship. *Is this Kay're the same person?*

Besides the emperor, only he and his wife knew of Kay're the adult. He contacted his wife on the *Tigerii* and conveyed his suspicion of the child being the adult Kay're. And that Jesus could be her father. They both concluded time travel was a nightmare never to be revisited again.

"Comm," called Tr'Tala. "Have you tried contacting the child recently?"

"I have, and have done so frequently, Supreme Commander. I don't think she knows how to answer the annunciator."

"Try again. Maybe with luck, she will answer."

"Yes, sir. Trying again."

Little Kay're pouted at the chirping, small metallic disk in her hand. She didn't know how to stop the noise, or to call the nice man that could return her home. She pressed her fingers all over the disk. "Hello, hello. Can anyone hear me?" There was no answer, and finally, the chirping stopped. She tucked the disk into her coin bag and continued her walk.

"Sir, still no answer," said the comm-officer.

"Very well," Tr'Tala snorted. "Do you have a fix on her?"

"I do, Supreme Commander. She is in a town called Hamat."

"That is where Lt. Nh'Got was when she reported in one hour ago. Is she still there?"

"I am checking. Unbelievable! Her annunciator and the child are very close to each other. Maybe they are together."

"Hail Lt. Nh'Got now."

"Hailing." A pause. "Sir, she isn't answering."

"What?"

"Sir, she isn't answering. Maybe something happened to her."

Tr'Tala cursed and slammed a fist into the chair. "Keep trying."

Z'mia's annunciator vibrated and vibrated as she soaked in the warm spring. She had it set to vibrate so as not to startle any locals. It was in her clothes, lying on the ground. In the darkness at the far end of the hot spring, a small Kay're slipped into the water unnoticed. Joyfully, she swirled the surface with her hands and closed her eyes. Immediately, she was running to a bright light radiating love.

CHAPTER THIRTY-SEVEN
Passover

It was dark when Kay're, Z'mia, and Mary emerged from the hot spring and dried themselves off. As Z'mia was dressing, she felt her annunciator vibrate. She didn't want to answer it in the presence of Mary.

"I have a call from the ship," Z'mia whispered to Kay're.

Kay're nodded. "Mary let's walk to the well for a drink." Kay're took the lead with Mary walking with her.

Mary stopped as she noticed Z'mia lagging behind. "Are you coming, Z'mia?"

"Ah, I need to relieve myself," Z'mia replied. "I'll catch up with you at the well." Mary nodded. She and Kay're walked off, and Z'mia hurried into the nearby bushes. She called her ship and found out that the child, Kay're, was very close by. Z'mia told the Supreme Commander she, her friend, and another woman were soaking in a hot spring. Tr'Tala said the girl must be in the spring too.

"I'm not there now," Z'mia said.

"Then hurry there and find the girl. I need to talk to her. She doesn't know how to answer the annunciator."

"Yes, Supreme Commander," Nh'Got replied and rushed back to the spring. It was now completely dark, and she could only make out a few figures in the moonlight. The spring was big, and she scurried around its edge, eyeing the few people still there. She didn't see a child and called the ship to see if they had a fix on her.

"The child is about two hundred meters south of you and moving," said the comm-officer. Tr'Tala hovered over the officer's shoulder with anticipation.

"Got it. I'll be in touch." Lt. Nh'Got closed the link.

She started moving that way but stopped as Kay're called out her name. She had a dilemma. Go after little Kay're or return to Kay're and Mary. She paused. Better to let Kay're know her little self is nearby and she what she wants to do.

She had a dilemma. Go after little Kay're or return to Kay're and Mary. She paused. *Better to let Kay're know her little self is nearby and she what she wants to do.*

"Here," she called out in the darkness.

Kay're and Mary came to her side. Kay're kind of wiggled her head as an unspoken question of what was going on. Z'mia bobbed her head. "I needed to rinse a bit after relieving myself and then something caught my attention."

"What did you see?" Mary asked.

"Some movement caught my eye. But in the darkness, I couldn't figure out who or what it was."

"We better get back," Mary said. "Could be a lion."

"Your probably right. Let us go," Z'mia said.

As they walked back to Mary's home, Z'mia whispered to Kay're that her little self was at the hot spring. Kay're nodded. Once home, they relaxed, though Kay're was worried about her little self being alone at night. Cleophas told his guest that Passover would be celebrated in four days. Tomorrow, he would go into town and buy a spring lamb that he would slay and prepare for the Passover meal. Mary would gather all the leaven used for making bread and go to the market the day before Passover and sell it. After Passover, she would repurchase the leaven.

"What is Passover?" asked Z'mia.

"It's the festival, which commemorates the liberation of our people from Egyptian slavery," Cleophas replied. Z'mia gave him a bewildered look as she lacked knowledge of Earth history. Cleophas saw the expression and gave her and Kay're a brief history lesson on Israel's captivity in Egypt. He included the story of Moses and the plagues cast on Egypt and the parting of the Red Sea. "Since that time, Passover is celebrated every year. Z'mia, this is more proof that God exists," Cleophas finished with a smile.

"Is your story true or folklore?" she questioned. Kay're had a concerned look on her face but said nothing.

"It is factual," he assured. "Now Kay're, what is bothering you?"

Kay're shrugged. "Your history lesson helped me remember some things, and they're not pleasant." She remembered Jesus's passion and crucifixion happened during Passover week. Was it this week? Or next year? Maybe two years from now? "I'm all right. Every one of us has had sad life experiences, but we go on knowing and they're not pleasant." She remembered Jesus's passion and crucifixion happened during Passover week. *Was it this week? Or next year? Maybe two years from now?* "I'm all right. Every one of us has had sad life experiences, but we go on knowing happy ones are around the corner." She smiled her reassurance.

"That's true," Cleophas admitted.

"I'm so glad my husband's story has helped you remember some things," Mary said. "I see it as another sign from God."

"I hope so," Kay're said. "But tomorrow, Z'mia and I need to leave. I fear people in the hot spring saw that we have short hair and might have figured out why the Roman soldiers had them remove their head coverings. Some might report us to the Romans and if they come here, you could be in trouble for housing us." It was a partial truth. She and Z'mia needed to get to Jerusalem to see if Jesus died this week. She would tell Z'mia about it once Cleophas and Mary retired for the night.

Everyone bid each other good night and Z'mia and Kay're were alone. Z'mia contacted her ship and explained why she couldn't search for little Kay're. She still didn't tell Supreme Commander Tr'Tala that the adult Kay're was the friend she was traveling with to avoid complicating questions from him why adult Kay're was here. Kay're herself didn't know. Until she did, she would keep Kay're's identity secret. She assured Tr'Tala that with her friend they would try to find the child tomorrow. Tr'Tala said the priority was to find Tl'Rak and Jesus. The child could wait, but if found along the way, all the better. Z'mia closed the comm-link.

"Our priority tomorrow is heading to Jerusalem," Kay're said flatly. "It's there that we will find both Tl'Rak and Jesus."

"Why do you say that?"

"Jesus's crucifixion was during Passover week in Jerusalem. Three days later he rose from the dead. I remember this from the Bible. You said Tl'Rak read the Bible."

"So he claims."

"Then he knows that this could be the Passover week that Jesus dies and then rises. He will be in Jerusalem waiting for his opportunity to kill Jesus before the Romans crucify him."

"Of course. But what did you mean by 'this could be the Passover week'? Is there another?"

the Romans crucify him."

"Of course. But what did you mean by 'this could be the Passover week'? Is there another?"

"From what I recall, Jesus preached to the people three years before he died. We don't know which of the three years this week's Passover is taking place in. Based on the miracles you saw, this is his final year, and his death will occur four days from now."

"And Tl'Rak will be ahead of us and waiting. It'll be a three-to four-day journey from here if we don't get delayed by something. Now I wish we had the horses."

"Let us hope our journey is uneventful. We need to leave early in the morning."

Z'mia agreed with a nod, and they settled down for sleep.

Tl'Rak finally made it out of the mountains. It was late afternoon when he spotted a town ahead. He didn't remember going through this town when he and Nh'Got traveled from Jerusalem to the Sea of Galilee. His concern was that he had traveled beyond Jerusalem. He entered the town and went to the well. There, he asked a local what town he was in. Jericho was the reply.

"Where is Jerusalem from here and how far?"

The man pointed west. "About a half a day's walk. Are you going there for Passover?"

"Passover?" Tl'Rak mused.

"Yes, Passover. You must be a gentile. I'm not talking to you anymore." He walked away.

Tl'Rak sat on a stone, contemplating the word Passover. "There is something about Passover. What is it?" he said to himself. There was a pause, and then he smiled. "Yes, yes!" He pulled out a piece of goat meat and chewed on it while eyeing a place to spend the night. He saw a place under some trees. There he settled with a pledge to find Jesus tomorrow and return glory to himself and Valerii.

After her bath in the hot springs, little Kay're left town and found shelter under a rock outcropping. The night air was cool, and she was shivering. "Lions, where are you?" she called out into the night. Soon she had an answer. Roars came from a distance, and her four-legged friends arrived. They curled up next to her to provide comfort and warmth.

CHAPTER THIRTY-EIGHT
Swim Time

At sunrise, Kay're and Z'mia were already trekking to Jerusalem. The going was slow as they stayed off the main road to avoid Roman soldiers. They were certain dedicated patrols would be looking for them.

At the end of an uneventful day, the women camped at the edge of the hills. Z'mia checked in with the ship and found out they had travelled twenty-five kilometers today. There was no change in the status of the ships. She informed Tr'Tala of their need to get to Jerusalem in three days.

"Excellent deductive reasoning, Lt. Nh'Got," praised Tr'Tala.

"Sir, actually it was...." Kay're shook her head no.

"It was what, Lieutenant?" Tr'Tala asked

"A good thing I remembered that Commander Tl'Rak told me he had read the Bible. It helped me to fill in the blanks."

"That is good. But you need to make better headway tomorrow if you want to reach Jerusalem in three days."

"Yes, Supreme Commander. Do you have a fix on the girl?"

"We do. She is ten kilometers ahead of you and moving toward Jerusalem too. I have been thinking about the child. If you stop Tl'Rak from killing Jesus, the child will see her father crucified by the humans. It would be a terrifying scene to witness for a child, let alone an adult."

Kay're paled on hearing that they believed she was Jesus's daughter. With her memory impaired, she wondered if the assertion was true. Jesus was God. Yet did he sire a daughter while on Earth? Another question she needed an answer to.

"Sir, but according to their Bible, he rises from the dead in three days," Z'mia said.

"Do you think the child knows that?"

Z'mia looked to Kay're for help as she was the child. Kay're nodded.

Z'mia looked to Kay're for help as she was the child. Kay're nodded.

"I think so, sir." *I hope so,* she didn't add.

"Still, it would be a terrible thing to see, even knowing your father rises from the dead," Tr'Tala said. "After his burial, he will beam-up to the ship in orbit for resuscitation and three days of rest. Then he returns to Earth to make it look like he rose from the dead for the sake of Bible history."

"Sir, this is all predicated on believing the girl is Jesus's child. She may not be."

"I think she is, for reasons I cannot tell you now," Tr'Tala countered.

"Really? I mean, yes, Supreme Commander," Z'mia corrected herself.

"Yes, really," Tr'Tala said, unhappy with Nh'Got breaking formality.

"Now, Lieutenant, rest, and make better time tomorrow." The link closed.

"You look ill," Z'mia said to Kay're, who was trembling.

"I'm shocked to hear that I could be Jesus's daughter."

"I'm sorry you heard that," Z'mia said soberly. A pause. "Anyhow, tomorrow we need to use the road, Romans or not."

Still shaken, Kay're nodded. "Your supreme commander, his voice sounds familiar to me. What is his name?"

"Sen Tr'Tala."

Kay're squeezed her eyes tight in deep concentration. "I have heard that name before but can't place it."

"If you have, then that would make you a time-traveler from my time." Z'mia still felt bad about her friend hearing she may be the daughter of Jesus. But why was she here when little Kay're was present at the same time? Did one of them come to Earth by chance? Or was Kay're the spouse of Jesus? "Oh my!" she blurted out.

"What is it?" Kay're questioned her friend.

"Something came to me," Z'mia replied, trying to cover for herself. She couldn't tell Kay're what she had just thought after the latest revelation. *What should I say?* "I concluded that you or your child self is here by mistake," she finally said, hiding some truth. She only hoped Kay're wouldn't look into her mind for the actual answer.

"Yes, I concluded the same when I first saw my little self," Kay're said, but sensed Z'mia was holding something back. She decided not to embarrass her friend by

"Yes, I concluded the same when I first saw my little self," Kay're said, but sensed Z'mia was holding something back. She decided not to embarrass her friend by pressing her for the rest of the story.

"Kay're, can I ask you a personal question?"

"Sure, ask away."

"Do you believe you're married?" She wondered how Kay're would reply.

"I cannot remember. But I keep pondering why I know your supreme commander. And what were the circumstances that made me think so? I'm going insane from my inability to recall anything."

"It appears some of your memory is coming back. Your belief that you know Supreme Commander Tr'Tala is proof of that. Maybe in the morning, more of your memory will return. Let's get some sleep." Z'mia also mulled over what Tr'Tala was holding back and why.

The sun was a ball of orange over the eastern horizon when Kay're and Z'mia awoke. They moved onto the main road to Jerusalem. The road was devoid of activity and the two women walked briskly heading south. As the sun peaked in a blue sky, the women took a break under some trees. To their luck, one tree bore figs, which was a treat from dried fish and stale bread.

"I'm going to call the ship to check our progress," Z'mia said. The comm-officer noted they had moved slightly over ten kilometers.

Supreme Commander Tr'Tala was listening. "At your current pace you will make Jerusalem the night before Jesus's execution," he said, butting in. "You could be too late."

"Why is that, sir?" Lt. Nh'Got asked.

"I did my homework last night reading parts of the Bible that focused on Jesus's death. On Thursday, Jesus enters Jerusalem for something called the Passover feast. After eating, he and some of his disciples head to the Mount of Olives to pray. There, an angry mob arrests him to begin a sham trial leading to his execution. Tl'Rak knows this and will be in that crowd. He will shoot and kill Jesus. At that point, time changes." He paused, allowing the gravity of his point to sink in.

"You need to pick up your pace to make Jerusalem by mid-afternoon," he continued. "Once in Jerusalem, you must find Tl'Rak and stop him. Finding him may be difficult, so I would lie in wait where Jesus is having his Passover meal. Tl'Rak he continued. "Once in Jerusalem, you must find Tl'Rak and stop him. Finding him may be difficult, so I would lie in wait where Jesus is having his Passover meal. Tl'Rak will be nearby."

"Understood, Supreme Commander," Lt. Nh'Got replied. "Sir, do you have the current location of the girl?"

"One second." A pause as he checked with the comm-officer. "She is four kilometers ahead of you and moving. You may overtake her."

"Sir, if we catch up with her is there anything special I need to know about her?" Another pause.

"Lieutenant, are you still traveling with your friend?"

"Yes, sir. She needs to find Jesus too; we are helping each other."

"Why does she need to find Jesus?"

"She has a serious brain affliction that affects her cognition and memory. There are no healers here, so she hopes Jesus will cure her."

"I see, but she may slow you down and frankly, I don't trust the people of this period."

"Sir, she is very trustworthy and helpful. She knows many of the locals. These locals provided food and shelter for us."

"Does she know you are an alien and from the future?"

"Yes, sir. She has watched me call the ship and talk to you. I had to explain what I was doing and why I needed to stop Tl'Rak. She is okay with that. She believes there are more inhabited worlds in the sky."

"That is interesting. Does she have a name?"

"Pardon me, sir. We need to get moving instead of talking." Z'mia bit her lip, hoping she was not insolent. It was her way of not telling Tr'Tala that her friend was Kay're too.

"Of course. Get moving. What is her name?" he persisted.

"It's Lady," she said, giving the title without the "Kay're."

"Lady?" Tr'Tala sounded the word out, but failed to get a further reply as Z'mia closed the link and looked at Kay're who was holding mouth trying not to laugh out loud.

"I couldn't tell him your name," Z'mia said. "It would confuse things even further."

even further."

Kay're laughed. "Everything is confusing right now."

"Do you think your memory has improved from last night?"

Kay're shook her head regaining her composure.

They continued their fast walk to Jerusalem. After several more kilometers, the road came alongside the Jordan River. "It's really beautiful here. I would love to jump in to cool off and bathe," Z'mia said.

"I would too. But time isn't a luxury we have. Wait, I hear horses. They are moving fast! They must be Roman horsemen!"

"Oh no. There is no cover. What do we do?"

"Go for a swim," Kay're said. She took Z'mia's hand and jumped into the water. On surfacing, Z'mia coughed out water. "Over there." Kay're pointed to her right. "Let's get behind those reeds."

They positioned themselves behind some tall reeds for cover. Sure enough, several Roman soldiers galloped toward the women's position. On approach, they slowed. The women ducked low in the water. With only their eyes above the surface, they couldn't see the soldiers.

To the women's misfortune, the soldiers stopped. "It's still a long way to Galilee," said one Roman. The horses need water. While they drink, we eat."

"I want to cool off," another voiced.

"Sure, why not," clipped the leader.

Z'mia cursed silently. This wasn't the delay they needed. Kay're took her knife and cut two reeds. She gave one to Z'mia and showed her how to use it as a snorkel. Z'mia nodded, and the women submerged and used them to breathe.   T h e y could hear the soldiers jumping into the river and splashing around like children. After what seemed like an eternity, the soldiers waded out of the water and redressed. Kay're pointed to the surface and she and Z'mia poked their heads above the water. The soldiers sat and ate, wasting more time. Finally, they remounted and galloped off. Kay're and Z'mia waded to the riverbank and up onto the road.

"Whoa! That was refreshing," Kay're said, running her fingers through her wet hair.

Z'mia chuckled. "You have a funny way of dismissing serious situations. I like your style. You know we would be a wonderful team zipping around the galaxy dealing

Z'mia chuckled. "You have a funny way of dismissing serious situations. I like your style. You know we would be a wonderful team zipping around the galaxy dealing with problems. Kay're and Nh'Got, super sleuths at your service."

Kay're laughed. "That would be fun. We would have to get a spacecraft and some sort of communications device so people in need could contact us. And you would have to leave your military unit and I—I'm not sure what I'd do."

"I can leave my service. I see little future in it. Subterfuge and extortion are the only ways to advance in rank. That's not my style."

Kay're nodded. "What about a ship?"

If you're Jesus's daughter that should not be a problem, Z'mia thought but didn't say. "Somehow, we will get one. If not, then we can hop on space freighters or use privateers to get around. Of course, this all depends on what you do when you're normal and back in our time."

"Of course," Kay're echoed. "What we need to do is get moving. We've lost over an hour." As if on cue, Z'mia's ship called, wanting to know why they weren't moving. Nh'Got explained the why, and they started again to Jerusalem.

CHAPTER THIRTY-NINE
Super Sleuths

As twilight approached, little Kay're continued following the road to Jerusalem. She had heard that Jesus was there for a celebration. He was her last hope of getting the lights to turn on so she could go home. Sleeping on the cold ground and being pursued by evil men was exhausting and terrifying. She longed for hugs and love from her parents.

Walking on, she again sensed a threat from behind. She paused and looked back to see several people riding horses. They were not soldiers, but local men with three women. They seemed ordinary enough, yet she sensed danger. Being too tired to run, she moved off the road to let them pass; at least she hoped they would.

One rider galloped ahead and came up to her side. "Child, are you alone?" Kay're didn't reply nor look up at him. She continued walking. "I asked you a question. Answer me!" She kept silent as she moved forward. The rider reached down to grasp her, but she ducked under his arm. The man moved his horse to block her. With her path hindered, she looked up to the man and read his intentions to kidnap her. She placed a painful thought in his mind. He shook his head to clear it and cursed at her. Then, she mentally told the horse to rear up and run away. The horse obeyed and came up on its hind legs, throwing the man. His head whiplashed against the ground and lay still. The horse bolted off.

Seeing what happened, two other riders raced toward her. Kay're was defenseless. One came to her side and scooped her up. He settled his horse as the other riders tended to their fallen friend.

"What did you do to him?" the rider demanded.

"Nothing. The horse got frightened, and the man fell off."

"How is he?"

"He is alive. Just knocked out," the other replied. Using his canteen, he doused water onto the man's face. He came around holding his head.

doused water onto the man's face. He came around holding his head.

"My head—it hurts," he moaned. "What happened?"

"Your horse spooked, and you fell off and hit your head."

"Oh," he groaned, holding his head. He tried to stand, but his knees gave out, and he collapsed to the ground.

"Sit here for a while. I will find your horse."

The man holding Kay're lowered her to the ground and dismounted. "Who are you and where are your parents?" Kay're kept silent. "You'll answer me, or I'll beat it out of you." He raised a threatening hand.

"I'm Kay're, and my parents are far away," she pouted.

"Why are you traveling alone?"

"I'm lost and I'm going to town to find Jesus so he can help me get home."

The man laughed as the other rider with the three women trotted up. "Who is she?"

"Another to add to our collection." He chuckled and continued, "She is alone and likely going to Jerusalem to find the one called Jesus of Nazareth, so he can help her home. Well, that won't happen." He took a length of leather from his waist and bound her wrists. The girl sneered at him as he hefted her up onto a horse ridden by one woman. The three women had their hands tied.

They waited until the other returned with the missing horse. Fifteen minutes later, the searcher returned without the horse. "I can't find it," he said.

"Okay, free up a horse by doubling up the women." He walked over to his fallen friend and eyed him. "Do you think you can ride?" The man nodded and stood. He was wobbly. "You're in no shape to ride. It's near sunset. We will camp for the night. Get the women down and let them refresh themselves and give them something to eat. Not too much, though. Then tether them together, including the girl."

As night fell, the women and little Kay're sat tied together around a fire. The men were on the other side, drinking wine and swapping stories. The man with the head injury lay quiet. Kay're sensed the presence of lions in the area and thought about shouting for them, but decided against it. They might attack the women too, something she didn't want to happen. Then she remembered the silver disk. If she could contact the voice in the sky, maybe they could help. But with her hands bound silver disk. If she could contact the voice in the sky, maybe they could help. But with her hands bound tightly, it was impossible to reach for it. She laid down for the night.

Behind schedule, Kay're and Z'mia Nh'Got tracked the road by the light of a half-moon. They had been walking for two hours when they noticed a light flickering ahead. They stepped off the road and into the trees, approaching the light. They saw four men, three women, and a child around the campfire. The women and child were bound together with their wrists tied. There were six tethered horses

"What do you think?" Z'mia asked.

"Human traffickers."

"What are human traffickers?"

"Kidnappers who sell women and children off to be used as prostitutes or slaves."

"Children, too?"

"Sadly, yes."

"That poor child. I wish I could see her face."

"You don't need to. That child is me."

"No! We have to rescue her and the women," Z'mia whispered through clenched teeth.

"We will. The men are drinking—likely wine. Soon they will be drunk and sleeping. Then we make our move. You better turn off your talking device before it beeps, giving us up."

Z'mia nodded and silenced her annunciator. They listened to the men talk.

"We need to get that fire roaring," one of the men said. "There could be lions in the area. The fire will keep them at bay." Two of the men got up, collected tree branches, and fed the fire, then they sat and continued drinking.

One hour went by and the men were snoring. Kay're and Z'mia circled back and came up from behind the women. They were sleeping too. Kay're tapped one on the foot to wake her. The woman's head rose, and Kay're put a finger to her mouth, signaling her to remain quiet. The woman nodded, and Z'mia woke the others in the same way. When she came up on little Kay're, the girl woke and looked into her eyes. It was the same eyes that she met on the road to the miracle of healing and feeding. She could feel the girl's presence in her mind—now it was thankful and gentle.

a finger to her mouth, signaling her to remain quiet. The woman nodded, and Z'mia woke the others in the same way. When she came up on little Kay're, the girl woke and looked into her eyes. It was the same eyes that she met on the road to the miracle of healing and feeding. She could feel the girl's presence in her mind—now it was thankful and gentle.

Kay're glanced at herself. Their eyes and minds joined, and they exchanged smiles. Kay're and Z'mia took their knives and cut the women and girl loose. They crept up to the horses. "Can you ride?" Kay're whispered to them. They nodded, and Kay're and Z'mia helped them onto the horses. As they did so, one horse spooked and whinnied. The sound woke one man.

"Hey!" he exclaimed. "Get up! The women are getting away!" The men awoke groggily and stood. "Let's get them."

"Here, take this money bag," Kay're said to her little self. "You and the women will need it. Follow the road to Jerusalem and don't stop for anyone." The girl nodded and Kayre lifted her onto a horse, gave her the reins, and slapped the horse on the rump. Off it went, with the women joining up with her. The remaining horses followed, leaving Kay're and Z'mia facing four men, though one was staggering.

"You take the two on the left and I will take the others," Z'mia said.

"Okay. This should be easy. They're fat and out -of -shape, not like the Roman soldiers."

"I'm so mad now I could scream," Z'mia said through gritted teeth.

Kay're laughed. "Go for it, girl!" The men moved toward them with knives showing.

Kay're struck first with a flying front snap kick to one man's face. He howled in pain, his nose was broken, and gushing blood. As she came down, she did a spinning back fist to the other man's head, staggering him back. She finished him off with a sidekick to the belly. He fell into the fire. The wineskin he carried burst, and the wine ignited, engulfing him in flames. He rolled over screaming and then got to his feet and started running. He didn't go far. Consumed with fire, he face-planted into the ground.

The man with the broken nose had somewhat recovered and slashed wildly at Kay're with his knife. She bounced away and then did a reverse spin kick to his head. She heard the crunch of his facial bones. He went down, unmoving.

wildly at Kay're with his knife. She bounced away and then did a reverse spin kick to his head. She heard the crunch of his facial bones. He went down, unmoving.

The first man Z'mia encountered was the leader. He slashed at her, but she adroitly sidestepped the knife and landed a kick to the side of his knee. It collapsed, and he wailed in pain, hitting the ground. The man with the head injury approached wobbly, and repeatedly swiped his knife at her. She evaded each slash, playing with him. With the fire at her back, she held her ground. The man cursed and jabbed his knife at her. She grasped his extended arm, pinned it against her body, and came down hard with her elbow on his upper arm. She heard it snap. The man bellowed in agony, dropping his knife. Z'mia, using the same elbow, brought it up and crashed it into the side of his head. He staggered and fell face-first into the fire. He was now a funeral pyre.

The man with the collapsed knee raised himself to a crouch position.

He hefted his knife into a throwing position aimed at Z'mia. He never got the chance to throw it. Kay're landed an axe kick to his head, her boot cracking his skull. He fell dead on the spot.

"You saved me!"

"Like you did me when we fought the Romans," Kay're said, smiling.

Z'mia looked around at the carnage and chuckled. "Whoa! Now that was exciting."

Kay're laughed. "Now you got it, girl!"

"The super sleuths of the galaxy save the day again. We are a great team. Super 'K' and Super 'Z.'"

"How about 'Special K' and 'Super Z,' as in Zarda," Kay're suggested.

"Who is Zarda?"

"Zarda is a Greek goddess in human mythology. She's the Power Princess known for her superhuman strength, speed, and agility. She appeared in American comic books in the earth's twenty-first century. Gee, some of my memory is coming back!"

"That is wonderful," Z'mia said and gave Kay're a hug. "I like your suggestion—Zarda! Super Z! What is a comic book?"

"It is hand-drawn figures and pictures that tell a story, published on paper, and sold in stores. Children are the major buyers. Of course, now it's all on the and sold in stores. Children are the major buyers. Of course, now it's all on the computer. And I remember this! Much of my memory is coming back, but I still don't know why I'm here and how I got here."

"I have a feeling it will all come back to you." A pause as they sat down to let their adrenaline settle. "Do you think we can find the other two horses?" Z'mia asked, looking around.

"Maybe in the morning. They're likely halfway to Jerusalem."

"It's sad that you had to send your little self away."

Kay're just bobbed her head. "We'll meet up in Jerusalem. I am sure of that."

"Are you sure?"

"Hmm. I think so," she replied, looking around at the fallen men. "Three are dead for sure. I will check the other one." She went to the man. He was on his back, unmoving, his face disfigured and oozing blood. Stooping down, she checked for a pulse in his neck and glanced at Z'mia, shaking her head. "I'll take his money bag. I gave mine to my little self. We'll need money for food and lodging."

"I will check the unburned one," Z'mia said. She went to the leader and took his money bag.

"We super sleuths have had enough for this day," Kay're said, returning to her friend's side. "Let us call it a night."

"First help me get this guy out of the fire. The burning flesh is nauseating." Z'mia said. Kay're nodded. Using a tree branch, they pushed the man out of the fire and dragged him by the feet to his smoldering comrade. Then they reclined by the fire.

"At least we will sleep warm tonight," Z'mia beamed.

"The heat feels good," Kay're said with a thin smile, but worried about her little self.

CHAPTER FORTY
Raw or Roasted

Under the light of a half-moon, the three young women and child rode at a brisk pace, throwing caution to the wind. In the darkness, the riders could hit low-hanging branches or fall off as the horse stumbled over something. After they had put a safe distance between themselves and the kidnappers, the pace slowed to a walk.

"Now what?" asked one woman, panting from the rough ride.

"I suppose we could camp here," said another. "After all, we have the horses. Even the riderless ones followed."

"There," said the child, pointing ahead to a flickering light.

"What do you think?" asked the oldest of the women.

"Let's dismount and sneak up and see who is there," suggested another. Leaving the horses behind, they snuck up on the light. It was a campfire.

"Roman Soldiers," whispered one woman.

"We can't get around them unseen," said one.

"Do you think we can trust them not to hurt us—or worse— if we approach and tell them our story?" another woman wondered.

"You have no choice!" came a rough male voice from behind. They turned to face two Roman soldiers with lances. "Move ahead," he directed with his lance. They obeyed and entered the campsite. "Decanus Varius, look what we found."

The young decanus, who was reclining by the fire, jumped up to greet the unexpected guests. "So, what do we have here?" he said, appraising the women and especially the child.

"We found them with their horses sneaking up on us," said the sentry.

"Who is to speak for you, women?" Varius asked.

"Since I am the oldest, I will," she said boldly, taking a step toward the decanus.

decanus.

"Okay, let's hear your story," Varius prompted with a wave.

"We escaped murdering kidnappers, took their horses, and rode swiftly until we saw your fire."

"Just like that?" Varius mused, smiling.

The women nodded.

"How many were there? And why are they murdering kidnappers?"

"Four men. They killed my parents and took me and my sister." She gestured to the youngest woman.

"And they killed my father and brother while we were working in the field and then...." The woman choked up.

"And you?' Varius looked at the child, wondering if this was the one Centurion Marcus was after.

The child looked up to the sobbing woman and placed a thought in her mind that they were sisters.

"She is my little sister," the woman said, and continued weeping. The child grasped her at the waist, securing the white lie.

Varius sucked in a breath. It was a sad story to hear. He continued with his questions. "And they let you take their horses and ride off?"

"We had help," the eldest said.

"Yes, we had helpers," echoed the other women.

"Oh, more than one. So, who assisted your escape?" Varius continued.

"Two women," the oldest replied.

That response piqued Varius' attention, along with the soldiers listening.

"You say two women?"

"Yes, yes, two women," the other woman said, and the child nodded.

"Where are these women now?" Varius continued. The women dropped their heads. "Well?"

"They're probably dead," the oldest said and began weeping.

"Why do you say that?"

"When they cut us free, they helped us up onto the horses. In doing so, one horse neighed, waking the kidnappers. They came at us, and the two women slapped our horses to gallop off. We rode away and left them to those murderers."

slapped our horses to gallop off. We rode away and left them to those murderers.”

“They were defenseless,” sobbed another woman.

“And when did this happen?”

“Tonight, about two hours ago.”

“Can you describe these two women? Any of you can answer.”

“It was dark, and things were moving fast, and, well, I don’t think any of us got a good look at their faces,” the eldest replied.

“I noticed one woman had short hair,” said the youngest woman.

“And the one who woke me had a very kind voice,” added the older woman.

“And they were tall,” said the third.

“Interesting,” Varius said, nodding. “I have heard enough. It is late. We will check out your story in the morning.”

“In the morning!” they exclaimed in unison.

“The murderers are abusing the women now, if they aren’t dead already. You need to ride now!” the eldest woman said, worry creasing her face.

“I don’t think so,” Varius said. “They are dead.” He glanced at his second in command, who nodded. “Sentries, take the child and women over there and make a fire for them. See to their comfort.” Two soldiers escorted the guests to the side.

When the women and child were out of hearing range, the second said,

“Decanus, they’re the two women we are after.” Varius agreed with a nod. “And sir, and when you said, ‘they were dead,’ you meant the men.”

“Of course. If those two women can take down eight lancers, they wouldn’t have any trouble taking these men out. I suspect we’ll find their bodies tomorrow.”

“And the two women?”

“They likely moved off into the hills knowing someone would come looking for them. We won’t find them on the road, especially tonight.”

“And the child and the three women?”

“Very sad situation. Let them go in the morning,”

Morning broke over Israel. At the campsite, Kay’re stretched the aches from her body. Z’mia was sitting and staring at the smoldering fire.

“With the warmth of the fire, I slept pretty well last night,” Kay’re said, yawning.

“I did too,” Z’mia agreed. “But I’m hungry. I wonder if these men left any food in

Morning broke over Israel. At the campsite, Kay're stretched the aches from her body. Z'mia was sitting and staring at the smoldering fire.

"With the warmth of the fire, I slept pretty well last night," Kay're said, yawning.

"I did too," Z'mia agreed. "But I'm hungry. I wonder if these men left any food in these bags."

"Let's check," Kay're said, and they each took a bag.

Kay're produced a small loaf of bread and a piece of dried fish. "Do these people eat anything else? Do you have the same?"

Z'mia looked in her bad and smiled. "I'll trade you."

"Oh no!" Kay're exclaimed, shaking her head. "What do you have? Let me guess, fried locusts."

Z'mia pulled one out. "You guessed it."

"They're kind of crunchy and tasty," Kay're teased.

"They may be tasty but bad for my bowels." She placed a hand on her belly. "I will take the fish." She tossed the bag to Kay're.

"We will share the fish and bread," Kay're said. "And I still have figs." They sat and ate.

"Look," Z'mia pointed to the sky. "Those big black birds."

"The buzzards. They smell death and are waiting to feast."

"Today they will have a choice—raw or roasted flesh," Z'mia said, looking over at the dead men. A pause. "Oh, I forgot to turn on my annunciator. The ship has probably been calling and they may think I'm dead. I'm going to contact them."

"Supreme Commander," the comm-officer spoke. "Lt. Nh'Got is calling."

"I have it here," he said. "Lieutenant, report."

She filled him in about their encounter with the child, three women, and four kidnappers. She detailed how she and her friend helped the women and child escape and their fight with the men."

"Lieutenant Nh'Got I am impressed, and with your friend, too. I didn't know that you were skilled in the martial arts."

"I am, sir, as is my friend. She is more skilled than me."

"How is it that this local woman of this time is an expert in martial arts?" Tr'Tala

"I am, sir, as is my friend. She is more skilled than me."

"How is it that this local woman of this time is an expert in martial arts?" Tr'Tala asked with suspicion.

"Sir, she isn't local to Israel, but from another locale on Earth. As a youth, she learned martial arts. It's part of their religious training." Z'mia glanced at Kay're for assurance and got a nod.

"I see," said Tr'Tala. "You said her name is Lady?"

"Yes, sir. Lady. That is her name."

"Ask him about the child," Kay're whispered.

"Sir, have you been able to establish contact with the child?"

"We have tried, but she still hasn't figured out how to answer. She is about nine kilometers from your position and moving south, likely to Jerusalem. You need to get moving now."

"Yes, sir. Moving now."

"Good. We'll track both of you and keep you informed. Tr'Tala out."

"I'm relieved knowing my little self is okay and heading to Jerusalem."

"And the three women are probably with her too," Z'mia said. "We better get going."

"We need to head into the hills up to that high spot," Kay're said, pointing upward. "We can view the road for kilometers and see if anyone is coming or going. I have this feeling that my little self and the woman encountered Romans last night. They told them about the kidnappers and us. The soldiers will head this way not so much to check their story, but to find us."

"You think so? It will cost us time."

"I do. Time wasted is time saved if we encounter Romans on the road."

"You're right. To the hills." They climbed over rocks and through scrub vegetation to a height that provided a view of the road.

"There!" Z'mia exclaimed. "I see riders coming up from the south."

"Looks like Roman horsemen."

"You were right; Romans. We better get behind some cover." They bellied down behind some large rocks and watched the horsemen approach.

"One soldier is pointing up," Z'mia noticed. "Do you think they saw us?"

"He's pointing to the circling buzzards," Kay're said, looking up to the sky.

"He's pointing to the circling buzzards," Kay're said, looking up to the sky.

The soldiers went at a gallop and reached the campsite. Already buzzards were picking on the dead. The birds danced away as the soldiers approached the bodies.

"Not pretty, Decanus," commented the second officer.

Decanus Varius nodded. "They did a number on these guys. Two burned and beaten; the others had caved-in faces and heads. Anyone recognize them?" They shook their heads.

"They don't have money pouches and their canteens are empty," appraised one soldier.

"So, the women are not only killers, but thieves too," said the second.

"I wouldn't call them that," Varius corrected. "They defended themselves from murderers and kidnappers; the worst of humanity. They did us a service. They took their money and water with them as they move on."

"To where, sir?" the second asked.

Varius looked at the ground and noticed unusual foot tracks. There was a forefoot print, a gap, then a heel print. There were two distinct sets. "Let's follow these tracks." Walking, the soldiers followed them to the edge of the hills.

"They're up there somewhere," Varius said, looking up toward the women's position.

"Decanus, are we going up to find them?" the second officer asked.

"No need to. They are heading to Jerusalem."

"How do you know, sir?"

"Because I am a decanus." He gave the man a wry smile. *And soon to be a centurion.* The soldiers mounted and rode back to Jerusalem.

"I thought they saw us and were going to climb up to get us," Z'mia said.

"That young leader, he is smart. He knows we are heading to Jerusalem, and that is where he is going pronto. He'll inform Centurion. They'll be ready and waiting for us. Our task to find Tl'Rak and Jesus just got more difficult."

"But we are the 'super sleuths' of the galaxy! Special Kay and Zandra! Nothing will detour our mission," Z'mia boasted.

Kay're chuckled. "Okay, Zandra. We can return to the road. There won't be any Romans on it."

Kay're chuckled. "Okay, Zandra. We can return to the road. There won't be any Romans on it."

CHAPTER FORTY ONE
Betrayed

Commander Tl'Rak's plan to kill Jesus was simple: shoot him when he left his last supper for the Mount of Olives. All he had to do was find the house Jesus and his disciples had reserved for the Passover meal, lay in wait, and slay him.

Though Tl'Rak's mind was perverse, it was also photographic. He remembered everything in the Bible. In the Book of Luke, Jesus laid out his plans to celebrate the Passover meal before his crucifixion. He instructed Peter and John to walk into the town and they would meet a man carrying a water jar. They were to follow this man to his house. In an upper room, they would celebrate the Passover meal. The only problem was the town for the meal wasn't given. Tl'Rak needed to know the town so he could watch out for the man with the water jug meeting the disciples.

He presumed it to be Jerusalem, but it had nine gates. The Bible lacked a notation of what gate. He couldn't monitor each gate for the meeting. It would be pure luck if he picked the right one. How would Jesus's disciples know which gate to enter through? Too complicated. It had to be another town.

He pondered the situation. *The meeting house had to be close to the Mount of Olives and its Garden of Gethsemane. The Mount of Olives lies between Jerusalem and the town to the east. Was it that town? I remembered walking through it on his way to Jerusalem. It was a smaller town, with one main road in and out. I recall a grove of trees that bore fruit. It was meaty and lacked sweetness. The fruit had to be olives, for the Mount of Olives. Of course, it had to be the town mentioned in the Bible.* He hurried from Jerusalem to the town called Bethany.

Early Thursday morning, Tl'Rak went to the Mount of Olives. There he found a high perch that gave him a view of the road in and out of Bethany. He watched and waited.

watched and waited.

The Bible was true. Two men entered the town from the east and greeted a man carrying a water jar. He scurried down from his position to follow them but lost them as he entered the town. He cursed himself for being slow. The town was small yet had several streets that crisscrossed with many buildings. He eyed the structures, focusing on those that were multistory. The Bible said Jesus's Passover meal would be in an upper-level room. That was still a problem, as many of the homes were two or more levels.

As he mused the situation, two men rounded the corner. They were the ones that greeted the man with the water jar. He let them pass and backtracked after them to find several two-story homes but no men. They had to be in one of the houses. It didn't matter which one, Jesus and his disciples would have to pass this way to reach the Mount of Olives. Tonight, he would hide in the shadows, wait for Jesus, and fire! If Jesus used another home other than one of these, he still had time to run over to the Garden of Gethsemane and lay in wait. If the Bible remains true, Jesus would go there to pray before a disciple named Judas betrayed him to the mob. He would kill Jesus before that occurred.

Little Kay're and the women left the Roman campsite at sunrise and rode toward Jerusalem. At mid-afternoon, they entered Bethany, and decided to stay there for the night. They found a room at an inn, paying with the money adult Kay're had given to her younger self. Little Kay're had passed that money bag to the women. She still had the small money sack taken from one man eaten by the lions.

Before settling in for the night, the women and child went to the market. They purchased unleavened bread and some lamb for their Passover meal. While in the market, Kay're spotted the man she had given food to in Nazareth. He was the same one Jesus had healed, and who had tossed away the talking disk. Even from a distance, she sensed his evil thoughts about Jesus. *Jesus must be nearby or he wouldn't be here. I'll look for him after we eat.*

It was late afternoon when Decanus Varius led his troops into Jerusalem. He dismounted and walked over to Centurion Marcus's tent. Marcus had seen him ride

ride in and was waiting.

"Decanus, you have returned empty-handed; no child, no women."

"We didn't see the child, Centurion. But the women will be in Jerusalem tomorrow," he declared with confidence.

"Really," Marcus said, taking a seat behind his desk. "Why so?"

"Sir, last night we found three women and a child sneaking up on our camp. I questioned them. They told me they escaped four murdering kidnappers with the help of two other women. One rescuer had short hair. The other woman's looks, they're not sure of, only that she was tall, like the other one. The escapees feared with tears that these two women gave their lives for them. I thought otherwise, knowing these two women were the ones you sought. They would easily deal with those four men.

"At dawn, I released the three women and the child and took my men north to investigate. I found the campsite and four dead men. Two were burned beyond recognition and the others had crushed faces and head wounds." He paused to catch his breath. Marcus had a thin smile on his face, pleased to know the woman were alive.

"Then I saw two distinct sets of footprints that had to be the women leading south to the hills. It was then that I knew they were heading to Jerusalem. All we have to do is wait for them to arrive and arrest them."

"Why do you think they are coming to Jerusalem?"

"Sir, their trail of beaten and killed men follows the route of the one called Jesus of Nazareth.   Jesus is in the area for the Jewish Passover. The women will be here tomorrow!"

"Decanus, your reasoning is sound," Marcus praised. "I trust you to post sentries to be on the lookout for these two women. I have a feeling the child will be here too. Refresh yourself and then assign your men."

"Yes, Centurion," Varius said boldly. He gave a breast salute and departed.

Marcus leaned back in his seat and smiled. "Leadership has a way of maturing a young officer," he told himself. "And tomorrow the women will stand here before me." Marcus took a long drink of wine; unknowing tomorrow would change his life forever.

The sun was beginning to set when Kay're and Z'mia Nh'Got plopped down on a log to rest and eat. Z'mia checked in with her ship. Tr'Tala told her she was fifteen kilometers from a town called Bethany and that the child was there, too.

"What do you think?" Z'mia asked wearily.

Kay're sighed, exhausted. "Tl'Rak hasn't made his move yet, or we wouldn't be here. But he will tonight, likely at the Mount of Olives."

"Why there?"

"As I remember in the Bible, Jesus had his last supper tonight, a bit after sunset. After the meal, he, and the disciples head to the Mount of Olives to pray. While Jesus prayed, his disciples fell asleep and only woke when the mob led by Judas came to arrest Jesus. The mob will take Jesus to Jerusalem for trial and then execution tomorrow. Tl'Rak's best chance to kill him will be while he prays tonight."

"Do you think we can make the Mount of Olives before Jesus gets there?"

"Maybe if we make a fast pace. Do you have the energy?"

It was Z'mia's turn to sigh. "We are super sleuths and we have to save the day again. Let us go."

At sunset, Tl'Rak took a position behind a cart near the homes he had seen in the morning. He hoped Jesus and his disciples would choose one of them to use for their Passover celebration. Tl'Rak waited, and then Jesus and twelve men appeared and headed to one home. They disappeared inside. Tl'Rak grinned. "Have your last supper, because that is what it will be—your last!"

The three women and little Kay're had their Passover meal. The women gave extra thanks for their escape. With tears, they asked God to show favor to the spirits of the two women who saved them. After the meal, little Kay're said she needed to step outside. She held her belly, showing nature was calling. They told her to be careful in the dark.

Little Kay're scurried around town searching for Jesus and the evil man. She saw the evil one behind a cart. Staying in the shadows, she moved closer to him. While she was sneaking up on him, Jesus and his disciples emerged from a house. They started walking toward her and the evil man.

house. They started walking toward her and the evil man.

Tl'Rak bobbed his head as he saw Jesus and his people leave the home. Jesus was in the lead. Even in the dark, Tl'Rak had a perfect shot. Slowly, he withdrew the blaster from under his cloak. He set it to its highest setting. The shot would blast Jesus to pieces. There would be no doubt of his death and no way to resuscitate him.

As he brought the weapon up, he heard the word, no ring in his head. Then he heard it again, but louder. He shook his head to clear it.

"You must not hurt Jesus," came a small voice from behind. He turned to see a small girl staring at him. Her eyes fixed on him and froze his thinking. Seconds passed, and he twisted his head to free his eyes and mind.

"You," he whispered so as not to give his position away. "You're the child who gave me food at the well."

"And you are the one Jesus healed by a miracle. Why do you want to hurt Jesus, who saved you from dying? Why? Why?" She placed the words in his head.

"Go away," he said softly with a wave of his hand.

"No!"

Tl'Rak raised his free hand to hit her. The child backed away, but kept feeding his mind with *Why? Why?*

Again, he shook his head and glanced back to the street. Jesus had passed by and his followers were surrounding him. He missed the kill shot. Screwing his face in anger, he turned back to the girl, but she had disappeared.

Little Kay're raced to the next street, hoping to intercept Jesus. But Jesus wasn't there. Panting out of breath and in desperation, she ran to the next intersection; no Jesus there. In the dark, she had lost her sense of direction. She stood alone in the middle of the street. Tears welled and rolled down her cheeks. She cried out, "Jesus, where are you?" The night didn't answer. She kicked the dirt and ambled down the street.

Tl'Rak followed Jesus and his followers to the Mount of Olives. Just as the Bible said, Jesus left his disciples to pray and after a while returned only to find them sleeping. He returned to his place of prayer.

In the distance, Tl'Rak could see torches approaching. The mob led by Judas Iscariot

In the distance, Tl'Rak could see torches approaching. The mob led by Judas Iscariot was coming. Judas would betray his master with a kiss, and the mob would arrest Jesus. "Too bad," Tl'Rak whispered to himself. "For history's sake, I would have enjoyed seeing the betrayal. And the servant, having his ear cut off and healed by Jesus. But it won't happen. I'll have to watch the shock on everyone's face when they see Jesus blasted to bits." He let out a guttural laugh.

Being some fifty meters away from Jesus, he inched closer and waited for Judas to plant the kiss. After which, he would shoot, and the debris of Jesus's body would cover everyone. He smirked and pulled out his blaster.

With feet sore, legs heavy, and winded, Kay're and Z'mia Nh'Got made Bethany. At the town's well, they drank to the fullest. It was dark and the only lights were from the homes that were observing Passover. As they filled their canteens, a man came for water. "Excuse me, where is the Mount of Olives?" Kay're asked the man.

"Just west of here. Stay on the road. It will be on the left." He drew water and left the women.

"We know that Jesus is still alive as we are still in the present," Z'mia said.

"But for how long?" Kay're asked. "Let us get moving before everything changes."

They hurried their pace. Soon moonlight showed olive trees dotting the mountainside. Up ahead, they saw a large grove of trees in a flat area. Amongst the trees, there was a lone figure creeping.

"Tl'Rak," Z'mia whispered. "I recognize his figure."

"That must be the Garden of Gethsemane," Kay're said in a low voice.

"Jesus must be there praying."

"Look!" Z'mia exclaimed. "Up the road, lights are moving this way,"

"Must be the crowd led by Judas Iscariot coming to arrest Jesus. I'm sure Tl'Rak must have seen them too. He will act soon. We need to intercept him."

"I'll do that," Z'mia said, tapping her chest. "Then you come up from behind him and jump him."

"Okay. Let us go," Kay're said eagerly, smiling.

Z'mia raced toward him. "Commander Tl'Rak," she said, stepping in front of him.

Z'mia raced toward him. "Commander Tl'Rak," she said, stepping in front of him.

"Nh'Got," he said with a wry smile. "I don't have time to listen to your story. Step aside. I have a mission to complete."

"You mean to kill Jesus of Nazareth?" she said, holding her ground.

"And return glory to Valerii!" He pushed past her.

As he did so, Z'mia grasped him by the arm.

"You fool!" he sneered and raised his hand holding the blaster to club her. Before the blow landed, Kay're hit him with a flying tackle. They both thumped to the ground the blaster flying from his hands. Hitting Tl'Rak was like running into a tree. He was thick and strong; it took her breath.

Tl'Rak got to his knees and glanced at the sprawled women. "It's you!" He pointed at Kay're and looked around for the blaster. It was next to Nh'Got. He scrambled up and went for it. As he did so, Kay're tripped him. He went headlong to the ground right to the weapon. He smiled, grasped it, and then yelped as Z'mia brought her boot down on his hand. In anger, he swiped his free hand and hit her in the leg. She stumbled back and fell.

Flexing his hand, he picked up the blaster and stood to kill Kay're. As he turned toward her, she jumped up and placed a snap kick under his chin. His head whipped back, but he held steady. He pointed his weapon at her. The shot never came as Z'mia tackled him in the legs. Again, he stood his ground, but it gave Kay're time to do a reverse jumping spin kick. She caught him flush on the temple. He staggered, his eyes rolling up. Finally, he fell and lay still in the night air.

"Is he dead?" Z'mia asked, gulping air.

Kay're reached down and checked for a pulse. "He is still alive." She took the blaster from his hand and gave it to Z'mia. "Better for you to have it."

"The crowd is here," Z'mia said, taking the weapon.

"Let's watch," Kay're said. They scurried into the trees and saw Jesus standing before the mob. Then a man approached Jesus and kissed him.

"You betray the Son of Man with a kiss?" Jesus said to Judas. One of Jesus's followers drew a sword and cut off the high priest's servant's ear. The crowd became more incensed. Jesus then touched the man and healed his ear, quieting the mob.

crowd became more incensed. Jesus then touched the man and healed his ear, quieting the mob.

"You have come out as if I am a thief with swords and clubs," Jesus said to the chief priest and elders. "Daily I was with you in the temple and you reached out with no hands against me, but this is your hour and the power of darkness."

The mob didn't respond to him but led him away to Jerusalem. Kay're and Z'mia noticed a single man following them. "Who is that?" Z'mia asked.

"I think it was one of his disciples, the one called Peter. We better get Tl'Rak tied up."

They returned to where they left him, but he wasn't there. Z'mia grimaced. Once again, she had let him slip away. "I need to call the ship." She sighed, knowing Tr'Tala wouldn't be happy.

Aboard the *Lionare,* everyone was pensive. They knew that if Tl'Rak killed Jesus Christ, this could be the night that changed their lives forever. "Supreme Commander, Lt. Nh'Got is calling. You have her, sir."

"Lieutenant Nh'Got, report."

She managed a dry swallow. "Supreme Commander, we have stopped Tl'Rak." She paused for another swallow. Tr'Tala blew out a breath of relief. "Sir, we saw Jesus betrayed and arrested by his people and led away to Jerusalem as written in their Bible. Tomorrow the Romans will execute him and then his people bury him in a tomb. While in the tomb, he will transport up to the ship in orbit for resuscitation. Three days from now he will return to earth for his resurrection."

"Good work, Lieutenant. Is Tl'Rak dead?"

"No, sir. We knocked him out. But he slipped away while we were watching the mob arrest Jesus. I have his blaster!" she exclaimed quickly to soften Tr'Tala's displeasure. There was a long pause.

"Lieutenant, that means Tl'Rak is still a danger. If I remember correctly, Jesus remained on Earth for forty days before he returned to his world. So Tl'Rak has that many days to hunt him down and kill him."

To her surprise, he didn't berate her for allowing him to escape again. "Supreme Commander, without his blaster it will be very difficult for him to kill

"Supreme Commander, without his blaster it will be very difficult for him to kill Jesus. His followers are always surrounding him," Lt Nh'Got countered.

"But it's not impossible," Tr'Tala said.

Then the comm-officer interrupted him. "Supreme Commander, I have been studying the Bible since our arrival here. After Jesus's resurrection, his body changes into a glorified one. With this body, he is only recognizable to those he chooses, mainly his apostles and a few select men and women. That will leave out all others, including Commander Tl'Rak. Lt. Nh'Got, and her friend. The time continuum will be safe."

"Yes, I remember reading that too," Tr'Tala agreed. "I wonder if he is a shape-shifter too? Lt. Nh'Got did you copy this?"

"I did, sir. I'm sure Commander Tl'Rak read the same. I wonder if he will remember that fact."

"If he remembers or not, I want him dead or secured in bindings waiting for transport to the ship." His voice remained calm. "I don't want to hear again that he has escaped."

"And you will not, Supreme Commander," Nh'Got assured.

"Good. Lieutenant, as unpleasant as it will be, I want you to witness the execution of Jesus and his burial. Then I want you to keep watch on his tomb for his return in three days. He may reappear as he was and then shape-shift. So, be alert. Jesus will leave the tomb in some form. I want you there to see, but keep yourself hidden from his view."

"I will, sir."

"Lieutenant Nh'Got, I will hold you to your word. Get some sleep. Tomorrow and the next few days will be long for you and I take it, your friend."

"Sir, she will be with me."

"Okay. Tr'Tala out."

"He took the news of Tl'Rak's escape better than I thought he would," Z'mia said. "What do you think, sleep here tonight or go to Jerusalem?"

Kay're sighed. "Jerusalem will be too dangerous tonight. Roman soldiers will be all over the place with Jesus there and the mob. I'm tired. Let's stay here. No one will be around here anymore tonight. Can that weapon start a fire?"

"It can. I agree we should stay here. Tomorrow there will be a crowd following Jesus to his execution. We can blend in with them to witness his death if you want to. But I have to see it."

"I will be with you. As your commander said, it won't be pleasant to see."

Z'mia nodded. "Let us gather some wood for the fire." They did, and Z'mia used the blaster to start a fire. They would have a restless sleep with thoughts of tomorrow's event playing in their heads.

CHAPTER FORTY TWO
Death on a Cross

After a long day, Centurion Marcus finally reclined on his cot for a night's sleep. If what Decanus Varius said was true about the two women, they would stand before him in his tent. He was unsure whether to bring charges against them. Surely the soldiers beaten and maimed by the two would want them tried. If the soldiers pressed him, he would threaten to charge them with assault with intent to rape the women. But what to do with the women? He would undoubtedly grill them on the standards of who, why, where, and what.

As he lay staring upward, he could still see the one woman's face and hear her voice in his head. She had a beautiful face, kind eyes, and a benevolent mind. Yet he knew she was deadly if threatened. And where did she learn to fight like a caged lion? Certainly not in Israel, where women were subservient to men, as were all the women he knew. This woman wasn't. What about the other woman? Another skilled fighter, but lacking the ability to enter one's mind. Were they sisters?

Then there was the child. She had the same face, eyes, and mental ability as the one woman. Again, he wondered if they were the same person. He shook his head, knowing that was impossible. *Yet, the woman knew new about my encounter with the child when she almost took my life. Too many unknowns and questions.* He smiled. "Tomorrow I will have answers. Varius, you had better be right," he said to an empty tent.

As he closed his eyes to sleep, a loud commotion sounded outside his tent. He heaved a breath, grabbed his sword, and went outside in his underclothes. There was a large crowd passing him. He saw Varius outside his tent and called to him, "Varius what's going on?"

"I don't know, sir," he replied hurriedly.

"Find out and report to me."

"Yes, sir. Let me change into my uniform."

"Find out and report to me."

"Yes, sir. Let me change into my uniform."

Marcus nodded and returned inside and sat on his cot. He brushed a hand through his hair and sighed. "No sleep tonight." It would take Varius several minutes to investigate, so he got up, poured himself some wine, and sat at his desk. Thirty minutes passed before Decanus Varius announced his presence.

"Sir, I have found out that the Jewish religious leaders have arrested Jesus of Nazareth. The charge is blasphemy against their teachings. They want him executed and are bringing him before Pontius Pilate to have him sentenced to death."

Marcus shook his head. "Unbelievable. They're nothing but pompous hypocrites. It makes me sick seeing them walking around in flowing robes with a holier-than-thou attitude. They fear that Jesus will usurp them, relegating them to common Jews. He has committed no crimes against the empire, and Pilate will wave them away."

"I'm not so sure, sir," Varius countered. "I have heard rumors that Pilate doesn't want any troubles with the locals. He wants Herod and Rome to believe that he is doing a good job of keeping the peace and stability here."

"Just wonderful," Marcus said, taking a swallow of wine. Jesus had healed him, and he had great respect for the man and wanted nothing bad for him. He even wondered if Jesus was God. And if he was, why would he allow all this to happen to him? "Well, let's hope Pilate has a spine and refutes them and releases him. If he affirms the sentence, it may stir up more trouble than the man's death is worth. I understand Jesus has a large following and has miraculously healed many. They'll be unhappy with his death."

"Sir, Pilate probably hasn't thought that far ahead. He thinks the death of another Jew will not matter if it maintains the status quo in Jerusalem."

Marcus nodded, though disturbed by the idea. "Varius, those two women may be here now. They may have infiltrated the crowd that brought in Jesus."

"Yes, sir, that is a possibility." Marcus gave him that certain look. "Yes, sir, I will take some men and search for them now."

"If you find them, send someone to let me know. I want you to place them in a holding cell until morning, then bring them here. I want a night's sleep before questioning them."

them in a holding cell until morning, then bring them here. I want a night's sleep before questioning them."

"As you command, sir," Varius said with a salute. He left the tent and Marcus returned to his cot. He laid down, but the thought of Jesus' execution bothered him greatly. And with the women possibly being here now, there was no way he could sleep. He rose, dressed, and walked into the night to join the hunt for them.

He searched the shadows and the streets of Jerusalem without fear. With soldiers all around the city, a shout would bring them to his assistance. He also knew the women reacted only when threatened or assaulted, that, he wouldn't do. With Jesus's arrest and the commotion around it, he decided not to press any charges against the women. All he wanted to do was question them.

He felt a personal connection to the woman who entered his mind. Though she almost killed him, he found her alluring and attractive. She was a woman he could fall in love with. After many minutes of searching, he found himself on the fringe of the palace courtyard. There he spotted Decanus Varius and waved for him.

"Your report?" he asked the decanus.

"I and my men have found no trace of them, but there are several women around the fire. They could be among them." Varius pointed them out.

"I see them," Marcus said. "We'll watch them for a while before we move. Position your men at all access points. If they respond, they aren't to hurt the women. Just surround them. Understood?"

"Yes, Centurion."

"Okay, give the word, then return here. I'll wait for you." Varius returned a quick salute and disappeared into the darkness. Marcus assessed the women in the courtyard. Most were short in stature and some had long hair flowing from under their headdress. Two women sat by the fire with their heads down. *Could they be the women?*

Varius returned to the centurion's side. "The men are in position," he said.

"Those two women sitting by the fire." Marcus pointed them out. "Do you recognize them?"

Varius squinted his eyes and shook his head. "I can't tell in the low light. Shall we approach them?"

"Yes, now."

you recognize them?"

Varius squinted his eyes and shook his head. "I can't tell in the low light. Shall we approach them?"

"Yes, now."

As they moved, one woman standing by the fire pointed down at a man who was sitting. "You were also with that Nazarene, Jesus," she accused him.

"I don't know what you are talking about," the man denied, and got up and went to the courtyard entry. Then another woman approached him.

"This man is one of them," she accused. Again, the man denied it. In the background, a rooster crowed.

Marcus and Varius held their position, watching the scene play out. Then a few more accused the man. "Surely you are one of them, for you are Galilean."

The man began calling down curses and swore at them. "I don't know what you are talking about." Then a rooster crowed for the second time, and the man departed quickly.

Marcus and Varius approached the fire where the two women sat cross-legged. "Have you no accusation against that man?" Marcus asked them. They kept their heads down and said "no" in unison.

"Show me your faces," Marcus demanded.

The women looked up. One woman's face was youthful, but sun-baked with wrinkles. She was a field worker and not the woman he sought. The other was older and also showed signs of a field worker. Likely the mother of the other. Marcus shook his head and walked away with Varius at his side.

"I am calling it a night," Marcus said. "You had better be right about your claim that the women will be here." He left Varius standing mid-salute. The decanus let out a sigh and he went to his tent. He would be up before sunrise looking for the women. He hoped he wasn't wrong.

Managing only a few hours of sleep, Varius was up before the sun. He went to each of the nine gates to check with the sentries. None of them had seen women matching the description given to them. The main gate held a large crowd that was heading to the palace courtyard. He followed and went inside to talk with his contact there.

He was another decanus who assisted Pontius Pilate. He told Varius that Pilate

He was another decanus who assisted Pontius Pilate. He told Varius that Pilate wanted Jesus released, but the Jews wanted to put him to death. Pilate planned to give the Jews a choice of whom to release; Jesus the Nazarene or the notorious criminal Barabbas. Surely, they wouldn't want Barabbas released to continue his murdering, thieving ways. If they chose Barabbas, Pilate's next move would be to have the Nazarene flogged and parade him before the Jews. He hoped the sickening sight of a beaten, half-dead man would show them that Jesus wasn't the king of the Jews or a God. They would dismiss him and go home.

"Let's hope it doesn't come to that," Varius said. "The man is innocent."

"We'll see. These locals are a stubborn lot."

Varius nodded and thanked his friend. As he was leaving, there was a chant from the crowd, "Crucify him!" Varius shook his head and hurried to inform Centurion Marcus.

Marcus was up when Varius announced his presence. "Come in," Marcus said. Varius entered and related the news about Jesus.

"This is getting out of control," Marcus said while munching on figs.

"I agree, sir. The man is innocent."

"Any word about the women?"

"I checked with the men at all the gates and nothing, sir."

"It is early yet. They'll probably enter through the main gate and mix in with the crazies that want Jesus dead. We need to keep a sharp eye on that gate. Okay, let's go. But I want to swing around to the palace to see what is going on with my own eyes."

The sun was already over the horizon before Kay're and Z'mia Nh'Got stretched the weariness from their bodies. The fatigue from yesterday's long journey and fight with Tl'Rak made for a long sleep. Nh'Got checked in with the ship for a status update and everything was the same. Tr'Tala said the child was moving toward Jerusalem.

"Look. Many people are heading toward Jerusalem," Z'mia said.

"Likely heading toward Golgotha, the place where they will crucify Jesus."

"We slept well past sunrise. Do you think they have already crucified him?"

"It happens around mid-morning," Kay're replied, looking up at the sky. "Judging by the sun's low position, it's still early. We had better get moving."

"We slept well past sunrise. Do you think they have already crucified him?"

"It happens around mid-morning," Kay're replied, looking up at the sky. "Judging by the sun's low position, it's still early. We had better get moving."

They ate a few olives from the trees and headed to Golgotha. They mixed in with several other men and women heading the same way. All had sober faces, no doubt followers of Jesus. The women didn't see the child.

Marcus and Varius reached the palace courtyard. The crowd there kept chanting, "Crucify him! Crucify him!" Pilate was standing on a portico and waved his hands at them. "Who do you want to be released? Barabbas, or Jesus the Nazarene?"

The crowd shouted, "Barabbas!"

Pilate turned around and motioned to the soldiers. They brought the Nazarene out onto the palace steps. He was wearing a scarlet robe and a crown of thrones. The soldiers stripped the robe from him, revealing his severely scourged and bloody body. He was weak and could barely stand. Marcus shook his head in disgust. Varius held a shocked face.

"Is this the man you want me to crucify?" Pilate asked. "Is this the King of the Jews? I hardly think so."

The crowd continued their chant, "Crucify him!"

Pilate sighed and washed his hands in a bowl. He nodded to the soldiers who placed the robe back on the Nazarene. They led him from the palace steps and through the crowd that shouted insults and spat upon him.

"This is a mockery of justice," Varius said.

"Not only that, but an insult to us as Roman soldiers," Marcus added. "We stand for honor; not anymore." The word echoed in his head and he remembered the woman. *I dishonored myself when I first encountered her. Lust got the better of me and three of my men paid with their lives because of it, and I almost too. She had honor and showed mercy.* He blew out a breath and noticed Pontius Pilate motioning for him. Marcus acknowledged and told Varius to wait while he went to see what Pilate wanted.

"Centurion Marcus," Pilate said to him from his seat. "I have a job for you. As you know, the self-proclaimed 'King of the Jews' will die this morning. The two criminals you brought in a few weeks ago will join him. They are of no significance.

you. As you know, the self-proclaimed 'King of the Jews' will die this morning. The two criminals you brought in a few weeks ago will join him. They are of no significance. But the Nazarene's crucifixion is significant to everyone, both for and against. I want you to provide perimeter security until he is dead."

"As you command," Marcus said without emotion.

"I see on your face that you don't agree with the death sentence of the Jew."

"I will carry out your orders."

"Come now, Marcus, you can speak freely," Pilate urged him on with a hand wave.

"What I feel or believe is of no consequence. I'm loyal to the empire and follow orders."

Pilate smiled. "That's a clever response. Marcus, I have received excellent reports about you from the short time you have been in Israel. And couriers from Rome say you are held in high favor there. Also, they say there are rumors of a promotion for you and a recall to Rome. That is good news for you."

"Governor, the winds of power in Rome frequently change direction."

"Yes, they do. I'm impressed with your cunning and loyalty. I would hate to lose you to Rome. I can see a promotion for you here. Now to another matter. Those two women and child you are after, I would like to question them myself." A pause. Marcus blinked, surprised Pilot knew of them.

"I have ears all over Israel. Nothing escapes me. On my word as governor, I won't harm the women."

"Yes, Governor. And the child?"

"Oh, I would like to see how cute she is and ask her a few questions. Then I will return her to your custody."

"And what will happen to the women after you question them?"

"I won't turn them over to the Jews. Mostly, it will depend on their answers. Centurion Marcus, you have a job to do, so go do it."

Marcus gave a salute and left, feeling disturbed by what Pilate may do to the women. He rejoined Decanus Varius and told him about his new task. "Muster up a dozen men on horseback and meet me at the main gate." Varius saluted and hurried to the barracks. Marcus went to get his horse.

saluted and hurried to the barracks. Marcus went to get his horse.

Kay're and Z'mia Nh'Got kept up with the group heading to Golgotha. Many people were whispering their lament that the great Teacher was going to his death. When they reached the skull-shaped hill of execution, they saw Jesus of Nazareth there. The soldiers were stripping off his robe. His back was to Kay're and Nh'Got.

"Oh, my!" Z'mia exclaimed softly. "They beat the flesh off his body! I want to blast those filthy Romans for what they have done." She reached under her dress for the weapon.

Kay're touched Z'mia's hand. "No. And the worst is yet to come," she demurred. They watched as the soldiers forced Jesus down onto a makeshift wooden cross. They drove nails through his wrists and feet; blood spewing from the sites. Jesus writhed in pain. Kay're and Z'mia winced at the barbaric sight. Z'mia fumed and again wanted to blast the soldiers. She sucked in a breath and exhaled her anger. Kay're held a stoic face, though inside she was angry and fighting back tears.

The soldiers hoisted the cross-bearing Jesus and secured it in the ground. Nailed above his head was an inscription, INRI. It translated to Jesus of Nazareth, King of the Jews. Women in the crowd wept openly.

Paraded through the crowd by the soldiers were two other men carrying their crosses. Kay're recognized them as the robbers that had jumped her. One caught sight of her.

"There's that woman," he muttered through his pain. The other turned his head to Kay're and swore at her. The people around Kay're looked at her. They were wondering if she was the woman of the rumors; the one who had beaten these two men to the point of death. She kept her head down, hiding her face.

Centurion Marcus, who was on a horse behind the crowd, saw several people turn and stare at one person. He hadn't heard the prisoner curse, nor could he see who the people were looking at. He moved his horse through the crowd for a look, but a loud voice caught his attention.

"This is no place for a child! Get her out of here!"

Marcus glanced that way to see the back of the child moving into the throng of people. He guided his horse in that direction. "Where is that child?" he asked.

One man thumbed toward the back, and Marcus dismounted and walked his

"This is no place for a child! Get her out of here!"

Marcus glanced that way to see the back of the child moving into the throng of people. He guided his horse in that direction. "Where is that child?" he asked.

One man thumbed toward the back, and Marcus dismounted and walked his horse to the rear. He didn't find the child and remounted and surveyed the area. He didn't see her, nor any women resembling the two he sought. His attention returned to the execution.

The soldiers had pushed the criminals forward and crucified them; one to each side of Jesus. As the three hung in agony, many people approached and hurled insults at Jesus. The Jewish chief priests and elders also mocked him, saying, "He saved others, but he can't save himself! Let this Messiah, this king of Israel, come down now from the cross, that we may see and believe."

Even one crucified with Jesus also heaped insults on him. The one on his left side said, "Aren't you the Messiah? Save yourself and us!"

The other to Jesus's right rebuked his fellow thief. "Don't you fear God? You are under the same sentence. Our punishment is just. We are getting what our deeds deserve. But this man has done nothing wrong." He glanced at Jesus and said, "Jesus, remember me when you come into your kingdom."

Jesus turned his head to him. "I tell you the truth, today you will be with me in paradise."

Kay're, upon hearing this, shivered. She remembered putting her boot to the thief's throat and looking into his eyes, knowing his destiny was death on a cross.

Time seemed to creep as Kay're and Z'mia soberly gazed at the horror of death by crucifixion. After many minutes, Jesus uttered, "I thirst."

The soldiers then offered him sour wine on a sponge and mocked him. "If you are the King of the Jews, save yourself." They laughed and hurled further insults. Centurion Marcus could only shake his head in disgust. Another display of dishonor.

Then three women approached the cross. Kay're recognized two of them: Mary of Magdala and Mary, the wife of Cleopas. "I don't know the other," she said to Z'mia.

"That's Jesus's mother, Mary," said a young man. He joined the three women at the foot of Jesus' cross.

Jesus upon seeing them said, "Woman, behold thy son!" After that, he said to the said to Z'mia.

"That's Jesus's mother, Mary," said a young man. He joined the three women at the foot of Jesus' cross.

Jesus upon seeing them said, "Woman, behold thy son!" After that, he said to the man, "Son, behold thy mother!" The man placed an arm around Jesus's mother.

Time passed and more people insulted Jesus and left. Many stayed waiting to see if there would be a miracle while others waited to see him expire. Centurion Marcus and Decanus Varius continued their watch over the onlookers. They kept a keen eye out for the child and the two women. Varius was anxious and becoming more so as the minutes passed. He had assured Marcus the women would be here, and up until now, they were absent, at least from his and Marcus's view.

Kay're and Z'mia kept their heads down and looked forward. They knew the centurion and his men were watching and looking for them. Occasionally, the women would give sidelong glances to assess the crowd and soldiers' positions. Both were concerned that Tl'Rak was in the throng somewhere and could act.

At about midday, Jesus cried out with a loud voice, "My God, my God, why hast thou forsaken me?" Quickly, from the west dark clouds rolled in, plunging all of Israel into darkness. Lightening roiled across the sky and thunder rumbled. Everyone on Golgotha felt the sudden change in the air. Many mumbled to each other. Some fled while others hurled more insults at Jesus.

He again looked up and declared, "Father, forgive them; for they know not what they do."

Centurion Marcus nodded. He felt deep sadness watching the man that saved his life die in such an agonizing way. As time passed, the darkness deepened, and lightning increased in frequency and intensity. Those on the cross could barely gasp a breath. Death was coming soon, and everyone knew it.

Now a hooded figure walked into the crowd. He moved his way to the front and fixed his eyes on Jesus, whose head was down. The man turned his head to the left; his eyes met Z'mia Nh'Got.

"Tl'Rak," Z'mia whispered to Kay're. "To our right." Kay're stepped forward a bit to get a look at him. The man sneered at her. Kay're wanted to place the thought *we will get you* in his head but refrained.

"What do you think he is up to?" Z'mia asked.

forward a bit to get a look at him. The man sneered at her. Kay're wanted to place the thought *we will get you* in his head but refrained.

"What do you think he is up to?" Z'mia asked.

"Waiting for Jesus to die and then follow to his burial site."

"Probably to steal his body or mutilate it before it transports up to his ship," Z'mia conjectured.

"More like lying in wait for three days and jumping Jesus when leaves his tomb," Kay're offered. "We'll be there and stop him. You have the weapon to do so."

Decanus Varius noticed Tl'Rak walk to the front. It was hard not to. Tl'Rak was a big man. Varius saw him look to his left and hold his gaze at someone. "That large man up front," he said to Marcus. "He is staring at someone."

"I see," Marcus said. "Two tall figures and they're looking back at him. They have to be the women."

"Do you think he's in league with them?"

"Maybe. Let's watch before we make our move. They're not going anywhere now. We'll also take the man. Alert your men. Be discreet about it so as not to alarm the man or women."

"Yes, sir," Varius said, smiling. He felt relieved that the women were here and soon to be in custody. After a few minutes, Varius returned to Marcus's side. "All is ready." As they watched the three, the child came to the man's side. She stared up at him and the man touched his head.

"Repent! Repent!" Were the words he heard a voice in his head. At first, he thought it was Jesus who put the words in his mind but sensed a familiar presence at his side. He shook his head to clear it and looked down. "It is you," he said to the child.

"You need to ask for forgiveness before Jesus dies," the child said with tears.

"Why, so you can stop sniveling? Because of you, he is dying a terrible death. I could have made it painless and instant. So, keep crying and watch your hope of getting home die," Tl'Rak said with a smug chuckle.

"You're a very mean man," the girl declared, wiping her eyes.

"Soon I'll be even meaner," he said to her and glanced back at Nh'Got and her friend. Her friend's eyes bore into his and he shivered.

"You're a very mean man," the girl declared, wiping her eyes.

"Soon I'll be even meaner," he said to her and glanced back at Nh'Got and her friend. Her friend's eyes bore into his and he shivered.

"You will never get the chance. My tears will be yours," he heard in his head. Again, he shook his head and realization took hold. With mouth agape, he looked down at the child, but she had left him. He turned to look for her, but hesitated as Jesus spoke.

"Father, into Thy hands I commend my spirit," Jesus said in a loud voice.

Now across the heavens, lightning spread. Bolts struck the ground in various places, creating thunder cracks that the Earth had never heard before. The ground heaved and rolled violently, throwing those on horseback to the ground. Graves below Golgotha were opened, revealing the dead. People began shrieking and tried to run, but fell because of the quaking. There was no immediate escape from the displeasure of God.

CHAPTER FORTY THREE
Three Days

The quake subsided, and people were stumbling to stand. Many who were unhurt ran from the mountain of death. Several on horseback suffered injuries, some knocked unconscious. Decanus Varius lay moaning in pain, his face bloodied on one side. Centurion Marcus sat dazed.

Kay're and Z'mia Nh'Got stood and dusted themselves off. Looking around, they saw the carnage of the Roman horse soldiers. There wouldn't be any danger from them. Searching for the centurion conducting the execution, they saw a man trembling in fear.

"Truly this was the Son of God!" he cried out. He dropped to the ground and his men huddled next to him. After a few minutes, he stood. "Let's get this over with." He nodded to one of his men. One soldier took a club and broke the legs of one thief to quicken his death by suffocation. Though nearly dead, he howled in agony, causing Kay're and Z'mia to shiver.

The cruelty of humanity was unsettling. When the soldier was about to hit Jesus, another soldier stopped him and jabbed his spear into Jesus's side. When Jesus did not flinch, the soldier with the club moved on to the other thief and swung his club again. The distinct snap of bones brought out a last wail of pain. Thus ended the execution of two men, guilty of crimes against Rome, and one man guilty of being the Son of God.

Kay're now wished she would have ended the thieves' lives on the trail to spare them the horror of crucifixion. But to do so would have changed the time continuum. Her consolation: one man gained paradise. Sadly, the other man was condemned to eternal damnation and pain. She looked back at the centurion she had battled previously. Her younger self was standing in front of him.

The child bent down and touched the centurion's face. His eyes fluttered. He could see the blurry outline of a face. He reached out to touch it. What he felt

felt was velvet soft and wet with tears. He knew it was the child. She placed a relaxing thought in his head and the pain subsided; her face came into focus.

He saw a weak, forlorn face with tears streaming down her cheeks. He could feel her sadness over Jesus' death. He managed a smile. "I know. I feel the same," he said to her. She willed a smile. Marcus tapped her on the shoulder and looked past her to see the woman that stirred his emotions staring at him. He then heard "thank you" in his head and wondered if she was thanking him for his gentleness with the child. Or was she simply being kind? He nodded at her. She returned the same. Marcus tried to stand, and as he did, wooziness overcame him and he settled back to the ground. The child touched him on the forehead and left him.

Z'mia Nh'Got noticed Tl'Rak again. He was disheveled with a bloody gash on one cheek. He stood staring at Jesus, who hung motionless on his cross. Two other men stepped past him, moving toward Jesus's mother, who sat on the ground before her son. Z'mia sighed in relief as she recognized one man as Joseph of Arimathea. He had helped her with Tl'Rak on the road to meet Jesus on the mount. The other, she didn't know. They went to Mary of Magdala and John who were holding each other. She nudged Kay're, who was watching her younger self move away.

"I know that man," she said, pointing to him.

"I know him too," Kay're replied. "I met him on the road. He is Joseph of Arimathea. I don't know the other."

Joseph and his friend stooped to talk to Jesus's mother and then approached the centurion. They talked a bit, and the centurion motioned his soldiers to bring a ladder to the cross bearing Jesus. Joseph and his friend mounted the ladder and began, with great care, taking the body of Jesus down. The centurion hammered out the nail from Jesus's feet. Using a very long strip of linen with broad straps fastened to it, Joseph and his friend lowered the body. They then wrapped the body in linen and placed it on a sheet in his mother's arms.

Kay're and Z'mia were crying, completely overwhelmed with sorrow. They wanted to pay their respects to Mary but held back, giving the grieving mother time with her son. After a while, Joseph, his friend, and the Centurion removed the body from Golgotha to a garden area. There, they placed the body in a tomb.

From a distance, Kay're and Z'mia had followed the burial procession and watched Jesus being placed in the tomb. The men sealed the tomb with a large rock. Then the mother time with her son. After a while, Joseph, his friend, and the Centurion removed the body from Golgotha to a garden area. There, they placed the body in a tomb.

From a distance, Kay're and Z'mia had followed the burial procession and watched Jesus being placed in the tomb. The men sealed the tomb with a large rock. Then the centurion and his men stood guard. Joseph, his friend, Mary, and John departed the garden.

Also following from a distance was Tl'Rak, and behind him was the young Kay're.

"I should blast him now!" Z'mia exclaimed.

"Not now," Kay're cautioned. "It would disturb the reverence of the burial. He wants to see the location of the tomb so he can make his move in three days. We'll be waiting for him." Z'mia nodded and called her ship to update Tr'Tala.

"Jesus is dead and buried," she somberly said. "His execution and the two others were horrible. I wanted to blast the Roman soldiers for their brutality."

"Of course, you did," Tr'Tala said. "Your military training did you well to hold steady."

"Yes, sir," Nh'Got said. "Sir, before Jesus died, the sky turned very dark with thunder and lightning. When he died, there was a great earthquake."

"We saw the darkness cover not only your area, but the entire planet. Our sensors picked up the quake that rippled the entire planet. Are you and your friend unhurt?"

"We're okay. Tl'Rak witnessed the execution and sustained a head injury. The moment to shoot him was inappropriate. Did the ship's sensors pick up transporter activity from Earth to the spaceship?" she asked before Tr'Tala could berate her for not killing Tl'Rak.

"We didn't detect any." He sounded irritated. "But we will continue to watch."

"Sir, Jesus has been dead for over an hour and sealed in his tomb. He must have transported up!" She didn't want to say, "Are you sure you didn't pick up transporter activity?"

But Tr'Tala heard it in her inflection. "The sensors didn't register any transporter energies or any space distortions!" He paused to let his tone of displeasure sink in.

But Tr'Tala heard it in her inflection. "The sensors didn't register any transporter energies or any space distortions!" He paused to let his tone of displeasure sink in.

Z'mia glanced back at Kay're who mouthed, "Jesus is God." Z'mia didn't want to believe it though her mind was beginning to waver. *Jesus may indeed be who he claims to be; the Son of God.*

"Lieutenant, what is your plan now?"

"We will wait in hiding near the burial tomb for the resurrection in three days. Tl'Rak will make his move then to kill Jesus."

"And you suspect he will do that?"

"Yes, sir. It will be his best opportunity. When he makes his move against Jesus, I will take him down."

"And Jesus?"

"I will confront him and have our ships released."

"I hope so. This situation has gone on long enough. I want it wrapped up in three days. I'm counting on you."

"Yes, sir. I won't let you down." Silence, and it was deafening.

"We'll contact each other if either of us discovers anything new. Tr'Tala out." The comm-link closed.

Lieutenant Nh'Got blew out a breath of relief. "Ideas?" she asked Kay're.

She looked up to the hills and motioned with her hand. "Up there, overlooking the tomb. We can see what everyone is doing. I suspect Tl'Rak will do the same, so let's stake out our position before he does." They made their way up a hill and took cover under some trees and bushes. After taking their positions, they watched Tl'Rak stroll casually into the garden. He nodded respectfully to the centurion.

"Leave! You have no business here," the centurion said to him.

"I'm here to make certain you buried the zealot," Tl'Rak replied. "There are rumors he may not be dead and moved to a house to care for his wounds."

"He is dead! I oversaw his execution and buried him here. You are interfering with official business. Now move on, or I will have you arrested and crucified."

Tl'Rak smiled thinly. "That won't be necessary." He turned and left the garden, but not before surveying the area. Kay're and Z'mia watched him walk toward the Mount of Olives.

Tl'Rak smiled thinly. "That won't be necessary." He turned and left the garden, but not before surveying the area. Kay're and Z'mia watched him walk toward the Mount of Olives.

"He was doing recon," Z'mia said.

"I agree. He'll take a position before dawn amongst the trees and pounce once the stone blocking Jesus's tomb moves."

"He'll need a weapon to overtake the three Roman soldiers and kill Jesus," Z'mia said.

"That is another reason he walked into the garden. The man is shrewd and knew we were watching him. He's counting on us to follow him out of the garden, and when we pass his hiding place, he'll jump you and take your weapon. But we won't play his game. Let him sit and wait. You'll get him in three days."

"Good thinking," Z'mia said. "If I ever want to be a ship commander, I need to think ahead like you and Tl'Rak. I hate to give him any credit."

"Well, after he figures out that we aren't falling for his trap, he'll think of another way to get your weapon. It is his only hope to overcome the soldiers and kill Jesus. We must be on guard at all times."

Z'mia nodded. "Do you think he saw us up here?"

"Not us, per se. It's more likely he was looking for the place we'd hide to view the tomb."

"Which is the place we're at now," Z'mia said. We need to move."

"Put yourself in Tl'Rak's shoes," Kay're suggested. "He'll know we're on to him and that we'll move from our general hiding place here to another. So where do you think that will be?"

Z'mia glanced around the garden and burial area and pointed to a group of trees on the hillside opposite them. "There."

"And that's where he'll make some sort of move on us to get the weapon," Kay're said.

Z'mia smiled. "But we won't be there. We'll stay right here."

"Right," Kay're agreed. "I hope he is as cunning as we play him up to be."

"What if he thinks we know this and will come here instead? It's like being a step ahead of us."

"That could be. He doesn't know me, but you. You are his subordinate in rank a step ahead of us."

"That could be. He doesn't know me, but you. You are his subordinate in rank and age. Because of that, he won't give you credit for thinking that many steps in advance. He'll go to the trees on the other side."

"So, what do we do when he goes there?"

"Be on guard here. He'll be furious when he discovers we bested him again. Angry people do stupid things. From here we can see the whole area, including the way up here. After all, you have the weapon."

"And I'm ready to use it on him and will do so as ordered."

"Good. It is getting late. The sun is setting. According to Jewish law, tomorrow is their day of rest. Nothing will happen tonight or during the day tomorrow. Tl'Rak will still lay in wait tonight in hopes you make your move on him during the dark. When the day breaks, he'll give up on you coming and formulate plan B, his attack on us on the other side. Of course, we won't be there. He'll sleep there and prepare himself for the resurrection the following morning. Nevertheless, we need to be on guard tonight. I will take the first watch for a few hours, then you until morning."

"No, no," Z'mia protested. "You have done all the thinking. You should rest first."

"Okay," Kay're said with a smile. "Let us eat first, then I will call it a night. Wake me in four hours."

Z'mia's watch passed without incident. She woke Kay're and offered her the blaster. She declined, saying she didn't feel comfortable holding it. Soon, the young lieutenant was asleep. Kay're positioned herself on a boulder that gave her a view of the garden and anyone coming up the hill toward her. Climbing to their position wouldn't be a quiet one, as it took physical effort with several grunts. And loose stones and rocks made crunching sounds. She was confident no one would get the jump on her and if someone tried, they would feel a boot to their face.

She fixed her gaze on Jesus's tomb, bathed in the glow of the Roman campfire. Two soldiers stood sentry on either side of the tomb while two others and the centurion slept around the fire. She wondered if Jesus was in the tomb. Had he regained life and somehow exited it to another place or time only to return for his resurrection? Though her mind was still clouded, she believed Jesus to be the Son of

Had he regained life and somehow exited it to another place or time only to return for his resurrection? Though her mind was still clouded, she believed Jesus to be the Son of God.

Z'mia and her commander believed him to be an alien. One with extraordinary power and transported to the small spaceship above the earth. Currently, they lacked evidence to prove the possibility. Would it be forthcoming, two mornings from now, with Jesus's resurrection?

After a few hours, there was a sound from the other side of the garden. The soldiers on guard noticed and woke the centurion. He and two other soldiers moved toward the sound. In the dim light, Kay're noticed a figure moving in the opposite trees. Was it Tl'Rak? If so, he was one step and a day ahead of her calculation. When Z'mia awoke, they would need an alternative plan to deal with him.

The soldiers entered the trees and after a few minutes emerged with a small child in hand. Kay're's heart skipped a beat as she recognized her little self. What were the soldiers going to do to her? She glanced down at Z'mia who was sound asleep. The commotion in the garden didn't wake her. Kay're focused on Z'mia's blaster. She could use it to rescue her child self. Yet she knew it wouldn't be necessary.

The centurion set the child down by the fire and offered her something to drink. He spoke to her, but Kay're, from her position, couldn't hear what was being said. Within a few minutes, the child reclined and the centurion placed a blanket over her. She remembered another centurion doing that to her many years ago. It was an unblocked memory, and it brought a smile to her face. The centurion, who was an executioner, was now a man of gentleness. Kay're believed Jesus's crucifixion had a profound effect on him.

After a few minutes, the centurion and two guards were once again asleep. Kay're relaxed and wondered about her past and how she, as a child, ended up on Earth during this period. Or was she, as an adult, out of place and time? She struggled to remember, but nothing came to her.

Morning broke, and Z'mia yawned herself awake. "Did anything happen during your shift?" Kay're pointed to the garden. "The child!" Z'mia exclaimed. The little girl was still asleep as the soldiers milled around the campfire.

"The soldiers found her roaming on the other side of the garden."

"Did they hurt her?"

The little girl was still asleep as the soldiers milled around the campfire.

"The soldiers found her roaming on the other side of the garden."

"Did they hurt her?"

"No. The centurion gave her something to drink and covered her with a blanket."

"That was nice of him. Jesus' death affected him for the better."

"I think so," Kay're agreed.

"Any sign of Tl'Rak?"

"Nope. He's laying low now. This evening it will be different."

"I'm hungry," Z'mia said, patting her tummy.

Kay're chuckled. "I still have a few locusts. You're welcome to them."

"Anything else?" Z'mia looked panicky.

"A few olives and dates. You can have them. I will go over to the other garden and gather more for our lunch and dinner."

"Do you still have money?"

"I do."

"How about stopping in town to purchase something more substantial?"

"That is a good idea. I will see if I can find Mary of Magdala and the others and offer our condolences."

"That would be nice. Be careful. Tl'Rak could be stalking around looking for us there."

"I will, and you be watchful here." Kay're started down the hillside to town.

It was the Sabbath, and in Bethany, shops were closed and everything was peaceful. Few people were out in the morning. Those that were, were drawing water or tending to livestock. Kay're spotted Mary of Magdala at the well.

"Mary!" Kay're called out.

"Oh, Kay're," she returned, dropping her bucket and rushing to greet her friend. They hugged. Mary wiped tears from her face. "They killed the Lord. They killed Jesus," she cried.

"I know, we saw. Z'mia was with me. It will be okay." Kay're smiled, not telling her that Jesus would rise tomorrow. Mary would find that out on her own.

"How can you say that?" Mary demurred. "He is dead!"

"If you believe He is the Son of God, then He is alive," Kay're soothed.

own.

"How can you say that?" Mary demurred. "He is dead!"

"If you believe He is the Son of God, then He is alive," Kay're soothed.

Mary managed a smile. "Where is Z'mia?"

"She is in the garden overlooking Jesus's tomb. She wants to make sure nothing happens there. Her crazed superior is still out there. He may attempt to remove the body."

"Did the Romans post guards?"

"They did, but Z'mia's superior is crafty and may figure out a way to get rid of the soldiers."

"Then it is good that you and she are there. What are you doing here?"

"I came to look for someone selling food. But I forgot that this is your Sabbath day and that no shops are open."

"Come with me to join the others. We have plenty of food." Mary led Kay're to an upper room. Inside, she saw forlorn faces. There was the smell of despair in the air. Mary introduced her to eleven men who were Jesus's chosen apostles and Mary the mother of Jesus. She knew the other women present. Kay're came up to Mary, the mother of Jesus, and hugged her and expressed her condolences. She wanted to place a thought in her mind that everything would be fine, and she would see her son again, but held off.

"I believe Jesus is the Son of God," she said to Mary and the others. "One day He will return in glory to rule over all that God has created." Her claim brought smiles from all. "My friend who is near Jesus's tomb expressed her sympathy too."

"Please, sit and sup with us," said Peter. Kay're accepted and Peter gave the blessing and passed around bread and dried fish. Kay're stowed some of her food into a bag." Peter noticed.

"Eat to the full," he said. "We will give you more for later on."

"This is for my friend."

"Then here, let me give you more for her and yourself." Kay're handed him the bag, and he filled it with bread and fish.

"You're most kind," Kay're said. "Please take these coins not for payment, but for your ministry to come and care for Mother Mary." She gave him her coin bag. Dumbfounded, Peter accepted. The rest of the meal passed in silence. After eating, but for your ministry to come and care for Mother Mary." She gave him her coin bag. Dumbfounded, Peter accepted. The rest of the meal passed in silence. After eating, John sang a psalm.

"I need to leave now. My friend is hungry and is likely worried about me," Kay're said. "Thank you for sharing your food and company. I consider all of you as my friends." Mary of Magdala guided her outside.

"Mary, believe me, everything will be okay."

"I believe you." Mary smiled and hugged her friend.

As Kay're was leaving town, she noticed Tl'Rak at the well. He was rinsing the dried blood from his head. He noticed her and paused. They shared a stare.

Tl'Rak heard in his head. *Your plan has failed. Jesus is God and you cannot kill Him. Don't harm Nh'Got or you will die!* Kay're nodded to him and left him with mouth ajar.

She rounded a corner, climbed a building, and ducked down to see if Tl'Rak was following. He remained at the well, grinning. He took a long draw of water and walked in a direction away from the garden tomb. Satisfied that he wasn't a threat now, Kay're returned to the hill.

"There you are!" Z'mia, exclaimed, relieved. "I was worried something bad had happened to you."

"I saw Mary, and she invited me into a room where I met Jesus's mother, eleven of his disciples, and other women. They invited me to eat with them and they gave me more food."

"Let me guess, bread and fish?"

"You got it, unless you want some locusts." Kay're chuckled and opened the bag. Z'mia eagerly took a hunk of bread and some fish. "I saw Tl'Rak in town. He was at the well, tending to his head wound."

"Did he see you?"

"He did, and I placed a warning in his mind to stay away from you or die."

"How did he take it?"

"He left the well with a sadistic grin. I think he took it as a challenge."

"Then he'll be here tonight."

"We can count on it. I hope he heads to the opposite side first."

"If he comes up this way, he's a dead man," Z'mia said, patting the blaster.

"If he comes up this way, he's a dead man," Z'mia said, patting the blaster.

"I don't see the child," Kay're said quickly, her eye searching the area.

"She went into the bushes an hour ago and hasn't come back. I thought she was going to relieve herself and return."

"Did she have anything to eat before she left?"

"The centurion gave her some bread and what else—fish." Z'mia laughed. "I wonder what she's doing. She seems to appear when major things are happening or about to happen. It's like she has precognitive abilities."

Kay're smiled. "She is a curious girl. I have a feeling she will be back soon."

"I hope she doesn't run into Tl'Rak. He could hold her hostage for leverage against the soldiers."

"That is my thought too," Kay're said, worried. "I hope you're a good shot with your blaster. It may come down to an exact shot." Kay're gave Z'mia a hopeful glance. She returned a curt nod.

Evening came, and all was quiet. The soldiers remained on guard and a campfire lit the garden. The child hadn't returned. Tl'Rak had yet to make his move, though both knew it was coming.

"One of us needs to get some sleep," Kay're said.

"I can't sleep," Z'mia returned. "I'm too hyped up with anticipation of Jesus reappearing and Tl'Rak's move. How about you?"

"The same," Kay're admitted, focusing on the opposite hill.

After a few hours of waiting and watching, a rustling came from the opposite hill. The light of the campfire showed the child. She was walking toward the soldiers. The centurion rose to greet her. Suddenly Tl'Rak came rushing out and grasped the girl and placed a knife to her throat.

"Stand back," he ordered the centurion and soldiers who had drawn swords. He looked up at Kay're and Z'mia's position. "I know you two are up there. If you want to see the child live, throw down the blaster."

"Can you get a shot at him?" Kay're asked.

Z'mia raised the blaster. Tl'Rak was one step ahead. He ducked down, head level with the child, making a kill shot difficult in the dim light. The centurion was looking up at the women, wondering what the evil man wanted.

Desperately, the child planted distracting thoughts into Tl'Rak's mind. Kay're could

Desperately, the child planted distracting thoughts into Tl'Rak's mind. Kay're could sense what her little self was doing and added further confusion to it. He shook his head to clear them.

"I know what you are doing!" he shouted. "Stop or I will kill her and you will die too!" Kay're let loose his mind. The child backed off too. "Now throw down the blaster!"

"Do it," Kay're said to Z'mia.

The weapon clattered between Tl'Rak and the centurion. Still holding the knife to the child's throat, he edged toward the weapon. "Pick it up," he told the girl, loosening his grip on her. She did and handed it to him, but he still held her.

"Release her!" Z'mia shouted.

"Nh'Got, you are a fool!" He laughed out while stepping back with the girl. As he did so, the child placed a foot behind him, tripping him. Falling, he lost his grip on the child. She ran to the soldiers. They came at Tl'Rak, but he was up quickly and attempted to shoot them. The weapon didn't discharge, as Nh'Got had powered it down. With no time to turn it on, he ran back to the hill. Spears came flying, one glancing off his right shoulder, ripping flesh. It took all his strength to keep hold of the blaster. The centurion and two soldiers followed but couldn't find him in the darkness. They returned to the campsite. The child sat sniffling back tears.

"I screwed up again," Z'mia demurred. "He will blast Jesus when he comes out of the tomb and we can't do a thing to stop him."

"We still have time."

"But he has the blaster. If he killed your little self, would you have died, too?"

Kay're returned a resigned look.

"Of course," Z'mia answered her own question. "I'm sorry I asked."

"I can't say don't worry about it. I'm worried, not so much for myself but for my younger self."

"What just happened confirms Tl'Rak knows you and the child are the same person."

"It does. But Tl'Rak doesn't know what time period I am from. Or my little self. That might give him pause about killing either one of us. Certainly me, knowing my death could alter the time continuum and wink him from existence."

"Do you think that even entered his mind?"

"It does. But Tl'Rak doesn't know what time period I am from. Or my little self. That might give him pause about killing either one of us. Certainly me, knowing my death could alter the time continuum and wink him from existence."

"Do you think that even entered his mind?"

"I don't know, but I hope so."

Z'mia blew out a breath and looked to the east. "The sun is starting to come up. We've got to figure out a way to stop Tl'Rak, and soon."

"Let's go down to the tomb. I will confront him, and you—" Kay're failed to finish her sentence as the ground began rumbling.

"Another quake!" Z'mia exclaimed.

The ground shook, but not violently as before. They braced themselves and looked down at the garden area. The Romans were up and steadying themselves. Little Kay're sat staring at the tomb. Tl'Rak stumbled from the opposite hill with the blaster at the ready.

"I think this is it—the resurrection!" Kay're exclaimed, shaking. The ground stopped moving and a large ethereal figure appeared at the tomb's entrance. The Romans and Tl'Rak fell to the ground like dead men.

"Oh my," breathed Z'mia and she went limp, Kay're catching her. She lowered her to the ground. Refocusing on the figure, she knew it was an angel; beautiful with large wings.

The angel looked down at the girl who was now standing. "You're a child of the Lord. Blessed are you, for there are two of you at the same time." The angel looked up to Kay're's position.

"Is Jesus alive?" the child asked.

"He who is Wonderful, the Counselor, the Prince of Peace is alive!" declared the angel.

"And will you move the stone from the tomb?"

"I will, but you must sleep now."

"I want to see Jesus so I can go home."

"Child, you are in human form. Your eyes are incapable of looking upon the Almighty God in His glory and splendor. You will go home. Now both of you must go to sleep." Again, the angel gazed up at Kay're.

"Okay," the child mumbled. "Do you have a name?"

you must go to sleep." Again, the angel gazed up at Kay're.

"Okay," the child mumbled. "Do you have a name?"

"I am Gabriel." He smiled and wrapped a large wing around her and she went limp. He gently guided her to the ground.

Kay're looked with mouth ajar. She gasped as another angel appeared at her side. He wasn't as big as Gabriel, but just as beautiful. "I know you," she said.

The angel smiled. "We have met before. It is now time." Like the other, he wrapped a wing around Kay're and her eyes closed and knees buckled. He moved her to the ground.

CHAPTER FORTY FOUR
Awakenings

As the sun started winking over the eastern hills, a light brighter than the sun shone. The great luminosity awakened little Kay're. She placed her hands over her eyes to shield them. Then the morning was normal again. She sat up and looked at the tomb, and it was open with the large stone laying off to the side. Scrambling to her feet, she ran to it. Pausing with apprehension, she poked her head inside to see to see if Jesus was there but saw an angel sitting on a stone slab.

"Gabriel," she called out to the ethereal figure.

"It is you, child." The angel gave her a smile.

"Jesus isn't here! Did the evil man shoot him and make him disappear?" She looked fretful.

"No, child. Jesus has overcome death. He has risen!"

"I need to see Jesus so I can go home!" she exclaimed, worry still creasing her face.

"You will go home," Gabriel assured. "Now you must leave before the others wake up and take hold of you."

"Where do I go? I want to go home!"

"Go to town. You will find peace and safety there. Hurry."

"I will. Thank you, Gabriel." The child hurried away, passing the sleeping Romans. Then she came upon the snoring evil man and stared at him for several seconds. She could read his dreams and they were as evil as him. She reached down and took his blaster and eyed it. Holding it with both hands, she pointed it at his head.

"You deserve to die," she whispered to him. Slowly she put pressure on the trigger—then released it. Keeping the weapon, she raced off toward Bethany.

The Romans yawned away their sleep. The centurion saw that the entrance to the tomb was open. He hurried to it, peeked in, and staggered back. "Men!" he shouted. The others were sitting, shaking the grogginess from their heads. "The body entrance to the tomb was open. He hurried to it, peeked in, and staggered back. "Men!" he shouted. The others were sitting, shaking the grogginess from their heads. "The body is missing! Let's get out of here, lest we get blamed for it." The Romans scurried away toward Jerusalem.

Tl'Rak fluttered his eyes open as the soldiers ran past him. He shook his head and forced himself into a sitting position. The nightmare of the child shooting him in the head still resonated. He sucked in a breath, exhaled, and saw the entrance of the tomb open. He remembered the huge ethereal figure and...nothing until his dream and awakening. He mumbled some oaths, stood, and went to the tomb. "It's empty," he said aloud. "That is why the Romans ran away."

He missed his opportunity to blast Jesus. He swore again and felt for his blaster. It wasn't at his waist. He panicked and scanned the ground. The weapon was missing. *The Romans didn't stop to pick it up, meaning Nh'Got must have taken it. No, she didn't take it, nor did her friend,* he corrected himself. *She would have shot me or at least bound my wrists and feet. The child took it. She was present when the figure appeared and, now she has disappeared. Did she try to kill me with it? That would explain the dream. Or did she plant it in my mind?*

He looked up to the hillside where Nh'Got and her cohort hid, but didn't see them. They were up there, and concluded the other woman and the child were the same. *How could they exist at two different ages at the same time? Unless the older one was from the future. But how far into the future; before, during, or beyond my time?* His mind was spinning. *Eliminating the child would change the future. If she was before my time, I wouldn't exist. Not a good option. I need to capture either and force answers from them. Then I will decide their fate.*

"Jesus, you are still my target, a god or not," he yelled out. He grinned, hoping the women heard his cry, and would follow him. He would lie in wait and then jump them. Then he would get answers from the mind prober. After one last glance at the women's position, he moved off to Bethany.

Though deep in slumber, Kay're's mind was active. Here and there she raced, searching for the door that opened to the wonderfulness of peace and love. Rounding another corner, she saw a distant light and reveled in joy. She had found it! With quick strides she ran toward it, and the light grew brighter and brighter. Then an

Though deep in slumber, Kay're's mind was active. Here and there she raced, searching for the door that opened to the wonderfulness of peace and love. Rounding another corner, she saw a distant light and reveled in joy. She had found it! With quick strides she ran toward it, and the light grew brighter and brighter. Then an angel appeared, and she stopped.

"It's you. The angel I encountered before."

"It is me," he acknowledged. "It's not your time to see the Son of Man coming in His kingdom."

"When will it be my time?"

"Only God the Father knows." The angel pointed to the left, and another hallway appeared. "There, your past to the present."

"Thank you." Kay're turned and made her way down the fresh path. Looking right and left, her life passed. Her first breath of life and cry gave her pause. She saw herself in her mother's arms and father smiling. Next came her first steps and fall. She picked herself up and waddled on. The first few years and milestones flashed by. Then there was the swirling light. She ran toward it, disregarding her father's warning.

"No, Kay're, no!" he shouted. She looked back and him, giggled, and reached out to the light and disappeared. She emerged into an unknown land and time. The swirling light behind her winked out.

Kay're sucked in a breath. She and her little self were together in the here and now. Timewise, over twenty-five hundred years separated them. Next came her first meeting with Jesus. His voice echoed in her head. *Truly I tell you, some who are standing here will not taste death before they see the Son of Man coming in his kingdom.* She saw herself shake from the experience as her mind opened to a new world. Jesus calmed her with his words, "Do not be afraid, I am with you always." She sighed and continued on.

Centurion Cassius Marcus appeared. She first met him at two different ages in her life. In their first encounter, he placed a cape over her. The second time she almost killed him. The thought saddened her heart and brought tears. He proved himself to be a caring, gallant, and proud man. She sucked in a breath, wiped the tears from her cheeks, and moved on. As the years passed, she saw herself grow and face challenges. Many she overcame, some not. Her accomplishments and abilities she saw herself grow and face challenges. Many she overcame, some not. Her accomplishments and abilities amazed her.

Moving on, she saw the faces of those she had encountered. So many beautiful smiles and people. Again, she dabbed away tears as her heart felt the pain of loss. "So many," she cried. The tears dried as unpleasant moments appeared, some even evil. She remembered dealing with them; justice prevailed.

The years moved on. Events and people came and went. The experience was like the man in the novel, *The Time Machine,* by H.G. Wells, that she had read the book many years ago. The character sat in his time machine and pushed the control forward, and the years flashed past him.

Now the end neared, and her heart skipped a beat. There he was! His smile melted her on the spot. His twinkling eyes made her swoon. Mark Ross had entered her life. He existed both at a young age and as an adult. Yet no sooner had he appeared than circumstances took him away, breaking her heart. He left her a gift that gave her hope for the future.

With her heart racing, she ran down the hall searching for him. She passed other events in her life as if they were insignificant until she saw him again. They met and married. This time she cried in joy.

Breathing heavily with happiness, she saw there were but a few steps to go. She took them and saw herself sitting in a spaceship. A man in uniform said he had a very important mission for her. She was to go back in time to stop a madman from killing Jesus Christ and altering the time continuum. If the flow of time changed, the hall of her memories and everyone would change or never be. Beyond this point, the hall stretched on in pure white. She continued, but the angel appeared, blocking her way.

"There is nothing more to see," the angel said.

"The hall extends further, and I want to go on."

"The rest of the hall is your future that you will fill in. You must return to your human self for this to happen."

"But the hall goes on and on. Does that mean my future does the same?"

"Only the Almighty Father knows. Are you ready to return?"

"It is so beautiful here. I would like to explore other pathways."

"And you will when it is your time. Now it is time to return to your human

"And you will when it is your time. Now it is time to return to your human life."

"Kay're, Kay're, wake up," Z'mia urged, gently shaking her friend's shoulders. Finally, Kay're's eyes fluttered open to see Z'mia's pensive face.

"Is something wrong?" Kay're asked, sitting up.

"Everything. I woke up to see you crying in your sleep. And look, the tomb is open! The Romans, Tl'Rak, and the child are gone."

"Did you see them leave?"

"No. I just remember a big ghostly figure appearing and then nothing."

"You passed out, and I caught you," Kay're said. "Then I fell asleep too."

"Did you see that figure?"

"I saw two. One that put us to sleep and the other when I was a child. His name is Gabriel. He moved the stone, and Jesus rose from the dead and left the tomb."

"I take it this angel told you his name, and you saw him move the stone and Jesus come alive and leave," Z'mia said skeptically.

"He told me his name, but I didn't see him move the stone or Jesus rise from the dead."

"Then how do you know Jesus rose from the dead? He could have beamed down from the spaceship and used some device to move the stone. The figure could be a hologram. Of course, you don't know what a hologram is." Z'mia Nh'Got was trying to convince herself that Jesus wasn't God but an alien as a god wouldn't allow himself to be killed.

"I know what a hologram is, and Jesus isn't an alien and didn't beam down from that spaceship. That ship is mine." Z'mia's jaw dropped in amazement. Kay're smiled and nodded.

"All this time you have held this from me."

"I didn't know it until just now. In my sleep, the other angel entered my mind and released my memory. I remember who I am, my past, my present, and why I am here."

Z'mia looked at her, unsure of what to believe. She was going to quiz Kay're more, but her annunciator beeped. She answered. "Lt. Nh'Got here."

Kay're more, but her annunciator beeped. She answered. "Lt. Nh'Got here."

"Where have you been?" Tr'Tala boomed. "I have been trying to contact you for two hours."

"Supreme Commander, I was unconscious from the moment of the—I am not sure."

"We registered another ground quake in your area. Shortly thereafter we saw a blinding light from your position. Give me a report."

"Sir, we felt the quake but after that everyone went unconscious." A pause.

"Did you see Jesus appear?"

"No, sir. But his tomb is open. Did you notice any activity from the other spaceship?"

"Negative."

"Supreme Commander Tr'Tala," interrupted Kay're, speaking Valerrian. She activated the annunciator in her ear.

"Who is this?"

"I'm Lt. Nh'Got's friend."

Tr'Tala put a fist to his mouth in thought. He vaguely recognized the voice. Where did he hear it? He touched an icon on the command chair and his wife's image appeared on the main screen. "Commander," he addressed her, "I am patching through my conversation with Lt. Nh'Got's friend. I had heard her voice before but couldn't place it. Maybe you will recognize it."

"I will listen," she replied.

"Lieutenant Nh'Got, give your friend the annunciator so I can communicate clearly with her."

"No need to," Kay're cut in. "I'm using my own." With that, Z'mia's mouth slackened again. "Is the small spaceship still cloaked?"

"It is," Tr'Tala replied.

"Good, now watch," Kay're said and wrinkled her forehead as if in deep thought.

"The ship has appeared!" Tr'Tala said, astonished. Immediately, he knew who he was talking to. His wife knew, too.

"Sen, I know who it is."

He smiled. "I do too. Kay're, or should I address you as Mrs. Kay're Ross?"

"Sen, I know who it is."

He smiled. "I do too. Kay're, or should I address you as Mrs. Kay're Ross?"

Lieutenant Z'mia Nh'Got's went slack-jawed. Was her friend, the wife of the famous famous UPA Captain Mark Ross? Kay're had read her thoughts and nodded. Z'mia was speechless.

"Kay're is fine, Sen," she replied. "And hello, Te'ana."

"It is good to hear your voice again," the Valerrian returned.

"Enough of the pleasantries," Tr'Tala said. "What are you doing here?"

"The same as you; to stop your renegade officer Tl'Rak from changing the timeline. He can't kill Jesus now, but he can kill other significant people and alter the continuum."

"And how do you know Tl'Rak cannot kill Jesus?"

"Jesus is God," she simply answered. "In his human form He was mortal, but not now since He has risen in His eternal form."

Tr'Tala shook his head. He still believed Jesus to be an advanced alien, but where was his ship? Did he need a ship or was it cloaked somewhere in orbit?

"Kay're, to debate Jesus as God is pointless. As you have pointed out, Tl'Rak is still a danger. He has to be neutralized, and Jesus found and forced to release our ships. Are you familiar with our situation?"

"I am. Have you tried to move your ships or transported from them since the resurrection?"

"I haven't. Give me a moment to check our status. Helm, move the ship ahead dead slow."

The helmsmen returned the order and worked his hands on his board. He shook his head.

Tr'Tala sighed. He touched a button on his chair. "Transporter room. Lock on Lt. Nh'Got. Bring her aboard." There was an acknowledgment of his order. Pause.

"Transporter room to the bridge. The transporter is still inoperative."

"Kay're, do you copy?"

"I heard. I will attempt to transport to my ship. Stand by." She gave the command, and her ship's computer activated the process. She remained on the planet. "No go, Sen."

command, and her ship's computer activated the process. She remained on the planet. "No go, Sen."

"Kay're, you need to find Jesus and ask him if he is holding our ships." Nh'Got dipped her head, knowing the Supreme Commander had lost confidence in her.

"Lieutenant Nh'Got, my order to you hasn't changed. You are to find and neutralize Commander Tr'Tala. If you and Kay're need to work together to achieve both directives, then do it. I want to put this time travel business to rest once and for all and go home."

"I will complete your order," Nh'Got clipped, feeling uplifted by Tr'Tala's command to her.

"Sen, the girl," whispered his wife, but all heard.

"Kay're, I have been in contact with a small girl on the planet that has Tl'Rak's annunciator. For a human, she speaks Valeriian. She says her name is Kay're." He let the name hang in the air, waiting for a response.

"The child is me," Kay're said flatly.

Z'mia Nh'Got now questioned if little Kay're came from the future. Or was she from this time? If the latter, adult Kay're would be very old! "Oh my," she blurted, staring at her friend.

"Lieutenant Nh'Got, what is it?" Tr'Tala asked.

"Nothing, sir. It's just amazing that Kay're is here on the planet at two different ages." It was a white lie. She didn't want to tell her commander of her suspicion, though maybe he was thinking the same.

"Okay," Tr'Tala said. "According to the Earth Bible, Jesus will be on the planet for forty more days. You must find him and force him to release our ships. If you can't do this, we all die here, unless you, Kay're, have other information." He had concluded the same as Nh'Got: Kay're was very old. If so, she must know the outcome.

"Sen, I know what you and Lt. Nh'Got are thinking. Time is fluid, and my being here at two ages is part of how the time continuum plays out. If Tl'Rak kills someone significant, it will change. It's up to Lt. Nh'Got and me to make sure it doesn't." She omitted giving her age.

Tr'Tala knew she was withholding the fact, but did not press it. "Kay're, does

Tr'Tala knew she was withholding the fact, but did not press it. "Kay're, does Tl'Rak have any idea you and the child are the same?"

"He does. I could read his thoughts to that fact."

"Does he know you are a UPA agent?"

"I don't think so."

"Yet he must know you are from some point in the future. If he eliminates the child, he removes you and alters the time continuum and it will not be for the good."

"I have thought of that."

"Then you need to find your little self and protect her and yourself if that makes any sense."

"It makes perfect sense. I still think Tl'Rak believes he can kill Jesus. He knows the Bible and that Jesus will be here for forty days. Jesus will be his primary target. But, if the opportunity avails itself, he could kill others like Jesus's apostles. They were instrumental in the formation and growth of Christianity on Earth and its history. Killing one or more of them will change the time continuum."

Tr'Tala blew out a breath of exasperation. "You two have jobs to do. Get to it. Keep me informed. Out."

"Now what?" Z'mia asked.

"Down there," Kay're pointed. Two men were running toward the open tomb with a woman following. One man out-ran the other, reaching the opening first. "They're two of Jesus's disciples. I saw them both when I went into town yesterday. One is Peter. The other, I don't know his name."

"I remember them, too, when I met Jesus and his followers at a campfire. And that is Mary of Magdala."

They watched the men enter the tomb, one by one, as Mary hung back. After a few minutes, the men left, leaving Mary standing outside the tomb crying. Then she went inside. Suddenly, to their amazement, they saw a man appear at the tomb's entrance.

"That's Jesus!" Kay're exclaimed.

"He had to beam in," Z'mia said wide-eyed. "He has to be an alien." He appeared to be holding a conversation with M ary. Then he disappeared, and Mary ran from the tomb.

Mary ran from the tomb.

Z'mia wanted to contact her ship, but Kay're read her thoughts and placed a refraining hand on her friend's arm. "It won't do any good. Let's eat to renew our energy and think of a plan."

CHAPTER FORTY FIVE
Specter of the Child

Kay're and Z'mia walked toward Bethany. Their eyes were constantly searching for Tl'Rak. "He could hide anywhere and shoot us," Z'mia said.

"I think he probably went to town looking for Jesus or where his disciples are staying. I know the place. Let's head there. The women will be there too."

"What if he is already in town waiting for us to lead him to the place where everyone is staying?" Z'mia asked. "He'll barge in and start blasting. Maybe we should stay out of sight, observe, and when Tl'Rak appears, make our move."

Kay're smiled and nodded. "Now you are thinking like a commander. If he's there, he'll see us. That we can use to our advantage. We'll make sure he follows us and then lead him into our snare."

"We can't be too conspicuous, or he will know we are setting a trap."

"Good thinking. I suggest we enter town from the rear, find the highest rooftop, climb up, and watch for him."

They did just that. From their perch, they could see most of the town. They kept a keen eye on the place where the disciples were in seclusion with the women, and the town's well.

"He'll need to drink," Z'mia said.

"And we will too," Kay're said, jiggling her canteen. "Mine is almost empty."

"Mine too. And that includes food. I'm getting hungry. We only have a few locusts." She gave Kay're a quizzical look. Kay're nodded while watching the well.

The sun passed the midpoint and coursed across the sky to the horizon. As darkness closed in, Tl'Rak appeared at the well. He looked around and scanned the buildings. Kay're and Z'mia kept a low profile. Satisfied, he drank, filled his canteen, and washed his wounds. Two men at different times came to the well to fill water bottles. Neither paid any attention to Tl'Rak, though each acknowledged him with a nod, drew water, and left. Tl'Rak watched them disappear into single-story homes.

to the well to fill water bottles. Neither paid any attention to Tl'Rak, though each acknowledged him with a nod, drew water, and left. Tl'Rak watched them disappear into single-story homes.

Again, he scanned the buildings. "Look at him," Z'mia said. "He looks smug and arrogant. He is such a tard!"

Kay're chuckled. Tard was Valeriian for a horse's rearend. "Like he knows we are watching."

"He wants us to see him. Well, we have. Now we need to go down there and take him out."

"Whoa, girl. He has a blaster. We have bare hands and two small knives. There is no way we would get close enough to him before he fires on us. We need a long-range weapon."

"Like a spear."

"Can you throw a spear from here in low light and hit him?"

"Not from here. But at street level I could. You could distract him, then I would run out and fling it."

"When I distract him, he shoots me. Your spear hits, likely not an instant kill. He turns and blasts you. The score—two dead women and one dead bad guy. I dislike how it adds up." Kay're blew out a breath. "Besides, you don't have a spear."

"We could steal one from a Roman soldier."

"We could, but he'll not be here when we return. We'll have to let him go tonight. Look, he is withdrawing to that covered stall."

"I see it. There is a donkey and two smaller animals there. He's settled into the straw amongst them."

"The two smaller animals are goats. He was probably there the whole day."

"He has a view of the well. If we go for water, he will see us, run out, and blast us."

"That's what he was hoping for during daylight," Kay're surmised. "But when we didn't show up, he had to change his strategy. That's why he came out into the open. He wanted us to see him and where he will spend the night. He is banking on us sneaking up on him in that stable where he hopes to get the drop on us."

"But that won't happen." Z'mia thinly smiled.

"Right. Put yourself in his shoes. What would be your plan to get the jump banking on us sneaking up on him in that stable where he hopes to get the drop on us."

"But that won't happen." Z'mia thinly smiled.

"Right. Put yourself in his shoes. What would be your plan to get the jump on two weaponless women?"

"I would pile up the straw in the shape of a body and drape it with my cloak to make it look like I was sleeping. Then hide in the shadows or behind one of the sleeping animals and wait."

"That's what I would do," Kay're agreed. "But we won't fall for it."

Z'mia nodded. "What do you have in mind?"

"Like we did on the bluff overlooking the tomb. We spend a restful night while he stays up waiting for us. Tomorrow when we are fresh, he'll be asleep or dragging his sorry behind. Then we can make some sort of move."

"But we could lose him," worried Z'mia.

"I don't think so. He'll be here waiting for Jesus or his disciples. We can go now to the Mount of Olives and camp there. There is food on the trees. Then in the morning retake our position here."

"But we need some water. Look! At the well."

"My little self," Kay're bemoaned. "That's not smart of myself."

"She needs water like we do," Z'mia said. "Tl'Rak sees her. He is coming out!"

"Kay're, run!" shouted her older self. The child looked up at her, as did Tl'Rak.

"Run, child!" Z'mia screamed. The shouts made people open their doors and peer out into the dimness. Some came out to see what was causing the commotion.

The girl held her position and pulled out the blaster and pointed it at him. He froze.

Is it active? he wondered. The child could read his mind and thumbed the weapon, and Tl'Rak had his answer. He could hear the distinctive hum of the blaster powering up. The sound stopped. But at what setting? He didn't want to find out. "Child, drop the weapon," he said with authority.

"No! You are an evil man!"

"You're not a killer. Give me the weapon." He had softened his voice to gain her

"Child, drop the weapon," he said with authority.

"No! You are an evil man!"

"You're not a killer. Give me the weapon." He had softened his voice to gain her confidence. Then he heard words in his mind: "I have killed before and will do so again." He knew it was not the girl who placed the thought. He looked up at the roof.

Kay're stared into his mind. "She will shoot you. I know, for she is me."

Tl'Rak wet his lips and wiped them with a wrist. He thought of rushing her. She would startle and hesitate in shooting, giving him time to secure the weapon from her.

"Don't even think it," Kay're called down to him. "Kay're, if he takes a step, shoot him. Our lives depend on it." The girl never looked up to her older self. She clenched her jaw, leveling the blaster. She was steadfast and Tl'Rak knew it. Slowly, he backed away, then dove into the stable.

Little Kay're turned and ran in the opposite direction. Kay're and Z'mia lost track of her as she ran into a crowd that had gathered on the street.

CHAPTER FORTY SIX
The Vision

Kay're and Z'mia mingled amongst the crowd searching for the little one. She had turned into a ghost, disappearing into thin air. Kay're focused her mind, hoping to gain a mental connection with her little self. She failed to establish a link.

"Where would you go? Or do you remember?" Z'mia asked.

"This is all happening in real-time, so there's no past to recall. Where I would go—I'm not sure. Perhaps to the disciples and women."

"Let me contact the ship. They can get a fix on the annunciator."

"Go ahead." Just as Z'mia was going to make the call, a familiar voice called out.

"Kay're! Z'mia!" They turned to see Mary of Magdala rushing toward them. Her face beamed with joy and she hugged both women.

"Kay're, you were so right. Everything happened like you said. I saw the Lord! He talked to me!"

"That's so nice," Kay're said. "Has he visited the disciples and his mother?"

"Oh, yes. Within the hour! He appeared out of nowhere, then after a few minutes, disappeared. It was sad that He left, but so reassuring to know He is alive and the promised Savior, the Christ."

"You say He just appeared, like how?" Z'mia asked "Were there any sparkling lights?" She still questioned whether Jesus was the Son of God.

"No lights. He just appeared as we were sitting on the floor. His sudden appearance startled us. We had the door and windows locked in fear of the Pharisees breaking in and taking us. Then when He bid us good night, He disappeared. But He is the Son of God. He can do all things."

"Mary, did a little girl run to where you are staying?" Kay're asked.

"No. But I saw her confront that wicked man you're after. Then she ran past

past our place toward Jerusalem. I feel so sorry for her. I hope she gets home okay. Do you know her?”

“We do,” Kay’re confirmed. “I’m related to her. I need to find her before that evil man does. He still thinks he can kill Jesus, but we know that isn’t possible. But he will harm anyone associated with Him, including His mother, the disciples, you, and the child. She has a close history with Jesus. And she has no home here and her parents are far away.”

“Oh. If she knows Jesus, He will protect her,” Mary assured. “He loves the children.”

“Still, we need to find her,” Kay’re said. “I can take her home.”

“Of course,” Mary concurred. “Do you have a place to stay tonight? If not, you can stay with us.”

“Thank you,” Kay’re replied, taking hold of Mary’s hands. “We can’t do that. Doing so could place you and everyone’s safety in jeopardy. That evil man is likely watching us now and will follow us to where you are staying. We will leave, but you need to blend in with the crowd before heading back to the disciples. We’ll see each other again. I promise.”

Mary nodded and pulled her scarf up to cover her face. She turned and mixed in with a few locals before vanishing into the darkness. Others were returning to their homes.

“Do we go to Jerusalem?” Z’mia asked.

“No. I don’t think it will be safe there. The Romans are probably in a foul mood over the disappearance of Jesus’s body. They’ll be on high alert, stopping anyone they suspect of being a supporter of Jesus. And the centurion is still searching for us. Also, Tl’Rak, if he is watching, will trail us. We don’t want to lead him to the child. Let’s go to the Mount of Olives as we planned. If he follows us there, he will have a big problem.” She beamed a smile.

“He doesn’t have the blaster,” Z’mia said with a broad grin. “He will have two big problems—us! Let’s go.”

First, they headed toward the stall that Tl’Rak had fled back to. If he was still there, watching, all the better. They would eliminate him once and for all. Steadying themselves for an attack, they entered. None came. Tl’Rak had left. Kay’re laughed. “We tried. This might be a good place to spend the night.”

Kay're laughed. "We tried. This might be a good place to spend the night."

"No way," Z'mia protested. "This place stinks and there is animal waste all over."

"I didn't notice the smell. We stink just as bad," Kay're joked.

Z'mia sniffed herself. "I'm bad. Still, I don't want to spend a night with animals. Let's fill our canteens and go to the Mount of Olives."

"Okay. There's an old torch." Kay're pointed to the corner. "We can use it for light. We need something to start the fire."

"There is a smoldering torch across the street," Z'mia said. "Maybe it still has an ember to start this one."

"I hope so," Kay're said hopefully. "Let's find out." To their relief an ember glowed. The used it to ignite their torch and went to the well and filled their canteens. Then they hiked to the Mount of Olives.

Centurion Cassius Marcus lay on his cot, staring up. He had a headache from his fall due to the earthquake. The quake also allowed the girl and two women to escape. Now there were rumors that someone, or some people, had taken Jesus's body. Yet others were saying Jesus had risen from the dead—that he was indeed the Son of God. Even Centurion Longinus, who supervised the crucifixion, confessed that now. *Could the Nazarene be the Son of God? He miraculously healed my windpipe and saved me from death. Only a god could do that!* He felt his neck and shook his head. *On top of that, people were claiming the dead had left their graves and were walking around.* He took a deep breath and closed his eyes. Tomorrow at sunrise, he would renew his search for the women and child. He also wanted to find that big man who seemed to be in league with them.

Kay're and Z'mia made camp on the Mount of Olives. They sat around a fire, munching on dates and olives. Their ears were keen to listen for anyone approaching. The hours passed, and finally, they succumbed to the day's events.

After a peaceful night, morning broke with bright sunlight. The women stretched out their kinks from sleeping on hardpan. They finished their stash of fruit and refreshed themselves.

"I have been thinking about Jesus," Z'mia said, starting the conversation. "If he is fruit and refreshed themselves.

"I have been thinking about Jesus," Z'mia said, starting the conversation. "If he is God, what form does he now have? Where does he go? When and where will he appear? How are we going to find him?"

"I have been thinking the same. It has been a while since I read the Bible. I do remember, after his resurrection, he appeared to five hundred at once and to the apostles at the Sea of Galilee. That's where we need to go."

"I bet Tl'Rak remembered the same and will head there too."

"Likely. We can kill two birds with one stone."

Z'mia wrinkled her forehead. "I'm not familiar with the term—kill two with one stone. We don't want to kill Jesus."

Kay're laughed. "It means we can accomplish two things at the same time—meet Jesus and confront Tl'Rak."

"I get it. Let's go."

During the night, the only place where little Kay're felt safe was Cassius Marcus's tent. She found the Roman camp and slipped past the sentries to the man's tent. Peaking under the canvas, she found him asleep, and crawled inside. She came to his side and placed a pleasant thought in his mind. He would have pleasant dreams all night long until sunrise. Looking around the tent, she saw his cape, took it, draped herself with it, and fell asleep.

Morning light filtered into Marcus's tent. He moaned a joyful sound, opened his eyes, and smiled. He had a restful sleep despite all the troubling events of the past few days. And his headache was gone! And there was the blissful and happy dream!

Chariots that flew like birds and shining buildings reached to the sky. They were all glass and glistening metal. The streets were not dirt, but made of some hard grey material.

The people, and there were many, some even looked non-human, wore strange looking clothes. Many women wore skin-tight leggings and sleeveless tops and were beautiful. It was odd that most men passed them by without even giving them a thought. Everyone seemed content and went about their business without a care. No one ever looked over their shoulders for someone coming from the rear to do them harm.

without a care. No one ever looked over their shoulders for someone coming from the rear to do them harm.

And there was music and singing coming from some buildings. In others, I saw people staring at moving images that hung in the air. Many were drinking amber-colored liquid from clear glasses. Some cheered as they watched the moving image, which appeared to be a competition of some sort.

One man walked by and said, "Nice costume. It looks like the real thing from the ancient Roman Empire—centurion rank with a sword. Are you an actor in the play Julius Caesar by William Shakespeare down on 12th Street? I love the line, 'Cowards die many times before their deaths.' Is that one of your lines?"

I shook my head, not knowing what he was talking about. The man smiled and walked on. Across the street was a park with various leafy trees and blossoming flowers. Children were playing and from a swing, a girl waved to me. It was her! The small girl that could enter my mind. I remember waving back and hurried over to her.

She giggled and said, "Centurion Marcus, you made it."
I said to her, "I did. Where are we?"

"The future, of course." She continued swinging. "You look so funny dressed the way you are. The people are staring at you."

I recall looking around and seeing people gawking at me. Some children came running to me and were feeling my uniform. Mothers came to my rescue, taking their children by the hand and apologizing. One woman said, "You must be an actor in the play, Julius Caesar. What a wonderful adaptation of Shakespeare." She took her child back to the play area.

Then little girl came to my side. Her bright eyes gazed into my mind and I felt rejuvenated. She took my hand. "Come, let us walk to the river and get ice cream." She hummed a tune, and we walked on. I wondered what ice cream was.

"Centurion Marcus, you must do something with your clothes," she said to me, laughing. She was right. I was out of place. Nearing the river, she ran ahead and disappeared. The dream ended and emptiness and sadness ensued.

Marcus sighed and swung his legs over the cot to a sitting position. He noticed his tent looked different from last night. "My cape," he said to himself. "It's hanging over a chair and not on the hook." He glanced at his table and saw that the dates

Marcus sighed and swung his legs over the cot to a sitting position. He noticed his tent looked different from last night. "My cape," he said to himself. "It's hanging over a chair and not on the hook." He glanced at his table and saw that the dates and bread were missing. In their place were pits and crumbs. He looked down to see small footprints and smiled. *The child was here! She had planted the dream in my mind. To do so, she must have had a frame of reference for that time and place. Is she from the future? If so, her older self is too. And how did they get here?* He sat at the table and pondered the small footprints, and it hit him. Did the child or her older-self take him forward in time? He felt energized and jumped up from the table. His only mission now was to find them. He had to verify the vision. If that meant being derelict of his other duties, so be it. He dressed quickly, and stepped out into the morning light.

"Centurion Marcus," said a decanus running up to him. "Pontius Pilate wants to see you now."

"Great," Marcus mumbled. "Do you know what he wants?"

"No, Centurion. He requests your immediate presence." Marcus nodded and followed the junior officer.

"Cassius Marcus," Pilate addressed from behind his breakfast table.

"Where is the child? The women?"

"We had them until the earthquake at the time of the Nazarene's death. It knocked everyone to the ground and the child and women escaped."

"Yes, I too toppled to the floor. I want them found."

"It is my top priority. I was about to resume my search when you summoned me."

"Good. Now you have another duty. Find the Nazarene's body. I take it you heard it is missing."

"I have, and rumors of the dead rising and roaming the city."

"That is most disconcerting. I saw someone I had crucified walking outside the palace. How could that be?"

"I don't know."

"Speculate."

"I'm a soldier and deal with facts."

Pilate waved a hand. "Marcus, you are always so politically correct. Do you think the

"I'm a soldier and deal with facts."

Pilate waved a hand. "Marcus, you are always so politically correct. Do you think the Nazarene called Jesus is the Son of God as his followers claim? Do you believe he rose from the dead and caused others to do so?"

"No god would allow his son to die. To what end?"

"You have a point. Go find his body and find the child and women."

"Sir, may I suggest having Centurion Longinus find the body. He was the one conducting the crucifixion and guarding the grave. That would free me up to find the others."

"I would, but he is missing too. My ears tell me he believes the Nazarene is the Son of God and is out searching for him to be one of his followers. For desertion, he can follow him to the cross. If you see him, take him into custody."

"As you say, sir. May I leave to start the search?"

"Go."

Marcus saluted and left. He gazed out into the courtyard to see if the child or women were there. He doubted they would be, but one never knew about the mysterious trio. They weren't present. He made his way to Decanus Varius's tent to see if he was fit to join the hunt; he was. They gathered their troops and rode out of Jerusalem.

CHAPTER FORTY SEVEN
Close Encounters

Kay're and Z'mia Nh'Got made their way toward Galilee, where they hoped to encounter Jesus and Tl'Rak. The going was slow as they stayed off the roads and trekked through the hills. This was necessary to avoid frequent Roman patrols, with Centurion Marcus leading some. It was obvious he was looking for them. Several times he had his men dismount and search amongst the bushes, rocks, and trees. The women's cunning kept them a step ahead and out of sight of the Romans.

Yet Marcus was shrewd and backtracked, hoping to catch the women off guard and in the open. His ploy almost succeeded. The roar of a nearby lion gave warning, and the women quickly ducked behind boulders as the Romans rode by. The Centurion heard the lion, and he brought his patrol to a halt.

"What is it, Centurion Marcus?" Decanus Varius asked.

"You heard the roar?"

"I did. We are many and the lions will keep their distance."

"That's not the point," Marcus said, scanning the area. "You remember the child and her command of the lions. Well, she must be close by, and the lion gave her a warning." *Or the women, too.* He hadn't told Varius that he suspected the child and one woman were the same. How it was possible, he didn't know. Either one or both with the other woman could be nearby; maybe the man too.

"Of course, Centurion. I should have made the connection too."

Marcus shook his head. "We know you're here," he called out. "Come on out now. It will be easier, and you won't get hurt." Marcus did a 360 on his horse. The hills remained quiet. He shouted again, "I'm going to send my men in after you. Things could get rough!" Not a sound.

Kay're and Z'mia exchanged glances. The situation didn't look good. To their rear was a steep climb that would leave them exposed. If they came out, there

there would be too many men to fight.

Marcus directed some men to the trees on the opposite side of the road. Others, he told, to search the rocks where Kay're and Z'mia hid. He and Varius stayed mounted, observing. With swords drawn, the soldiers neared.

"We need a miracle," Kay're said in a soft voice. As if on cue, soldiers came running from the trees, a pride of lions ambling behind them. The unmounted horses spooked and raced off. Marcus and Varius controlled their steeds and backed them away. The soldiers scrambled to the rocks and upward. Those near the women paid them no heed, climbing over them in panic. Kay're and Z'mia had to duck their heads to avoid getting kicked.

"Come on, let us get out of here!" Kay're said, scurrying to the road toward the lions. Z'mia lagged, unsure if they were the friendly beasts. "It will be okay." Kay're waved for her friend. "They're the same ones you met before and won't hurt us."

Z'mia swallowed dryly and followed.

Marcus and Varius held their position and watched the women mingle amongst the lions. Up ahead in the trees, a man stood. The animals and women hurried toward him, while some cats loped toward the rocks to stand sentry. When the women and pride joined the man and they disappeared into the trees. It was only then that the remaining lions ran off to join them.

"That man has the same power over the lions as the child," Varius said. "Do you think he is the girl's father?"

"I don't know," Marcus replied, straightening himself in the saddle.

"And the women weren't afraid of the lions. Do you think that man is the husband of one of them? And the women are sisters?"

Varius is making sense, Marcus told himself. But he knew that the child and one woman were the same. The other woman could be the girl's mother and the man her father. But what of the other large man? How did he fit in? More questions without answers. The situation was becoming more complicated by the day. He very much wanted to follow them. He looked to the rocks to see Rome's finest soldiers cowering.

"Come out!" he shouted. "Find your horses."

"Will we follow them?" Varius asked.

"Will we follow them?" Varius asked.

"We will. Help the men round up the horses."

"Thank God the lions showed up," Kay're panted as the cats nuzzled her. Z'mia gingerly tapped one on the head, and it purred.

"God works in mysterious ways," the man said with a thin smile. He appeared to be in his thirties. "The lions take to you and your friend. They can sense your kindness and love for God's creations."

"They sense the same in you too, sir," Z'mia said, still warily eyeing the beasts.

"They have been my friends for many years. The Romans are seeking you." It wasn't a question.

"Yes," Kay're said. "We are outsiders and have disrupted their apple cart— and they don't like it."

Z'mia made a quizzical face, unsure of what her friend was referencing.

The man laughed. "The fruit has caused humanity much turmoil."

"I understand completely," Kay're said with a smile. She glanced at her friend, who shrugged. "Z'mia, I will explain later."

"We better get to the rocks before the Romans come after us," Z'mia said, pointing ahead at them.

"It'll be a few hours before they gather their horses," the man said plainly. "We'll be okay for some time. Where are you women heading?"

"To the Sea of Galilee," Kay're answered.

"You're not Galileans. What do you seek there?"

"How do you know we aren't from Galilee?" Z'mia asked.

"You said you were outsiders."

"We seek Jesus, the risen Lord," Kay're said boldly.

The man smiled. "I see. And you?" He looked at Z'mia. "You don't share your friend's beliefs."

"My mind is still open about his claim to be the Son of God."

"Yet you follow this woman on her quest."

"I'm her friend, and we stick together," Z'mia said. "We can have varying opinions and still be friends." The man smiled and reached down and ruffled the opinions and still be friends." The man smiled and reached down and ruffled the mane of the pride's leader. The big cat roared with delight.

"And what of you?" Z'mia queried.

The man ignored the question and pointed ahead. "There's a clearing. I have been traveling for many hours and would like to eat. Let's rest there and sup. Do you have food?"

Kay're was suspicious of the man when he brushed off Z'mia's question. As she tried entering his mind, a wave of vertigo unsettled her. She stumbled, and the man caught her.

"You need nourishment," he said.

"Kay're, are you okay?" Z'mia asked, concerned.

"I'm fine," she puffed. "Thank you for catching me. I guess in all the excitement my blood sugar levels depleted. I have some bread and locusts."

"And I have dried fish and dates," Z'mia added.

The man grinned. "Then we will dine to the full."

They sat in the shade of a tree. "I have a friend who dined on locust and honey," the man said, crunching on one.

"I'm sure the honey made the locusts more palatable," Kay're said. She chuckled and popped one in her mouth. Then she remembered in the Bible that John the Baptist ate locusts and honey. Herod had him beheaded before Jesus' crucifixion. Was this man referring to him? If so, did he know that the man was dead?"

"What is honey?" Z'mia asked, breaking Kay're's thoughts.

"It's a very sweet, viscous substance made by bees; a flying insect that has a stinger," Kay're answered.

"We have similar on my pla—place of residence," Z'mia said. She caught herself, not wanting to give herself up as being from another world. Of course, she knew the man would likely not believe her if she tried to explain. He would consider her mentally disturbed.

"In some places, they are called 'kadees,'" the man said. Z'mia's mouth gaped. That was the Valeriian name for bees. She glanced at Kay're who tilted her head, acknowledging her surprise too. "In other places, their names are tsis'na and nyuki," he quickly added. Both women shook their heads, as they didn't recognize those words.

and nyuki," he quickly added. Both women shook their heads, as they didn't recognize those words.

"The bread," he said, holding out a hand. Kay're nodded and gave him the small amount she had. He held it and looked up to the sky and spoke words unrecognizable to Kay're, Z'mia and their translators. He broke it and gave each a piece.

"I see you still have the Roman canteen."

Kay're's mouth gaped. "Have we met before?" The man smiled and disappeared, leaving both women slack-jawed. The lions roared.

"That was Jesus," Kay're breathed. "I didn't recognize him."

"Neither did I," Z'mia added. "He somehow blocked our minds of his identity. I'm contacting the ship." She did and learned sensors hadn't picked up any transporter activity at their location. The Supreme Commander was none too happy that they had let Jesus slip away. The link closed with Z'mia grimacing, knowing she had let her commander down again.

"We'll find him again," Kay're encouraged. "We know what he looks like anew. Now, are you a believer?"

Z'mia blew out a breath. "He is convincing. I'm keeping an open mind. We better get moving before the Romans show up. That centurion is persistent." Kay're nodded, and they finished their meal and hastened their walk toward Galilee. The lions followed.

From a high perch in the hills, Tl'Rak had seen the women's encounter with the Romans and the man. When he saw him disappear, he knew the man was Jesus. With a smirk, he followed the women from a distance.

Tl'Rak knew he couldn't get to them, with the beasts staying at their side. His hope turned to the child. She had to be in the area searching for her older self or Jesus. When she walked out into the open, he would grab her and retrieve his blaster. Then use her as a bargaining chip to force Jesus to appear so he can shoot him. At the very least, have the woman surrender to him in exchange for the child's life. He would force answers from either or both, then kill them. As for Lt. Nh'Got, she forfeited her life from the time she betrayed him on the ship. Suddenly, he felt renewed vigor and hastened his walk to keep up with the women.

On the second day, the lions separated from the women and moved toward women.

On the second day, the lions separated from the women and moved toward Tl'Rak's position. That caused him to retreat quickly. He ran and scrambled amongst the rocks until his lungs burned. Exhausted, he turned and saw the lions in the distance. They had settled in the shade of a rocky outcropping. There was no way he could follow the woman. For the time being, he would lose track of them. He continued backtracking to put more distance between himself and the beasts.

For the next three days, the women ducked in and out of hiding from the Roman patrols. As before, Centurion Marcus had his men dismount and search the hills and trees. The soldiers were sloppy in the hunt. They seemed to be looking over their shoulders more than beating the bushes. Lions, not ladies, were on their minds. As a result, they missed a couple of opportunities to catch the women.

Sunset on the fourth day with the Romans far away Kay're and Nh'Got made a camp on a hilltop. It would be another frosty night without fire that could give away their position. They sat in silence, eating the last of their food.

"Kay're, do you think, or can you sense, if Tl'Rak is following us?"

"The day we met Jesus, I felt someone, likely Tl'Rak, following us. After the lions left, I didn't sense his presence."

"Do you think they got him?"

"I don't think so. I would have felt that too. The lions scared him off."

"But he will be back," Z'mia said.

"We can count on that. He believes we are his best chance of finding Jesus."

"Or your little self. He wants to kill you."

"I know. And you, too." Kay're ate her last locust.

Z'mia nodded solemnly.

The sunrise brought warmth to the chilled women. Weary to the bone, dirty, and hungry, they stood and surveyed the surrounding area around them. Not a soul in sight.

"Do you sense anyone?" Z'mia asked, still worried Tl'Rak could close ready to jump them.

Kay're sucked in a breath, held it, and closed her eyes. "No one," she finally said.

"We need to find some food," Z'mia said.

ready to jump them.

Kay're sucked in a breath, held it, and closed her eyes. "No one," she finally said.

"We need to find some food," Z'mia said.

"Agreed." Just then, Kay're's belly rumbled. "I think the Sea of Galilee is on the other side of those distant hills." She pointed to the east.

"That is a good half-day walk," Z'mia breathed.

"But I have friends there. They have food and there is that hot spring we can soak in."

"I can't wait. I'm sore and stinky. Let us hurry." She took the lead. Kay're chuckled and kept pace with her friend.

CHAPTER FORTY EIGHT
Water and Wine

Late afternoon found Kay're and Z'mia Nh'Got on a hill overlooking the Sea of Galilee. From their position, they could see from north to south the towns of Magdala, Tiberias, and Hamat. In Tiberias, they saw Roman soldiers camped with many relaxing in the town's hot springs.

"Ugh. We won't be bathing there again," Z'mia demurred.

Kay're nodded. "The southernmost town, Hamat has hot pools. I soaked in ones dedicated to women. We can go there."

"Do you have friends there?"

"I do. A nice man named Cleophas and his wife Marry."

"Then what are we waiting for?" Z'mia said eagerly.

"For the sun to go down. If we descend now, someone, namely the soldiers, might see us."

"I am starving," Z'mia said wearily, sitting down.

Kay're nodded, joining her. "There's a cricket next to you. They're edible."

Z'mia gazed at the insect and swallowed dryly. "I'll pass. You can have it."

Kay're chuckled. "I can wait."

When the sun slipped below the horizon, they made their way toward Hammet. The going was slow in the dim light. By the time they approached the edge of town, it was dark and only a few people were about. Some were at the well drawing water, and the others at the springs that were on the other side of town. Keeping their heads low, the ladies walked toward a long-needed bath.

As they neared the women's pool, they heard clopping from behind. Turning, they saw Roman horsemen coming up the street. Quickly, they ducked into a nearby animal stall that held lambs. Lying low in the hay, they watched the Romans ride past led by the centurion that was hot on their trail. Several soldiers held torches for light. The men pulled up to the women's spring and dismounted.

soldiers held torches for light. The men pulled up to the women's spring and dismounted.

"Look! They are making the women get out of the water," Z'mia whispered.

"The centurion is searching for us," Kay're said. "See, he's dismissing the old ones and inspecting the others, focusing on their hair length."

"And more than that," Z'mia said, "look how the men are staring at the naked women."

"Disgusting. I hope the centurion has learned his lesson and will reprimand his men."

"Woman," Centurion Marcus addressed one of them. Both Kay and Z'mia could hear his voice. "Have you seen two tall women that are strangers to your village? They have short hair." The woman shook her head. "I want an answer, not a head shake. I'm going to ask all of you. Did any of you see these women or an unaccompanied small female child?" The women exchanged glances with each other and in unison mumbled, "No."

"So, you did see them or the child," Marcus accused. "You gave yourselves away." He pulled out his sword and put its point to a woman's throat. "Do you want to change your answer?"

"We saw one woman with short hair about two weeks ago. And there was a small girl that was without a parent. But not since."

"Not two women?"

"No, no. Only one," they chorused.

"Was this one staying with anyone in town?" There was silence until the sword touched the throat again.

"Cleophas and his wife."

"Lead me to their home."

"May I dress?"

Marcus nodded. "Go ahead."

"We have to get to Cleophas and warn him," Kay're said, hurriedly, worry etching her face. "Let's scoot out the back."

They ran to Cleophas' home and found it dark. Kay're knocked on the door and called out his name. There was no answer. "I'm going in." She pushed open the door. "Cleophas, Mary." Still no reply. She searched the rooms, finding them empty.

door and called out his name. There was no answer. "I'm going in." She pushed open the door. "Cleophas, Mary." Still no reply. She searched the rooms, finding them empty.

"Kay're! The soldiers are coming."

"The bedroom window," Kay're said, pointing to it. She opened the wooden panel, and they slipped through as Centurion Marcus entered the house. He heard a noise from the back room and rushed in to see the window open. Stepping up to it, he peered out and saw two figures scurrying away.

"It's them!" he shouted and raced outside and mounted his horse. He led his troops around back and up the hillside path. After several paces, he stopped and ordered his men to dismount and search the area. With torches in one hand and swords in the other, the men beat the bushes and stumbled over the rocks.

Kay're and Z'mia crouched behind a large boulder. They could hear the Romans drawing closer. Kay're peaked out to see a single torch approaching. "One is coming," she whispered, her body tensing ready for a fight. "He may not see us." Z'mia nodded nervously, and grasped a good-sized stone.

The soldier was about to pass by but caught his foot in a hole and fell into Z'mia. She clutched him and placed a hand over his mouth and then used the stone on his head. He went limp.

Kay're took the torch. "Is he still breathing?"

"Yes. Should I finish him off?" Z'mia asked in a low voice.

"No. No more death. Take his water bottle and that bag. It may have food."

"Atilius," called out an approaching soldier.

The women exchanged glances. Kay're shrugged. "Here," she gruffed in her best imitation of a man's voice and waved the torch. "Z'mia, get ready."

"Atilius, are you okay?" the soldier asked, seeing his comrade's legs sticking out from behind the boulder. He bent down to check on him and saw stars.

Kay're smiled. "You're good with that rock. Get his water and food bag, and let's get out of here." They extinguished the torches and crept their way up the hillside.

Marcus frustration grew as the soldiers weren't having luck capturing the women. "Decanus, recall the men. We'll not find them in the darkness." Varius dismounted and walked up the hillside and ordered the men to return to their horses.

women. "Decanus, recall the men. We'll not find them in the darkness." Varius dismounted and walked up the hillside and ordered the men to return to their horses. The troops mustered and took charge of their mounts. Yet, two horses remained without riders.

"Who's missing?" Marcus asked, fearing the worst.

"Atilius and Callius," Varius replied. He shouted out their names. The air remained quiet.

Centurion Marcus sighed. He knew the women had got them. "Take the men and search for them. You two stay here." He pointed to two of the soldiers. Varius and the others took to the hills.

After twenty minutes, Varius and the men returned supporting their missing mates. "Report," Marcus ordered.

"We found them unconscious. I got them back with splashes of water on their face. Someone hit them in the head." The two men had blood on the side of their heads. Varius had removed their helmets. "They didn't see who hit them. And whoever it was took their canteens and food bags."

"Is that true?" Marcus questioned the men.

Both nodded while holding their heads. "It is," Callius mumbled, and his legs gave out.

"Get them on their horses. We are returning to camp." Marcus pulled on his horse's reins and turned back to town. "Another missed opportunity," he mumbled to himself.

From the hill, Kay're and Z'mia watched the Roman torches retreat to town. "They'll be back in the morning," Kay're said. "Let's see what is in the bags."

"I see dried meat and some sort of grain cakes," Z'mia said.

"Same here." Kay're bit off a chunk of meat. "Tastes like bacon."

"Whatever it is, it's salty, but satisfying," Z'mia said. She then took a swallow from the canteen. "Hey, this isn't water. Hmm. Wine. How about you?"

"Water," Kay're said, and took a long drink.

"Is wine a standard drink for a soldier?"

"I don't think so. Likely one of those guys was a wino."

"What's a wino?"

"A drunkard."

"I don't think so. Likely one of those guys was a wino."

"What's a wino?"

"A drunkard."

"Ah. I know what you mean. Let me have some of your water. Do you want a drink of wine?"

"Why not? It'll relax me." They exchanged canteens. After a while, they were sleeping.

CHAPTER FORTY NINE
Barabbas

Higher up the hill, a figure watched the women dispatch two Roman soldiers. He grinned with satisfaction and slowly crept toward them. His crawl stopped as the torches went dark. "Of course," he whispered to himself. "The light would give them away." He waited, and the Romans returned to retrieve the fallen. The women had retreated, but to where? He resumed his crawl to their last position, hoping to find them.

The wine went to their heads, and they succumbed to its effect. Kay're and Z'mia Nh'Got were sound asleep and didn't hear the approaching man. In the dim moonlight, he assessed their placid faces. He crouched down and touched Nh'Got's hair. The softness of it gave him pause, as it had been some time since he was with a woman. She stirred a bit but relaxed in slumber.

He glanced over to the other woman. Equally beautiful, yet different. Her breathing was slow and deep. *How could you allow yourselves to be caught off guard after evading the soldiers?* He shook his head and pulled out his knife. Turning it in one hand, he reached down and took hold of the canteen lying next to the woman. He took a long draw. It wasn't water! *No wonder the women are out. The wine is potent but satisfying, another missed pleasure.*

Never taking his eyes off the women, he settled onto the ground with his back against a rock. After more gulps from the canteen, his mind started lusting for the women. He shuffled on all fours toward them.

Once again, Kay're found herself running down a white corridor. Turning a corner, she faced the same angel. "My, you're persistent," the ethereal one said. "I told you it isn't your time."

"I know. My spirit is weak, and the draw of pure love is overwhelming. I must

must find Him.”

“You have found the Prince of Peace on Earth—rejoice. Until the appointed time that only the Father knows, hold steadfast in your belief in the Son of Man.” The angel paused and looked down. “There is danger!” He disappeared and Kay’re winked open an eye to see a dark form hovering over Z’mia. Quickly, she snapped out her left foot, hitting the figure in the head. Blackness replaced the lust in his mind, and he fell onto Z’mia. Panic replaced her dream. She screamed out and pushed the load away.

“Tl’Rak!” she panted.

“No. Not him,” Kay’re said, studying the man’s face that was bleeding from the nose.

“Another thief,” Z’mia said, shaking her head that was dizzy from the wine.

“Worse. He was about to….”

“Thanks,” Z’mia said, sitting. “Whoa, that wine put me out.”

“Me too.”

“How did you wake up in time?”

“The angel warned me. We better get this guy tied up. I still need to sleep off the wine.”

“He was about to rape me. He doesn’t deserve to live. If he is dead, we can sleep in peace and not have to worry about him.” She spotted his knife and picked it up. Kay’re shook her head. “Then let me castrate him!” Z’mia said.

“Whoa! That’s extreme. If I was a man, I would rather be dead.”

Z’mia studied the man, took the knife, and slit the man’s tunic to the groin. She paused, then cut several strips for bindings.

“Girl! I thought you were going to do it.”

Z’mia chuckled. “Don’t tempt me. Let’s hog-tie him.” They did, gagging and blindfolding him too. Satisfied, they returned to their dreams.

Grunts and groans at sunrise woke the women. Their unwanted guest was struggling against the bindings. Kay’re took his knife and cut loose the blindfold. She chuckled. “You’re lucky to be alive. When I told my friend that you were about to molest her, she wanted to cut off your….” She pointed the knife to his groin. His face paled. “But she was too drunk from the wine and her hand was too shaky to do the job.” She looked over to Z’mia and winked. “Is your hand steady now?”

groin. His face paled. "But she was too drunk from the wine and her hand was too shaky to do the job." She looked over to Z'mia and winked. "Is your hand steady now?"

Z'mia grinned from ear to ear. "It sure is." She showed him an unwavering hand. "Let me have the knife." Kay're tossed it to her. Z'mia held it up, the sun reflecting off the blade into the man's eyes. She walked over to him and hunched down, waving the knife in his face. His eyes were wide with fear and he shook his head and grunted through the gag. She moved the knife to his groin. The man twisted his body away. "Kay're, he is too squirmy. Hold him still."

"He might head butt me," Kay're said.

"I can take care of that," Z'mia said. She moved the blade to his throat and held it there. The man's face was ashen. She moved the blade up to his chin. The point drew a few drops of blood. With a quick swipe, she cut loose the gag. He gasped in relief.

"Enough, who are you?" Kay're asked. It took a minute for him to regain his breath.

"I'm Barabbas."

"Barabbas!" Kay're repeated.

"Do you know him?" Z'mia asked.

"I know the name and its historical significance." Barabbas' eyebrows peaked. "Barabbas was the one Pontius Pilate freed, paving the way for Jesus's crucifixion. Are you that man?"

He nodded.

"You have no shame. You should feel blessed," Kay're said. "The crowd spared your life for the Son of God, and still, you are acting badly."

"I didn't intend to harm you last night. I admire you, women, for what you did to the Roman soldiers last night. I saw you hit them in the head with a rock. I despise the Romans as much as you. And you're the women rumored to have taken down a whole troop of Romans. Is it true?"

"It is," Z'mia gruffed. "You're no better than them. You tried to rape me last night!" Her eyes narrowed in furry. "I should've killed you!"

Barabbas cringed. "I apologize for my behavior. The wine, it went to my head, and I lost control."

head, and I lost control.”

“Enough,” Kay’re cut him off and gave Z’mia an apologetic look.

Z’mia shook her head and sucked in a breath to compose herself.

“Barabbas, if we free you, will you behave?” Kay’re asked.

“You have my word.”

Kay’re cut the bindings and Barabbas groaned as he stretched out his arms and legs. “Do you have any water?” She handed him the Roman water bottle. He took long draws. “And food?” Z’mia tossed him a few dried locusts. The man eagerly downed them. Z’mia grimaced watching him eat them.

“You dislike them?” he said to her.

“I prefer other foods,” she answered, still feeling anger toward the man. He shrugged. “Are there more?”

“Hold out your hands,” she said, and emptied the bag of locusts. One after another he popped them into his mouth, then paused.

“I’m sorry. I forgot about you,” he said to Kay’re. “Please.” He offered her the rest.

“No. You can have them all,” she said, smiling.

“You know, the entire Roman army is after you. You two aren’t safe in all of Israel. If I were you, I would leave this land quickly. If you can, get across the Sea of Galilee and head east.”

“We have business here,” Kay’re said. “We can’t leave until we take care of it.”

“What kind of business would you have? Women aren’t business people unless....”

“Don’t think it,” Z’mia cut him off. “We’re not that kind. Before we leave this land, we have to find the one called Jesus Christ.”

“So, you too have heard the rumor that He has risen from the dead.”

“It’s not a rumor,” Kay’re said. “We have seen His resurrected self. But he left us before we could conclude our business with Him.”

“What business would a mere man or woman in your case have with the Son of God?”

“It is personal,” Kay’re said.

“You’re diseased and need healing!” He backed away.

“We’re not,” Z’mia corrected. “We need his help to leave this land.”

"You're diseased and need healing!" He backed away.

"We're not," Z'mia corrected. "We need his help to leave this land."

"I told you, cross the sea and head east. The Roman Empire doesn't extend past the Sea of Galilee."

"Reaching the shoreline is the problem," Kay're said, stretching the truth. "We were down in Hammet last night and the Romans saw us and chased us up this hill."

He chuckled. "So, you think, Jesus of Nazareth will wink you across."

"Something like that," Kay're replied. "After all, He is the Son of God and anything is possible with God."

"He rose from the dead!" Z'mia added.

Barabbas rubbed his chin. "That is true. You two have great faith." He then turned his head. "I hear someone coming." All eyes looked down the hill. Roman soldiers were at the base, led by the centurion. He pointed up the hill and several men dismounted and started upward. The centurion took the rest of the horsemen north and up the road.

"He's going to cut off our retreat," Z'mia said.

"Romans are smart," Barabbas said. "There's a small cave up the hill shielded by an outcropping. It is hard to find. I will take you to it and you can hide there. Then I will return here. When the Romans come, I will tell them you headed north at sunrise. They will scurry down to their horses and catch up with the centurion and relay the information."

"What about you?" Kay're asked.

"Thanks to them, I'm a free man. They don't want me. Their focus is on you. Once they leave, I'll return and give you the all-clear."

"Barabbas, you are favored in God's eyes," Kay're said. "He uses you to complete His will. Your release from prison was necessary so His son, Jesus, could die for the forgiveness of sin. And now, He uses you to save us from the Romans. God the Father will use you in the future. For what, only He knows. There is a proverb that says, trust in the Lord with all your heart, and do not rely on your own understanding. In all your ways acknowledge him, and he will make straight your paths. Remember this always." She leaned over and kissed him on the cheek. "Please, take us to the cave."

him on the cheek. "Please, take us to the cave."

CHAPTER FIFTY
Rebirth

*T*he Romans were quick climbers led by Decanus Varius. Kay're and Z'mia had barely squeezed into the cave before they heard the soldiers confronting Barabbas. "I recognize you," Varius said. "You're Barabbas. The one released instead of Jesus, the Nazarene. He died so you could live."

"I'm a free man," Barabbas claimed, moving away from the shaded cave entrance. "I have committed no crimes since then. Why do you come after me?"

"We don't want you," Varius replied, eyeing the man's bruised face. "We're looking for two women that are in the area. Your face tells me that you encountered them."

"I did. Last night these wild women jumped on me and beat me. One even attempted to cut my throat. See my wound." He lifted his chin to show the decanus the blood crusted cut.

"I know these women. They wouldn't attack you unless they had a reason. You forced yourself on them, didn't you?"

Barabbas cleared his throat. "Why would I accost two helpless women? The people gave me a chance to redeem my life, and I will not jeopardize that."

"These women are far from helpless," Varius countered. "You attacked them, and they got the better of you. You're lucky to be alive."

"Believe what you want. I'm innocent of any crime."

"So where are the women?"

"I don't know. They hogtied me, blindfolded me, and put a gag in my mouth. Just before sunrise, one said, 'We need to head for Capernaum.' Then I heard them walk off. I lay quiet until the sun's rays filtered through the blindfold. Then, I freed myself and they were nowhere in sight."

Varius scanned the area. He saw no women, only rocky hills, brush, and sky. "Barabbas, commit no more crimes, or you will hang on a cross. Men, back to the to the horses."

"Stay put," Barabbas warned the women through the side of his mouth. "I don't trust the Romans. They could double back." After the Romans rode away, he gave them the all-clear. The women crawled out and saw the dust of the Romans riding northward. They sighed, relieved. Neither relished the thought of another fight with them.

"Thank you, Barabbas," Kay're said. "Here, take this canteen and food bag."

"But you'll need them."

"That's okay. They're extras we got from the Roman soldiers," Kay're said, smiling. "May God bless you."

He was speechless as he stood watching the women descend the hill. He looked inside the food bag, found dry meat, and ate a portion, washing it down with water. He then headed north to Capernaum to see what the Romans would find there.

"Decanus Varius, aren't we going to join up with Centurion Marcus and tell him where the women are going?" asked one of his men.

"We don't have time to do that. The women will escape us again. We need to overtake them and wait for the centurion. We'll receive the glory for capturing them." *Or the wrath of Marcus for going solo.*

Varius's plan was to head to the home of the prostitute, Mary of Magdala, and lay in wait. One woman had stayed with her and he figured both would return. When they did, he and his men would spring out and capture them. He had a nagging question in his mind. Were he and his five men capable of handling the women and capturing them alive? If the women died in a scuffle, his life would end. If they got the better of him, again his life would end. Both were no-win solutions. He had to take them alive and stay alive himself. He made his first command decision and waved his men on.

Kay're and Z'mia entered Hamat that was now void of Romans. The locals were going about their morning chores. The women returned to Cleophas's home to find it vacant. The back window was still open, which meant Cleophas and Mary hadn't returned.

to find it vacant. The back window was still open, which meant Cleophas and Mary hadn't returned.

"I need that bath," Z'mia chimed.

Kay're chuckled. "Let's go."

There were a few women with children in the spring. They were bathing the children and refreshing themselves. One woman said, "You are the women the Romans are after. You should leave before they return."

"We saw them from the hillside," Kay're said. "They are heading toward Capernaum and won't be back today. Has anyone seen Cleophas and Mary?"

"Not since Passover. We don't know when they will return."

"There is a rumor that they have seen the Teacher—alive after His crucifixion!" another exclaimed.

"He is alive," Kay're confirmed. "We have seen Him too. And we need to find Him again. Have any of you seen Him?"

All shook their heads.

"My husband heard someone say that the Teacher was in Capernaum yesterday," said an elder woman. "Maybe that's why the Romans headed that way."

Kay're and Z'mia exchanged glances. "We need to bathe first," Z'mia said.

Both entered the water. "Whoa, this is wonderful," Z'mia cooed, sitting in the warm water.

"It is," Kay're agreed, sinking to her neck. "I have been thinking. We shouldn't go to Capernaum. Jesus may not be there. After His resurrection, He appears when and where He wants and to whom. Like on the road, when the Romans had us cornered. Then He just disappeared."

"What do you suggest?"

"We head back to Bethany via the road. The centurion and his men will be in Capernaum searching for us. When they don't find us, they will search the surrounding area. It will take days to do so. In Bethany, there will be few or no Romans. If there are any, they won't know what we look like. So, we should be safe."

"Why Bethany?" Z'mia quizzed.

"The Mount of Olives is there. That's where Jesus ascends into heaven. We'll certainly see him."

Z'mia nodded. "Tl'Rak will know that too."

"The Mount of Olives is there. That's where Jesus ascends into heaven. We'll certainly see him."

Z'mia nodded. "Tl'Rak will know that too."

"We'll arrive before him. When he shows up, we'll take him down." She made a slash motion across her throat.

"He may be there already, waiting for us and Jesus."

"That is a good point. He's crafty. We should count on it and approach cautiously."

Z'mia bobbed her head. "You know, I could sit here in this water forever." She sighed and let her head lay against the pool's rim.

Kay're smiled, and climbed out of the water. "And you will if we don't get to the Mount of Olives and take care of business." Z'mia cringed and pushed herself up onto the bank.

After their bath, they purchased food, refilled their canteens, and began their journey. For the first few hours the road was devoid of activity. Then they heard the gallop of horses. They were Romans, four in number. Without cover, they lowered their heads and moved off the road to give the riders room to pass.

The soldiers slowed down and pulled up next to the women. "Have you seen any other soldiers in the area?" one asked them.

"We have," Kay're answered. "North of Hamat. We heard that they were heading to Capernaum."

"Why are you not looking up at me?"

"We are humble women and respect your authority," Kay're replied, head still down.

"And you will curse us when we leave. What are your names and where are you from?" he pushed. They didn't reply. Kay're could read dark intentions in the man's mind. She coughed and brought her hand up to cover her mouth and in doing so nudged Z'mia.

"I asked you questions." He dismounted. Kay're sensed his ugliness increasing. She also read the mind of another soldier. He thought that they were the wanted women.

"Again, we are humble women but hard-working," she said. "Look at my hand as proof." She raised it and thrust it into his throat. The man gasped and fell to hand as proof." She raised it and thrust it into his throat. The man gasped and fell to his knees. Quickly, she pulled the reins of the nearest horse and twisted them. The horse and rider came down. She kicked him in the head and he went limp.

Z'mia had the clue and was ready. When Kay're acted, she yanked on the reins of a horse, spilling both horse and rider. The man got trapped under the horse and was yelping in pain. She silenced him with a foot to the jaw and dove and rolled. And just in the nick of time, as the fourth Roman had his sword out and swiped at her but missed.

He quickly turned his horse toward Kay're. She too ducked and rolled, evading the man. Determined, he spun his horse around to attack again. Z'mia had gathered a sword, held it up over her head to parry the strike. She did and fell to the ground from the force of the blow. Swiftly, he guided the horse around to see the other woman holding a sword. He raced toward her and swung his sword. Kay're dodged it and backhanded her sword, severing his foot. He wailed in pain as the horse race on but fell off, grabbing at the stump. Blood was spurting out.

Kay're came over to him. "Help me," he pleaded. She started to kneel, but hesitated as she sensed more danger. She turned to Z'mia who was dusting herself off. One soldier had regained consciousness. He staggered to his feet, pulled out his dagger, and threw it, hitting Z'mia in the lower right chest. Z'mia clutched her chest and inadvertently activated her annunciator.

Aboard the *Lionare,* the comm-officer noticed Lt. Nh'Got's annunciator was open for conversation. He hailed her but got no response. It caused him concern and he called out, "Supreme Commander, Lt. Nh'Got's annunciator is open, but she isn't responding. I fear something has happened to her."

Tr'Tala turned to him and noticed the apprehension on the man's face. "Put her annunciator on the speaker," he said, unsettled. Everyone on the bridge became attentive and inched up on their seats to listen to what was transpiring on the planet's surface.

"Kay're!" Z'mia yelled, pulling out the dagger. She fell hard onto her back.
Aghast, Kay're ran with a sword to the Roman who threw the dagger and thrust the blade under his sternum and upward. She left it there and ran to Z'mia. The soldier

Aghast, Kay're ran with a sword to the Roman who threw the dagger and thrust the blade under his sternum and upward. She left it there and ran to Z'mia. The soldier stumbled and fell to the ground with the blade coming out his back.

On a hillside near the road, Tl'Rak watched the skirmish. He was further impressed with the women's fighting ability. They did a number on him and had just taken out four soldiers trained to fight with swords. He was thoroughly enjoying the moment. His mood dampened when Lt. Nh'Got went down from a knife.

"You fought a good battle, Nh'Got, but you were careless," Tl'Rak told himself. "You should always finish the enemy. This is what happens when you don't. Well, one less person to worry about." He grinned. "Now, I just need to get answers from you, mysterious woman. Then I will end your life."

He started moving down the hillside, then abruptly stopped as he heard a child's voice in his head. "No! You are an evil man!"

He immediately recognized it. He glanced back to see the girl holding a rock. His blaster was on a strap dangling from her neck. "Child, you will pay now!"

She threw the rock at him. He ducked and started up the hill. She raised the blaster and fired. The shot hit stones just in front of his face, throwing debris into it. He cursed and rubbed the dust from his eyes. When they cleared, he saw her disappear over the ridge.

"Oh, Z'mia," Kay're cried, tearing open the tunic to assess the wound. The wound was bubbling blood. She could hear a sucking sound with each breath Z'mia took. Those on the *Lionare* heard the same. They moved to the edge of their seats with faces showing deep concern.

Z'mia was pale and weak. Kay're used the same knife that had hit her friend and cut a section of cloth from her tunic and placed it over the wound. "Hold this," she said and took Z'mia's hand and draped it on cloth. She then ran over to one of the dead Romans and unbuckled his belt, stripped off the canteen, food bag, and scabbard. Using the knife, she cut off a length of his uniform and ran back to Z'mia. "Kay're, I won't make it." Her voice was weak.

"Hush. You will." She tossed the original cover and fan-folded the Roman cloth into a bandage and placed it on the wound. She wrapped the belt around Z'mia and food bag, and scabbard. Using the knife, she cut off a length of his uniform and ran back to Z'mia.

"Kay're, I won't make it." Her voice was weak.

"Hush. You will." She tossed the original cover and fan-folded the Roman cloth into a bandage and placed it on the wound. She wrapped the belt around Z'mia and cinched it tight over the bandage.

"Kay're, I am glad to have you as my friend."

Kay're smiled. "And you as my friend." She could sense Z'mia's life fading with each breath. She took her canteen, cleaned her face, and gave her a sip of water.

"We were good super sleuths," Z'mia managed.

"We still are and will be again." Kay're eyes were misting. In her lifetime she had seen much death and lost many close to her. Yet there was something very special about Z'mia. Her death would rip her apart. "Z'mia, I'm so sorry." She wept and held her friend's head in her lap.

High in space, Subcommander M'Catis had a tear in his eye. He had developed a great respect and fondness for the young lieutenant. He judged her to be an exceptional woman.

Kay're didn't hear the approaching footsteps. "We know you," came a voice.

She looked up to see the men that she had supper with. They were Jesus's apostles. "Peter," she said, acknowledging him. He and the others came to her side and stooped.

"This woman. We know her. Jesus invited her to our campsite one night. We suppered together. Is she your friend?" Peter asked.

"She is," Kay're acknowledged, wiping the tears from her eyes.

"She looks bad," said another apostle, feeling Z'mia's skin and putting an ear to her chest to listen to her heart.

"A stab wound to the lung," Kay're said, sniffling back tears.

"I'm Luke, a physician. This is grave. I can do nothing for her." On the *Lionare,* there was a gasp from the comm-officer. M'Catis wiped away tears. Tr'Tala held a passive face, though his heart ached for the brave lieutenant.

"You have so little faith," came another voice. All eyes turned to see Jesus standing before them. He knelt next to Z'mia. "This one has great faith. She called out to me when she was thirsty. She brought her enemy to me for healing. Daughter," He said

"You have so little faith," came another voice. All eyes turned to see Jesus standing before them. He knelt next to Z'mia. "This one has great faith. She called out to me when she was thirsty. She brought her enemy to me for healing. Daughter," He said to her. Z'mia's eyes opened weakly. Everything was blurry, but she recognized the voice. Suddenly a feeling of love flushed through her body. She managed a thin smile.

"Who do you say I am?"

"The Son of God." Her voice was faint.

All on the *Lionare* exchanged glances and murmurs crisscrossed the bridge. Tr'Tala waved a hand to hush them. He leaned forward to better listen to what was being said.

"Your faith has healed you." Jesus said, touching her wound. He stood and vanished.

Z'mia's color returned. She coughed, then took a deep breath. Kay're cut the belt and checked the wound. It was closed and disappearing. "You're going to be okay! We'll be super-sleuthing again. Rest."

Cheers echoed across *Lionare's* bridge. Tr'Tala still stoic, didn't silence them. *Could this man called Jesus Christ be the Son of God? Or was he still just a benevolent alien? But did he release my ship?* He turned an ear to listen further.

"We have witnessed the Master perform many great signs since He has risen," said the youngest man.

Kay're remembered reading that Jesus performed many miracles in the presence of his disciples that weren't recorded in the Bible. "You must be John."

"I am. You are Kay're. Mary of Magdala speaks well of you."

"Mary is a very kind woman. How is she doing?"

"She is well and rejoicing with Mary, the mother of Jesus, and the other women."

"That is nice." Kay're smiled and noticed the Roman soldier who had the horse fall on him crawling away. "Excuse me," she said and went over to him. One of his legs was limp. She stood over him.

He looked up at her, his face pained. "I saw Him appear and disappear out of nowhere. He's the Nazarene we crucified. He healed that woman. Is he truly the Son of God?"

out of nowhere. He's the Nazarene we crucified. He healed that woman. Is he truly the Son of God?"

"You saw, you heard. What do you believe?"

"That He is God's son. How do I receive healing for my broken leg?"

"You have received healing," Peter said, walking up. "Your soul now has eternal life in paradise with Christ."

The soldier managed a thin smile. "But my leg, it still hurts terribly."

Peter looked up to the sky and prayed and positioned his body in such a way that his shadow covered the man. The soldier's eyes widened, and mouth gaped. He touched his leg and felt no pain. Peter reached down and pulled him up to a standing position. "Go, my brother, and delight in the glory and power of Jesus Christ. Be a soldier for Him and Him alone."

"Thank you," he said, hugging him, something a Roman would never do with a Jew. He found his horse and rode off toward Galilee.

Kay're excused herself and ran over to the Roman with the severed foot. He was pale and unmoving. There was a large pool of blood at the base of the affected leg, and the hemorrhaging had ceased. He had bled out. She stared down at him and shook her head.

Peter and Luke came up to her. "We saw everything. You defended yourself and unfortunately, people died. They're in God's hands now. Come, let us rejoice in the rebirth of Z'mia, a new daughter of Christ."

CHAPTER FIFTY ONE
The Past is Now

Tl'Rak saw the child disappear behind an out-cropping. He paused and studied the terrain. "I'll cut you off!" he shouted and moved on a diagonal. Rounding a large boulder, he reached out and grasped nothing but air.

"What? Where are you?" In the distance to his left, he saw birds scatter from the hillside. There amongst the rocks, the girl scurried. She was agile and quick, and catching her on the run would be impossible. He would follow her, knowing she would fatigue, stop, and fall asleep. He had the stamina and will to go on until she was in his grasp.

Before returning to Z'mia's side, Kay're glanced at the hillside. She had seen her little self shoot at Tl'Rak and disappear over the ridge. Tl'Rak unhurt, clawed his way after her. Kay're desperately wanted to sprint up the hill to help. Instead, she sucked in a breath and followed the men to Z'mia but not after sneaking another peek at the hillside.

The disciples were sitting around Z'mia. They were in awe of Peter's healing of the Roman soldier. When they saw the trio approaching, they stood with John helping Z'mia up.

"Peter, you have the gift of healing," Andrew, his brother, said.

"We all do," Peter confirmed. "The Master told us so. He said nothing will be impossible for you if you have faith the size of a mustard seed and believe in God Almighty. I now have that faith. Andrew, you have it too. You all do!" He hugged his brother. "Let us sit and sup and rejoice in the risen Lord."

"The Alpha and the Omega, the beginning and the end, the first and the last," Kay're said. Eyes fixed on her. "It's a quote from Jesus."

"He said this to you?" John asked.

She smiled at him. "And He will say it to you too." She didn't want to tell him he would hear these words in a vision and write them down. John nodded.

"Z'mia, how do you feel?" Kay're asked her.

"Like a new woman." She tapped her chest. In doing so, she closed the comm-link to the *Lionare.*

Aboard the Valeriian ship, the comm-officer noticed the link had closed. "Shall I get her back?" he asked the Supreme Commander.

"No," Tr'Tala answered. "Helm, try to maneuver the ship."

The helmsman worked his board and shook his head. "No response, sir."

"Jesus isn't kind to us," he breathed, retreating to his cabin. He contacted his wife and gave her a rundown of current events.

"Sen, I'm sure everything will turn out okay," she encouraged, hoping her words weren't empty.

"I hope so," he replied, sighing. She blew him a kiss. He returned the same.

"Kay're, you have eaten little, while Z'mia has partaken as if it was her last meal," Peter said. "Your face was joyous and now you look unsettled. What has changed your spirit?"

"I'm looking at those dead soldiers. I'm responsible for their deaths. I started the fight." It was half true. She was more worried about her little self with Tl'Rak on her trail. She wanted so much to race ahead, to help and take Tl'Rak out once and for all.

"Kay're, if you didn't act first, they would have captured us and done worse," Z'mia countered.

"She's right," John agreed. The others chorused their agreement. "They could have ridden past but they didn't. They stopped for only one purpose."

"We know, John," Peter interrupted.

Kay're nodded and looked skyward. Buzzards were circling. "We have to bury or burn them." She pointed up to the sky. "If they are here, the Romans will see them and come."

Without tools to dig, they dragged the dead to the base of the hill and gathered rocks to cover them. It took them over an hour to complete the burial. Peter concluded with a prayer and said to the women, "We're going to Galilee. Will you gathered rocks to cover them. It took them over an hour to complete the burial. Peter concluded with a prayer and said to the women, "We're going to Galilee. Will you join us?"

"What will you do there?" Z'mia asked.

"Most of us are fishermen. We'll fish and spread the good news of Jesus rising from the dead," Peter answered.

"And maybe Jesus will appear to us again," Andrew added.

"I'm sure He will," Kay're said, smiling. She remembered the Bible story of the men fishing and seeing a man on the shore waving to them. At first, they wouldn't recognize Him as Jesus. He would tell them to let down the nets again and they would catch many fish. Then they would recognize Him.

"We have business in Bethany," she continued. "We need to take leave now before the Romans show up and find us here." They bid each other farewell and parted ways.

"If you're sure they will see Jesus again, why aren't we going with them?" Z'mia asked.

"Because Tl'Rak is up there in the hills chasing my little self. They both appeared after you went down. My little self shot at him with the blaster but missed and ran off. He took off after her."

"Let's go," Z'mia said, starting the climb. She moved like a cat, as if nothing had happened to her. Kay're kept pace. Atop the ridge, they saw no one. Footprints didn't show on rocks and stone. The child and Tl'Rak could have gone in any direction.

"What do you think or remember from your past?" Z'mia asked.

"My past is now, so I lack recollection. I would head to where it all began."

"Where is that?"

"The hills near Capernaum."

"Where the Romans went?"

Kay're nodded. "They're searching for us. When they don't find us, they will leave and head back to Jerusalem. By the time we get there, they'll be gone."

"I hope so," Z'mia breathed. "I'm not looking for another fight, except with Tl'Rak."

Decanus Varius found the home of Mary of Magdala vacant. That was okay with him. It was all the better to set up his trap. He cracked open the window and lit an oil lamp. As evening approached, it would look like someone was home. The two women would surely invite themselves in.

He had two of his men take the horses down to Capernaum to keep them out of view. When they returned, he positioned them and the others in hiding around the house. Then he took his stealthy place and waited.

Sunset, and still no one appeared. "Surely, the women would be cautious and wait until full darkness," he told himself. The Romans waited and waited until the oil lamp went out. "Maybe that's the sign for the women to approach the house," he whispered, and motioned to the men to be ready to move. The women never appeared, and he and his men kept vigil for a few more hours. The air remained still. Not one person showed up.

Finally, Varius gave up. "Come out, men. They're not showing. We will camp inside the house. In the morning, we will get the horses and rejoin Centurion Marcus." It was a thought he dreaded. He had his explanation and hoped it was good enough. His excuse played over and over in his mind and kept him from a restful sleep.

CHAPTER FIFTY TWO
On the Hunt

Centurion Marcus and his men searched the hills without sighting the women. Nor did they see the small girl. Mid-afternoon he called a halt and he and his men rested and ate. He wondered if Decanus Varius had any luck in finding the women. As the sun continued to move west, there was no decanus or any of his men. It was disconcerting, as they should have shown up by now. *Did they encounter the women? If so, did they fall victim to them?*

Marcus couldn't wait any longer. He had to know. "Mount up, men," he ordered. They backtracked north. On the way, they spotted a lone man on the road. Marcus rode up to him. He recognized the man as Barabbas. He was the one the crowd demanded be released and Jesus of Nazareth crucified. The crucifixion of the one who saved his life, still disturbed him.

"You're Barabbas," Marcus said to him.

"That is my name," he huffed. "Are you going to arrest me? Like, I told the other Roman officer, I have committed no crimes since my release."

"The other Roman, was he alone or with other soldiers?"

"He had men with him."

"Where and when? Were there two women with them?"

"What is it with you Romans and two women?" Barabbas answered. "Just leave me alone." He walked past, but Marcus blocked him with his horse.

"I asked you some questions. I want answers." Marcus put a hand on the hilt of his sword.

"I saw them on the hillside south of here early this morning."

"You saw who?" Marcus demanded, becoming frustrated.

"Romans!" Barabbas shouted. "The leader, a young one, asked me about seeing two women. I haven't seen any women for weeks. Now may I pass?"

"Go," Marcus said, waving a thumb. Barabbas walked away, hiding a smile of of satisfaction for again outwitting the Romans.

"Centurion, do you think he is truthful?" asked one soldier.

"If he has lied, he will die," Marcus replied. "To the south, quickly."

As they rode, Marcus monitored the sky for buzzards. They were a sign that something was dead, or nearly so. In the distance, there were a few high in the sky. Were they gathering for Varius and his men, victims of the women's fury? He hoped not. Nor did he want the women dead. He needed to question them, especially the one who had invaded his mind.

Z'mia contacted the *Lionare.* Supreme Commander Tr'Tala took the call and sighed relieved that the young lieutenant was well. He left the comm open for everyone to hear. Smiles broke across the crew's faces on hearing Lt. Nh'Got's strong voice. She assured Tr'Tala that she was fit and on the trail of Tl'Rak. She wanted to know if they still had a fix on the girl's annunciator and her heading. They did, and the child was traveling toward Jerusalem.

Kay're heard the conversation. "That's interesting. I thought she would head to where it all began."

"Where it all began? I don't understand," Z'mia said, her

"It's the place where I returned to yesterday."

Z'mia gave her a quizzical look.

Kay're laughed. "Just as Tl'Rak, you, your supreme commander, and I came back in time, so did my little self. We adults traveled back intentionally. Little Kay're arrived by accident. Then again, maybe not." She shrugged.

"Where is this place?"

"Toward Capernaum. I hope we can catch up to her before Tl'Rak does. They have about an hour head start. Come on! We need to hurry our pace. Z'mia sighed and quick-stepped it to keep up with Kay're who was walking briskly.

Marcus made it to where he and Varius split for their hunt. The buzzards were still soaring overhead. He had his men dismount and search the hillside. After an uneventful hour, he recalled them. The birds had departed, and that was a good sign. But where was Varius? Where did he go? He looked down to spit and noticed horse tracks.

noticed horse tracks.

"Of course," he blurted out.

"What is it, Centurion?" asked the senior enlisted man.

"Horse tracks!" Marcus replied. "Look, our fresh ones and those over there are older. They are heading north. I know where he is heading."

"Where, Centurion?"

"To the one called Mary of Magdala. The women must have gone there to see her. She was at the Nazarene's crucifixion. Varius figured it out too. Barabbas saw the women. I noticed he had cuts and bruises on his face, likely from a fight he had with them, and ended up on the short end. I am surprised they didn't kill him. He must have seen them move to the north and is following them, likely to seek revenge. Varius must have noticed his battered face too and forced information out of him about the women. Men, we have to ride fast."

With the sun slipping below the horizon, little Kay're was bone-weary. She desired to sleep under the stars and dream of happy times. Yet she knew the evil man was still following her and wouldn't stop until he caught her.

"I need to find Jesus so he can turn on the lights so I can go home," she told herself, and took another step, then another. Finally, fatigue overcame her will. She curled up under a tree and fell asleep.

For a spaceman, Tl'Rak was an able tracker. He had learned the skill from his father while hunting with him as a child. Tracking footprints in the rocky hills was challenging. The child left none. Only subtle clues in the positions of rocks and stones showed him someone had trekked over them. He followed the trail and after several hours, he sat for a rest. It surprised him that the child had such stamina. Any normal child, especially a girl, would have stopped to rest after only two hours. This child was special. Besides her mental ability, she was physically strong like her older self. But she was still a child and no match for him. He had to get the drop on her before she could use the blaster.

Now the sun had set, and the light was a shade of purple. Moving in the dark would be dangerous as he knew large beasts roamed the area at night. Ahead, he could see the hillside flattening to some trees. He would settle there for the night, and

Ahead, he could see the hillside flattening to some trees. He would settle there for the night, and with luck, the girl would too, and maybe even start a fire with the blaster. It would make the catch easier. He scanned the area for a campfire. There was none.

"She's cunning," he told himself. "A fire would be a give-away or a trap! It's good that she didn't ignite one." In the darkness, he stumbled down the hill to the trees. There he found one with an ample trunk and sat, leaning his tired body against it. He ate a small meal and lay down. Soon he was snoring, not knowing the girl was sleeping ten feet away.

It was dark when Centurion Marcus reached the outskirts of Magdala. He had his men dismount. They would approach the town on foot so as not to arouse anyone. There it was, Mary's house. There was a faint light flickering inside.

"Someone is home," Marcus whispered. "I want the women alive. You four, go around the back." He pointed to them. "The rest of you are with me. We're going through the front door." They crept up to the house. Marcus waited until his men were in position in the rear, then drew his sword and burst through the door. To his surprise, he faced not women, but Decanus Varius and his men lounging and eating. Varius's jaw slackened, and he stumbled over a man to stand. Righting himself, he saluted his commander. The others stood to attention.

"Varius, you're fortunate it was me that caught you off-guard. If it was the women, you and your men would be *dead!*"

Varius managed a swallow. "Understood, sir. It won't happen again."

Marcus waved a dismissing hand. "Tell the ones out back to stand down," he said to one of his men. "Everyone can sit and relax." He reclined too. "Give me a report."

Varius filled him in about the events since they split earlier in the day. He also explained his decision to go off on his own to capture the women. He hoped it was good enough.

"Varius, I give you credit," Marcus praised the junior officer. "I would have done the same even if it one-upped my commanding officer. It's a means to secure promotion. In this remote land where opportunities for advancement are slim to none, one does what one must. It was a good try. I agree, the women aren't coming here. Barabbas lied to us. He pointed us in the wrong direction. The women likely have done the same even if it one-upped my commanding officer. It's a means to secure promotion. In this remote land where opportunities for advancement are slim to none, one does what one must. It was a good try. I agree, the women aren't coming here. Barabbas lied to us. He pointed us in the wrong direction. The women likely tore into him but showed mercy by not killing his sorry butt. In gratitude, he didn't give them away. He won't get mercy from me for his lying tongue. We'll rest here tonight and restart the search at daybreak."

Kay're and Z'mia called it a night when darkness covered the land. They found a cozy spot on the hillside. Z'mia called the ship and found out the child had stopped moving some six kilometers from their position.

"As a child, you moved like one of those large cats," Z'mia said. "Moving six clicks in a standard hour through these hills is impressive."

Kay're laughed. "I can feel it in my legs now." She massaged her thighs. "Not as young as I used to be. Let's eat and get some sleep. I want to be moving at sunrise. I'm sure Tl'Rak will be too."

"So, you think he hasn't reached her?"

"Do you think he could cover that same distance over the same time?"

"Not with his weight and age. He's strong, but not in that great of a shape. Walking and crawling in these hills is exhausting. It's way different from exercising on the ship. And we don't have the best nutrition here to maintain our strength. Unless he's moving in the dark, he will be a few clicks behind your little self."

"You don't think he's moving now?"

"No way. The only thing he is doing is snoring. By the way, do I snore?"

"I haven't noticed. Have any of your boyfriends ever mentioned that you do?"

"What boyfriends?" she demurred. "On a spaceship, they don't exist, and I've been in space most of my adult life. At the academy, ah, the few encounters I had, none of them spent the night. Well, they couldn't anyhow. Before the academy, I was a wallflower, absorbed in my studies and prepping myself for the rigors of it. I lacked a boyfriend. When I entered the academy, I wanted to be ready and first in my class. Those that made eyes at me, I looked the other way. I had a few lapses. I'm not that experienced in love."

ready and first in my class. Those that made eyes at me, I looked the other way. I had a few lapses. I'm not that experienced in love."

"You're young and beautiful. You will find love," Kay're assured.

Z'mia grunted. "Not if we don't get off this planet."

"Look at it this way, if we don't, there is always one of those Roman soldiers. That young officer that rides with the centurion. He's handsome. You two would make a pleasant couple."

"He wants to kill me," Z'mia jested.

"Oh, I'm sure you could turn on your feminine charm and twist him around your finger. You will be his centurion."

"Just what I need. Well, he is kind of cute, for a human. I thought you were going to say I should go after the centurion."

"No, he is mine." Kay're giggled, though inside she knew it wasn't a joke.

Z'mia rolled in laughter and Kay're joined her. They laughed themselves to sleep.

A loud guttural sound woke little Kay're. She grabbed the blaster and sat up. The noise continued rhythmically but didn't advance on her. Slowly, she crept to the sound. There he was, the evil man, sleeping on his back, puffing away. She backed up past arm's length just in case he wasn't asleep and studied him. What was he thinking? She entered his mind to find out. Quickly, she broke the link as the image was disgusting. He was dreaming of naked women dancing around and kissing him and worse.

"Yuck," she whispered, and looked at the blaster and then back at him. "Can I do it? Should I? If I do, you will never hurt Jesus," she whispered to him. She lifted the weapon with both hands, placed two fingers on the trigger, and pointed it at him. Her hands trembled and tears rolled down her cheeks. After a few breaths, she lowered the weapon and wiped her eyes clear.

Showing on the side of the blaster were four small green lights. In the sunlight, she hadn't noticed them. Above the trigger was a button. She touched it and only three lights glowed. Again, she pressed the button and two lights showed. Then again, one lit, and again, none. The weapon also lost warmth. She knew it was turned off. She pressed the button again and heard a faint hum, then a green light

She knew it was turned off. She pressed the button again and heard a faint hum, then a green light appeared.

Suddenly she realized the man wasn't snoring anymore. She glanced at him to see his eyes opening and focusing on her. "You," he snarled and pushed himself up. In a panic, she raised the blaster, pulled the trigger, and a green halo bathed him. He fell back, still. She scurried back a bit with the weapon still pointed at him. The man didn't move.

"Are you dead?" she asked. He didn't respond. She focused on his mind. It was empty of thoughts. Standing with the weapon still pointed at him, she came to his side and nudged him with her foot. Still no movement. She knelt and put her hand on his chest. It was moving. He was alive. She let out a sigh, relieved.

"Why am I happy you aren't dead?" She yawned. "I'm tired and need to sleep. But how long will you sleep? Maybe not long enough." She hefted the weapon and discharged it. The green halo reappeared and faded fast. She checked his chest. It was moving. Satisfied, she curled up next to him and fell asleep.

CHAPTER FIFTY THREE
Moving On

At sunrise, the Romans walked to Capernaum to gather their horses. Centurion Marcus and Decanus Varius both felt rejuvenated after spending the night in a warm house instead of outdoors or in a tent. Varius couldn't remember the last time he'd spent a night in a solid enclosure. Such was the life of a junior officer.

"What is our destination, Centurion?" he asked.

"Hamet. The women have friends there. They may be there."

"I'm curious, sir," Varius continued. "It's obvious that these two women and the child are from a foreign land. If they intended to meet the Nazarene Jesus, why are they still here when the man is dead? What is their endgame?"

Marcus tried not to show his annoyance at being questioned so early in the morning. Varius was an irritant, but he had a keen insight. "Perhaps they, like the others, believe the man rose from the dead and they need to see him again. As for their purpose, I don't know, but I want to. They have to answer to those questions and for the attacks on our men."

"Centurion, I don't understand how they have power over the lions. And the ability to fight better than a man. And how do they keep slipping past us all the time?"

"Varius, in time, we will have all the answers."

"Yes, sir. Oh, sir...."

"Stow it, Varius." He cut him off with a quick wave. The decanus bobbed his head. He wanted to know if the women would be scourged and crucified for their crimes. It wasn't his desire. Their beauty and extraordinary abilities had infatuated him. He had never encountered women like them, and it appealed to his manly desires. The thought of seeing them whipped until their flesh tore from their bodies made him cringe. If they survived, their execution would be too much for him to too much for him to take. He shook his head to clear the thoughts.

They reached Capernaum and rode south toward Hamet all the time watching for the women and Barabbas. Centurion Marcus wanted him to face crucifixion for all of his crimes. He would bring fresh charges of lying to a Roman officer and aiding and abetting the criminal women. Even now, he could hear the spikes pounding into the man's wrist and feet, and his howling agony.

"Oh, my head," Tl'Rak grumbled, holding its sides. Overhead the sun was climbing, and the light hurt his eyes. His headache was akin to a drunken hangover. He remembered waking in the middle of the night and seeing the child. She had the blaster pointed at him, then nothing. He concluded that the child shot him. Thankfully, she had it set to the lowest setting. *Was it on purpose? Or was I just lucky?* He shivered in thought and sat up and surveyed the area.

The child was nowhere in sight. He noticed her little footprints heading southeast, and they appeared a few hours old. He cursed himself for being careless. Gingerly, he stood and started following the girl's trail.

Both Kay're and Z'mia had a restful sleep. Z'mia admitted she was sore at the wound site, although there was no trace of the injury. She checked in with the ship and was told the annunciator was moving ten kilometers southeast of them.

"Wow!" Z'mia exclaimed. "Your little self has put another four clicks in before we even woke. She is still heading toward Jerusalem."

"And Tl'Rak is probably hot on her heels," Kay're said, stretching. She then popped a locust in her mouth. "Want one for the road?"

"No way. I still have a cake left and some dried meat. We better get going if we're going to catch them."

"We still have to be careful. The Roman, who rode off toward Capernaum, will likely run into the centurion and his men. He'll tell them what happened to him. I'm not sure how the centurion will take it."

"He won't be happy that we killed three of his soldiers," Z'mia concluded.

"That's for sure. I wonder if he will acknowledge that Jesus rose from the dead and is the Son of God. After all, Jesus had healed him, and now one of his men had received miraculous healing. That same man witnessing your healing. I hope it dead and is the Son of God. After all, Jesus had healed him, and now one of his men had received miraculous healing. That same man witnessing your healing. I hope it brings compassion and forgiveness to the centurion's heart. If it does, then he will understand we fought his men in self-defense."

"He may understand, but he is a soldier and has to answer to authority. I'm sure his superior will be enraged when he learns we dispatched three more of his men. Like it or not, he will follow orders. Just as I did when Tl'Rak started his journey of madness."

Kay're nodded. "You're right. Let's get moving."

Late afternoon found the Roman soldiers led by Centurion Marcus outside of Hamat. He was frustrated he hadn't seen Barabbas. Nor did he and his men see the girl or women. He hoped his luck would change in Hamat.

As they approached the town, they saw a gathering of townspeople. They surrounded someone who was speaking. Marcus wondered in that someone was the crucified Nazarian alive and well. In his disbelief, he saw a Roman soldier was talking.

The man noticed the centurion and excused himself. "I'm Junius." He saluted Marcus.

"What are you doing here? And where is the rest of your patrol?" Marcus questioned.

"Centurion, the rest of the patrol is dead. Killed by two women."

Marcus straightened up in his saddle at the news. Varius pulled his horse up next to the centurion to listen.

"Give me a full accounting," Marcus ordered, dismounting.

"Centurion, two days out from Jerusalem, we came across two women and recognized them to be the ones you seek. Before we could take them into custody, one punched our decanus in the throat and killed him. She then pulled my horse down, and it fell on me, breaking my leg. The other women did the same with Gnaeus's horse. He recovered and threw a dagger, hitting her in the chest. She fell and looked dead. The woman who pulled my horse down, battled Fabius and cut off one of his feet. He bled to death. She then raced over to Gnaeus and ran a sword through him. Finally, she went to her friend and tried to save her, but there was nothing she could do."

to Gnaeus and ran a sword through him. Finally, she went to her friend and tried to save her, but there was nothing she could do."

Marcus's heart sank in despair. He hoped she wasn't the one who had entered his mind. "Okay, go on."

"Then as I watch her hold her dying friend, this man appears out of nowhere. At first, I did not recognize him, but then I realized who it was—the crucified Nazarene named Jesus. He knelt next to the dying woman and touched her. Immediately she was healed! Then he disappeared. As this was going on, a bunch of men showed up. They were Jesus's followers. One named Peter cast his shadow on me, and instantly my leg healed. He called me brother and told me to delight in the glory and power of Jesus Christ and be a soldier for Him and Him alone. I was telling people of what I saw, and my healing, and that Jesus is the Son of God."

Marcus was speechless. Jesus was alive! Only a god could rise from the dead, heal both friend and foe, and appear and disappear in a blink. "And what of the women?"

"I don't know, sir. I jumped on my horse and rode off, ending up here."

"Why here and not return to Jerusalem and report the killing of our men?"

"Centurion, my head was spinning in confusion and wonderment. I didn't want to go back to Jerusalem. Everyone there would think I'm crazy. Of course, they would send out troops to investigate. I didn't want that. The one woman who started the fight didn't come across as a bad person. I know that sounds strange. She could have finished me off but didn't. I just rode until I arrived here. I submit myself to your judgment." He bowed his head, awaiting the centurion's sentence. He knew his misconduct was a capital offense. The centurion had the right to summarily execute him on the spot. He waited to feel the cold steel penetrating his abdomen.

"Get your horse and join up," Marcus ordered.

The man heaved a sigh of relief. "By your command, Centurion." He ran off to retrieve his horse.

"Centurion, he deserted his patrol," Varius said. "Why didn't you execute him?"

"What did he desert? His patrol was dead. He did us a favor by not returning to Jerusalem. Surely, Pilate would order a large posse to hunt the women down. They would get to them before we did and likely torture the women and then execute him?”

"What did he desert? His patrol was dead. He did us a favor by not returning to Jerusalem. Surely, Pilate would order a large posse to hunt the women down. They would get to them before we did and likely torture the women and then execute them. All our questions would go unanswered. Is that what you want?”

Varius shook his head. "No, sir,” he replied, relieved that the centurion had no interest in harming the women. At least not until he had questioned them.

"If you had said yes, then you would execute Junius yourself,” Marcus said and paused to let his words sink in. "The sun will set soon. We'll camp here. Tomorrow we will ride fast to Jerusalem.”

CHAPTER FIFTY FOUR
We Meet Again

After two days of travel, Kay're and Z'mia Nh'Got had only gained four kilometers on the little girl. The child kept a steady pace to Jerusalem, a sign that Tl'Rak hadn't captured her. They didn't see any sign of him but believed he was between them and little Kay're.

"Kay're, I'm going to need a fresh pair of boots once I get back on the ship, if I ever do," Z'mia commented, sitting on a rock. She had taken off her boots to massage her aching feet. "Look, the sole is wearing thin."

"Mine too," Kay're said, checking her boot soles. "This is the most walking I have ever done in my life."

"And you have two lives. Double the walking." Z'mia started chuckling. "I think I hear something." She quickly put her boots back on. To the west, they could see a cloud of dust.

"Romans," Kay're said. "Up into the rocks now." They hurried and found cover amongst the boulders. They were so dust-covered they blended in nicely with the barren, brown, and gray hillside.

Indeed, it was the Romans led by the centurion with the young officer at his side. They rode by without noticing them. Kay're attempted to read the centurion's thoughts but he rode by too swiftly. When the patrol was well down the road, the women peeked out from their hiding spot. They noticed the Romans slow from a gallop to a trot and then stop.

"Centurion, what is it? Why are we stopping?" Varius asked.

"I have a feeling the women are around here. I think we passed them." He didn't tell him that the woman may have entered his mind.

"I see nothing," Varius said.

Marcus ignored him and rode to the rear and scanned the area. He saw nothing and his mind was now his alone. "Another missed opportunity," he told himself, and rode back to the front.

"I didn't see anything," he told Varius and waved his troop forward. They rode off at a slower pace, all the time surveying the hillside for the girl or women.

The night was creeping in from the east and little Kay're was shivering. Her hunger and the cold sapped the strength from her small body. Having only water, she wondered if she could make it to Jerusalem. Ahead, she noticed an unmoving flickering light. She waited until full darkness before creeping up to see who made the fire.

Sitting by a campfire were an old man and his donkey. She knew who it was and walked into the fire's light. Her approach startled the man. He jumped up with a hand on his knife.

"Don't be afraid," she said to him. "We have met before."

The man eyed her. "Yes, of course," he said, smiling. "You're the child with the woman and the injured man. Come and warm yourself." She sat and focused on the fish that was cooking on the fire. "Oh, forgive me. You must be starving."

"I am. And cold."

"The fire will warm you and the fish will fill your tummy. It's ready." He handed her the fish on a stick.

"But you must have some too."

"We can share." He smiled to her and divided the fish. "I'm not like Jesus. I can't make this lone fish turn into many."

"You know He is alive," she said.

"I know, child. He rose from the tomb I placed him in. How do you know He is alive?"

"I have seen Him. But only for a moment. I need to find him so that he can make the lights appear so that I can go home."

"What lights are you talking about?"

"The ones in the mountain that way." She pointed to the east.

"I have never seen lights in the mountains."

"They only come on when Jesus wants them to."

"I see. So, the lights will show you the way home when they appear?" Her story amused him.

"I see. So, the lights will show you the way home when they appear?" Her story amused him.

She shook her head. "Oh no. When they come on, I will run through them and return home."

"Hmm. And where is your home?" She pointed to the sky. *Poor child. Just like the last time we met when I asked her where her parents were. She must miss them badly.* "Child, when Jesus calls you, as He will I one day, we will see the lights and go up to our heavenly home."

"I hope He calls soon. I miss my parents and friends so much."

"I miss mine too," he consoled. "But I hope He doesn't call you or me too soon."

"Why? I want to go home now, not later."

"We have much life to live. I need to proclaim Jesus's resurrection, and through Him one gains eternal life. Of course, you want to grow up to be an adult."

"I will up there." Again, she pointed to the sky.

"If it is God's will. By the way, you never told me your name. Do you have a name? Mine is Joseph. Do you remember it?"

She giggled. "Of course, and my name is Kay're."

"Kay're," he repeated. "It's a beautiful name for a beautiful girl. I met another person with the same name. She is most extraordinary and beautiful, as are you. You two seem so alike."

"I know," little Kay're said and took a bite of the fish.

"You do?"

She nodded, finishing her fish.

"How?"

"Oh look!" She pointed to the moon. It was starting to eclipse with a quarter of it covered.

"I've seen this before," Joseph said. "Soon the whole moon will turn the color of blood. It is an example of God's power."

"Maybe. But it is simply the Earth moving between the sun and the moon. The Earth casts a shadow on the moon as it does. See the curve of the Earth on the moon."

Joseph looked up, bewildered. "Kay're, everyone knows the sun revolves around the

the moon."

Joseph looked up, bewildered. "Kay're, everyone knows the sun revolves around the Earth and the Earth is flat."

She giggled. "Joseph, you are so funny. The Earth is round, not flat. You can see its round shadow on the moon. If the Earth was flat, the shadow would be a straight line. And the Earth goes around the sun, as do the other planets. Didn't they teach you that in school?"

Joseph's mouth was agape. The child had made a logical point. "They didn't teach us about the sky and stars," he answered.

"You went to a poor school. I'm sleepy." She yawned and curled up by the fire. Sleep came quickly to her.

Joseph took a blanket and covered her. "Such a sweet and innocent child." He looked up to the moon again. It was half dark. As the child said, the darkness had a curve to it, like a ball. *Is she right? She is a most unusual child. I will ask her again in the morning how she knows the woman of the same name.*

Tl'Rak finished another frustrating day tracking the girl. Her trail was growing cold. Climbing the rocky and steep hills drained him. He wondered if his inability to stay on her trail was from fatigue. His eyes were having difficulty discerning signs of her movement. Was she jumping from rock to rock, leaving no ground evidence to pick up? Regardless, she was heading toward Jerusalem, likely to see Jesus ascend into heaven.

As he sat, he noticed the moonlight fading. He looked up to see a lunar eclipse. "An omen," he said to the darkness. "I hope a good one, and tomorrow I will have the child in my grasp." He leaned back against a rock and closed his eyes.

"Centurion Marcus, do you think God is angry at us and has caused the moon to grow dark like that?"

Marcus shook his head. "I don't know." His thoughts were on the women and child.

"Centurion, it seems every time the moon grows dark something bad happens. Remember, the moon went dark shortly before Augustus died. Many said it was an omen of his impending death. Do you think it is an omen for us?"

happens. Remember, the moon went dark shortly before Augustus died. Many said it was an omen of his impending death. Do you think it is an omen for us?"

Marcus looked up at the moon. "It's strange that this is occurring. Every time we have gotten close to the child or the women, some force of nature blocks us. The storm popped up when we were at the river where the child was being baptized. She escaped us. Then the lions appeared when she was out in the open. Again, she escaped. The women were at the crucifixion of Jesus.
They evaded us when the ground quaked and lightning and darkness covered the land. Now we are on the verge of taking hold of all three of them."

"Is this a sign that we should give up the chase?" Varius asked.

"We aren't giving up the hunt," Marcus replied bluntly. "It could be a good sign that we are close to catching the three of them. Anyhow, I have seen this before and nothing bad has happened. In a few hours, the moon will be normal. We will be okay. In the morning, we will continue our search for the girl and women."

Varius shivered, "I hope you're right, Centurion." He placed his hands over the fire to warm them. Marcus drew a long swig of wine, hoping that the eclipse was a good omen.

Kay're and Z'mia had settled down for the night. Both were lying on their backs staring up at the lunar eclipse. "Have you ever seen anything like this?" Kay're asked.

"I have on Valerii. Some still believe in superstition and think it's a sign of something bad about to happen. Stupid people."

"Right now, on Earth, no one knows what causes eclipses. Many believe they are signs of God's anger with humanity. And like some of your people, a precursor to something disastrous." "Well, something disastrous is happening!" Z'mia exclaimed. "We are almost out of food and water."

"True," Kay're admitted. "I'm down to two locusts. One for you and one for me."

"I'll wait for lunch. Maybe we will find some berries or those things you call figs."

Kay're laughed. "I'll save one for you, just in case."

Z'mia chuckled. "Thanks. Oh, we're such sorry super sleuths."

Kay're laughed. "I'll save one for you, just in case."

Z'mia chuckled. "Thanks. Oh, we're such sorry super sleuths."

The sun was up an hour before Joseph finally came out of his dream state. He yawned and stretched, and a smile broke out across his face. "I've never slept so soundly. The dreams I had were wonderful," he said to the world. He glanced over to the campfire. It was smoldering, and two buzzards had replaced the child. They were eyeing him.

"Shoo! Fly away," Joseph said, waving a hand. "I'm not dead yet. Find a meal somewhere else." They obliged him and flew off. He sat up and looked in all directions for the girl but didn't see her. He called out her name several times. The air remained quiet. Returning his gaze to the campfire, he noticed the cup and reached for it. Inside was a hunk of bread and some drops of water.

"Oh my," he whispered. "Child, you drank from the cup Jesus used at his last supper. And you left me some bread. Very symbolic." He said a blessing and ate the bread and sipped the few drops of water left inside the cup. Then he took it to his donkey and stored it in a pouch. Panic came over him.

"The vials!" He shuffled through the pouch and felt for them. He sighed in relief. Both were there. He took them out and checked to see if their seals were intact. They were, and he jiggled them to see if the blood he had collected from Jesus's dead body was still present. He heard the blood move in both and placed them inside the cup and closed the pouch.

Returning to the campsite, he kicked dirt onto the warm embers to smother them. Again, he called out for the girl. There was no response. Satisfied that she wasn't in the area, he took hold of the donkey's reins and walked off toward Galilee.

Tl'Rak was up and moving as the morning sun winked over the horizon. He wanted to close the distance on the girl and hopefully catch her off guard. Getting the blaster was his priority. Without it, the girl was harmless and he believed Jesus was too, before his ascension. Of course, with the blaster, he could finish off Nh'Got if she wasn't already dead and force the woman and child to give up information. Then he would dispose of them and begin his move to take control of the Earth. No one could challenge him as long as he had the blaster.

It took him most of the morning to descend from the hillside to the road give up information. Then he would dispose of them and begin his move to take control of the Earth. No one could challenge him as long as he had the blaster.

It took him most of the morning to descend from the hillside to the road leading to Jerusalem. He stooped and scrutinized the footprints in the dirt. There were several sets, some very noticeable. One set was the size of a child's heading eastward. He smiled. They had to be the girl's, but they were many hours old. If he hurried his pace and traveled in darkness, he could catch up to her. They were still a day's travel from Jerusalem. If luck was on his side, she would be asleep and easy to capture.

After two hours of brisk walking, he spotted a man and his four-legged animal coming his way. He slowed his pace and waved the man down. "Traveler," he addressed the man, and smiled to gain his trust. "May I bother you for a drink of water? My supply is nearly gone and it is still a two-day walk to the next town."

The man nodded to him. "Certainly," he said and retrieved his water bottle from his donkey and gave it to the stranger. As the man drank, he recognized him. "Ah, we meet again. You're the man that Jesus healed. I remember encountering you with a woman. She told me robbers stabbed you, and you were dying. The woman and I got you onto my donkey and took you to Jesus for healing. On the way, a small girl joined us. It appears that you are doing fine."

Tl'Rak eyed the man and thought he looked vaguely familiar. "Yes, I remember. You were most gracious in helping me. What is your name?"

"I am Joseph of Arimathea and I'm glad I could help you. And praise God for your miraculous healing. And what is your name?"

"Tl'Rak of Valerii." He thumped his chest and bowed.

"Tl'Rak, I have never heard of Valerii, but then I haven't traveled far and wide. By the way, where is the woman you travel with?"

"Joseph of Arimathea, she is in the Galilee area searching for that girl that gave me aid. I'm traveling this way, hoping to find her. You know she is alone, and I and the woman, want to give her a home with us." He felt pleased with himself, knowing how good of a lie it was.

"Oh, that is very kind of you two. I saw her last night. She came to my campsite, and I gave her food and drink."

"Where is she now?"

"Where is she now?"

"I'm not sure," Joseph said, pulling on his beard. "When I rose this morning, I didn't see her. She is a sad child, missing her parents greatly. They must be dead."

"She told you such?" Tl'Rak asked.

"Not directly. When I asked about her parents, she just points to the sky and says they are there. Of course, that means they have died and gone to heaven."

"That's interesting," Tl'Rak mused. "Did she say anything else?"

"Let me think." Joseph paused in thought. "Well, last night she told me the moon went dark because the Earth was round and casting its shadow on the moon. And that the Earth revolved around the sun. I thought the Earth was flat, and the sun revolved around the Earth. When I told her that, she told me I went to a poor school. Thinking about it, she made sense and may be right. What do you think?"

"I think she's right," Tl'Rak said. *I wonder what school she went to, to know that. Surely not one on Earth at this point in its history. Are her parents in a spaceship above Earth now? If so, that could be the reason I couldn't beam back to the ship and why it isn't functional.*

"Did she say where she is heading?" Tl'Rak continued.

"To find Jesus so he can, as she says, make the lights appear so she can go home. Such a confused child."

"Make what lights appear?"

"Lights in the mountain that way." Joseph pointed toward Galilee. "When they appear, she will run through them and return home. Oh, I hope you will find her and give her a wonderful home."

"So do I," Tl'Rak said, looking to the northeast, his mind racing in thought. *A transporter? Or a space portal? I need to find those lights! And Jesus must be an alien that moves about the galaxy using a portal or giant transporter. I may need him alive and force him to activate the portal and send me to where and when I decide or tell me how to operate it.*

"Do you think the girl headed back toward those mountains?" Tl'Rak asked.

"It's possible," Joseph answered. "She is a determined child. I'm heading that way. Would you like to join me? I could use the company. My donkey is a poor conversationalist."

Why would she turn around and head back to the mountains by the sea?

asked.

"It's possible," Joseph answered. "She is a determined child. I'm heading that way. Would you like to join me? I could use the company. My donkey is a poor conversationalist."

Why would she turn around and head back to the mountains by the sea? She knows Jesus ascends into the sky from Jerusalem and wants to get there before he does. But why is she here, and her grown self too? Is the grown one here to rescue her?

"Joseph of Arimathea, thank you for your offer. If she is heading that way, my lady friend will catch up to her. I will continue toward Jerusalem."

"In that case, I wish God's blessing on you. May our paths cross again. Good day." Joseph dipped his head and led his donkey forward. Tl'Rak watched the man walk away and then picked up his pace toward Jerusalem. He had renewed vigor, but cursed himself for not asking Joseph if he knew the child's name. It could be a clue to her identity, where she came from and when. It wasn't from the current Earth.

CHAPTER FIFTY FIVE
The Holy Grail

Kay're and Z'mia kept a steady pace on the road without fear of the Romans back-tracking. Up ahead, they saw a man walking his donkey toward them. Both recognized him as a person they had met before. They hurried to him.

"Joseph!" Kay're called out, waving a hand.

Joseph beamed a broad smile as he recognized the women. "Kay're, it's so good to see you."

"And you too, Joseph." She gave him a hug.

"And you are the woman that was with the dying man," Joseph said to Z'mia. "I didn't catch your name."

"It is Z'mia Nh'Got," she replied with a smile and bowed to him.

"A most unusual name. Much like your friend that Jesus healed. I met him a few hours ago."

"You saw Tl'Rak?" Z'mia asked, impatiently.

"Yes, that is the name he used. He told me he was searching for the little girl that was with you at the healing. He wanted to give her a home, and you would be there too. I saw the child last night. She found me and stayed the night. We talked about how the Earth casts its shadow on the moon last night. She says the Earth is round and revolves around the sun. I believe her."

"She is right, Joseph," Kay're said, smiling at him and holding his gaze. Immediately, Joseph knew the child and Kay're were the same.

He gasped. "How is it possible?"

"It is, Joseph. The how is too long to explain. It's urgent that we find her, and before Tl'Rak does. He wants to harm her. Did she tell you where she was heading?"

"She didn't say. But she was adamant about going home to see her parents in the sky. And to do that, she needed to find Jesus so he could make the lights appear in the sky. And to do that, she needed to find Jesus so he could make the lights appear in the mountains by Galilee. When the lights appeared, she would run through them and go home. It makes little sense. Are your parents dead and in heaven?" He pointed to the sky.

"Joseph, they are alive. And yes, they are in the sky."

Joseph looked up to the blue sky and shook his head. "How? Where?" he mumbled.

"God made many planets that have people on them like you, me, and Z'mia. She and I are from faraway planets and we too want to go home. And like my little self, we need to find Jesus so he can make it possible for us to go home."

Joseph looked up to the sky. "Jesus is God. The creator of everything. With him, nothing is impossible. Praise be to God."

"Amen," Kay're said. "Joseph, I'm so glad your mind is open to the greatness of God and all that He has done."

"Joseph, which way was Tl'Rak heading?" Z'mia asked.

"To Jerusalem. I hope the child isn't heading that way."

"I suspect she is," Kay're demurred, shifting her gaze in that direction.

"Then you must go now and rescue her."

"Joseph, could you spare us a small portion of food?" Z'mia asked, eyes pleading.

"I have little after sharing with little Kay're and water with Tl'Rak. But what I have is yours." He went over to his donkey and took his food bag and brought it over to Kay're and Z'mia. "Help yourself," he said and handed the bag to Kay're.

She opened it and her eyes grew wide in astonishment. "Joseph, you have several cooked fish and two loaves of bread."

"What?" he exclaimed and looked in his bag. "This morning, I had half a fish and a small piece of bread that I was saving for later. And now...."

"You have a miracle from God," Kay're said. Z'mia's mouth gaped. "How much more do you need to see to believe that there is a God, Z'mia?"

"I'm not sure what to say," she returned, looking in the bag herself.

"Say you believe," Joseph said, grinning. "Here, take two fish and a loaf of bread." He placed the food in Kay're's bag. "Now you must go and find yourself. May our paths cross again, and God bless you."

bread." He placed the food in Kay're's bag. "Now you must go and find yourself. May our paths cross again, and God bless you."

"And God bless you, Joseph," Kay're said, giving him another hug. "You are such a good man."

Z'mia gave him a hug too. "Thank you, Joseph. May God bless you."

They departed, and after several steps, Kay're turned around and looked back at him and said, "Joseph, the holy grail and his blood will protect you and give you a long life with miracles, like you witnessed today." She waved and continued her walk to Jerusalem with Z'mia at her side.

Joseph walked away, shaking his head. "What did she mean by the holy grail? The blood, I understand. Is the cup the holy grail? And how did she know I had them? Maybe, she will tell me the next time we meet."

"What, is the holy grail?" Z'mia asked as they continued along.

"It is the cup Jesus used at his last supper before his crucifixion. Joseph used it to collect Jesus's blood when he hung on the cross. There is much legend and lore about it throughout Earth's history. The grail is said to have the miraculous power to heal all wounds, grant eternal youth, and grant everlasting happiness to whoever holds it. The cup or grail is the most sought-after relic from this time. Whatever Joseph did with it, he kept its location a secret to his death."

"Wow!" Z'mia said. "One thing is for certain, Tl'Rak didn't know this, or he would have taken the cup from Joseph."

"You're right. Just another reason we need to take him down."

Z'mia nodded.

Then Kay're took a fish and loaf of bread, said a prayer, and divided it, giving Z'mia her share to eat. They ate as they trekked on to Bethany.

CHAPTER FIFTY SIX
Friends and Foes

The walk to Bethany was taking longer than expected. The constant passing of Roman patrols kept the women off the road and hiding from view. Obviously, the Romans were hunting for them. They saw the soldier who was miraculously healed with Centurion Marcus and his men. He must have identified the women as the attackers of himself and comrades.

Of all the patrols, Centurion Marcus led only one, accompanied by his handsome decanus. Z'mia wanted to know his name. She had developed a physical attraction to him. Kay're teased her about it. Z'mia said she was being practical; saying she would need a mate if there was no going home. The decanus was the logical choice; young, handsome, and strong. Z'mia told Kay're to latch onto the centurion. Then the foursome could run away to another part of the world and live happily together. Kay're didn't tell Z'mia how close her vision was to reality, though she missed her husband, Captain Mark Ross.

"So, Z'mia, how are you going to seduce that young officer?"

"First off, I'm going to need a bath! No man will want to get close to me, or you, smelling like a goat."

Kay're chuckled. "Unless they are drunk."

"But they're no fun then. They slur their words and fall asleep too soon."

"I thought you told me you had minimal experience in romance."

"I'm a quick learner."

"Okay, then what?"

"I need to get him alone and...." Suddenly, the sound of running horses cut her answer short. Ahead, a dust cloud was moving their way. Quickly, the women ducked into the scrub brush just off the dirt path. Several Roman soldiers galloped past them.

Kay're giggled. "Z'mia, your future husband was leading them."

"I saw. They're in a hurry. I wonder why?"

"Maybe they had a hot tip that we were somewhere down the road. Let's go. We can make the Mount of Olives before dark."

Continuous Roman patrols also slowed down Tl'Rak. The first two he encountered stopped him. They wanted to know if he had seen two women in the area that were foreigners. He told them he saw them heading toward Galilee. In his perverse way, he wanted to eliminate the women himself, though he knew Nh'Got was probably dead already. First, he needed to find out the identity of the woman who entered his mind. By sending the Romans off the trail, it would give him time to capture the child. He knew that if the Romans caught the child's older self, they might kill her. Her death would cause the child to wink out of existence, and with it his hope of leaving this planet and time.

As a third patrol neared, he recognized the centurion leading the men. He was the one hot on the trail of Nh'Got and the woman. He was the same officer at the crucifixion who eyed him and likely considered him a cohort of the women. This Roman he needed to avoid or face capture and possible execution. He didn't fear death, but not by the ghastly method of crucifixion. It was a scene that would live forever in his mind.

Quickly, he sought cover behind a tree. The Romans rode past without noticing him. No sooner had he resumed his trek than another patrol approached from his rear. Without hesitation, he ran for cover, but not quick enough. They rode up to him and had lances pointed at his chest.

"Why are you running from us?" demanded the lead officer.

"I thought you were bandits out to kill me," Tl'Rak replied. "It has happened before, and I barely survived the attack. I didn't want to have it happen again."

"Do we look like bandits?" the officer persisted.

"Sir, when I see a cloud of dust heading my way, I don't take chances and run for cover."

"You look suspicious. Maybe you are a bandit."

"Sir, I'm a simple man on my way to Jerusalem in search of work. Look, I have nothing to hide but my canteen that is almost empty." Tl'Rak raised his arms, showing his tunic and water skin. "It's still a walk to Jerusalem. Could you fill my

I have nothing to hide but my canteen that is almost empty." Tl'Rak raised his arms, showing his tunic and water skin. "It's still a walk to Jerusalem. Could you fill my canteen?"

The officer mulled over Tl'Rak's response and nodded to one of his soldiers. "Fill his canteen."

"Thank you, sir." Tl'Rak bowed his head, placating the officer. "By the way, have you or your army found a small lone child?"

"What is that to you?" asked the officer.

"Nothing. Before you arrived, another Roman patrol stopped me and asked me if I had seen that child. I'm concerned for her safety and hope you have found her. You know, with all the large beasts and bandits in the area, it's not safe for her."

"We have not," the officer replied dryly and turned his horse. He and his men rode off.

Tl'Rak laughed and sat next to a tree. "These Romans are so gullible." With sunset near, he would spend the night here.

With her small size, little Kay're easily avoided detection by the Roman patrols. Her heart skipped a beat when she saw Centurion Marcus ride by. She had developed a fondness for him. He would be her father if she couldn't return home.

The twilight brought a chill in the air. She shivered and wondered if the weapon she took from the evil man could make a fire. Before the sunlight disappeared, she gathered twigs and dried grass and formed a pile. With the weapon out, she eyed it, thumbed a button, and heard it hum to life. A green light glowed, and she pointed at her pile of twigs and depressed the trigger. A green beam shot out and bathed the twigs in a green halo that quickly disappeared. No fire started. She thumbed the setting to two green lights and fired the weapon. This time the wood-pile started smoking and then a flame appeared. She jumped up and down in glee and scurried off to find more twigs for her fire. After a while, the stress of the day overcame her will to stay awake, and dreams filled her head.

Before the sun breached the eastern horizon, both Kay're and Z'mia were up and moving toward Bethany. Z'mia checked in with the ship to learn their status remained the same. The child was now fifteen kilometers ahead of them and moving.

Before the sun breached the eastern horizon, both Kay're and Z'mia were up and moving toward Bethany. Z'mia checked in with the ship to learn their status remained the same. The child was now fifteen kilometers ahead of them and moving.

"Your little self is an early bird," Z'mia said. "Most children stay in bed well into the morning unless prompted by their parents to get up. Not you."

Kay're smiled. "Most children don't have a madman chasing after them. When this is over, I'm going to stay in my nice, cozy, warm bed until noon."

"If it ever ends," Z'mia countered. "What about your husband? He must be worried that you are missing."

"I don't think he knows I'm missing. Remember, we are living in the past. When we return to our time, it will be like we just left a minute ago."

"That is, if we can get back and to the right time."

"You have a point. We could return early or late. If we're late, then everyone's going to be concerned about us. If early, well, no one may know us, or like now, we will run into our younger self."

"This is so confusing," Z'mia said, shaking her head. "We've got to find Jesus before he leaves the planet and have him restore function to our ships so we can go home."

"Then you will leave your future husband back in time," Kay're needled.

"Well, I will take my chance for love in my own time."

"Or you could take him with you. Just beam him up." Kay're burst out laughing.

"I don't think Supreme Commander Tr'Tala will allow it. He will say the time continuum will change. I know a marriage of a Valeriian to a human, especially one from the past won't be approved."

"You could say the human going into the future with you is part of the normal flow of the time continuum. Maybe everything that is happening now is."

Z'mia blew out a breath. "I'm not sure of anything. I hope that us being stuck here isn't part of the flow of time."

"Me neither," Kay're agreed.

"Kay're, Z'mia" came a shout from the rear.

They turned to see the apostles trotting toward them. "You frightened us," Kay're said.

"Kay're, Z'mia" came a shout from the rear.

They turned to see the apostles trotting toward them. "You frightened us," Kay're said.

"Sorry," said Peter. "We saw you and needed to tell you the Romans are searching for you. Several patrols stopped us and asked if we had seen you."

"Of course, we told them no," added Matthew.

"I thought you men were heading to the Sea of Galilee to go fishing," said Z'mia.

"We went there," answered Andrew.

"And when we were out fishing, we saw the Lord appear and He walked on water to our boat," John said excitedly.

"And tell them what Peter did," Andrew encouraged.

"The Lord called for Peter to come to Him, and he left the boat and walked on water to Him."

Z'mia's face showed surprise, while Kay're smiled, remembering reading about the account in the Bible.

"Is it true?" Z'mia asked, looking at Peter.

Embarrassed, Peter nodded. "But I lost faith and began sinking. Then the Lord took my hand and guided me back to the boat. He is all powerful."

"So, why are you here, and not there?" Z'mia continued.

"The Lord told us to head to Bethany," Peter answered. "And we have been walking quickly and into the night before resting.

"Why isn't He with you?" Z'mia asked.

"He disappeared," John demurred.

"So, we are doing as He requested," Luke added.

Kay're felt encouraged that Jesus wanted the apostles with him for his ascension to heaven. She and Z'mia would be there too and hopefully meet Jesus and have him release the ships.

"May we join you?" she asked the men.

"Certainly!" they chorused.

The sun's rays landed on Tl'Rak's sleeping body. He stirred as the warmth felt good after a chilly night that caused him to shiver and burn more calories. The body's felt good after a chilly night that caused him to shiver and burn more calories. The body's response to the cold fatigued him even more. He fluttered his eyes open and stretched to find his muscles aching. Whether to get up or not was his quandary. He decided the hunt could wait. His eyes closed and snoring followed.

Around midmorning, the sound of voices stirred Tl'Rak from his slumber. His eyes snapped open as he recognized Nh'Got's voice. He rolled to his side and grasped his knife and saw several men mingling around Nh'Got and the mind probing woman. They were walking on the road and conversing. Then one man pointed his way. "Traveler, will you join us?" he asked.

Tl'Rak stood, and that gained the women's attention. "So, Nh'Got, you are alive after all!" he shouted to her. He gave her a wry smile.

"Let's get him!" Z'mia exclaimed, anger etching her face. Tl'Rak grinned and beckoned them, assured he'd fended them off. *I'll kill you, Nh'Got but not the mind prober. I need answers from her.*

She and Kay're started to move and Peter grasped Z'mia's shoulder, holding her back. The others blocked Kay're.

"The Lord said, 'Blessed are the peacemakers, for they shall be called children of God.' Is he worth killing?" Peter asked.

Z'mia wiggled out of Peter's hold and looked at Kay're. She shrugged.

"He is," Z'mia seethed, her fists clenching. She glared at Tl'Rak. He let out a guttural laugh. "He killed many of my people and is out to kill a little girl that is related to Kay're."

"Oh, Z'mia, trust in the Lord to protect the child," Peter continued. "That man will answer for his sins at the end of time."

"Z'mia, it'll be okay," Kay're said. "Let him go for now." Z'mia nodded. The men exchanged bewildered looks wondering what she meant by her statement. Kay're didn't tell them she and the child were the same person. All watched Tl'Rak run off with a smirk on his face.

"Come, let us continue on to Bethany," said John.

"Kay're, it's time to get up," her mother said, touching her shoulder. "It's a school day and breakfast is waiting."

She rubbed the sleep from her eyes to see her mother's face blur into darkness. She sat

She rubbed the sleep from her eyes to see her mother's face blur into darkness. She sat up and looked around to see dark ground, a few trees, and a smoldering campfire. She sighed, "It was all a dream." Sucking in a breath, she pushed herself up and restarted her trek toward Jerusalem.

Mid-afternoon found her in Bethany. She walked to the town's well for a drink and to refill her water bottle. While doing so, voices called out to her: "Child!"

Kay're looked up to see three women walking her way. She recognized them as the ones the bad men held captive and rescued by her older self and the other women.

"We were so worried about you," the older woman said. "You never came back that evening."

"Sorry," Kay're replied. "I saw someone I knew and tried to catch up to him, but I got lost."

"And for many days," added another woman.

"I saw the mean people kill Jesus and wandered around after that."

"Yes, we saw the crucifixion too," said the older woman. "Very sad. But we heard that He rose from the dead."

"He did. I saw Him!" Kay're exclaimed. "And I have been searching for Him. He can help me get home. Have you seen Him here?"

"No. Maybe He will return to the area as His mother is staying in Jerusalem."

"That's good. I need to find her and maybe she will let me stay with her. Then I will see Jesus for sure."

"Tomorrow we can all go to Jerusalem and look for her," the elder said. "Stay with us tonight. We have food and we will help you wash yourself."

"Okay." Kay're smiled and followed the women to their place of stay.

The three women and little Kay're were up at sunrise. They enjoyed a small breakfast and made the three-kilometer walk to Jerusalem. Arriving at the main gate, they notice Roman soldiers on sentry duty. They eyed everyone coming and going. Those with children were stopped and questioned.

"They are searching for me," she said.

"Why would they want you?" asked the oldest woman.

"Because the centurion wants me."

"They are searching for me," she said.

"Why would they want you?" asked the oldest woman.

"Because the centurion wants me."

"A Roman centurion wants you, for what?"

"I met him a few times, and he wants to take care of me."

"That seems odd," said another of the women. "But at least you will have a safe home and food."

"But I want to go back to my real home. And he won't let me. I can't let the guards take me. If they ask you who I am, please tell them I'm your daughter." She looked up to the eldest woman for her answer.

The woman smiled at her. "I will. Let's go." As they approached the gate, the soldiers dropped their lances blocking the entrance.

The lead soldier stooped down and stared at the little girl. Kay're pulled back from him and hugged the older woman's waist. "Mommy, he's going to hurt me."

"I'm not going to hurt you," he said, and stood. "Is this your daughter?"

"She is."

"And where is the girl's father?"

"Bandits killed him, and they...." She began to sob. The other women started sniffling back tears.

"You may pass," the soldier said, feeling bad for them. The women entered the great city of Jerusalem that was bustling with people.

"Let's go to the marketplace. It's in the upper part of the city. Jesus's mother may be there," the eldest woman said. They made their way there. Several Roman soldiers walked amongst the crowd of people buying and selling goods. They didn't appear to be searching for anyone.

The women and child mingled in the crowd but didn't see Jesus's mother. The eldest woman asked several people if they knew her and where she was staying. Most people shook their heads, while others spat on the ground. Obviously, the name of Jesus brought disdain. One woman stormed off toward a Roman soldier.

"I think she is going to report us to the Romans," the youngest said. They watched her converse with the Roman and point them out. The soldier quickly ran off toward the palace. After a few minutes, a centurion stepped out.

"It's him," Kay're said. "The centurion who wants me. I've got to leave." She ran off watched her converse with the Roman and point them out. The soldier quickly ran off toward the palace. After a few minutes, a centurion stepped out.

"It's him," Kay're said. "The centurion who wants me. I've got to leave." She ran off into the crowd as the centurion, soldier, and snitch approached the marketplace. In fright, the women scurried off too.

"Where are they?" Centurion Marcus demanded.

The woman turned in all directions searching for the girl and the women. "They've run off."

"Soldier," Marcus said to the man. "Go to the main gate and tell the guards to stop and hold any women with a child. Then go and repeat the order to the guards at the other gates."

The soldier saluted and ran off.

"Do you know these women?" Marcus asked the tipster.

"Never saw them before or the girl. Must be out-of-towners."

"If you see them again or the girl, give a report to the nearest soldier. There could be a reward for you."

She bowed to him and stepped away, leaving the centurion scanning the crowd. After several seconds, he returned to the palace.

The three women escaped the city in the nick of time. They looked back to see the messenger soldier arrive and deliver the centurion's order. On their walk back to Bethany, they worried about the child, and hoped she found Jesus's mother or made it out of Jerusalem.

Little Kay're had jumped into a hay wagon and watched and listened to the centurion. She had to get out of the city, but not through the main gate. The sentries there would recognize her. When the centurion returned to the palace, she popped out of the hay and asked a local for the nearest gate. He pointed to the west, and she ran off in that direction.

The gate was open, and two soldiers stood on either side. Kay're hid behind a corner of a building and pondered how to get through it without the soldiers seizing her. She noticed that foot traffic was low, with only a few soldiers going out. She had to make a move before the messenger soldier came to this gate.

"The weapon," she told herself, and pulled it out from under her tunic. She thumbed gate.

"The weapon," she told herself, and pulled it out from under her tunic. She thumbed it on, and two green lights showed. She raised the weapon to eye level and started to step out into the open, but hesitated and ducked back in. "Too strong. I don't want to kill anyone." She touched the other button and three lights illuminated. "Oh, too much!" She pressed the button until it cycled to one green light. Satisfied, she held it behind her back, stepped out, and walked to the gate. The soldiers noticed her and moved to block the entrance.

"Halt there, child," one said, and he started walking toward her. As he did so, Kay're brought the weapon out and depressed the trigger. The green beam shot out and the soldier fell to the ground. The other guard rushed toward her, and he met a green beam too, joining his partner on the ground. She looked around to see if anyone else was coming. There was no one, so she ran up to the first soldier and put a cheek to his chest. His heart sounded strong, as did the other soldier's when she checked him. She ran through the gate.

CHAPTER FIFTY SEVEN
Another Cold Night

Little Kay're had run through the gate to see the Roman army bivouac. Thankfully, the few soldiers there didn't see her, and she found cover in some bushes. Soon, the messenger soldier would alert them after finding the two sentries unconscious. Then he would run to the centurion and appraise him of the situation and all soldiers would search for her.

On tip-toes, she made her way down the hillside on a diagonal to the soldiers. Halfway down the slope, she heard the messenger soldier call out to those in the camp to come to the gate. When they passed by her, she ran to their campsite and to the familiar tent of the centurion.

She snuck in under the backside and saw fruit and drink on the table. It was as if the centurion expected her, and she helped herself to the fruit. The cup held wine, and she dismissed it. After eating her fill, she filled her food bag, ducked out of the tent, and scrambled up the hillside to a hiding place. From this spot, she could see Roman activity. She hoped they would think she had run down the hill and to the next village and head there.

"What happened here?" Centurion Marcus asked the two stunned guards.

"Centurion, I'm not sure," one answered, holding his throbbing head. "All I remember was this small girl approaching the gate. I told her to halt, and she pointed something at me, and then—I don't remember."

"What did you see?" Marcus asked the other guard.

"Centurion, I saw the child and, when Florin fell, I ran to him and then—I don't know. And I also have a terrible headache."

"What did the girl look like?" Marcus continued, perturbed.

"Small, like a typical child," Florin said.

"Be more specific," Marcus demanded, glaring at the two men.

"About three cubits tall, slender, dirty white dress. She had dark hair," the second guard answered.

"Did either of you sense something like a voice in your head before you went unconscious?"

"No, sir," they answered in unison.

"Did any of you other soldiers see this girl?" Marcus asked the troops from the camp.

"Negative," came the voices of the men.

Marcus shook his head, walked out of the gate, and scanned the area. If the child was out there, he didn't see her. "Okay, everyone, return to your duties." He trudged down the hillside to his tent, all the time keeping his mind alert to an intrusion. Those from the bivouac returned to their places.

Marcus entered his tent and sat at his table. He reached for some grapes, only to find the bowl that held them and other fruits empty. "You were here," he mouthed and glanced around the tent. All his other possessions were in place. He noticed small footprints in the dirt that led to the back of the tent. "In and out like a cat." A smile broke across his face. "And what other powers do you have to render men unconscious?"

He rose from his chair and went outside to call for a soldier to bring him more fruit. As he was about to call for the man, Decanus Varius rode up.

"Varius, anything?" he asked.

"No, Centurion," Varius replied, dismounting.

"The child was inside the walls of Jerusalem and came out of the gate above us," Marcus said. "She rendered the two guards there unconscious by pointing something at them. Then she snuck into my tent and took all my fruit."

"Sir, shall I muster men to search for her?" Varius asked.

"I don't think it will do any good," Marcus said. "She is clever and will evade us. And this new power she has makes her more formidable." *And why didn't she and her older self use it before?*

"Varius, send someone to Jerusalem to replenish my fruit and bring us some roasted meat. We will dine together."

"Yes, Centurion," Varius replied with vigor, feeling uplifted with the dinner invite.

dinner invite.

Tl'Rak hustled away from Lt. Nh'Got and her friend. Sundown had him on the Mount of Olives. There, he nourished himself by eating olives and figs from the trees, after which he made his way to Jesus's tomb. In the dim light, he could see the tomb was still unsealed and there was no one around. It would be a good place to spend the night.

He stepped up to it and peered in, and his eyes grew wide. On the burial slab sat a luminescent figure. It looked up to him and glowed with brightness like the sun. Tl'Rak shielded his eyes with his arm. The figure raised a hand, propelling the visitor backward. He fell onto his back, and everything went black.

Kay're, Z'mia Nh'Got, and the disciples trekked leisurely to Bethany. With the going slow, they set up a campsite for the night several kilometers outside of Bethany. Andrew started a fire for warmth and to cook fish.

Both Kay're and Z'mia relished the taste of roasted fish that was moist and tender. It was better than the standard dried smoked fish. Kay're placed her bread on a stick and toasted it over the flame. The men stared at her, unsure of what to make of it.

"Try it," she encouraged and handed Peter a piece of her toast.

He took a bite. "This is good," he said with a nod and started toasting his own bread. The others did the same.

After the meal, the disciples sang a psalm and then bedded down for the night. The women found a comfortable spot on the other side of the fire and reclined.

"Finally, a night with heat," Z'mia sighed.

"It does feel good," Kay're said, turning onto her side facing the fire. She closed her eyes to sleep and hopefully another journey down the pathway in her mind. Suddenly her eyes snapped open. She could feel the ground rumbling, and not from an earthquake, but from pounding hooves. She sat up.

"What is it?" Z'mia asked.

"Approaching horses. Don't you feel it?"

Z'mia turned a cheek to the ground and popped up. "Romans!"

"We got to get out of here, now. Hurry," Kay're said, standing. Z'mia came to her feet

"Approaching horses. Don't you feel it?"

Z'mia turned a cheek to the ground and popped up. "Romans!"

"We got to get out of here, now. Hurry," Kay're said, standing. Z'mia came to her feet and together they started running into the trees.

The commotion stirred the disciples. "What are you doing?" Peter asked.

"Romans are coming," Kay're shouted. She and Z'mia disappeared into the darkness just as four Roman horsemen made the campsite.

The decanus leading the group dismounted and stepped into the light of the fire. Peter stood first to greet him, and the others came to his side.

"Oh, it is you again, the followers of the one called Jesus," the decanus said and waved to his men to dismount.

"Yes, I remember you from yesterday," Peter said.

"I am going to ask you again. Have you seen the two foreign women or a lone girl?"

"We have seen them," Peter answered.

In the darkness, Kay're and Z'mia watched and listened. "Is he going to give us away?" Z'mia whispered.

Kay're shrugged. "I hope not."

"Around sundown we met," Peter continued. "We shared a song and a meal, and they left us heading that way." He pointed up the road. "I'm surprised you didn't see them."

"They probably saw us coming and ducked into the shadows," the decanus replied as a lion roared in the distance. The sound gave the Romans pause. "We will spend the night here. Let us stoke your fire. It will keep the lions away." He directed his men to gather more wood to feed the fire. With the fire roaring, they fixed their horses to the trees, had a meal, and made their sleep arrangements. Sentries rotated for the night.

"Another cold night," Z'mia sighed.

"But not here," Kay're said. "In the morning, they may come here to relieve themselves."

Z'mia nodded. "Where to?"

"This ground is heading up a hill. Let's climb for a bit and find a secure spot. At morning's light, we can observe the Romans and see where they are heading.

spot. At morning's light, we can observe the Romans and see where they are heading. When they leave, we will continue to Bethany."

CHAPTER FIFTY EIGHT
Return to the Mount

Centurion Marcus stood outside his tent in the cool night air. He gazed out at his troops that were relaxing after another day of work. Some were gathered around a campfire talking, while others were casting lots. Many soldiers had already bedded down for the evening. "The life of a soldier," Marcus said. He sucked in a breath of crisp air, went back inside, and sat on his cot. He suspected the girl would return to his tent this evening and planned to stay up waiting for her. After a few hours, the sound of songs and voices subsided. The quietness of the night got the better of him and he reclined and began dreaming.

Slipping past the night sentries, little Kay're made it to the backside of the centurion's tent. She listened for any sounds of movement and heard none. Satisfied it was safe, she ducked her head under the tent and peered in. In the dim light of an oil lamp, she saw the centurion sleeping on his cot, his chest rhythmically risings and falling. She crawled in and saw bread, dates, and water on the table. They were arranged as if they were for her. She helped herself, filled her food bag, and then tiptoed to the centurion.

In the pale light, she stared down into his placid face. He looked so much like her father, and tears welled in her eyes. She wanted to hug him and kiss him on the cheek. Bending down to do so, she pulled back as he stirred. He didn't wake.

Little Kay're settled her flight reaction and ever so gently placed a hand on his forehead. He didn't move from her touch. She held her hand there for a minute and grinned as she saw a thin smile parted his lips. He twitched once but she held her touch. After a few seconds, she withdrew her hand and crawled out the backside of the tent.

"Come, Centurion Marcus," said the small voice.

"To where?" he asked curiously.

The little girl giggled. "To the lights."

The little girl giggled. "To the lights."

"What lights?"

"Oh, you know. The ones in the mountain."

"Which mountain?"

"The one near the great sea where the valley is. Come now! You have to go through the lights."

"Why?"

"Because you have to. I'm going through them, and you have to follow me." She held out her small hand to him. "Come Centurion Marcus."

"Centurion Marcus," the voice repeated. "Centurion Marcus, are you awake?"

He fluttered open his eyes to see the inside of his tent sunlit. "I'm here," he rasped and popped out of bed. "Come in."

Decanus Varius entered. "Sir, I didn't see you at the morning report and thought maybe something happened to you."

"I'm okay," he said and went to his table for water and fruit. There was no fruit or bread, and the water cup was empty. "She was here last night."

"Sir, who was here?" Varius asked with eyes wide with curiosity.

"The child. I suspected she would be here and placed food out for her. She took everything, and I missed her again." *And she placed dreams in my head.*

"Sir, she can't be far off; likely up in the hills. I will send out a search party."

"No. Let her be. Most important are the two women. Any news on them?"

"Livius and his men rode in a few minutes ago. They didn't encounter them but they came across some of Jesus's followers outside of Bethany. The same ones that Junius claimed healed him. They saw the women earlier yesterday but didn't know where they were heading. Your orders, sir?"

"Continue with standard patrols with sharp eyes out for the women. Again, if they are sighted, send a rider back to inform me. Have the others keep the women in view until I arrive. I want you to stay in camp and keep order. First, I want you to get someone who knows the Galilee area and have him report to me now. Have him bring a map too."

"Yes, sir," Varius replied. He saluted and left the tent wondering why Marcus needed a map of the area, as both knew it well.

First, I want you to get someone who knows the Galilee area and have him report to me now. Have him bring a map too."

"Yes, sir," Varius replied. He saluted and left the tent wondering why Marcus needed a map of the area, as both knew it well.

The morning's bright sunlight finally stirred Kay're from her sleep. She rolled to her side to see Z'mia sitting against a rock munching on dates. Kay're smiled at her and sat up.

"Did you have one of your dreams again?" Z'mia asked.

"If I did, I don't remember. How long have you been up?"

"About a solar hour." She tossed Kay're a date.

"Why didn't you wake me?"

"You looked so peaceful I thought you were traveling in your brain and talking to the angel or God."

"If I talked to God, I'd remember," Kay're replied dryly, looking down at the vacant campsite. "Everyone is gone."

"I woke to see the disciples walking toward Bethany. The Romans were nowhere in sight. Look! Here come some now."

Kay're turned toward the west and studied the approaching horsemen. "I count ten."

"Looks like they are stopping at the campsite."

They watched as the lead Roman dismounted and eyed the ground. He saw something and started walking their way.

"He's following our footsteps," Kay're said, stooping down. Z'mia did the same. At the edge of the incline, he stopped and gazed their way. The women ducked their heads and listened for him to call for his men to make the climb. Kay're nodded to Z'mia and she reached down for a fist-sized rock. Kay're grabbed one too. They were ready for another battle with the Romans.

"At least we hold the high ground," Z'mia whispered, and Kay're nodded. They steadied themselves and waited. After a minute, they heard horses trotting off. Both peeked out to see the Romans riding off into the sunrise.

Kay're sighed. "That was close. I didn't relish another skirmish with them. If we had to fight, I would have peed my pants. Well, at least on my tunic." She burst

If we had to fight, I would have peed my pants. Well, at least on my tunic." She burst out laughing.

Z'mia laughed too. "Better go behind a rock."

Kay're continued laughing as she disappeared behind a large boulder. After a few minutes, she returned and with Z'mia descended to the road and toward Bethany.

Holding his head, Tl'Rak groaned. He opened his eyes to see a blue sky. The brightness of the morning hurt his eyes and increased the pain in his head. He turned his head toward Jesus's tomb to see it unchanged from yesterday.

"What was that inside that caused me to black out?" he mumbled to himself and forced himself to stand. Still looking at the open tomb, he answered his question. "It must have been one of the angels that greeted Mary Magdalene when she went to the tomb. But that angel is only an alien, albeit a powerful one."

He debated whether to look inside again but his throbbing headache told him not to. He turned and gazed around the area. "I have to find a hiding place near the top of the Mount of Olives and wait for Jesus to arrive. Then I will get him before he ascends to the sky."

Little Kay're stretched herself awake to see the sun overhead. Peeking out from her hiding place above the Roman camp, she saw normal activity. She didn't see the centurion but assumed he was still in his tent as two men approached it and entered. It was time for her to move and she crept sideways toward the Mount of Olives. There she would be safe for the rest of the day and night. She hoped to spot Jesus and seek his help.

"Centurion Marcus, this is Akim. He knows the Galilee area and has helped us in drawing maps."

"You didn't bring any maps," Marcus gruffed. "I wanted a map of the Galilee area."

"Centurion, tell me what you seek, and I can make the map," Akim said.

"Is there a mountain in the Galilee region where swirling lights appear at certain times?"

"Is there a mountain in the Galilee region where swirling lights appear at certain times?"

Akim blinked and glanced at Decanus Varius, who shrugged. "Centurion, I have never seen such a sight nor is there any lore about such an appearance."

"I can believe that," Marcus agreed. "But is there a certain mountain that has a valley running near it?"

"There are several in the Galilee area. The most notable one is called Arbel and has the Valley of the Doves at its base. The path that runs through it goes from Nazareth via Cana to Magdala. There are many caves in the valley that can be used for refuge. If you've been in the Galilee area, it's not hard to miss."

"I know that mountain," Marcus said. "That has to be it!"

"Do I need to draw you a map, Centurion?"

"No. You have been most helpful. Varius, see to his needs. Dismissed." The two men left, leaving Marcus to his thoughts. He sat at the table and pondered whether to ride to the mountain or stay in camp waiting for news about the two women. It's possible the women were already at Mount Arbel or heading there. As for the girl, on foot, it would take her more than a week to reach the mountain. By horse, he could be there in two days. He decided to stay in camp for a few more days.

Kay're and Z'mia arrived in Bethany at sunset. Only a few people milled about. Most were refreshing their water jars at the town's well.

"What do you think?" Z'mia asked.

"Are you asking about a place to stay?"

"Yeah. I don't relish another night outside."

Kay're looked around. "Well, there's that stable over there. The hay is soft to sleep on and it will be warmer with the animals giving off body heat."

"I'll pass. I don't trust them if you know what I mean. I already smell bad, and I don't want them adding to it."

Kay're chuckled. "As if it would make a difference." She sniffed her arm-pit and cringed. "Well, we can still make the Mount of Olives and hold up where we did the other time. There is food on the trees and maybe we'll see Tl'Rak and catch him off guard. I'm sure he's there."

"Let's go," Z'mia agreed.

catch him off guard. I'm sure he's there."

"Let's go," Z'mia agreed.

They made the Mount as the sun winked out for the day. Cautiously, they made their way into a grove of date and olive trees and helped themselves all the while keeping an eye out for Tl'Rak. The air had an eerie silence to it. Anyone trying to sneak up on them would be noticed.

"Where do you think Tl'Rak is hiding?" Kay're whispered.

"On the hillside opposite, where we hid the last time," Z'mia said, pointing up and to the west. "We could circle from behind and get him."

"He may be planning on it," Kay're cautioned. "Better for us to get some sleep as he will be restless waiting for an attack that won't happen."

"And in the morning, we can devise a plan to bring him out in the open and take him out once and for all," Z'mia said, grinning.

"Sounds good to me." Kay're yawned and slumped to the ground for a night's sleep. Z'mia joined her.

CHAPTER FIFTY NINE
Ascension

*T*he sound of clattering horse hooves woke Kay're and Z'mia. Staying low, they watched a group of Roman horse soldiers ride by toward Bethany. When they were out of sight, both women stood and gazed at the far side of the mountain, hoping to catch a glimpse of Tl'Rak. To their dismay, they didn't see him.

"He's keeping low a profile," Z'mia said, shaking her head.

"More like he's sleeping. Check in with your ship to see if they have a lock on my little self."

Z'mia did and learned the ship's status remained unchanged and the child was three hundred meters to the west. She turned to Kay're. "That places her likely near Tl'Rak. Do you think he has her?"

"I don't think so. If he did, he'd bring her out into the open again as a bargaining chip."

"For what? He'll have the blaster. We don't have anything he wants."

"Me," Kay're said, touching her chest. "He wants both of us together."

"Why?"

"To answer all his questions. Why we're here, and what date we're from. He can't afford to kill either of us until he has the answers, lest he winks out of existence. Maybe he thinks we can help him get off the planet and back to his time or another in the future."

"So, what is our plan?" *I hope you have one!*

"We need to move up the mountain to higher ground. There we will have a better view of the garden and the road. Then we can plan accordingly. If luck is on our side, we will see Jesus."

"Sounds good. Let's gather some more fruit and move."

After a restless night waiting for Lt Nh'Got and her friend to approach, Tl'Rak

After a restless night waiting for Lt Nh'Got and her friend to approach, Tl'Rak dozed off. Not even the morning light could keep his eyes open. As he snored, little Kay're snuck up, appraised him, and entered his mind. This time, it was blank of thought.

Tempted to place some horrid thoughts in his head, she giggled. Tl'Rak made a guttural sound and Kay're pulled back with a hand on the blaster. He turned to his side and continued his slumber.

"You're evil," she whispered and placed a thought of the devil with a pitchfork poking him. The thought made her giggle again. She left him, moving laterally along the hillside to find some figs to eat.

Kay're and Z'mia reached high ground on the Mount of Olives, where they had a view of the surrounding area. As they paused to look around, their hearts skipped. Just above them, they saw Jesus and his disciples.

"How did they get by without us seeing them?" Z'mia asked.

"They must have come up that path." Kay're pointed to the left. "It's partially hidden by the trees."

"We need to go to him," Z'mia said eagerly.

"We're too late," Kay're said, and pointed to Jesus.

They looked at Him with His arm outstretched. Then He drifted up into the air. Higher and higher He went to meet a white cloud that appeared. Jesus entered the cloud and both raced high into the sky and finally out of sight. Then two men in white apparel appeared with the disciples.

Kay're and Z'mia stood dumbfounded from the sight of the ascension and the sudden appearance of two men.

"They must be angels," Kay're said.

Z'mia wanted to answer, but a cry from the other side of the mount interrupted her thought. She and Kay're turned to see who was calling out. They saw little Kay're running toward the disciples.

"No, Jesus! Don't leave!" the child shouted as tears streamed down her face. "Please come back! I need you! Jesus!"

"He's not coming back," came a harsh voice.

Little Kay're tensed as she recognized the voice. She reached for the blaster.

Little Kay're tensed as she recognized the voice. She reached for the blaster.

"I will take that." Tl'Rak grasped her arm and spun her around. He ripped the blaster from her hand. "Now let's go." He pushed her ahead

Kay're and Z'mia started running toward him. He fired the blaster at them. The shot missed, exploding a rock at their feet. They dove to the ground.

Z'mia cursed and peeked up to see Tl'Rak and little Kay're disappearing into the trees. "Now what? He has you and the blaster."

"But not Jesus," Kay're replied, standing. Worry creased her face. "I know where he's taking her."

"Where?" Z'mia asked, wiping the dirt off her face.

"He is taking her to the rock wall that has the portal. There, he hopes she or I will open the portal to affect his escape from Earth. With me in tow, his going will be slow. The intuition of my younger self is good. She will understand that we will reach the portal and arrive there before she and Tl'Rak do. Along the way to the portal, she'll make the journey difficult, allowing us the opportunity to reach our destination ahead of them."

"But he has the blaster, and we have knives and stones as weapons. We won't get close enough to hurt him," Z'mia demurred.

Kay're looked up to the sky again. Jesus and the cloud had long disappeared. The disciples came to their side, minus the two angels.

"We saw the evil-doer take the child," Peter said. "Fear not, the Lord will protect her."

Kay're managed a thin smile.

"I hope," Z'mia said dejectedly.

"Jesus's ascension will heal your hearts," Peter encouraged. "Like his resurrection healed his mother's pierced heart."

"Pierced," Kay're mumble and smiled. "That's it! Thank you, Peter. You gave us the answer to our need to save the child. We must go now. God bless all you. Z'mia let's go." She started trotting down the mountain with Z'mia hurrying to keep up.

"What is it?" Z'mia panted.

"I will tell you later. Right now, we need to get to the Roman camp outside of Jerusalem."

outside of Jerusalem."

Aboard the *Lionare* and *Tigerii*, the ascension of Jesus didn't go unnoticed. All eyes stared at the viewer that showed a sun like brilliance coming up from Earth. Then, enormous ethereal beings rush to its side and together they move toward the ships.

Supreme Commander Tr'Tala jaw gaped at the sight, and he shielded his eyes from the brightness. He rose from the command seat and moved closer to the viewer. To his surprise, the glowing manifestation and beings didn't stop at Kay're's ship. They continued at a swift pace into deep space. In seconds, the brilliance looked like a distant star and then disappeared.

"Te'ana, did you see that?' he asked his wife through his annunciator.

"I did! I think it was Jesus with angels at his side. Some of the crew say the huge ethereal figures were the same ones that surrounded our ships when we arrived."

"I concur. I'm going to contact Lt. Nh'Got and see if she saw the ascension from her position. I will keep the channel open for all to listen. Comm-officer get me Lt. Nh'Got."

"I have her, sir," he replied quickly.

"Lieutenant Nh'Got, I believe we just saw Jesus rise from the planet with angels greeting him. He was as bright as the sun and disappeared into deep space. What did you see?"

"Sir, we saw him lift from the surface into a cloud and disappear. That is all I can report."

"Did you see Tl'Rak?"

Z'mia grimaced and glanced at Kay're for support. Kay're shrugged, unsure of what to say. "Sir, we saw Tl'Rak. He grabbed Kay're's little self and took off into the trees." She took a breath and continued. "But we have a plan to get him before he escapes the planet." It was a lie, and she cringed telling it. They hadn't formulated a plan.

"He has the blaster!" Tr'Tala blurted. "You let him get away with it and you didn't get Jesus to release our ships." A pause. Z'mia winced from the rebuke.

"And what is this about Tl'Rak escaping the planet?" he asked.

"Supreme Commander Tr'Tala," Kay're said, coming to Z'mia's rescue. "There is a time portal near here. It is how my younger self arrived on Earth. Tl'Rak rebuke.

"And what is this about Tl'Rak escaping the planet?" he asked.

"Supreme Commander Tr'Tala," Kay're said, coming to Z'mia's rescue. "There is a time portal near here. It is how my younger self arrived on Earth. Tl'Rak has surmised there is a time portal from his encounter with an old man and his donkey who told him about me and the lights appearing in the mountain. He will force her to take him there so he can make his escape. But she doesn't know how to activate it. He'll find this out and wait for me and Lt. Nh'Got to arrive. Then he will use my little self as a hostage and force me to activate the portal. But we'll be there before he arrives and surprise him, saving the day."

"Kay're you're full of surprises," Tr'Tala said. "Even if you stop Tl'Rak, that doesn't help us. We're still dead in space."

"Have you tried moving your ship?"

"No. Hold on. Helm, maneuvering thruster forward."

"Yes, sir," clipped the helmsman. He touched the controls, and the ship moved ahead.

Tr'Tala sighed relieved. He smiled and asked his wife, "Te'ana, can you move the *Tigerii?*"

"One second," she replied. "We've moved!"

"Lt. Nh'Got, stand by to be transported."

"I'm waiting, sir," Z'mia replied, beaming a broad smile.

Kay're held a reserve look and said, "I'm checking my ship to see if I can transport up."

Tr'Tala gave the order to transport Nh'Got to the *Lionare*. After a few seconds, Tr'Tala asked his transport chief, "Do you have her?"

"No, sir. Transporters are still inoperative."

Tr'Tala slammed a fist down on the armrest. "Lt. Nh'Got, it's still a no go. How about Kay're?"

"Sir, her transporter is inoperative too." Her smile disappeared. "Sir, are you heading back to Valerii?" Her voice was hurried as she worried about being abandoned by her people.

"Lieutenant, the mission isn't finished. You still have a job to do. I won't desert any of my officers. If you and Kay're have a plan, I suggest you get to it pronto."

desert any of my officers. If you and Kay're have a plan, I suggest you get to it pronto."

"Yes, sir!" Z'mia exclaimed, feeling relief.

Z'mia closed the link and took a deep breath. "He still has confidence in me."

Kay're grinned. "He knows we are super sleuths. Now let's sneak over to the Roman camp."

CHAPTER SIXTY
Bows and Arrows

"Centurion Marcus! Centurion Marcus, come out quick!" Decanus Varius shouted.

Marcus hustled out of his tent. "What is it?"

"Look!" Varius pointed to the sky above the Mount of Olives.

Marcus shielded his eyes from the sun to see a man suspended in the air drifting upward. "How is that possible?" He was slack-jawed.

"I don't know, sir. Do you think the man is the Nazarene called Jesus? Many claim him to be the Son of God. Some say they have seen Him alive since His crucifixion."

Marcus didn't answer. He and everyone in the camp stood staring at the man rising to a lone cloud in a clear sky. Then he disappeared into the cloud, and it zoomed out of sight. They all stood dumbfounded.

"Only a god can fly and disappear," Varius mumbled.

Marcus continued his silence. He knew it was Jesus, but was He the Son of God, as His followers claimed? He had heard His followers say that God the Father lived in Heaven. *Did Jesus leave for Heaven?*

"Varius, muster some men to check the Mount of Olives. I have a feeling that the women and child are there."

"Yes, Centurion," Varius said and walked away with his eyes still fixed on the sky.

Marcus retreated to his tent and sat at his desk. "The Son of God," he mumbled and took a long draw of wine. "He healed me, and what did I do? I stood by and watched Him be crucified." He took another swallow of wine. "Thankfully, you overcame death and are going home to Heaven. And what is Heaven? Where is it? Can a mortal go to heaven? Can I go to Heaven? If so, how?" He paused and swirled the wine in his cup.

"More questions without answers. The woman and child may have the answer on how?" He paused and swirled the wine in his cup.

"More questions without answers. The woman and child may have the answer on how to get to Heaven. Maybe the dreams the child put in my head were of Heaven. And who are the other woman and man? How are they related to the woman and child? I have to find them!" He finished the wine, plunked down his cup, strode out of the tent, and called for an attendant to get his horse. He would join with Varius on the hunt for the child, women, and man.

Tl'Rak hefted the young girl up and draped her over his shoulder, pinning her flailing legs to his chest with an arm. She screamed and pounded her fists on his back. Ignoring her tantrum, he trudged down the mountain and into the trees.

"I'm going to put you down," he said. "Don't run off or I will use the weapon on you and make you go unconscious, like you did to me. When you wake up, you will have a terrible headache. Is that what you want?"

Kay're sniffled and remained quiet. She tried to enter his head.

"Don't do that," he growled, feeling her presence entering his mind. "I'll shoot you."

She broke the connection.

"Good. Now, I'm putting you down." He bent down on a knee and let her fall face first. Kay're placed her hands out to break the fall, then fell to her side and stood to see her captor pointing the blaster at her.

"I know what you want." Dhe pouted at him. "You want me to take you to the lights."

"That's right." He smirked. "Start leading the way." He waved the blaster, prompting her.

"It won't do you any good. I don't know how to turn the light on. Only Jesus knows, and He went to the sky."

"You may not, but your older self does. She will follow and I will be waiting. Get moving, and no funny stuff. Remember, I have the blaster and I will use it. I mean business."

She gave him an ugly face and shuffled ahead. Tl'Rak followed, feeling good he had the upper hand on the girl, her older self, and Nh'Got. He grinned as he good he had the upper hand on the girl, her older self, and Nh'Got. He grinned as he followed the girl.

"Look. Soldiers are heading this way," Z'mia said, pointing down the mountain.

"I see," Kay're replied. "They must have seen Jesus' ascension and are coming to investigate. They may think we are here too. Let's hide in the olive grove." They hustled to the grove and took cover behind trees. They watched the Romans dismount from their horses and trudge up the hillside.

"Your potential boyfriend is leading them," Kay're said and giggled.

"But I don't see the centurion. Oh my, they're stopping the disciples."

The decanus dismounted and held a conversation with Jesus's followers, with Peter taking the lead. They saw Peter shrug and point toward Bethany. The decanus glanced that way and waved to his men to follow him. The Romans rode toward the town.

"Good, they are heading away from us," Kay're said.

"Well, here comes the centurion." Z'mia pointed to him. They saw the centurion catch up to the soldiers, dismount, and talk to the decanus. The young officer motioned his hand to Bethany. The centurion shook his head in disagreement and pointed to the olive grove. He dismounted and led his horse in the women's direction. The decanus and soldiers followed.

"We need to get out of here," Z'mia said.

"I know just the place," Kay're said and hurried toward the Roman bivouac. Z'mia followed. They scrambled up the far side of the Mount of Olives to the place where little Kay're had hidden the night before. From there, they watched the Romans come out of the grove and stop. The centurion scanned the area and said something to the decanus. The officer saluted him and directed his men to their horses. They rode off toward Bethany. The centurion returned to the campsite and his tent.

At sunset, Decanus Varius and his men made their way back to the bivouac without captives. Centurion Marcus took the report and sighed disappointed. He took a long draw of wine to soothe his melancholy. Varius and his men joined the rest of the soldiers around the main campfire. After eating supper, they retired to their retired to their tents.

"Do you have a plan?" Z'mia asked.

"Yep. To secure weapons to use against Tl'Rak."

"The Romans have nothing to fight against a blaster."

Kay're smiled. "Yes, they do. They have bows and arrows. Have you ever done archery?"

"No, but I know what it is. It is a sport on our planet."

"Well, we're going to steal bows and arrows tonight and then head back to the mountain with the portal near Galilee. Along the way, we will practice shooting arrows. We have to be good enough to shoot Tl'Rak from twenty to thirty meters."

"Okay. I hope we don't get caught," Z'mia said, wetting her lips.

Deep into the night, Kay're and Z'mia moved down from their cover to the Roman bivouac. In the shadows, they saw only four centuries on duty, one at either end of the camp and two walking from one end to the other. They would meet at the main campfire and move past each other, only to turn at the end of the camp and repeat the walk.

The archers camped near the horses. Kay're and Z'mia made their way to the back of the archer's tent and listened for movement or talk; all was quiet. Kay're dropped to her belly and lifted the edge of the tent for a peek. It was too dark to see anything. She withdrew.

"I will have to do this by feel," Kay're said. "I think they're sleeping with their heads to the side of the tent with their gear next to them."

"That's a problem," Z'mia said. "If we work from the side of the tent, the sentries will see us."

"You're right. I will just have to slip in through the back and hopefully not bump anyone. Lift the edge in the middle."

Z'mia did, and Kay're crawled in and patted the ground. On either side, she felt feet and froze, hoping she hadn't woken anyone. The Roman to her left stirred a bit but kept snoring. The one on the right never moved. She inched forward with barely any room between the feet of the men. Still feeling her way, she felt the end of a bow. With both hands, she hefted it up and guided it in front of her, slipping it under she felt the end of a bow. With both hands, she hefted it up and guided it in front of her, slipping it under her belly. She then pushed it to the back. Z'mia felt it and pulled it out.

Kay're inched forward past the feet and tapped around for the quiver. She found it and maneuvered it to the center and pushed it under her torso back to Z'mia. One set down. On her other side, Kay're felt the end of a bow. She tried lifting it, but it didn't budge. She inched her way to the next soldier. Her hand found a bow, and this one had gear on it, as did the one on the other side. Frustrated, she came up to a squat and duck-walked until she felt another bow. This one easily gave way. Holding it in one hand, she felt for a quiver. She found it and placed it down with the bow. She knew two quivers of arrows wouldn't be enough. She and Z'mia would likely lose some practice shooting.

Kay're reached down to her left and felt another bow. Disregarding it, she tapped past it until she felt the quiver. Slowly, she pulled it to her. Now to get out. On her hunches, she grasped the bow and one quiver in one hand and the second quiver in the other and stood. She blew out a silent breath, feeling blood returning to her legs.

One foot in front of the other, she inched her way to the back of the tent. Stooping down, she handed one quiver to Z'mia, and then the second one. As she passed the bow, one end caught on a soldier's foot. She glanced back as the man woke and sat up, releasing the bow. This sudden movement caused Kay're to lose her balance. She toppled into the rear center post that held up the tent. It gave way, bringing the tent down on everyone. Quickly, she scurried out from under the leather canvas and told Z'mia to run. They ran between the horses and into the night as the Roman campsite woke to the turmoil.

After a few hours of sleep, Centurion Marcus sat up and looked around his tent. The oil lamp still burned, and the fruit on the table remained untouched. The child hadn't returned. "Might as well get some fresh air," he told himself and stepped out into the cool crisp night air. He sucked in a breath and surveyed the camp. The walking sentries met at the campfire and noticed Marcus; they saluted him.

"Carry on," he said with a half-wave. They continued their walk. He took a last deep

"Carry on," he said with a half-wave. They continued their walk. He took a last deep breath and turned toward his tent. Then shouts came from the archer's tent that had collapsed. In the light of the campfire, he saw two tall, slender figures carrying bows and quivers race from the tent, and disappear between the horses. He ran to the archers' tent as the soldiers were scrambling from under the leather covering.

"What happened?" Marcus asked as the soldiers stumbled to attention.

"An intruder knocked down the back support pole," a soldier answered.

"Did you get a good look at the person?" Marcus continued questioning, though he knew who caused the calamity.

"No, Centurion," he replied.

"Anyone?"

The other men shook their heads.

"What happened?" Decanus Varius asked, running up to Marcus's side.

Marcus held up a restraining hand. "Men, re-pitch your tent and inventory your gear. I suspect some of you are missing bows and quivers." The men nodded and started on the task. "You others, return to your tents."

"Varius, the two women caused the tent to collapse. They made off with bows and quivers of arrows."

"Why would they do that?" Varius asked, yawning.

"I don't know. Whatever their reason is, it must be very important. Otherwise, they wouldn't risk entering a tent full of soldiers to steal them."

"Centurion, I'll muster troops to search for them."

"No! You and the men will end up with arrows in your chests. Is that how you want to die?" His tone was sarcastic. "These women are dangerous and more so now. We will discuss it in the morning." He turned on his heels and retreated to this tent. Varius stood staring into the darkness with a hand over his heart. He managed a dry swallow and returned to his tent.

CHAPTER SIXTY ONE
Into the Darkness

Kay're and Z'mia ran toward Bethany as fast as they could. With lungs burning, they made it to the edge of town and collapsed against a building. Sucking in air, they listened for approaching horses. The air remained quiet.

"I can't believe they didn't see us," Z'mia gasped.

"They probably did and searched the adjacent hills. At sunrise, the calvary will be out looking for us."

"Then we can't travel on the main road to Galilee," Z'mia said, still breathing heavily.

"Especially carrying bows and arrows," Kay're added. "We'll stick out like lepers and the locals and travelers may give us up to the Roman patrols."

"Over there," Z'mia said, pointing to the left. "There's a path heading north. Looks like it leads to the hills."

"I see. Let's refill our canteens at the town's well and then follow it. Water sources may be scarce."

In the dim moonlight, Kay're and Z'mia trekked north. Two hours later, the sun peaked over the eastern horizon. With their position high on the hill, the site was spectacular. They sat on a rock and watched the splendor of the sunrise.

"We need to sleep," Z'mia said, and sighed.

"Agreed," Kay're said, surveying the surrounding hills. "Let's get off the road and up amongst these rocks. Hopefully, there is an outcropping for shade."

To their relief, they found a shallow cave big enough to hold them. They nestled themselves in and soon were sleeping. While they slept, small rocks rattled down from above. One hit Z'mia in the foot, waking her.

She nudged Kay're, who blinked her eyes open. "Someone is above us," she whispered. Both women reached for their knives and sat up. Scratching sounds from above indicated the intruder was inching down their way. They tensed, waiting sounds from above indicated the intruder was inching down their way. They tensed, waiting for the attack. Seconds later, a large male lion jumped down, blocking their escape. Other cats joined him. The male roared.

Kay're heaved a sigh of relief as she recognized her friends. Z'mia cowered in fear.   Kay're laughed. "It's okay. They're our friends." She crawled out and hugged the male lion. The beast purred in delight, and she stood and greeted the other cats.

Z'mia timidly joined Kay're. She held out her hand and the large male licked it. The females surrounded her, rubbing their heads against her legs.

Kay're stooped down and looked into the male's eyes and said, "Big boy, we need to sleep. Stay and keep watch." She kissed him on the nose and motioned for Z'mia to return to the cave. They slept in peace.

Following the night's chaos, Centurion Cassius Marcus had difficulty sleeping. The women escaping with bows and arrows replayed in his mind. *What is their endgame? Were they leaving Israel and needed them for hunting game and protection? And what about the girl? Was she going with her older self? Or was she heading to that mountain alone?*

He sat up in his cot. "The mountain," he said to himself. "They are all heading to the mountain. But why do the women need the weapons?" He walked over to his desk, sat down, and lit a candle. On a blank scroll, he penned an order, rolled it up, and sealed it with wax from the burning candle. To make it official, he impressed the wax seal with his centurion ring and placed it next to the fruit bowl. He stood, donned his uniform, and strapped on his sword. Then he stuffed his food bag with fruit and dried meat, and filled his canteen with water. He slung them over his shoulder and without a final glance around his tent stepped out into the night air.

The camp had settled down with only the sentries on duty. Marcus disregarded them and walked to his horse. He saddled it and then rode off past a bewildered guard at the north end of camp. The man held his salute as he watched the centurion disappear into the dark.

The sentries weren't the only ones who saw Marcus leave. Decanus Varius had difficulty finding sleep too, as the night's events replayed in his mind. He thought some cool air would clear it, and he would then easily fall back to sleep. Stepping out of his tent, he saw Centurion Marcus ride off into the darkness. Surprised, he called had difficulty finding sleep too, as the night's events replayed in his mind. He thought some cool air would clear it, and he would then easily fall back to sleep. Stepping out of his tent, he saw Centurion Marcus ride off into the darkness. Surprised, he called over one of the sentries.

"Do you know where Centurion Marcus is heading?"

"No, Decanus. He went straight to his horse and rode off."

"Did he say anything to the other guards on duty?"

"No, sir. He said nothing to anyone. Just left."

"Okay, carry on," Varius said and walked over to Marcus's tent, and entered it. The first thing he saw in the dim light of the burning oil lamp and candle was the sealed scroll. He picked it up and saw the notation on the outside: *Order of Promotion for Decanus Julius Varius.*

Varius swallowed nervously. He broke the seal, unrolled the document, and read the order promoting him to centurion. In disbelief, he shook his head and sunk into the chair that was now his. He looked around the tent and felt pride that he had earned Marcus's trust to command the Centuria of Jerusalem.

"Why did you do it? And where are you heading in the dead of night?" He sighed and looked around the tent. In the corner, he noticed small footprints. "The child," he whispered. "Of course. He must know where she and the women are heading. But where? And why are you going alone?"

He reached for the fruit bowl for a fig, but it was empty. "Marcus took all the fruit. He plans to be gone for a while." A pause and then a smile. "That mountain in Galilee! It must be the place." He stood, grabbed the scroll, and left for his tent. Minutes later, he was riding out of the camp.

CHAPTER SIXTY TWO
The Road to Mount Arbel

We'll stop here for the night," Tl'Rak said to the child. "Gather some wood for a fire. I will watch you and shoot you if you try to run off." He pulled out his blaster and waved it at her.

Kay're again gave him an ugly face and wandered off amongst the trees. Tl'Rak grinned as he watched her dutifully gather twigs and branches. Within minutes, both were sitting by a blazing fire. Tl'Rak tossed her a hunk of bread and a piece of dried fish.

"Child, how is it that you understand and speak Valeriian?"

"I learned it," she replied matter-of-factly.

"Where did you learn it?"

"In school. Where else would I learn it?"

"Indeed, that is the question," Tl'Rak mused. "What is your name?" He hoped it would give him a clue about her identity and where she and her older self were from. More importantly, he wanted to know what date they came from.

"I'm not telling you!"

"You will," he said and leveled the blaster at her.

"Shoot me!" She squeezed her eyes tight, waiting for the shock.

He chuckled. "You're brave and a fighter. I admire that." He crawled over to her. "Give me your hands." Kay're opened her eyes and extended her arms. He bound her wrists and ankles. "If you attempt to escape, I'll stun you and your head will hurt terribly in the morning. Now sleep."

"Mr. Bad Man, you know there are lions in the area. I can summon them, and they will eat you while you sleep."

"Lions? Ah, the large four-legged beasts. If they come, they will eat you too." He gave her a wry smile.

"They are my friends. They won't hurt me but eat you." She grinned at him and reclined. Tl'Rak wiped his mouth and looked around the dark surroundings.

at him and reclined. Tl'Rak wiped his mouth and looked around the dark surroundings. He reset the blaster to kill and moved closer to the fire and laid on his side.

The night seemed to last forever, as Tl'Rak kept an eye open for the lions. He only managed a few hours of light sleep. Though tired, he was glad when the sun peaked over the eastern horizon. Glancing at the girl who was still sound asleep, he envied her good rest. "Time to wake up," he said to her and reached over and cut the bindings securing her wrists and ankles.

She peeked an eye open. "Oh, I see the lions didn't eat you. Too bad." She sat up, rubbed her wrists, and cleared her eyes of sleep. "I need to go to the trees and then eat."

"Go, but I will be watching." He showed her the blaster.

When she returned, Tl'Rak gave her some figs to eat. "Now, are you going to tell me your name? And where are you from?"

"No," she squeaked and munched on a fig.

"You will in time. Let's get moving." He pointed the way.

Centurion Marcus reached Bethany in a matter of minutes. In the moonlight, he looked around for signs of the women. The town's streets were devoid of any people and quiet. He expected to have caught up to them here. They only had a twenty-minute head start and were on foot, and he was on horseback. "Where are you?" he asked the air. Slowly he guided his horse around town, searching the side streets and shadows. They had evaded him. Undaunted, he rode out of town on the main road and waited for them. They would have had to come this way if headed to Mount Arbel.

He settled in amongst some trees and watched. Soon his eyes became heavy, and he dozed off. He dreamed of the flying chariots and buildings of glass that stretched to the sky. The city's grandeur overwhelmed him. He turned to his left to see a magnificently landscaped park. Several children played on the lush grass, and he strained to see if the girl was among them.

"Centurion Marcus," came a voice. He turned around to see who was calling him. "Centurion Marcus," the voice repeated, and a hand nudged his shoulder. He opened his eyes to see the face of Decanus Varius.

shoulder. He opened his eyes to see the face of Decanus Varius.

"Varius," he mumbled, forcing himself to stand. "What are you doing here?" He didn't add, *in my dream.*

"I saw you leave camp and followed. I know where you are going and want to join you, if you allow me."

"I take it you didn't see the women or child?"

"No, Centurion."

"I take it you have had no sleep?"

"Correct, sir."

Marcus blew out a breath. "Okay, I will take the watch until sunrise, and then you relieve me while I sleep for a few hours. If you see anything, wake me."

"Yes, Centurion. And thank you." Varius lay on his side, feeling pleased Marcus accepted his presence. Tomorrow they would ride together on the road to Mt. Arbel.

Kay're and Z'mia slept well into the late afternoon. They woke to see the lions had disappeared. Both stretched the knots out of their bodies.

"It felt so good to sleep without shivering to stay warm," Z'mia said.

Kay're yawned. "That's for sure. Maybe we should travel at night and sleep during the daylight."

"But will we have the lions to watch over us while we sleep? With them around, nobody will approach us, and we will be safe."

"I don't think we can count on it. Let's eat and then get moving."

Centurion Marcus blinked his eyes open at about noon. He looked around and saw Varius tending the horses and waved to him. Varius nodded and guided the horses over to Marcus.

"Did you see the women or child?" Marcus asked, stretching the kinks out of his back.

"No, sir. Only a few locals. I asked them if they had seen two women with bows and they didn't. Of course, they may have but won't admit it."

"We're not welcome in this land, and they won't rat out anyone to us."

"Unless it is Jesus of Nazareth," Varius added.

"We're not welcome in this land, and they won't rat out anyone to us."

"Unless it is Jesus of Nazareth," Varius added.

"And the women aren't Jesus. They're more like folk heroes to the Israelites. I've heard the talk amongst them about how they bested our men and the two thieves. They won't give them up." He paused and asked, "Anything about the girl?"

"I asked about her too and nothing. Maybe they took the road north out of Bethany."

"And where does that lead to?"

"If you stay north, it goes to Nazareth. From there the road goes through the Valley of the Doves to Cana and then to Mount Arbel by the Sea of Galilee. But between Bethany and Nazareth, there is a branch of the road that goes east to Galilee. Do you think the women took the road north out of Bethany?"

"Well, they didn't come this way," Marcus said sarcastically and mounted his horse.

Varius agreed with a nod and hopped up onto his horse.

They galloped back to Bethany and up the north road. After two hours, they came to the town of Ramah and refilled their canteens. They asked several locals if they had seen the two women or a small girl traveling alone. As expected, the town's people denied seeing them.

"How far to the split in the road?" Marcus asked.

"If we rush, by sunset. The town Sychar sits near the fork in the road. Maybe the women will spend the night there."

"Not unless they can fly," Marcus said, wondering if he had made a mistake in promoting Varius to centurion. And did he even know it? "They're on foot, Varius."

"Of course, Centurion. Likely, they're just outside of this village settling down for the night."

"That's the first thing you have said that makes sense," Marcus said, eyeing the village's open-air market. Several stands were still open. "Let's get some local food and camp out on the other side of town in those trees." He pointed ahead.

Centurion Marcus extended his politeness by buying food for the two of them. He could have easily taken it without reprisal. This surprised the vendor, and he gladly accepted the Roman coins. Marcus noticed the man's pleased expression of them. He could have easily taken it without reprisal. This surprised the vendor, and he gladly accepted the Roman coins. Marcus noticed the man's pleased expression and asked, "Did you sell food to any other travelers today?" To avoid alerting the man of his true intention, he omitted mentioning women and child.

"No, Centurion. You and your friend are the only non-locals I have seen today."

"Okay. Let me have another loaf of bread." Marcus flipped him another coin, and he and Varius remounted their horses and rode out of town. They settled in for the night under a canopy of trees.

After refreshing themselves and eating, Kay're and Z'mia returned to the road heading north. They walked until sunset and didn't encounter anyone. Ahead, they noticed a few trees and beyond them a small village. Staying in the shadows, they approached and took cover behind some trees.

"No soldiers," Z'mia smiled.

"Hopefully just friendlies," Kay're said, smiling. "Let's hide the bows and quivers here and go in. Maybe someone will have food for sale and a place to stay."

They entered the town to see a cluster of men leaving a building. The men noticed them and headed their way. Kay're didn't sense they presented any danger. She and Z'mia held their ground as an elder man took the lead and motioned for others to surround the women."

"We mean you no harm," said the elder. "There's a Roman Centurion and a fellow officer camped just on the other side of town. I don't want them to see you. Let's move between the buildings." Kay're and Z'mia exchanged glances, knowing who the villagers were referring to.

"Did they ask about us?" Kay're asked.

"Yes, but they mentioned you would have bows and quivers."

"We hid them outside of town," Z'mia said.

"Are you the two women who allegedly defeated two Roman patrols?" asked a young man eagerly.

"We are," Kay're said. "I have a question. Were the two officers alone?"

"Yes," the elder replied.

"Are you going to fight the two Romans?" asked the same young man. "They won't

"We are," Kay're said. "I have a question. Were the two officers alone?"

"Yes," the elder replied.

"Are you going to fight the two Romans?" asked the same young man. "They won't be a match for you."

"Joshua, don't say such things," the elder chastised him. "Everyone is God's children. We don't advocate violence. Sorry," he said to the women. "How do you intend to deal with them?"

"We want to avoid them," Kay're said. "We are peaceful, but we will defend ourselves. Do you have some food and a place for us to sleep tonight? We have money to pay."

"The elder waved a dismissing hand. "I have an extra room and plenty of food. My wife and I would be honored to have you spend the night with us."

"Thank you," both women echoed.

At sunrise, Kay're and Z'mia were outside spying on the Romans. The two men mounted their horses and rode north. They didn't notice the women eyeing them from behind trees. Satisfied that the Romans wouldn't backtrack, Kay're and Z'mia returned to their host's house. They had breakfast and enjoyed conversing with the elder man and his wife. The man asked them where they were heading. Kay're said it would be best if they didn't know. Plausible deniability, if the Romans returned and asked questions.

After eating, the women retrieved their bows and arrows and using a knife carved a bullseye on a tree. They practice their archery at thirty meters. The first few arrows disappeared into the countryside. Then the arrows started hitting the tree. Finally, both became proficient in placing the shots in the target ring.

"Okay, Robin Hood, I think you got it," Kay're said, laughing as Z'mia shot one dead center.

"Who's Robin Hood?"

"A legendary fictional character from fifteenth-century Earth, known for his archery prowess. He used his skill with bow and sword, and with his band of merry men, to steal from the rich and give to the poor. They were heroic outlaws. Like us, hunted by the authorities."

"Did he have a close friend?" Z'mia asked.

"Oh, yeah! Little John, but he wasn't little. He was a large burly man."

"Oh, yeah! Little John, but he wasn't little. He was a large burly man."

"You don't fit that description."

"Well, there was his famous girlfriend, Maid Marion."

Z'mia rolled her eyes. "I still like super sleuths. Let's go."

The Romans leisurely ride to the town of Sychar was uneventful. They encountered a few travelers who denied seeing the two women or a small girl. They arrived in Sychar in the late afternoon. The town looked much like Ramah. At the open market, Marcus purchased food and queried the vendors if they had sold food to any other travelers. Two had, but the travelers were men.

Afterward, Marcus took the lead and questioned the town's elder about the women and child. The Jewish man had heard rumors about the women but hadn't seen them in this town. They left town and came to a fork in the road. One branch continued north to Nazareth and the other northeast to the Sea of Galilee. Off to the side was a water well made of stones.

"We'll camp here for the night," Marcus said. He pointed to some large boulders that had a few large trees overhanging them. "There we can see everyone who passes and stops at the well."

Varius made a fire, and both sat and ate. "Centurion, do you think the women are traveling to Mount Arbel via the road that follows the Jordan River?"

"That's a possibility," Marcus replied, pulling off a hunk of bread from the loaf he brought. "We should have encountered them on the road or in town."

"Sir, unless they saw us coming and hid," Varius countered.

"That's true but we can verify it," Marcus said and pointed to the rocks across the road. "Tomorrow at sunrise we will take positions up there in the rocks and watch who passes by during the day. If they or the child are using this road to Mount Arbel, we will see them."

Varius craned his neck around to look where Marcus pointed and smiled. "Yes, we'll see everyone coming and going from there. What about our horses?"

"There must be a place behind the rocks to tether them," Marcus said and stood surveying the area. He then peeked around the boulders that were behind him. "There is a small clearing. We will place the horses there. They'll be out of sight of everybody."

sight of everybody."

"Sir, I'm confident we'll see them tomorrow," Varius said, smiling. But the joy faded as he recalled the images of the crippled and wounded men after fighting the women. He didn't want to end up like one of them. "When we see them, then what?"

Marcus read Varius's mind. "I have no intention of picking a fight with them or even engaging them in conversation. We'll follow them at a distance and see what happens at Mount Arbel."

"Sir, that sounds good. That is, if they are heading there."

"I'm sure they are," Marcus assured. He didn't add that Mount Arbel could be the key to getting to a place of great wonder. A place where chariots flew, and glorious buildings touched the sky. Possibly the pathway to heaven, or heaven itself? Would he see Jesus?

With the girl leading the way, Tl'Rak's trek to the mountain with the lights was arduously slow. His fatigue from the lack of sleep, slowed him down. He couldn't sleep as his mind was always alert for lions, not knowing whether the girl would summon them. He heard their roar one night and it sent shivers down his spine.

At mid-afternoon, he ordered a rest stop. He leaned against a tree and dozed off without securing the child. The girl took advantage of it and sneaked off. After running twenty meters, the ground blasted away near her feet, freezing her.

"That's far enough!" Tl'Rak growled. "If you take another step forward, I'll stun you."

She shrugged and returned to the trees next to Tl'Rak. "You know, up till now I have been kind to you, keeping the lions away. Tonight, maybe not. It depends on how soundly I sleep." She smiled at him and reached into her bag for a fig.

"In that case, I will make you sleep soundly." He sneered at her, tapping the blaster.

"It will not matter. If you stun me, my mind will turn off and the lions will sense that. They will come to investigate. When you are asleep, they will sneak up and bite your neck." She bit into a fig for emphasis. "And eat you, just like I eat this fig." She grinned at him and put the whole fig in her mouth

Tl'Rak wetted his lips and wiped the sweat from his forehead. "You think you're so will sense that. They will come to investigate. When you are asleep, they will sneak up and bite your neck." She bit into a fig for emphasis. "And eat you, just like I eat this fig." She grinned at him and put the whole fig in her mouth

Tl'Rak wetted his lips and wiped the sweat from his forehead. "You think you're so smart. Well, I will get the last laugh."

"Does one laugh at the moment of death?" she asked, lifting her eyebrows, and reclined, leaving Tl'Rak pondering her question.

At sunset, Kay're and Z'mia left the road for the rocks to settle down for the night. Luckily, they found a patch of level ground for sleeping. Though the surface was hard and cold, their weary bodies gave way to somnolence.

They rose at sunrise and continued their walk. Around mid-day, they spotted a village. Again, they took scout positions and viewed its activity. All appeared peaceful, and they didn't see the two Roman officers. Carrying their bows, they entered the town and went to the well to refill their canteen. Their presence brought stares.

As they drew water, a boy ran up to them. "You must be the women who killed the Roman soldiers!" he exclaimed with a broad smile. "You even have their bows and canteens. Look!" he called out to the crowd that was gathering. "It's the warrior women!"

"That's enough," said a woman stepping up and grasping the boy by the arm. "Please excuse his enthusiasm."

"But it appears what he said is true," said a deep voice. An older man stepped forward. "I'm Rabbi Ben-Ami."

Kay're bowed to him. Z'mia noticed and did the same. "Rabbi, we acted in self-defense," Kay're said. "We don't seek confrontation or wish ill will to anyone. We come in peace."

"With bows and arrows?" the rabbi questioned.

"We took what was necessary for protection and survival," Z'mia said, and pointed to their Roman canteens.

The rabbi smiled. "Yes, the countryside is full of dangers, including Roman soldiers. Two passed through town yesterday and they inquired about you. They camped out by the fork in the road near Jacob's well."

you. They camped out by the fork in the road near Jacob's well."

"We know them and the place," Kay're said.

"They're after us," Z'mia added. "Are they still there?"

"We didn't see them this morning," another man said.

"Where do the roads go from the fork?" Z'mia asked.

"One to Nazareth and the other toward the Sea of Galilee. Where are you heading?"

"I'd rather not say to protect you," Kay're replied.

"I was in Capernaum two days ago," said a young man stepping up. "And there were many Roman troops there. If you go there, it will be dangerous for you."

"We expect danger wherever we go," Kay're said.

"You are smart," the rabbi said. "May God bless you on your travels. But first let us prepare a meal for you."

"You are most kind," Z'mia said.

After the meal, they bid their hosts goodbye. Minutes later, they came to the intersection. "I know this place," Kay're said, noticing the well off to the side. "My first day on the planet, I stumbled upon this well. I was so thirsty, to the point of collapse. At the well was a woman drawing water, and she told me, Jesus came to her and asked for water. When I heard that, I knew where I was and when."

"Then what?"

"I drank to my fill and took the fork to the northeast and Galilee."

"You know the way. Lead on."

"Let's drink from the well first."

The wooden bucket and ladle were still there. Kay're lowered the bucket, filled it, and pulled it back to the surface. She offered Z'mia the first drink, then took her turn. The water remained refreshing. As she drank, her mind felt something.

"I sense we are being watched," she said. "Don't look around. Here, take another drink." She handed Z'mia the ladle. "It's the centurion and his junior officer. They're behind the ridge to the left. I don't sense any danger. Let's pretend we don't know they're here. I'm going to rinse my face, then you do the same."

They splashed their faces and joked a bit, laughing. Then they walked off, taking the fork Kay're had previously used on her trek to Galilee. From above, Marcus and Varius watched, with satisfaction showing on their faces. When the women were out pretend we don't know they're here. I'm going to rinse my face, then you do the same."

They splashed their faces and joked a bit, laughing. Then they walked off, taking the fork Kay're had previously used on her trek to Galilee. From above, Marcus and Varius watched, with satisfaction showing on their faces. When the women were out of sight, they mounted their horses and followed them, staying out of view.

Sen Tr'Tala sat in his quarters having dinner with his wife. Of course, she was a holo-figure as was he on her end of the comm-link.

"Sen, since we have propulsion, have you considered sending a shuttle to the surface to Kay're's little self? Since Tl'Rak has her, the guards on the shuttle can take him out once and for all."

"I thought about it. He'd see the shuttle coming and lay in wait. When the guards step out, he will pick them off. And if there is a shoot-out, the girl could be killed in the crossfire or he will kill her out of desperation. If she dies, the time continuum will change. Everything will change and we may never meet, or worse, wink out of existence. I couldn't endure living without you!"

"That's so sweet, dear. I would miss you terribly. But I understand. It was a thought. Sen, take a shuttle over to the *Tigerii*. You can turn the *Lionare* over to Sub-commander M'Catis. Then together we can see this situation to the conclusion, whatever it is, holding each other's hand."

He sighed. "I miss feeling your touch. But I was thinking that you should take the *Tigerii* back to Valerii and our time."

"No way! I'm not leaving you," she protested. "Take a shuttle over to me, or I will take one to you."

"Te'ana, you can't leave your ship!"

"Then you come to me!" She batted her eyelids at him. He sighed again and nodded.

"It's getting close to sunset," Varius said. "What should we do?"

"Let's get closer and see what they are doing," Marcus replied. He prompted his horse to a quicker pace. After a short time, the women came into view walking down the road. Marcus dismounted and motioned for Varius to do the same. They prompted his horse to a quicker pace. After a short time, the women came into view walking down the road. Marcus dismounted and motioned for Varius to do the same. They followed at a distance until they lost them in the darkness.

"Do we go on?" Varius asked.

"Like two fools in the darkness? Don't you think they know we are following them?"

"They haven't shown the fact," Varius answered.

"Of course not. Skilled fighters give nothing away. They are probably waiting for us over the next hill. I don't want an arrow in my chest tonight. Do you?"

"No, sir," Varius said, again managing a dry swallow.

"Over there," Marcus said, pointing to a rock outcropping. "We will camp there for the night."

Marcus gathered brush and dried stubble and made a fire. Varius watered the horses and then took a place by the fire. Both men sat in silence wondering what the women were thinking. Unknown to them, the women watched them.

"Centurion, I will take the first watch while you sleep."

"No," Marcus said, waving a dismissing hand. "There will be no watches. Varius, if the women sneak up on you, do you think you could defend yourself against them? I couldn't, and I'm not sure either of us could go one one-on-one with them. I think we will be safe for the night. Let's get some sleep and be up before the sun."

"Looks like they are calling it a night," Z'mia said, sighing. She and Kay're saw the two men reclining next to a campfire.

"Sure does," Kay're agreed. "It's the centurion. The younger man is the one you have eyes for."

"It was only a thought," Z'mia said.

"I still think you two would make a great couple."

Z'mia chuckled. "Just like you and the centurion. Oh, I am sorry. I forgot you're married to Captain Ross."

"Forget it," Kay're said, tapping Z'mia on the shoulder. "We need to get some sleep. Tomorrow, we will reach the mountain. First, check-in with your ship and get a location for my little self."

some sleep. Tomorrow, we will reach the mountain. First, check-in with your ship and get a location for my little self."

She did and found out the child was twenty kilometers east of her position and unmoving. It surprised her that the comm-officer gave her the information and not Tr'Tala. Shrugging it off, she closed the link.

"We'll be at the mountain before she and Tl'Rak," Kay're said. "It will give us time to set up a position for a view of their approach and an open shot for you with the bow."

"Aren't you going to shoot?"

"No. Tl'Rak will call me out to open the portal. When the portal opens, he will make a run for it and may blast me and the child, or take the child with him. It will be up to you to shoot him before he does. The integrity of the future depends on you."

Z'mia sighed, realizing the weight of the past, present, and future depended on her aim and shooting skill. "Come on, let's find a place to sleep."

CHAPTER SIXTY THREE
The Valley of Doves

As the sun reached its zenith in a cloudless sky, Kay're and Z'mia could see the impressive sheer face of Mount Arbel. Ahead was the beginning of the eastern end of the Valley of the Doves. They entered, and Kay're led her friend to the base of the prominent mountain.

She pointed. "There, the portal."

"I see nothing but a rock wall," Z'mia said.

"Believe me, it's there. It can be opened by entering a code sequence or by someone activating it somewhere in the galaxy. That is how my younger self came to be in this land and time. Some portals require a gold disk-shaped key."

"How do you activate this one?"

"I hope it uses a code sequence."

"So where do you enter it and do you know what it is?"

"There should be a touchpad near the entrance. I don't know the codes. It varies according to your destination and date. Maybe I can figure it out once I find the touchpad."

Z'mia blew out a breath and wiped the sweat from her forehead. "I guess we better see if we can find it."

"First, find out how far Tl'Rak is from us."

Z'mia contacted the ship and gave Tr'Tala an update. He didn't care if the portal opened or not. The priority was stopping Tl'Rak. The annunciator on the girl indicated that she and Tl'Rak were at their current pace, one standard hour away from Mount Arbel.

"That doesn't give us much time," Z'mia said after closing the comm-link. "By the way, who built these things?"

"No one knows. There is one on another planet in UPA territory. That's the one my younger self came through." She didn't tell Z'mia the planet's name, as the UPA classified it top secret. "The portals are likely millions of years old. There may as the UPA classified it top secret. "The portals are likely millions of years old. There may be more on Earth or even on your planet Valerii. Do you know of any there?"

"No. If they exist on Valerii, they are a guarded secret."

"I understand. They could be used to travel back and forth through time and to hostile planets. The balance of power may shift to whoever controls these devices."

"And alter the time continuum," Z'mia added, shaking her head.

Kay're nodded. "That's for sure."

"But the UPA knows how to use them."

"They know of their existence, but not how to control them or how many there are and where. Pure luck activated the one I stepped through and I stupidly ran through it, not knowing the where and when. Anyhow, we better find a place to hide, one that will give you an open shot at Tl'Rak. After you take him down, then we can search for the touchpad."

"What if he demands you activate it first before he releases your little self? It's like do it or die."

"In that case, you better be a good shot. I will try to maneuver him for a kill shot. Over there in the trees. It looks like a good place to hide and shoot from."

From a distance, Marcus and Varius watched the women enter the Valley of the Doves. They dismounted and walked their horses into the trees and tethered them. Keeping out of sight by staying in the tree line, they made their way to Mount Arbel.

After a short walk, they saw the women standing in full view at the base of the mountain talking. The mind-probing woman constantly pointed to the base of the mountain. From their position, they saw nothing out of the ordinary. The mountain face was sheer with boulders and rocks at its base. Then the women scramble into the trees. One woman loaded her bow with an arrow and pointed it at the mountain. She repeated the action several times before lowering the bow but keeping it at the ready. "I'm wondering if that arrow is meant for us," Varius whispered.

"If it is, why didn't the other woman ready her bow for shooting? There are two of us, and they must know that. Most odd."

"Perhaps they just want to take one of us out, and deal face-to-face with the other," Varius conjectured.

"Hmm, I don't know. Nothing they do makes any sense."

"I'm wondering if that arrow is meant for us," Varius whispered.

"If it is, why didn't the other woman ready her bow for shooting? There are two of us, and they must know that. Most odd."

"Perhaps they just want to take one of us out, and deal face-to-face with the other," Varius conjectured.

"Hmm, I don't know. Nothing they do makes any sense."

"Maybe that does," Varius said, pointing to the eastern end of the valley. Coming into view was a large man and a young girl. He had a firm grasp on the child's wrist.

"It's them," Marcus said in a low voice. "The child! And the man we saw at Jesus's crucifixion. The women must be here to rescue the child. That's why they wanted the archery sets."

"But they're skilled in hand-to-hand fighting. They don't need bows and arrows to take him out."

"They must have a reason. I'm sure we will find out soon."

"Look, the girl is pointing at the mountain," Varius whispered, his face lighting up with excitement. "What is it about the mountain?"

"Something important to bring them all here. Let's see how this plays out."

"Where is the portal?" Tl'Rak growled, anxiously waiting to make his break through it to escape this planet and time.

"I don't know what a portal is."

"Then where do the lights appear?"

She pointed at the base of the mountain. "There."

Tl'Rak with the girl in tow, walked up to the mountain's base and studied it. He even rubbed a hand over the rock wall. Nothing happened. "Make the lights appear."

"I told you I don't know how," she pouted.

He twisted the girl around and faced the valley. "I know you are up there! Mind prober, the older self of this child, come and activate the portal, or I will kill you by killing the girl."

"What language is he speaking?" Varius asked Marcus. Both held bewildered looks.

"What language is he speaking?" Varius asked Marcus. Both held bewildered looks.

"I don't know. But I gather he's telling the women to come out into the open. See, the one with the bow has it ready. She's going to shoot him."

"But the other one doesn't, have her bow ready," Varius said, pointing at her. "Oh, look! She's coming out into the open."

"She's the bait and the other one will shoot the man when he gets closer," Marcus said.

"That's good strategy," Varius agreed. "But dangerous."

"Danger is their game," Marcus said, smiling. "The strategy is only good if the other can shoot straight and hit the man and not the child." They watched the scene play out.

"Shoot straight and true. I don't want an arrow in my back," Kay're said to Z'mia and placed her bow and quiver down. "I'm coming out!"she shouted and walked into the valley.

Tl'Rak pushed the child in front of him and pointed the blaster at her. "Any mind-probing or funny stuff, and both of you die," he said with a smirk.

"And you will wink out of existence," Kay're chided, and came to her little self and stooped down and touched her face. "Are you okay?"

"I am. He wants me to make the lights appear, but I don't know how."

"I know," she said, and patted her on the head. She stood and faced Tl'Rak.

"Who are you and where are you from and when?" he snapped.

"I'm from your past, present, and future," she replied and again stooped down to her little self. "You'll understand this," she said to her and sent a thought to Z'mia. *Shoot him!*

"That's not an answer!" he roared. "Activate the portal! Now!" As the words left his tongue, he felt the wiz of something zip past his head and then a thunk on the rock wall. Quickly he turned and saw a broken arrow on the ground.

"Nh'Got!" he yelled and whirled around. He noticed the glint of metal in the trees and fired his blaster at it. The ground and a tree exploded, sending the two soldiers diving for cover. "Romans!" Tl'Rak shouted and glanced around to see if there were others ready to shoot him. He ducked down and reached out to grasp the

the trees and fired his blaster at it. The ground and a tree exploded, sending the two soldiers diving for cover. "Romans!" Tl'Rak shouted and glanced around to see if there were others ready to shoot him. He ducked down and reached out to grasp the girl by the leg. She evaded his hand and jumped into the arms of her older self.

"Where's Nh'Got?" he asked, still sitting low.

"The Romans must have her," Kay're replied, looking down at the man.

"You brought them," he accused.

"No, they followed us."

"Open the portal! he demanded, wetting his lips nervously. "We can all escape them." Kay're held her position with the girl hugging her waist. "I swear I'll kill you if you don't open it." He pointed the blaster at her. "Now!"

Kay're hesitated, wondering why Z'mia didn't shoot another arrow. Maybe the Romans did get her. "Very well," she said, and walked up to the stone wall. Her younger self stayed at her side. Tl'Rak kept a low position.

Kay're surveyed the wall and plied her hands over the surface, finding no indication of a touchpad. If it was there, the wind and rain over eons of time eroded its presence. She reached for her canteen and poured water over the rock face to clean it of dust and grit.

"Yes, there it is," she said. To her right, she saw a faint sign of hieroglyphic symbols. She held her hand over them.

"Activate it!" Tl'Rak shouted. "Hurry, before the Romans come."

"It's not that simple," Kay're said. "If I randomly open it, there's no telling where the receiving gate is or it's time."

"I don't care," Tl'Rak said. "Just do it!"

Kay're sighed and mentally sent a message to Z'mia. *Be ready and shoot straight and true.* She looked down at her younger self and smiled.

"I know," the little one said. "I recognize the pattern." She stepped up to the touchpad and tapped four symbols. On cue, the stone wall hummed to life and a swirl of colored lights appeared. The child jumped up and down in glee. "I did it!"

Quickly, Tl'Rak stood and started running toward the lights. One step away from entering them, he grasped the child, then fell face-first to the ground. An arrow had pierced his upper right back. Little Kay're rolled away and her older self dashed up and secured the blaster that lay next to Tl'Rak. Kay're turned and waved to Z'mia.

away from entering them, he grasped the child, then fell face-first to the ground. An arrow had pierced his upper right back. Little Kay're rolled away and her older self dashed up and secured the blaster that lay next to Tl'Rak. Kay're turned and waved to Z'mia.

Marcus and Varius quickly dove behind some large boulders, sucking in air. "That's why the women needed the bow and arrows," Marcus huffed out of breath.

"That weapon," Varius wheezed. Marcus nodded.

"He must be from the gods," Varius continued.

"No, he's from the future. Most likely the women are too." He peeked out from behind the rock. "Look!"

Varius took a glance to see the lights of Mt. Arbel, a swirling ball of colored scintillations at the base of the mountain. "What's happening?"

"I don't know. Oh!" he exclaimed. He and Varius watched the man run toward the lights and grasp the girl, only to fall short of them with an arrow in his back.

"The other woman shot him!" Varius said, excitedly.

"He must be an evildoer," Marcus added. "Let's see what happens next."

Z'mia carrying her bow with an arrow ready, raced up to the two Kay'res. She stared down at the still figure of Tl'Rak and shook her head. "I wish it didn't have to come to this."

"You did what you had to do," Kay're consoled her. "If you didn't drop him, he would have taken me into the portal. Then he would be running amuck with a blaster in his hand somewhere in the galaxy. He could change the time continuum."

Z'mia nodded. "You're right."

"I'm thankful your aim was good. You cut it pretty close."

"Ahh," came a guttural groan from Tl'Rak. He inched himself up and rolled to his side. "Nh'Got, you shot me." He managed a weak smile. "Well, are you going to finish me off?" He glanced over at the swirling lights.

"Don't even think of it," she said, leveling her bow at him.

"Here," Kay're said and handed her the blaster. "Better for you to have it. It's set to kill."

Z'mia swung the bow over her shoulder and pointed the blaster at him. "I'm going

"Here," Kay're said and handed her the blaster. "Better for you to have it. It's set to kill."

Z'mia swung the bow over her shoulder and pointed the blaster at him. "I'm going to contact the ship."

"And tell that gutless traitor Tr'Tala you have won." Tl'Rak coughed, with blood trickling out of the corner of his mouth.

Z'mia ignored him and tried to contact the *Lionare*. She only got static. "Nothing."

"Let me try," Kay're said. She heard static too.

Tl'Rak weakly laughed. "You're both stuck down here. In time, you will die here too."

"The portal may be interfering with communications," Kay're said, and stooped down to her younger self. "It's time for you to go home."

The girl nodded. "Are you coming too?"

Kay're shook her head. "I can't come with you. Remember when Jesus opened your mind to the wonders of life and the universe?"

"Yes." She sniffled back her tears.

"Do you understand now why I can't come with you?"

"I do. I will miss you." Tears ran down her cheeks.

"As I will miss you." Kay're placed a hand on either side of the girl's face and said, "My knowledge is your knowledge. Everything I know, you know." She kissed her little self on the forehead. "Call him." Kay're stood and stepped away from the girl.

"Cassius Marcus come!" the child shouted and waved for him. "Come, Cassius Marcus, come!"

On the *Tigerii,* Supreme Commander Tr'Tala stood next to his wife who sat in the command seat. They and everyone else on the bridge watched one blip disappear. Then they saw another blip that was Lt. Nh'Got moved to it and disappeared too. He ordered the comm-officer to contact Nh'Got.

"All I have is static, sir," came the reply. "Do you want me to put it on speaker?"

"No. Keep the channel open and let me know if you contact her."

"No. Keep the channel open and let me know if you contact her."

"Supreme Commander," piped the tactical officer. "I'm picking up a large energy surge coming from Lt. Nh'Got's last position. It's interfering with the comm-link."

"The portal, it's activated," his wife said.

"It appears so," he agreed, his face wrinkled with concern.

"Tactical put a visual of the area on the main, full zoom."

"Yes, Supreme Commander."

Everyone stared at the primary screen, and it showed static.

"The portal," Te'ana said, tapping her husband's hand. "All we can do is wait."

CHAPTER SIXTY FOUR
Where Dreams are Made

"Centurion, how does she know your name?" Varius asked.

"I don't know. She wants me to come down."

"Of course, you aren't going?"

Marcus paused and touched his head. He heard her voice beckoning inside his mind. "I am," he finally replied, and stood. "Julius, did you get my scroll promoting you to Centurion?"

"Yes, sir, I found it in your tent. I have it in my bag. Thank you, sir."

"You earned it. Centurion Julius Varius," he addressed him with his new title. "Command by leading from the front, have self-confidence and moral courage. When there is indecision, rely on your gut instinct and don't second guess yourself." He extended an arm to him. "Take care of yourself."

Varius clasped Marcus' arm. They shared a smile, then Marcus broke the bond. The older centurion walked into the valley and up to the women and child. The girl took hold of one of his hands. He looked down at her and felt a calming presence in his mind.

He gazed up and faced the eyes of the woman that almost took his life but gave it back. "Who are you?"

"Someone who loves you," Kay're said with tears welling in her eyes. She kissed him on the cheek. "Protect, teach, and love her. She will give you so much more in return." She looked down at her younger self and nodded. "Time to go."

"Come, Cassius Marcus," the girl said and stepped up to the swirling lights. Marcus reluctantly followed at her side. The girl turned and gave a final wave and led the way into the portal. Marcus followed her and the portal closed, returning the mount to its normal state.

From his position, Varius stood slack-jawed from what he had seen. The man he admired disappeared with the child. He needed answers and started walking toward the women.

walking toward the women.

"Where did they go?" Z'mia asked.

"The first stop of several on the journey of a lifetime," Kay're said, wiping the tears from her eyes. "Look who is coming." She pointed to the young officer approaching them.

The young man, handsome in his uniform, with sandy blonde hair and blue eyes walked up to them. His eyes met Z'mia's and they held each other's gaze. Both their hearts raced; it was love at first sight.

"You are a most beautiful woman. What is your name?" Varius stuttered.

The words melted Z'mia. She had wished her entire life to hear those words spoken with innocence and sincerity. "Thank you. My name is Z'mia, and you are a handsome and gallant man. What is your name?"

Varius smiled. The words came out in Latin through her annunciator. "I am Julius Varius."

"That's a beautiful name," Z'mia said, blushing.

"Z'mia, they say love is blind, but not now," Kay're said. "It's time to go where dreams are made." Kay're walked up to the touchpad and tapped the hieroglyphics. The lights of Mount Arbel reappeared. "Here, take my food bag and coin purse. I won't need them." She handed them to Z'mia and then hugged her. Again, tears formed in her eyes. "I will remember you always. And who knows, maybe we'll see each other again."

"Oh, Kay're," Z'mia cried. "I will miss my super sleuth friend." They embraced again, and she then took hold of Roman's hand. Together they stepped into the whirling lights and vanished; the mount returning to stone.

Kay're stared at the rock face. She remembered the ending of a poem from nineteenth-century Earth. She repeated the words, "Though the night was made for loving, And the day returns too soon, yet we'll go no more a roving by the light of the moon."

She wiped the tears from her cheeks and quickly turned to Tl'Rak and said, "I can read your mind. It's not going to happen." She stepped up to him and placed a foot on his chest. He winced in pain. "Your knife," she said and reached under his tunic for it. She tucked it into her waistband and backed away.
"Supreme Commander Sen Tr'Tala, do you copy me?"

"Supreme Commander Sen Tr'Tala, do you copy me?"

"Kay're, I have you," Tr'Tala said, relieved.

"Tl'Rak is down. He is alive—barely."

The news brought cheers and smiles from all aboard both ships. He had ordered the comm-link open for all to hear.

"How?" he asked.

"Z'mia shot him with an arrow using a Roman archery set."

"Why are you calling and not Lt. Nh'Got?"

"Sen, she is gone."

Immediately, the jubilant faces on the ships disappeared, replaced by dour ones. Tr'Tala sucked in a breath and asked, "How did she die?"

"She's not dead. Just gone."

"What do you mean, just gone?" Tr'Tala asked.

"She went through the portal with a young Roman officer."

"She did what?" he voiced loudly.

"She chose happiness. It was love at first sight. Sen, you know the feeling."

His wife reached for his hand. He looked down at her lovely smiling face and nodded. "I do."

"Z'mia knew she couldn't bring him to the ship," Kay're said. "A Valeriian and human marriage, especially to a man from ancient Earth, would be forbidden. It was a matter of heart versus service to the empire. She chose the heart."

Tr'Tala's wife squeezed his hand firmer approving of Nh'Got's decision. "I understand," he finally said.

"Do you want Tl'Rak, or should I leave him here to die?" Kay're asked.

"I want him alive. Our transporters aren't working. I will send a shuttle down to your position."

From the corner of her eye, Kay're saw an ethereal figure. It was the angel from her dreams. He smiled at her, nodded, and vanished.

"Sen, your transporters are working. I will stand next to Tl'Rak so you can get a fix on both of us. Kay're out."

She walked over to Tl'Rak and said, "I quote from the Bible, Proverbs chapter eighteen, verses six and seven. A fool's lips bring strife, and his mouth calls for blows. A fool's mouth is his ruin, and his lips are the snare of his soul. You read chapter eighteen, verses six and seven. A fool's lips bring strife, and his mouth calls for blows. A fool's mouth is his ruin, and his lips are the snare of his soul. You read the Bible and know the words. You should have heeded them."

"Curse you!" he wheezed. "Kill me now!"

Before she could answer, they disappeared in a dazzle of light.

Amongst the rocks, a lone figure watched all that had transpired. The man was completely awed at what he saw. He stumbled into the valley and up to the rock face where the swirling lights appeared. He looked around to see if anyone was watching. Satisfied, he was alone; he took a deep breath and palmed the rock face. Suddenly, a swirl of lights appeared. He stared at them for a few seconds and like the others, he walked into them. Then Mount Arbel returned to stone.

Kay're and Tl'Rak materialized on the transporter deck. Sen Tr'Tala, his wife, a security detail, and medics stood waiting. Tr'Tala waved the medics and security to Tl'Rak who lay on the floor.

"Is he alive?" Tr'Tala asked the lead medic.

The man scanned Tl'Rak. "He is, Supreme Commander. The man has pulmonary edema and internal blood loss."

"Spare me the details," Tr'Tala said. "Can you save him?"

"I need to get him to sickbay," he said, avoiding the question.

Tr'Tala pursed his lips. "Get him out of here!" He turned to Kay're and managed a smile.

"Sen, Te'ana," she said, stepping up to them. "Forgive me for my unkempt appearance and body odor. I've not had a change of clothes since my arrival on the planet, nor a bath in many days."

"Oh, Kay're, don't worry about it," Te'ana said. "Come with me to my quarters. You can take a long hot shower and I will have a change of clothes for you. Then we will dine, drink wine, and you can tell us your story."

Kay're smiled. "You cannot imagine how I have longed for the comforts of our time. I was getting tired of eating insects."

of our time. I was getting tired of eating insects."

Te'ana looked at her husband and mouthed, "Insects!" He managed a dry swallow. She led Kay're to her quarters.

Finally, it was time for Kay're to return to her ship and head for the future. She, Sen Tr'Tala, and his wife Te'ana stood alone in the transporter room.

"Sen, what will happen to Tl'Rak?" Kay're asked.

"He will go on trial for treason and the murder of hundreds of Valeriians. He will be found guilty and, similar to Jesus Christ, handed over to the crowd for punishment. The crowd will be the families of those he murdered. Tl'Rak was right to ask you to kill him on Earth. He knows what the families will do to him and it won't be pretty."

"I understand," Kay're said, unmoved by what awaited Tl'Rak. "Well, I want to thank you again for your kind hospitality. We've got to stop meeting in critical situations."

"I know," Sen said. "Soon, I want you to come to Valerii as me and my wife's quests. We will dine and share stories. After which, we can show you the wonders of our planet. I'm sure the emperor wants to personally thank you for your role in stopping Tl'Rak. With her approval, I will award you the Valeriian medal of Highest Honor."

"That is very kind of you," Kay're said, smiling. "Truly, Z'mia Nh'Got deserves the award."

"And she will receive the same medal," Sen said. "And as her best friend, I want you to accept it for her. As you said, you may see her again. If you do, tell her she has been promoted to the rank of Sub-Commander and a ship of her own is in the future."

"That is nice. Sen Tr'Tala, you are a great man."

A pause as he let Kay're's praise sink in. Sen blushed and his wife kissed him on the cheek.

"And Kay're," Te'ana said, breaking the silence, "please bring your husband, Captain Ross, with you. I want him to see you accept the award and of course, share a conversation with him. Oh, there is something I need to ask you. I didn't ask at course, share a conversation with him. Oh, there is something I need to ask you. I didn't ask at dinner thinking it was inappropriate. Why did you take Centurion Marcus with you through the portal?"

"I needed him to protect, teach, and nurture me as I grew into a woman. And then to—love me. It was love at first sight."

Again, Te'ana reached for her husband's hand. He gladly took it and gave it a gentle squeeze.

"Kay're, bring your son too," Sen said.

Kay're laughed, and Sen and Te'ana exchanged puzzled looks.

"Did I say something funny?" Sen asked.

Kay're chuckled. "No. He hasn't been conceived yet."

It was Te'ana's turn to laugh. "Then, dear, I think you better get going and correct that issue."

"Oh, I intend to." She stepped up onto the transporter platform. "Until we meet again on Valerii." She waved to them, and Sen worked the transporter controls. She reappeared in her spacecraft and settled into her seat at the console. Earth rotated before her, and she felt a moment of sadness. "Goodbye, Joseph of Arimathea, Cleophas, Mary your wife, Mary of Magdala, Peter and the rest of the apostles, and the lions. I will forever remember our time together."

She adjusted her viewer to give her a view of both the *Lionare* and *Tigerii.* The ships broke orbit for their journey back to Valerii and their time. "Computer, load the program for the return trip back to twenty-fifth-century Earth."

"Program loaded, ready to execute on your command," returned the computer.

Kay're touched a tab on the seat's armrest and she was auto-buckled in. "Execute," she said, and the ship accelerated toward the sun.

Kay're's ship slowed to sub-light speed after rounding the sun. She shook off the dizziness associated with time travel and stared at the Earth. Within minutes, the planet grew in size, showing the continents.

"Did I arrive at the programmed time?" That was her main concern. She opened her comm and said, "Admiral Reid, this is Kay're. Do you copy?"

In the Situation Room, Reid had just gotten the okay from Kay're that opened her comm and said, "Admiral Reid, this is Kay're. Do you copy?"

In the Situation Room, Reid had just gotten the okay from Kay're that she was ready to make the jump back in time. He wished her God-speed. "Madam President, gentlemen, all we can do is wait and hope we don't wink out of existence." He blew out a breath and surveyed the anxious faces around the table. Then Kay're's face appeared as a holo-image center table. It took everyone by surprise.

"We see you, Kay're. Are you having mechanical issues preventing you from making the jump?"

Kay're chuckled. "I made the jump and spent almost two months on old Earth. I'm back to report that Tl'Rak has been stopped and is in custody on Valerii, facing charges of treason and murder. The time continuum is intact. All is well."

"Praise the Lord," Reid said. "From our standpoint, you were only gone seconds."

"I guess so," Kay're replied. "Your techies did a great job programming my ship's computers. They deserve a medal."

"And they will get them," the president said. "As will you for a job well done."

"Thank you, Madam President."

"I have one question now," the president said. "Did you see Jesus Christ?"

"I did and talked to him on two occasions. I saw His crucifixion, resurrection, and ascension into Heaven. He, and my time on old Earth, left a lasting impression on me. One I will never forget. If you don't mind, I want to see my husband, Mark. It's very important."

"You need to submit a report of your activities on old Earth," Reid said.

"Yes, I want to read it," the president added.

"Madam President, Admiral Reid, respectfully, I think it would be best not to have any hard copies of my journey. I will give you an in-person report."

The president and Reid exchanged glances. The president agreed, nodding. She knew the information must be very sensitive.

"Agreed," Reid said. "I think we can let you spend some time with Captain Ross and hear your report later." He glanced at the president, who again nodded.

"Thank you," Kay're said, beaming a large smile. "I won't be too long." She closed the link and had the computer search for Mark's ship. It was five hours away.

"Agreed," Reid said. "I think we can let you spend some time with Captain Ross and hear your report later." He glanced at the president, who again nodded.

"Thank you," Kay're said, beaming a large smile. "I won't be too long." She closed the link and had the computer search for Mark's ship. It was five hours away. "Computer, plot a direct course to the *Eagle*."

"Course plotted."

"Mark, here I come!"

EPILOGUE
New Life

Cassius Marcus and Kay're stepped out into bright sunlight on a grassy hillside. Overhead, Marcus saw the flying chariots. In the distance, he that reached the sky. The scene was like everything in his dreams.

"Is this Heaven?" he asked the child.

"No! No!" she pouted. "This isn't where I wanted to go. I must have touched the wrong symbols. We must try again." She turned and looked at the rock structure behind her.

"Let's go to the city," Marcus said. "Your older self left me in charge." He smiled at her. "And I don't even know your name."

"It's Kay're."

"Do you have a last name?"

"It's Enfield, but I go by Kay're. Okay, we can go to the city, if you let me have some ice cream and then we will return here and try different symbols."

"That's fair. But I don't know what ice cream is."

"It's something you eat; it's sweet and creamy. It's so good. You will like it. But you'll look funny wearing your uniform in the city. People will stare at you and think that you're weird."

"Really?"

"Yes, really. Oh, I need to change my clothes too. I look like a filthy rag doll. We'll find new clothes. Let's go." She took his hand, and they walked to the city of dreams.

"Where are we?" Julius Varus said, shielding his eyes from the sun's glare, unaware of what was behind him.

Z'mia Nh'Got scanned the barren brown landscape and did a double-take when she looked from side to side. Slowly, she turned to see a stone pyramid that seemed to touch the sky. She estimated it to be about one hundred and fifty meters that seemed to touch the sky. She estimated it to be about one hundred and fifty meters high and its base some two hundred meters. "Wow!" she exclaimed, and Varius turned, his eyes widened and mouth agape in amazement.

"This could be the Great Pyramid in Egypt," he said. "I have heard about it. Built twenty-six hundred years ago or more. There should be two others and a few smaller ones." He trotted to one corner with Z'mia following.

"I don't understand," he said. "This is the only one. Maybe we got here before the others were built. There are no people around."

"Where is Egypt?" Z'mia asked.

"On Earth, across the Mediterranean Sea from Italy."

"I know the place," Z'mia said. She stooped down and drew a map in the sand of the Mediterranean area.

"That's good," Julius said, and stooped down too and put a depression in the sand indicating their current position. He then drew a line from the point heading north to the sea. "It's the Nile River just east of here. We head towards it and follow it north to the city of Cairo. There should be people there."

Z'mia stood and looked at the cloudless blue sky. To her left, opposite the sun, a large half-moon filled the sky. Her jaw went slack. She nudged Julius and pointed at the moon. Again, his eyes widened in surprise.

"We are not on Earth," he mumbled. "Do you know where we are?"

Z'mia shook her head, activated her annunciator, and set it on speaker so Julius could hear too. "Lieutenant Z'mia Nh'Got calling the Valeriian starship *Lionare,* are you receiving me?" Nothing. She repeated the call without a response. "I'm going to set the annunciator to broadcast on frequencies across the spectrum. Maybe I will get someone."

Julius nodded. "I hope so. This heat is oppressive." He wiped beads of sweat off his forehead. "Survival will be an issue staying here."

"I agree. For anyone, this is Lt. Z'mia Nh'Got of the Valeriian starship Lionare. Can anyone hear me?" Again, silence. She repeated her general call.

This time a gruff voice replied, "Valeriian, we don't see your ship. Uncloak and surrender. Prepare to have your ship boarded. You are in Catarin territory."

Quickly, Z'mia closed the link. "Catarins! They were a long-time enemy of Valerii, but we have a peace treaty with them. Unless we are at war again or have of Valerii, but we have a peace treaty with them. Unless we are at war again or have arrived before the peace treaty."

"How long ago did you establish the treaty?"

"About four standard years ago. Before the treaty, we were at war for three hundred years. We could be on their planet or one of their claimed worlds. But when? We need to get out of here. I'm sure they will trace the origin of my call. But which way to go?"

"That way." Julius pointed to the south. "There are birds in the air. That means water or some source of food."

"Good call," Z'mia said. "Let's get moving and quickly."

Barabbas stepped through the lights into water, deep water. In panic he thrashed his arms, turning his body to face the lights, but they had vanished. He looked up to see the sunlight at the surface and wondered if he could hold his breath long enough to cover some forty feet. With scissor kicks and arms flailing, he propelled himself upward. As he neared the surface, the instinct to breathe was overwhelming. *Just a few more feet.* He breached with a gasp and sucked in both air and water, then sunk beneath the surface. Again, he kicked his legs, got his head above water for another breath, and slipped down below the water line. This time he lacked the strength and will to make another attempt for life. His arms went limp and floated out and up. Then a force hugged him and pulled him upward.

Overhead, Barabbas looked down on himself being hauled aboard a boat by three young men. He judged them to be teenagers. They laid him down on his back.

"He's not breathing!" said one of the boys. "I'm going to start CPR! I'll do the breathing. Terry, do the chest compressions. Dale, gun it to Beaver Island. There's a medical clinic there."

Dale shoved the throttle to full speed and the boat jetted off. As it did, Barabbas found himself speeding toward a bright pinpoint of light that grew in size and brightness with each passing second. Finally, the movement stopped and he fell to all fours. Immediately, he felt an extreme love and peace engulf him. He looked sideways to see the most beautiful place he had ever seen, filled with flowers and colors he had never seen before. It was awe-inspiring.

and he fell to all fours. Immediately, he felt an extreme love and peace engulf him. He looked sideways to see the most beautiful place he had ever seen, filled with flowers and colors he had never seen before. It was awe-inspiring.

"Barabbas," a voice called out to him.

He glanced up and his jaw went slack. "It's you, the Nazarene that was crucified in my place. Oh, I'm so sorry."

"Stand up, Barabbas," Jesus said, reaching down his hands. Barabbas took hold of them and Jesus pulled him up.

Barabbas smiled, looked around and asked, "Where am I?"

"You're in my kingdom."

"It's so beautiful here and I feel so much love. Thank you for bringing me here."

"Barabbas, you have to go back," Jesus said.

"No! No, Lord! I don't want to go back."

Jesus smiled. "I have used you to do my will on Earth, and you still have work to do for me. When it's your time, you will return here. Now go." Jesus raised up a hand. As quickly as Barabbas arrived, he departed.

The five-hour flight to her husband's ship, the *Eagle,* seemed to take forever. Kay're was anxious to see him and fall into his loving arms. During the journey, she thought back to her time in ancient Israel. Her meetings with Jesus, both as a child and adult, were life-changing. Then her mind shifted to Centurion Cassius Marcus. Her emotions welled up and a tear formed in her eye. She loved him like a father, and he was instrumental in her development as a woman and who she is now. She could never repay him enough for his love.

"And Z'mia. Where are you, my friend?" she called out and looked out into the blackness of space hoping for a reply. She saw only pinpoints of light. Then her heart raced. Ahead was the great starship *Eagle.* She hailed the ship.

Aboard the *Eagle*, Lt. Commander Abigail Canelli took the call. A smile creased her face. She had developed a strong friendship with the captain's wife and secretly hoped she would have the handsome Paul Goode with her. She liked the man who had shown her such a great time in the realism simulator, known as the realem, taking man who had shown her such a great time in the realism simulator, known as the realem, taking her to Paris, circa the early twentieth century. The young man reminded her so much of Captain Ross, who she admired greatly.

"Kay're," Canelli greeted her. "Good to hear from you. I have your ship on sensors."

From his command seat, Captain Ross perked up hearing Canelli address his wife. He swiveled his seat toward the comm-station. "Miss Canelli, put my wife on the main."

"You have her, Captain."

Ross turned his seat to the main screen to see his wife beaming a smile. She looked as lovely as ever. All the men on the bridge swooned over her beauty. "Free Agent Kay're, what can I do for you," he said, trying to hide his excitement.

"Captain, I'm requesting permission to bring my craft aboard."

"Is your visit for business or a social call?" he asked, hoping it was the latter.

Kay're laughed. "A bit of both," she replied, batting her eyes at him.

Ross blushed and felt the weight of the crew's amused eyes on him. They knew what Kay're had on her mind.

"Permission, granted." He stood and saw the smiling faces of his crew. "Gerry, you have the con."

"Absolutely, Captain," Commander Carston said, grinning. "And Captain, I'll cover your shift."

Ross gave him a wink and strode off the bridge. Minutes later, he and his wife were in his quarters. Kay're smiled at him, looked in his eyes, and thought of her son that would soon enter the world.

The Lights of Mount Arbel

Free Agent Kay're is commissioned to do time travel again, this time to the year 33 AD to stop a rogue Valeriian Commander, named Dhiel Tl'Rak, from killing Jesus Christ. As she begins preparations to beam down, she disappears in a sparkle, reappearing in Israel with short-term amnesia of where she was and when. She ambles off to find out answers to her memory loss. Unbeknownst to her, her five-year-old self has come through a portal to Israel at the same time.

Tl'Rak's ship arrives at Earth after destroying several Valeriian warships tasked to prevent his time travel. He and Lt. Z'mia Nh'Got transport to Earth to find Jesus and kill him, though the lieutenant along with other crew members are against his plot. Tl'Rak believes Jesus is an alien that has shaped the history of the galaxy and relegated the once proud warrior Valeriian Empire to a weak pacifist state. He believes killing Jesus will change the time continuum and return the Valeriian Empire to the great power it once was and he'd be honored as a hero for doing it. While on Earth, he is told his ship has been disabled by an unknow cause and can't move or transport anyone. He and the lieutenant are stranded on Earth. Tl'Rak believes Jesus caused his ship's malfunction and is more determined to find Him and force Him to restore his ship's power then kill Him.

The same happens to the ship sent to hunt Tr'Tala down. It's commanded by Te'ana Zh'Cata the wife of Sen Tr'Tala, the Supreme Fleet Commander. Unable to transport down to Earth, they must rely on Lt. Nh'Got to stop Tl'Rak. She understands this as does Tl'Rak. One night while sleeping, he abandons her. Nh'Got ambles around and meets Kay're. Together they hunt for Tl'Rak, Jesus, and little Kay're. During their search they fight Roman soldiers, unsavory characters, and interact with many of the biblical characters of the time. And they witness Jesus's death, resurrection, and ascension. The adventure gets more intriguing as Roman centurion and his faithful decanus are hot on their trail. Both men will play a prominently in Kay're and Nh'Got's life respectively. The story is a delightful read filled with suspense, moments of sadness and joy, and love.

ABOUT THE AUTHOR

Paul Varney was born in Toledo, Ohio, and graduated from Maumee High School in Maumee, Ohio, where he lettered in baseball and wrestling. He attended the University of Toledo and graduated with Baccalaureate degrees in psychology and nursing. Following these degrees, he completed his education at the University of Alabama in Birmingham, obtaining a master's degree in nursing as a nurse practitioner. He was commissioned as an officer in the U.S. Public Health Service and retired after thirty years of service at the rank of captain. He lives in Bradenton, Florida. *One Indiana Summer* and *The Lights of Mount Arbel* are the first two books in the series, with books three and four to be released in subsequent years. Another non-series action-packed sci-fi novel will be coming soon, too. When he is not writing, he enjoys flying on a flight simulator and keeping fit by cycling, golfing, walking, and weight training. He enjoys hearing from fans and friends.

COMING SOON!

Coming soon is the third book in the series, *Where Dreams Are Made.* The journey continues for young Kay're, Centurion Cassius Marcus, Valeriian Lieutenant Z'mia Nh'Got, Roman Decanus Julius Varius and Barabbas after they walk through the portal at Mount Arbel. Barabbas appears in the twenty-fifth century only to disappear again through the Lake Michigan Stonehenge portal with four FBI agents. Then a Coast Guard diver investigating this portal also disappears and ends up in the twenty-first century when teenage Kay're is making her presence known as the greatest woman golfer with the nickname "the Girl From Nowhere." Eventually, both mysteriously disappear, leaving the FBI scratching their heads. And Free Agent Kay're's adventures continue in the twenty-fifth century, and she worries about her friend Z'mia Nh'Got, who, with Decanus Varius, are stuck in unfriendly Catarin Space. They are surprised by unexpected quests and together they plot their return to the twenty-fifth century. Many new characters appear to add intrigue to the story.